KARIN TABKE

THE SENATOR'S *Daughter*

A CHIMERA
NOVEL

Previously published as *Rule of Law* (2018)
THE SENATOR'S DAUGHTER
Copyright © 2022 Karin Tabke LLC
All rights reserved.
ISBN: 978-1-957750-90-3

To my husband, Gary, without your love, protection and support, there would be no #Tabkestrong

To my sister from another mister, Sylvia, you are the wind beneath my wings. #Beachesbaby

AUTHOR'S NOTE

Thank you for taking time out of your day and money from your pocket to read *The Senator's Daughter*. Alana and Law have been with me through the best of times and the worst of times. Without them to fall back on, there were days I wasn't sure I could get out of bed much less write. But I did, because they called to me, needing me to help them help each other through their darkest hours. In return, they helped me through mine. We're here, battered, bruised and still afraid but knowing life has more in store for us. We need each other. We need you.

Thank you for being here for us.

~Karin

THE
SENATOR'S
Daughter

A CHIMERA
NOVEL

LAW

12:46 a.m.

He feared nothing.
He feared no one.
Not anymore.
Because he had lost everything.

HIGH ATOP HIS SEVEN-STORY COMPOUND, impervious to the wicked whip of the wind or the cold bite of rain that soaked through his clothes to his skin, Law cast his gaze toward the dark unsettled bay. Its churning calmed him in a way that placid water could not. Perhaps it was because there was so much unsettled within him.

His gaze moved to the lights that dotted the docks, glittering in the rain like terrestrial stars, outshone by the brilliant glow of the new eastern span of the Bay Bridge to the north.

Against the night sky, the bridge radiated energy, its majestic reflection rippling on the bay, a beacon to guests and locals alike. The constant stream of headlights and taillights flowing in both directions never ceased. Its rebuilding after the last big earthquake was an engineering marvel worth the extraordinary cost, connecting two very different cities.

San Francisco. The shimmering jewel of the west coast. A melting pot of citizens, crime and culture. Oversensitive and oversold, in his opinion.

He preferred the city that he had helped resuscitate. The one that pulsed angrily behind him. Oakland. Just as diverse. Just as cultured, and just as criminally sophisticated. The forgotten city. He'd taken advantage of that fact. It served him well these past years. It would serve him better in the years to come.

Tonight would mark his first preemptive strike to right a terrible wrong. Every thought, every move, every choice he had made since he was five years old served one purpose: vengeance.

Lightening struck the weather pole less than ten feet from where he stood. Sparks spewed from the violent impact, showering him in hot stabs of heat. Impervious to the pain, Law stood stalwart gazing at the bridge.

The wheels of revenge had been set in motion.

Like a shark swimming the dark waters in search of prey, he would strike.

His lips tightened when his cell phone vibrated in his hand.

The text from Unknown read: **Package located.**

Fifteen minutes later, his phone vibrated again. **Package secured.**

He smiled and tossed the burner cell into the bay. Stealing was so much more entertaining than going to the trouble of paying.

So was payback.

An eye for an eye. In his world there was no other way…

ALANA

1:04 a.m.

She was cold.
She was naked.
But not afraid.
Nothing scared her.
Because she didn't care.
Not anymore.

SHE WAS IN MOTION. Awareness slowly infused Lana's senses.

She was cold. The stench of body odor, urine and cigarettes clogged her nostrils. She opened her eyes to darkness. The hard metal she lay on gave no comfort to her twitching body. The rhythmic back and forth staccato of windshield wipers pounded in cadence to the dull throb of her temples.

The vehicle came to an abrupt halt, jerking Lana further from the warm safe place only a heroin fix could give her.

She was curled in a ball, hooded, gagged and bound, her

kneecaps pressed into her forearms, her elbows digging into her thighs.

Where was she? What happened? Was this part of rehab? Some ploy to make her so miserable she'd do anything for a fix? She wouldn't do it! Not again. So many times she had tried and failed. Damn Anton for getting her started. Damn her for not caring enough to stop.

Memories poured into her brain.

"Fuuuck," she breathed against the wet gag.

The pole.

The smell of expensive cigars, the deep thrum of male voices as they commanded her and the other girls to bend, grind, thrust, and prance for them. Hands sliding along her legs, squeezing her tits, checking her teeth as if she were a mare at auction. She'd allowed it. Welcomed it. Needed it. Along with the fix she so desperately didn't want to crave. Anton had shot her up after the man on the phone paid a ridiculous amount of money for her.

The euphoria that replaced the horror of being sold to the highest bidder had been instant.

And she lived for that shit. Would do anything for it. Anton made sure of it.

She, Alana Elizabeth Conti, the wild child of a conservative senator, was a groveling, utterly degraded, relapsed heroin addict. And now, the property of a complete stranger.

What had she done?

Lifting her head, she listened. The shrillness of an approaching siren abruptly silenced.

Hope injected her sluggish brain. Had daddy finally come to his senses and realized she was worth saving? Hope bloomed. "Daddy!" she cried against the soggy gag. "I'm here!" But no one heard her.

"Motherfuckers," the driver cursed. Cold air whooshed into

the vehicle when the driver rolled down his window and shouted, "Do you know who you're fucking with?"

A sudden hard staccato startled her. Metal hitting metal. *Ping. Ping.* Lana realized suddenly that the sound was bullets piercing the roof of what she was sure was a van. Tightening into the fetal position, Lana prayed. For survival. For death. Whichever would free her.

The van jerked into reverse, swerving then hydroplaning across the road. Squeezing her eyes shut, Lana braced herself as best she could before they hit something. Her body slammed hard into the sidewall of the van.

The driver cursed wildly, grinding the gears, jamming down on the gas, trying to blast out and away.

The van shot forward, slamming into something solid. Whiplashing her neck. Sheet metal banged and crumpled, deafening her as the back doors swung open. Cold air whooshed in, curling around her body, chilling her to the bone.

Strong hands grabbed her ankles and pulled her from the vehicle. Somebody held her close, surrounding her with instant warmth. Still stunned, she couldn't lift her head. Couldn't see him.

"You can't take her!" the driver screamed.

"Looks like we already did, amigo," a male voice with a distinct Latino accent answered. "Now shut the fuck up, and hand over the paperwork, Carson."

Not a name Lana had heard before.

"Paperwork?" Carson asked dumbly.

A suppressed gunshot erupted so close to Lana's head, her ears rang. Carson shrieked in enraged pain.

"Dude!" He was hysterical now. "You fucking shot me!"

"Had to, slowpoke. Now give me that."

Carson kept stalling. "Do you know who she belongs to?

You're dead if you—" Another gunshot immediately followed by another shriek of pain. "Here! Take the fucking contract!" Carson screamed.

"Grab it," her new captor calmly said to someone close by.

Lana was rearranged so that she was being held close to the warmth of the hard body striding away from the van.

"Got it, *bromista*," a new strange voice answered.

The man holding her pulled her tighter against him and called to Carson, "Tell Dragovich we'll be in touch." The van doors slammed shut.

"Who *are* you?" Carson screamed from the van.

The man holding her laughed. "Figure it out, *pendejo*."

"Is she alive?" another strange male voice asked.

"Yeah," her new captor said, moving quickly with her in his arms. "Did you get hit?" The man holding her demanded, shaking her slightly.

Shivering in fear, all Lana could manage was a weak shake of her head.

Metal doors opened. From his movement the man holding her stepped up, maybe into a truck? She was carefully deposited onto a hard surface. Instinctively Lana tightened into a ball. Her legs were pulled straight and strapped down, same with her arms. Terrified they might hurt her if she rebelled, Lana lay unmoving. Seconds later the familiar slide of a needle pricked her left arm and then a warm blanket was placed over her.

They were taking care of her in a weird way. Lana's mind began to drift. The black hood settled over her face.

"Daddy," she sobbed. "Is that you?"

"No, baby doll, I'm not your daddy," her new captor said, softly from beside her. "There's nothing he can do for you now."

Doors slammed shut. The shocks registered the weight of the driver as he settled in. In seconds they sped off into the night.

CHAPTER ONE

THE OPIATE GLOW that had cradled her had worn off. Cold seeped into Lana's bones.

The world was still and silent when she opened her eyes to blackness. Her senses, no longer blurred, were painfully heightened. With clarity came the fear she'd thought she was no longer capable of feeling.

Whimpering, she struggled to sit up but the restraints prevented her.

"Still with us?" her captor asked.

Lana nodded, realizing they were no longer in motion. "Please untie me," she managed, her voice muffled against the wet gag, thinking miserably that she sounded like a lost little girl.

The driver behind her head exited the vehicle.

The door at her feet was opened, making her tremble as cold air swirled beneath the blanket, around her ankles to her calves then between her legs. Hard shivers wracked her small frame. From outside, the mingled smells of exhaust and salt water rushed her senses. "C-c-cold," she muttered.

The straps were loosened then removed along with the blanket.

"Close your eyes," her captor said.

Immediately she obeyed.

"Don't open them until I say you can."

Lana nodded. Expertly, he untied the hood and lifted it from her head. The cold air that swirled around her sweaty head felt good. As quickly as the fabric was lifted from her head, he tied it around her eyes.

"Open."

The improvised blindfold was snug. She kept her eyes closed.

"Sit up," he commanded again.

As she struggled to rise, he pulled her by her bound hands to a sitting position, adjusted her torn dress before a body-warmed jacket was placed around her shoulders, its deep hood drooping over most of her face. Scuffling feet and the sounds of other people moving about told her she wasn't alone with her captor.

The sharp snap of metal being cut relieved the tension between her ankles. Strong arms carefully lifted her from where she had lain, and then from the vehicle.

"Try to stand," he commanded, setting her bare feet down on cold concrete. Wobbly, she grabbed at his arms to steady herself. She was still blindfolded, gagged, her hands bound and wearing what was left of the little blue dress she'd donned after the auction. She wished she could simply disappear in the heavy jacket that encompassed her.

The feeling of being utterly helpless and at the mercy of this unknown man terrified her.

A heavy rolling door lowered behind her, cutting off the hard chill of air. Still she shivered. Not unusual. Despite Anton's attempts to plump her up for the auction, her body fat was minimal. The byproduct of a heroin addiction.

"Walk," he said.

Lana took a slow careful step, her knees buckled, and her ankle went out on her. The circulation had been cut off. She could barely feel her toes.

She was hoisted up like a baby into strong arms.

"Check the equipment in with Lennon before you come up," the deep voice of the one holding her said. It was, she realized, the same voice she'd heard earlier. As the fog cleared from her brain she realized though it was the same voice, it was minus the accent.

"Someone get the cage door," he ordered.

A dull buzz preceded the slide of retracting metal bolts somewhere nearby. The sounds were synchronized, as if they were remotely unlocked by a mechanism, not by a human hand.

"He wants her in the asylum," a new voice said. Male, just as authoritative. Where was she and who was *he*?

Whoever was holding her reached forward and pulled. A heavy door slid along metal. They stepped up and stepped forward.

Whispers floated around her. The vibration of distant music pounded through her temples. Shards of psychedelic pain exploded in her eyes. Wincing, she tightened in her captor's arms, wishing she could wake up from this nightmare.

Machinery below them engaged with a rumbling noise, then suddenly they were catapulted upward. An elevator?

Several heartbeats later the lift eased to a stop. This time the sliding door was opened from the opposite side to the pulse of music and the sudden hush of voices. She caught a mixed whiff of booze, cigars, vape mist, musky perfume. Party time in hell. And she was practically naked except for the shredded dress that barley hung on to her small frame and jacket. Barefoot. Bare-assed.

The man holding her proceeded into the room. She felt a different energy as if it were a living, breathing thing: wicked-ness. It pulsed around her. Who were these people? What did they want with her?

As she tried to rearrange herself, his arms tightened. She felt suffocated by the damp blindfold. Trapped by the heaviness of the jacket. The soggy, filthy gag nearly choked her. Her breath caught in her throat and panic surged. Bowing her back, she dug her heels into a rock hard thigh and spun to free herself.

Her body struck the hard surface of the floor, pain shooting through her joints. As she rolled, the jacket slid from her body, the shreds of her dress twisted around her waist. Lana pulled her knees to her chest and looped her cuffed hands around them, burying her head between her elbows. It was the best defense against whatever was to come.

Huddled in a tight ball, her nakedness exposed, all she could think of was how she could get her next fix. How it would take her to the warm place she loved most. The place that didn't judge. The place that embraced her with no condemnation. A place of safety.

Not like where she was now. Soaking wet, blindfolded and gagged, her hands bound, stripped bare for the avid eyes of strangers. Unsympathetic strangers. She could feel the intensity of their vibe as the crowd closed around her. She had never felt more alone.

Or more betrayed. No one was going to save her. There wasn't a soul she'd come in contact with who she hadn't let down, hurt or disappointed. She was worthless. To her family. To her father above all. What kind of man sold his daughter to the highest bidder?

Heat permeated her chest. Spreading to her belly, then her limbs. A raging, angry heat that momentarily disoriented her with how alive it made her feel.

She'd *been* someone once. She'd loved and been loved.

She'd had a sister she cherished above all else. Who had cherished Lana as much in return.

A father she thought once loved her, and a mother…bile rose in her throat. A mother who—Lana forced the visions away.

None of it mattered. Because when she'd needed her father the most. The man who had given her life? He had crumpled her up like an empty wrapper and tossed her into the trashcan. Fuck her father. Fuck her mother. They could go to hell. She didn't need them. She'd proven it these last six years. She didn't need anyone.

Feminine laughter tittered around her. Heavy footsteps moved in closer. Instinctively, she knew she was surrounded. Not by friends. Not by kindness. By violence, barely restrained. Tensing, anticipating the worst, Lana waited.

"That can't possibly be her, True," a woman said. Her low husky voice shimmered with confidence. Lana shuddered, imagining her conjuring a spell over a crystal ball. "Law will be disappointed."

"We'll find out shortly," True said.

Hushed whispers floated in and out of range. Beside her, across the room, above her. The room was warm but she was cold. The suffocating air buzzed with tension. Who was Law? Why did he want her? If she disappointed him, what would he do with her? Or to her?

Lana felt fear again.

She had to find her way back to numbness. To that place where it didn't matter who touched her. It would be easier that way. Everything would be easier.

The voices quieted and the throbbing music died down as the ding of an arriving elevator sounded. Not the one she'd been carried into but a different one, descending on the opposite side of the room. Lana swallowed hard. An unexpected hush hung heavy in the smoke-filled air as unseen doors opened almost soundlessly.

Lana sensed the onlookers edging back, away from the man who was striding toward her.

He stopped.

"Remove the blindfold," a dark voice commanded.

Lana stiffened. That voice dove deep into her body, touching her invisibly. Entering her mind without asking. Searching silently—for what? Steeling herself not to hear was impossible.

Instantly her blindfold was tugged off, but Lana only shook her head, her eyes still closed. If she couldn't see them, they didn't exist. Right?

A stronger fear wormed its way into her heart.

"Uncuff her," the voice commanded again.

Her hands were immediately freed. The music no longer reverberated at low volume. Instead, an uneasy silence hung like a pall around her. The jacket she had been wrapped in was placed over her. And there she lay, like a baby, her eyes squeezed shut, still curled into a half naked ball, inner thighs stinging from her own urine. At least most of her was mercifully covered by the jacket.

What a spectacle she must be. Still the center of attention, and she had yet to move. The aches in her joints forced her into reluctant action. Little by little, she stretched her legs, then her arms, rotating her ankles and wrists, flooded by a pins-and-needles sensation as blood circulated again.

Pulling the thick jacket protectively around her shoulders, Lana opened her eyes. The room glowed with a silvery darkness.

The floor below her was smooth black hardwood. Jackboots all around. Some studded, some heavy, all black leather. Punctuated by sleeker, feminine versions in a myriad of colors and styles. She was surrounded. Utterly vulnerable.

Warily, she sat up. Cast her gaze to the floor, taking a minute more to collect herself. Lana figured she had two options: play weak and stay on the floor or stand tall and act tough. And it would be an act. She stood. Her knees shook, her body shook harder.

Like a little kid walking through a haunted house without a parent, Lana held her breath, anticipating the big scare. As she looked from face to face, each more hostile than the one before, the reality of her situation hit her with the force of a heart attack: She was living a nightmare.

Exhaling slowly, Lana bolstered her nerve. She'd survived life in a super-strict boarding school, on the streets and inside the Russian mob. She could do this. Starting with the man who'd given the order to uncuff her. Straightening her spine, she turned slightly and lifted her eyes.

A fierce green gaze bored into her as a rushed breath of shock escaped her lips. Life and death and everything in between seethed in those frightening eyes. He had seen hell. *Lived* through hell. Would put her or anyone who crossed him right there with him.

Never had she seen a soul so revealed in anyone's eyes. His compelling gaze held no shadows. Only fire. A dangerous fire.

She was about to get burned.

CHAPTER TWO

LANA DIDN'T NEED a neon sign to tell her the man before her was inhuman. It radiated off him in hot brutal waves.

She was afraid.

Not because he could break her in half with one hand. She knew instinctively that he could make her suffer in unimaginable ways, without a twinge of conscience, because he had none. She struggled for words to define him.

Unreachable. That fit. But it wasn't enough. She swallowed hard. Hazardous. Insatiable. He was all that and more. She could see it in his eyes. Feel it in his demeanor.

God help her, what had she done?

Her gasp of fear was muffled by the gag still in her mouth. He reached toward her, and she flinched. He stopped when she did, his eyes narrowing before he proceeded. Lana held her breath, unsure of what he might do to her.

He was massive. A full head taller than her five-foot four-inch frame. At least two hundred forty pounds of muscle. Jet black hair, blazing green eyes with black bordered gold striations, aquiline nose, and full cruel lips.

A faded scar ran down his forehead, just missing his left eye, through the dark stubble on his cheek to his mouth, giving it a predatory twist. A Glasgow smile.

She couldn't help looking at the rest of him. Shirtsleeves rolled halfway up. Long, muscular arms, heavily roped with veins, covered in intricate tattoos.

Black pants. White shirt. Black shoes. Custom made, by the looks of them.

The blunt tips of his fingers slid along the gag between her lips, and pulled it down. Instinctually, Lana licked her sore lips. When she did, her tongue caught his fingertips. Green eyes widened, pupils dilated. When they narrowed dangerously, she opened her mouth, drawing in a frightened breath.

"Sorry," she whispered. Not because she meant it. To save herself from what she saw in his eyes.

"Are you?" He demanded softly.

Swallowing hard, she nodded.

"Good. Because I own you," he rasped.

"No. You don't." A flash of pride made her risk talking back. To hell with the consequences.

He let it pass, to her surprise, studying her before he spoke again.

"Think so? But here you are. Signed, sealed, delivered. Every inch of you belongs to me."

Lana lifted her head and glared at him. "Is that how you get your jollies? Then take what you want, when you want it. That's the only piece of me you'll ever own."

To prove it to him and every other person in the room that she didn't care what they did to her, she shrugged off the jacket.

The twisted linen of her dress hung around her waist, barely covering her butt and thighs. It was barely there intact, shredded, compliments of that pig Carson, it emphasized her waist and breasts. Chin notched high, she stood quietly before him. Forcing her body not to tremble, Lana fought back the humiliation that threatened to undo her.

She willed herself to remember the proud, beautiful girl she'd once been. Before her downhill slide into addiction. And now this. She glanced sideways at the surrounding crowd. The scene was almost too bizarre to comprehend. Then looked back at him.

His iron gaze had moved down, taking her in so intensely that it felt almost physical.

She stepped back. His blazing green eyes met hers again, an unspoken question in their depths.

"Like what you see? You're not the first."

With his massive hands, he unwound the shreds of her dress from her waist. Panic infused her. Was he going to strip her completely bare?

When he pulled the fabric up to cover her breasts then proceeded to tie the ends together around her neck, Lana exhaled, relieved. It was short lived.

Taking her wrists into his hands, he pulled her against the wall of his body. Lowering his lips to her ear, he said just loud enough for the gawkers to hear, "I'll be the last."

His hot breath singed her cheek, causing her body to shake violently. Afraid of her reaction to him, she stood still, willing back the tears that stung her eyes. She hated herself right now. Instead of slapping the arrogant look off his face, she was crying. Blinking furiously to keep the tears at bay, Lana capitulated. "I don't care if you are."

He reached down and retrieved the jacket with his free hand and settled it around her shoulders. "You'll care," he said, moving her away from him.

When she stood rooted to the floor, unable to drag her eyes from his, he flashed a deadly smile, then looked past her.

"Treva, take her to the white room and stay put until I get there."

"The white room?" The other woman seemed surprised.

"Yes," he said, then looked back at Lana and warned, "Don't try anything. If you even look like you're leaving—" he inclined his head toward the ominous group surrounding them—"I'll let them decide what to do with you. Do we understand each other?"

CHAPTER THREE

TREVA FLASHED smoky hazel eyes at Lana, who couldn't move, didn't want to, suddenly ashamed of her pathetic, bedraggled state. The proud feeling of fighting back dissolved under the other woman's indifferent gaze.

Lana could only stare at the exotic bombshell's face. Smooth caramel skin, sweeping eyebrows, glittering cat eyes, high cheekbones, and pouty golden lips melded together in flawless symmetry. Thick black hair pulled back into a long glossy genie ponytail topped it off. Her only adornment, gold chandelier earrings that lightly brushed her neck.

Treva's clingy, spaghetti-strapped black gown was the height of designer chic, just right for a badass sex kitten. And Badass at the moment was not amused.

Lana would get no kindness from her. Well, Lana didn't need kindness. From anyone.

Hoping for a few more minutes of the here and now, terrified of what might lie ahead in the *white room*, Lana said, "Give me just a second, please."

Treva looked past Lana to Law for approval.

"You have ten seconds," he said.

Lana jumped at the sound of his voice. Turning his way, she caught her breath. The hair on her arms spiked. Where many guests or whatever the hell all those people were, had stood, now there were none.

Shadows moved in otherworldly waves behind beveled panels positioned at angles along the brick walls. Elaborate chandeliers hanging at different lengths from the ceiling flickered eerily. A long sleek black bar top ran the length of the back wall, edged by silver-studded black leather stools. Near that, black and grey suede sofas alternated with red brocade divans. Perfect for horny men traveling in packs funded by lavish corporate expense accounts, Lana thought, and bitches of the night striking come-hither poses. The Ultimate club featured similar set-ups and private nooks.

Marble tables bore vases overflowing with white roses accentuated by polished sterling candleholders. The white wax dripped in rippled streams down the metal, pooling on the tables.

Golden light radiated through the cut glass of bottles of expensive booze in front of the mirrored wall over the bar, creating artificial warmth. Someone appeared at last, a massive ghoul of a man. He stood behind the bar staring at her as he polished a glass.

Lana whirled back around to Treva, who eyed her warily. Shadows slipped around her. Whispers. The seductive laugh of a woman. The deep voice of a man. Low moans of pleasure.

What secrets did this mysterious room hold? And again, where was everybody?

Had she been drugged a second time without knowing it?

The deep bass of house music percussed beneath her feet. She finally noticed the floating stairway leading to a second-floor balcony.

Questions answered. Standing behind the twisted steel and dark wood railings, party people stared down at her. They were a fascinating combination of multi-pierced and tattooed men and dazzling women. Decked out in gleaming silk and studded leather, and sprinkled with diamonds—they were glamorous in a violent way. If that made sense. Nothing she was seeing did.

Each person in the room had an edge to them. All wore black, some with a flash of crimson or pearl. The men's hair-styles ran the gamut of dreads, half bald fades, to prohibition cuts.

Stripping in an upscale club like The Ultimate—and being expected to hustle on the side as well—had trained her to pick out designer style faster than any other girl. Clothes, shoes, watches...she was alert to the most expensive details of attire, sure signs of a worthwhile mark. Some customers were so obnoxious, they deserved to be taken advantage of. Though she never had.

That level of style was definitely on display here. With some freaky exceptions.

Most of the men wore tailored black suits with button down red shirts or slick black leather vests with red shirts, each one with the same insignia: a circle of flames around the head of some mythical creature. The exception to the rank and file was the green-eyed brute.

Who was coming down the stairs.

To see her? Yes. He strolled over to her and Treva.

Hello again. She didn't say it out loud. Just looked him over, seeing things she hadn't noticed until now.

Only his left ear was pierced with a small silver gauge. He was clean-shaven except for the shadow of a beard. His shoulder-length black hair looked a little damp, which might explain the thick waves. Nice. And also hot. But the intensity of his stare unnerved her to her core.

Treva reached out to take Lana's arm, but Lana snatched it away, summoning up the nerve to ask the man who thought he owned her what he intended to do with her. "Who are you? Where am I? Why am I here?"

Flames danced in his eyes. The sight triggered something deep and visceral in her. Fear, certainly. But also an exhilaration she couldn't define.

"You're here because you sold your soul to the highest bidder before you arrived, which was none of my doing." Law smiled malevolently. "He was careless."

Stepping toward her, he extended his hand.

Shaking, afraid of what he would do if she didn't, she took it. Turning her slowly around, he surrounded her, his body turning with hers. His free hand slid down her arm to her waist. Splaying his hand across her belly, he pressed her back against his chest. The steady thud of his heart reverberated into her skin, pulsing through her chest to her nipples down her belly to the core of her.

Licking her dry lips, afraid if she moved he would do something more, Lana stood statue still.

Raising her chin with his fingers so she could see the balcony above, he lowered his lips to her ear and said, "Now, you belong to Chimera. You no longer have a choice, actually. Who do you think you are?"

A captive and a slave. She got that. She was defenseless. The crowd stared down in silence. She was no match for any of them. Let alone all of them. The only way to survive was to get out. But how? The adrenaline rush she'd experienced when she'd come face-to-face with her captor had begun to wane. The need for a fix mushroomed. Despite the fear of her current circumstances, Lana fought back the craving. The last thing she needed was to get high. She'd never leave this place.

"Do you have a name, woman?" a severe male voice, with a hint of the islands, asked from somewhere behind her. Turning, Lana expected to see a tattooed Pacific Island fire dancer to go with the voice. But there was no one.

Wrong. She blinked when a man strode from the shadows.

He wasn't as tall as Law, but wider, heavily muscled, and older than Law. Her inclination that he was an islander was accurate. Sharp features cut into darkly tanned skin. Cold black eyes. Long dark hair pulled back by a leather cord.

No tailored suit for him. He was dressed for some other kind of business. The killing kind.

A long leather duster strained across his wide shoulders then tapered down his waist laying flat along his thick thighs and calves. His shirt and pants were black, his boots, just as black. His scowl, also black. No doubt his soul was too.

There was nothing soft or welcoming about him.

"I asked you if you had a name."

"That's none of your business." Her name was the only thing she had left.

The man's eyes narrowed. Lana pressed back into the protection of Law's chest.

He took another step toward her. Lana gasped and turned to Law, begging him with her eyes to protect her.

"Ty asked you a question," he said softly.

Lana shook her head. "I don't like him."

"Most people don't."

"Do you want to know why?" Ty said stepping closer to her.

Law's arm tightened around her waist.

"You forget where you are, Tyrus," Law said, his voice clipped.

Tension snapped between the two men. Lana's knees shook. From fear. From the cold. From the shock of her situation. She wished she could just slip away unnoticed into the shadows.

"I don't forget, Law," the hulk answered then backed up slowly into the darkness he'd come from.

Lana shook her head. He was just there and now he was gone. Looking up at the rail, she blinked. It was empty. Squinting, she could just make out translucent shadows. Were they fucking with her head or was she in the twilight zone?

"According to the paperwork, she goes by Brandi. Brandi Harper," someone said from behind them. "But I'm guessing that's an alias."

Breaking out of Law's hold, Lana whirled around to face the voice. It was True, the one who kidnapped her from Carson. Catching her breath, she stared wide-eyed at him. He was as tall as Law, as muscled and as intimidating. But the similarities stopped there. Whereas Law was dark and brooding, this man was bright and better tempered.

"It *is* Bran—di," she stuttered.

True's intense blue eyes held hers captive. "The name you were born with."

Did they know who her father was? Would they tell him she was here? A new fear engulfed her.

Lana stiffened her spine. "My name is Brandi Harper."

True shook his head. "There are consequences for dishonesty." He looked past her to Law. "I'll leave it up to him to decide what that consequence will be."

Lana whirled around to face Law. "It's Brandi, I swear it."

"Yeah? You have about thirty minutes to rethink your answer."

"Then what?" she asked.

"Then I will begin to apply pressure until you give me what I want."

"Torture? You're going to torture me until I tell you my real name?"

Law grinned. "Ah, now we're making progress."

Lana seethed. He'd tricked her! "Fine, my name is Fuck Off Fiona."

Law's eyes gleamed. "Game on. You now have twenty-nine minutes." He looked past her to Treva.

"Let's go," Treva commanded as she nudged Lana forward.

Jerking her arm away from the woman, Lana shook her head. "Don't touch me."

Treva smiled, malice lacing the curve of her Cupid's bow lips. "I've had a long night, and I've got the migraine to prove it." She nudged Lana forward. But she didn't move. Treva grasped her elbow. "Move, girl. Now."

"Easy now, Trev," True warned. "Law went to a lot of trouble to bring her here. Don't break her before he has a chance to."

The implication of True's words stunned Lana to silence. Turning, she raised her eyes to Law, searching for a hint of compassion.

She saw none. Instead his dark green eyes bored into her with violent passion.

The thud of her heart made it hard to breathe. The realization that she might never leave here of her own accord hit her hard.

A sudden wave of sickness hollowed out her soul. What could the devil possibly want with her? She was nobody to everyone. She was nobody to herself. She hadn't been anyone for a long time.

"What," she whispered to Law, "Are you going to do with me?"

"That remains to be seen."

CHAPTER FOUR

THAT REMAINS TO BE SEEN?

Had she been kidnapped by one sex trafficker for another? No, no, this gothic hallucination was much more advanced than simple sex for hire. It went deeper. Darker. Danger emanated from Law in ominous waves. His cryptic people: Chimera, elegant, evocative, enigmatic. Each and every one of them, most especially, Law, highly evolved.

Altruistic? Doubtful.

Criminal? Most certainly.

Chilling. Absolutely.

She didn't know what was real and what was imagined. The shadows and the whispers. The sensation of being watched. Evaluated. Judged for her worth—all of it was unnerving. Worst case scenarios flooded her brain. Flesh forcing flesh. Begging sobs and silent terror. Screams of pained pleasure and pleasured pain. Her screams. She had to get out of here, wherever *here* was.

Treva pressed her hand to the small of Lana's back, guiding her toward the stairway left of the bar. A black hole beyond.

Palpable malice radiated from the woman's warm palm to Lana's cold skin. When the blackness engulfed them, Lana whirled around, panicked, wildly searching for Law. Did he care that she was terrified? That she needed a fix desperately?

Deep in the shadows, the only clue to his presence was his burning gaze lasered on her. His power was intense. Drawing her toward him. She pushed back against Treva's steady hand, inexorably drawn to Law's dark allure.

Behind her doors opened softly. Treva nudged her away from Law to an open elevator that was anything but utilitarian. Soft black pin tucked leather enhanced with pearl rivets encompassed three walls. A thick mother of pearl handrail ran the length of the back wall.

"Back against the rail, *Brandi*. Hands behind you." Treva voiced the command so softly, Lana strained to hear her words.

Pushed into a figurative corner, Lana complied. As her back pressed into the leather, something grasped her wrists.

Crying out, she jerked away from the enslavement; pulling so hard she lost her balance and fell to her knees on the cold white marble floor. Pain shot from her knees up her thighs to the small of her back. Helpless, she clung to the rail, yanking at the shackles that had encircled her wrists as if by dark magic. Her weakness was growing. Coming down off a heroin high had become harder and harder.

"Your lack of dignity is appalling," Treva hissed. "Law's out of his mind to have risked so much for someone like you."

Off balance, Lana struggled to stand. "You don't know me," Lana defended.

"I know what I see."

The jacket slid from Lana's shoulders. Looking out to where Law stood in the shadows, his burning gaze piercing the darkness between them, she wished she could veil her own. Hide somehow. She fought the sensation that he was reading her mind. Thought by thought. Going deeper. All the way down to her soul.

Holding Law's gaze, defiant, Lana slowly stood. Her back arched as she pulled hard against the shackles, realizing for the first time they were lined with the same soft leather as the walls. But they were the real deal. She was a prisoner in the devil's lair. She screamed as the doors soundlessly closed.

Tears slid down her cheeks when the elevator glided upward. In the recesses of her mind Lana knew she should make a run for it. She had to get away. Find a place to hide, a place to recuperate, a place where she could find what she needed and break free of this nightmare.

The elevator came to a smooth stop. As it settled, Lana looked up at Treva who stood staring at her.

"I don't care what you think of me," Lana said. It was the truth.

"You won't care what anyone thinks of you as long as you think so little of yourself," Treva shot back, then pressed a hidden button on the right panel.

The shackles were withdrawn from Lana's wrists. She clutched the rail. Unwilling to let go.

Silently, the doors opened to a softly lit foyer. High polished marble reflected the electric flicker of wall torches. Treva's hand pressed Lana between the shoulders. "Go straight, there's a door across the foyer," she directed.

"I—don't want to," Lana breathed, resisting. "I want to go home."

"This is home for as long as Law says it is. Now move."

Vehemently, Lana shook her head. Turning to push Treva away, Lana stopped mid movement. The glitter of a blade held her at bay.

"I don't want to cut you, princess, but I will." She inclined her head toward the foyer. "Now go."

Swallowing hard, Lana preceded her across the cold marble to an extra wide, metal-strapped door.

Treva slid back a panel to the left of the door and quickly pressed a sequence of numbers. Several locks disengaged.

"Open it," she commanded.

Reluctantly, Lana turned the ivory knob and slowly pushed the door open. What the muted lighting revealed stopped Lana at the threshold. First to assault her senses was the dusky scent of the white stargazer lilies on the nightstand. Squeezing her eyes closed, Lana forced back the traumatic memories associated with the scent.

"Can, you—get rid of those flowers," she whispered afraid if she spoke louder she would scream the request.

"The flowers stay," Treva snapped, pushing Lana further into the room.

Fighting back a full-blown panic attack, Lana regulated her racing pulse. She could do this. Flowers couldn't hurt her.

Nodding, Lana said, "The room is nice."

"Glad you approve," Treva said.

It was spacious and decidedly feminine but not frilly.

Every corner was rounded, from the carved wooden bedstead to the walls, the armoire, the settee and the secretary in the corner. There was no window that she could see.

As she stepped deeper into the room, the large mirror on the wall over the dresser caught her eye. Peering intently at it, she had the uneasy feeling she was being watched.

The white on white fabrics, wood and paint suggested purity. Her gaze swept over the headboard to the artwork that hung above it. An alabaster relief of the curve of a woman's back and buttocks, the only color in the entire room, a wisp of crimson along the inner thigh of the relief. Sacrificial blood? Is this where the devil took his virgins?

Lana was anything but, in the physical sense anyway.

She suppressed a shudder. This room wasn't the serene sanctuary it appeared to be. It was a prison. Pointing to a second door she assumed was the bathroom she said, "Where does that go?"

"That remains locked from the other side."

Lana swallowed. No way out except the door she came through. Her fear, combined with the remnants of her last high, wreaked havoc in her stomach. Without a fix soon, she'd be in really bad shape. She could do it, she told herself. Stop cold turkey. She'd done it once before. Her gut tightened at the remembered bone deep pain. The clawing need, scraping at her belly. The sleepless nights that turned into days. The desperation for just a taste to get her over the hump. It had been excruciating. But she'd woken up one morning without the craving. She knew then she would be okay. Until Anton forcibly shot her up, keeping her high as a kite until the night of the auction. Forcing her to sign the contract for a fix.

She deserved what came after.

"Is—there a restroom I could use?"

She had to pee. She needed a drink of water and to wash the sweat from her face. And she had to think fast. The door to freedom was behind her. This would be her only chance to escape before Law showed up to exact his punishment.

Treva stepped past Lana to the tall armoire and pressed the middle of the full-length mirror flanking it. A faint click and it opened, revealing a spacious bathroom.

"There are clothes in the armoire. Find something to fit you. The bathroom has everything you need. I suggest you take a quick shower before Law gets here. He doesn't like dirty women."

Lana had no response to that. Nodding, she hurried into the bathroom, closing the door behind her and peed, her mind racing with ideas to get out of here alive. Flushing the toilet, she stood and quietly walked to the door. Silence. It was now or never.

"Oh my God! Treva, hurry!" she screamed as she opened the door.

When Treva came running through the doorway, Lana slammed the door hard into her head. The woman grunted from the impact, hitting the tile floor, out cold.

Lana didn't waste a second. Stepping over her, she tore through the armoire looking for something, anything that would fit! Ripping a red sheath dress from the hanger, Lana held it up to her body.

Too wide. She swore under her breath, tore off the shreds of her dress and yanked the new dress over her head anyway. Running back to where Treva lay, she yanked the black belt from the dress, quickly slinging it around herself. Stepping over the woman, Lana hurried to the mirror over the sink and checked her reflection. Gah! She looked like hell.

Pale skin, pale lips, dark shadows beneath her swollen blue eyes. Hair, a total mess. Quickly she splashed her face with cold water. Smoothing her hair back, she pulled it up into a knot. Pinching her cheeks, she dug for lipstick in the top vanity drawer, finding a tube of red and quickly applying it before she dashed back to Treva and pulled off her shoes. Flustered, unable to buckle them in her panic, she threw them across the room and emptied the bottom of the armoire.

"Yes!" she cried out in relief. A glossy black wig was neatly laid out in the bottom drawer. A few hard tugs and she was wearing it.

Treva groaned in pain.

Not wasting precious seconds of time searching for shoes that fit, Lana grabbed the heeled sandals and ran to the door.

Nervously she looked around for something to use as an improvised weapon when she remembered Treva's threat. She patted down the still-unconscious woman and found the knife, hiding it in the fabric folds of her dress, then hurrying back to the door.

Locked. There was no knob. Frantic, Lana ran her hands over the nearly invisible divide between its smooth surface and the walls. There had to be a way—ah, there it was. Pressing the heel of her hand where the knob would be, she felt an unseen mechanism inside move before the door swung open.

Quietly she closed the door behind her. Looking down the hall she inhaled deeply then slowly exhaled. Do or die. She could do this.

Hurriedly, Lana strapped the heels to her feet, and while they were slightly too large, she was intimately acquainted with challenging footwear. It was a given that the sexier the shoe, the more difficult it was to walk in.

Throwing her shoulders back, ever watchful, Lana sauntered down the low-lit hallway like she belonged there. As she rounded the corner, she nearly jumped out of her heels when the ding of the elevator reached her.

Law. That had to be him. Riding up to the white room. Expecting to see her, but not like this. Tiptoeing, Lana moved as fast as she could to the metal door at the end of the hall.

The door clicked open. She rushed through it. Heart thumping wildly, Lana flew down the stairway to the next floor. She would have continued downward but the stairs ended at a landing and another door.

Nervously, she tried the door. It was locked. Even worse, the stairwell was dark. Panic swarmed through her. She could go back the way she came but Law would see her. She couldn't magically make the door open. Looking up and down and all around, she had two options; stay where she was and use the knife to fight for her life or go back the way she came and make a run for it.

She'd go back. Just as she passed the door, she heard the click of the handle. Backing up so quickly she hit the wall with a loud whoosh, Lana stood perfectly still as the door opened in front of her. Silently she reached out for the handle as the person walked through, her presence for the moment undetected.

Whoever it was, male or female, was small like her. Lucky break. She pressed the tip of the knife into the person's back.

"Open the door."

The body stiffened. "Did Law send you?"

Lana flinched. Male. He sounded innocent.

"Yes, he did. He wants you in the white room."

Instead of forcing, she lowered the knife. Instinctively she knew that he wasn't capable of hurting her.

When he turned around and looked at her with unsuspecting brown eyes she knew she was right. He was an adult but no taller than her, his brown hair pulled back into a man bun. The area above his right eye was concave, along with a long scar that ran from it into his hairline. He'd either taken a hard fall or had been severely hit by something. He wasn't wearing black or red. Instead he was casually dressed in khakis, white button down shirt and loafers. He didn't belong in this sinister place.

He had to have felt the knife tip. But he didn't ask questions. Too shy? Too scared? Hard to tell.

Slipping from behind the door and then between him and the darkened room beyond the door he'd inadvertently opened for her, Lana smiled as he let her pass. "Law and I are playing hide and seek. Please, Jimmy?" She gave it a shot.

"I'm Monty."

"Yes, sorry. Law told me your name, I must have forgotten. My bad. Please don't tell him you saw me." She smiled. "Law always wins. This time he's going down."

"Huh?"

"Oh, it's just a game. Nice talking to you, Monty." She put a hushing finger to her lips and winked at him as she closed the door. When it was completely closed, she pressed against it, letting out a long sigh of relief.

A motion sensor somewhere inside the room gradually illuminated it, a weird electric blue like something out of a sci-fi movie. She was in a control room. Dozens of closed-circuit camera feeds were mounted above her, the screens tilted at an angle for optimum viewing. A long metal table held six desktop monitors, some with several active screens within their screens. The half a dozen keyboards were situated beneath the screens, each with its own laser mouse.

At the center of it all was a lone chair.

Holy shit. She'd stumbled into the nerve center of Law's cryptic world. No time to waste. Taking a deep breath, she proceeded into the room and stopped at the first monitor, touching a key.

The screen came to life, revealing saved social media pages and file documents. Squinting, she looked closer.

It all added up to a dossier of a local biker gang, *Los Coyotes*, in the city. She pressed the mouse and scrolled through about a dozen member profiles before moving on to another biker gang, Lucifer's Legion.

Ugh. Several of the Legion members frequented the Ultimate. They were in tight with Anton.

But her disgust turned to cold fear when she glanced at the next monitor on the metal table, appalled to see a freeze frame of her being pulled out of the van earlier tonight. She jabbed at the Enter key and the frame turned into video. Oh my god. Had he watched her kidnapping go down? How? A drone?

What the hell kind of man was Law?

She straightened, fighting back the fear, and stepped away from the monitors, looking around her instead. She took in a panoramic view of the Bay and yachts secured to a private dock. Was that black glass structure cantilevered out over the dark water a nightclub? Was that the music she'd heard when they pulled her from the van in the garage?

There was an outsize laptop left open by the expanse of windows. She jabbed at the keyboard, half expecting to see herself naked and writhing, but pulled up only security feeds of parking lots and a garage. Then a room full of men sitting around a card table with huge stacks of chips in front of them.

Gambling and gabbing, like idiots, unaware they were being watched.

Compelled to find out more, dreading what she might see, she hit a different key. The white room appeared. The feed was still. She could just make out Treva's bare feet, and part of the rest of her, sprawled on the floor near the bathroom. If Law had seen this, he evidently didn't care.

The hair on the back of her neck rose.

Good God, was he watching her now?

Backing away, Lana glanced around the room, feeling hidden eyes on her. Taking one last look at another screen before she hightailed it out of there, she stopped in her tracks. Her high school graduation photo. Like yearbooks, available online to anyone. But to see it here was a total shock. For more than one reason.

Despite the loneliness and isolation of boarding school, the girl with the broken smile in the picture had been happy that day.

She was free. Free to do as she pleased and answering to no one but herself. How wrong she had been.

Click. Go away, girl. *Click. Click.* The San Francisco Chronicle headline from six years ago flashed up on the screen: **The Senator's Daughter Presumed Dead**.

Staging her death. Survival at it's most basic. It was the only way she could escape the demons. But they had followed her. They were always there. Just below the surface, lurking— reminding her of what she had done.

Shaking off the shadows of her past, Lana clicked through several more pictures of herself, most of her at the club, on the pole or serving cocktails.

Apparently, Law had been watching her for some time. Waiting to make his move. She scrolled back several pages.

He wasn't just interested in her, apparently. She found an article on her father's appointment as chairman of the intelligence committee.

She knew her father had serious clout in the capital as well as a super high security clearance, but what was that to Law?

She pressed another key and all the screens fizzled into digital sparks simultaneously. What was the hell was happening? Too late, she noticed the tiny camera lights at the top of the screens. All green. All on.

More frightened now than angry, she moved around the room looking for another way out and nearly screamed with relief when she found a second door on the opposite side of the room. As she slowly backed out, she glanced over her shoulder and nearly fainted. Law's glaring face flashed on every screen in the room.

Lana bolted and ran straight into an alternate universe.

CHAPTER FIVE

THE THROATY MOAN of a tenor sax set the mood for the
sensual choreography playing out before her. A large yet intimate
room with a sunken conversation space dead center drew her
eyes to beautifully dressed men and women who mingled in the
softly lit room. Some of the woman, ethereal in their appearance,
looked as if they weren't quite real. Light shimmered through
their bodies and their eyes. She watched a lovely women press
her lips to a man's neck. When he turned to take her into his
arms, his hands moved through her as if she were a shadow. Or a
hologram?

The woman laughed, the sound soft, seductive. Retreating,
she tilted her head toward the wide flaring stairway. He looked
past her. Lana followed his gaze. Several beauties smiled down
from the balustrade balcony, the invitation not lost on anyone
who was paying attention.

Lured by the siren's call, he followed the gossamer woman
up the stairway where they were greeted by the others, and then
disappeared into the shadows. Total different vibe than the jack-
booted crowd. These people, an élite clientele, were here to be

served the finest libations, epicurean delights and beautiful bodies.

Thankful for the shrouded alcoves and low lights, Lana was able to blend in with her hasty disguise.

Low moans of pleasure floated around Lana, taunting her with the promise of rapture. The eroticism of the sound alone was an aphrodisiac. A woman's gasp as she climaxed followed by the deep satisfied groan of a man well pleased filtered from the walls.

Lana understood. This place was purely and simply a pleasure palace. Not, she realized, exclusive to heterosexual couplings. A striking woman dressed in a femininely tailored tuxedo took the hand of another woman, the look between them one of unmistakable desire. Their eyes locked as they floated up the stairway and disappeared.

Several men, wearing the same black suits with red shirts she had seen in the asylum, moved effortlessly behind a long gleaming bar at the far end of the elaborate room. Alluring women in sheer black togas trimmed with slim red shoulder sashes moved among the guests, seeing to their needs.

Lana blinked several times as she watched a toga-draped girl walk into a perimeter wall and disappear.

Shaking her head as she processed what she just witnessed, Lana closed her eyes and when she opened them, the girl had reemerged, her tray empty.

What was this place? Looking deeper into the shadow that surrounded the sunken space, Lana watched several other girls slip in and out of what looked like a solid wall. Stepping further into the enthralling room, Lana mentally prepared herself for anything. Law's world was as mysterious as the man himself.

The sax improvisation reached an intense crescendo, like hot sex set to music. An amazing soundtrack for what was, as far as she could tell, sophisticated debauchery for the elite.

She needed to walk through the room like she belonged, to the other side, which she prayed was the way out. Because there was no going back. Raising her chin, and avoiding eye contact, Lana focused on the goal. Stepping slowly down into the social area, she moved through the gathering.

When one of the toga-clad women asked if she would like a cocktail, Lana shook her head and continued moving. As she cleared the sunken meeting area, she turned and looked over her shoulder to the door she had come through, just as it opened. Heart racing, she turned forward and hurried. Several suited men were exiting an elevator straight ahead, no more than twenty feet from her. She needed to get on it before it closed.

Holding her breath, praying for success, Lana glided across the marble floor. Almost safe. She sighed with relief.

But the moment she entered the car, a hand touched her shoulder from behind. She stopped mid-step, terrified.

"Miss?" a deep voice asked.

Slowly exhaling, Lana put her foot down but didn't dare turn. If that was Law who had come through the door, he might be looking her way.

"Yes?" she softly responded, her voice tinged with a slight but authentic French accent. She had mastered it long ago—the daughter of the French ambassador to the US had been one of her middle school roommates.

"There is a gentleman here tonight who would like an introduction."

"*Non*, I am so sorry, I am not feeling well this evening. Perhaps another night?"

Lana glanced over her shoulder to see the man shrug nonchalantly and then withdraw.

She stepped all the way into the paneled car, coming face to face with another black suit, paired with a white shirt and bow tie. Not a guest. An elevator attendant. Well, hell. Someone had to push the buttons, right? He accepted her presence with a nod and asked, "Where would you like to go, mademoiselle?"

Smiling, she pursed her full lips into an award-winning pout, well aware that he couldn't help staring at her mouth.

"I am not sure which floor it is, but it would be the one to exit, please."

"Would you like us to arrange for a ride, or contact the parking valet or the dock steward?"

"The valet, *s'il vous plait*."

"My pleasure. If you would be so kind as to give me your remote code, the valet will have your car available as soon as you exit."

Lana swallowed and looked over her shoulder. No sign of Law. But she was running out of time. Clueless about a remote code, she said, "*Merci*, but that will not be necessary. My friend with the car will meet me outside."

He nodded, and pressed the Close Door button. Just as the doors began to close behind her, a deep familiar voice said, "Hold the elevator, Johnny."

Law.

Moving deeper into the corner of the car, her back to him as he entered, it was everything Lana could do to control her trembling. He was a foot away from her. Please, she prayed, don't let him get me.

"Which floor, sir?" the attendant asked.

"The Club, but hold the door, I'm waiting for someone," Law said.

"Of course, sir."

Fear tightened Lana's chest, making it difficult to breathe.

She didn't dare move. The intangible heat of Law's body wound around her. Power pulsed wildly from him. His spicy masculine scent stimulated her senses as surely as if he caressed her.

She could almost hear him laughing at her for thinking she could escape him.

No good would come of it if she allowed this man any part of her. The sexual spell he radiated would allow him to slowly possess her—mind, body and soul—until there would be nothing left of her.

"I am afraid, *monsieur*," she said softly to the attendant without looking up, "that I must be going."

"May I be of assistance?" Law said from behind her.

Shaking her head, she said, "*Non, merci.*"

Lana forced herself to remain erect, not slumped in fear. Ignoring Law, she sidestepped from the car, and hurried toward the bar. If ever she needed a drink, she needed one now. On edge, she watched a determined True stride out of the same door she and Law had come through, his head on a swivel, looking for someone. Her.

"Excuse me," she said to the bartender. "Could you direct me to the ladies' room, please?"

He pointed to the elevator. Oh no. Law was right where she'd left him, staring in her direction. "Go past the elevator, then straight back."

"Thank you." She couldn't move, not until Law was gone. But her flight instinct was too strong. And her hasty disguise wasn't the greatest. If he caught her, he would double down on her punishment. Inhaling deeply, she strode toward the hallway. Once she was out of sight, she bolted for the restroom.

The startled attendant, a plump woman in a modest uniform, quickly recovered when Lana burst into the room.

"May I help you, miss?"

"No, no, I just—never mind." She hurried to the first stall, pulled back the heavy upholstered door, slipped in, and closed the door behind her. Locking it, she plopped down on the toilet and exhaled.

Narrow escape. Closing her eyes, she leaned back, biting her lip, fighting the terror that gripped her. She was the hunted. If she was found, she would be—no, she couldn't think of that. It couldn't happen. Tightening her body into a ball, Lana fought the hysteria that caught fire inside her. He would do things to her, she just knew it. Things that would enslave her to him. Things that would control her, just as heroin had, but worse. She couldn't endure the punishment that would come if she were caught.

Agonizing seconds ticked by. Wrapping her arms tighter around her body to keep it from shaking, Lana inhaled a deep breath. Then another. Slowly, her courage returned. She could do this. She *would* do this.

"Miss," the attendant called. "Are you okay?"

"Yes, I just had to go so bad!"

Standing, Lana flushed the toilet then smoothed her wig. Pinching her cheeks, she licked her lips and opened the door. The attendant smiled and handed her a moist scented cloth.

"Thank you," Lana said as she took it. As she rinsed her hands, she eyed the array of hygienic and cosmetic sundries before her. Single-use tubes of lip gloss and mascara. Exactly what she needed. Plus mouthwash, breath mints, floss. And perfume samples, deodorant, tampons, nail polish remover and several other lady things.

Raising her gaze to the mirror, Lana didn't recognize the haunted face staring back at her. She had to blend in; she needed to clean up. Moving to the end of the long counter, she washed her face, and rinsed her mouth with mouthwash. Patting her skin dry, she got busy with the mascara and lipstick, generously applying both. Lastly, she dabbed the sultry perfume behind her ears. Smoothing her wig, and her improvised dress, she straightened and gave herself a second look. Better, but she still couldn't fool a trained eye. Her best plan of escape was to get down to the valet-parking stand, and slip away.

"Maris," she said reading the attendant's nametag, "I left my purse at the table. I'll be right back. I appreciate your discretion."

"No worry," the attendant reassured her. "Is there anything else I can do for you this evening?"

"Ah—yes. Which way to the stairway that goes outside?"

"The elevator is quicker."

"I'm claustrophobic. I always take the stairs when I can."

"OK. Then go past the bar to the left, you'll see the door. You'll still have to go past security to get out of the complex, though. Just let them scan your wrist."

Scan her wrist? Of course a man like Law would have his fingers on the pulse of every soul that entered his domain. What was he hiding that required such tight security?

Thanking the attendant, Lana peeked down the hall before she followed the directions given. Not looking anywhere but ahead of her, Lana moved as quickly as she could without drawing attention to herself.

When she opened the door to the staircase she almost screamed with relief, taking the stairs two at a time in a headlong rush. Freedom was only steps away, down a short hallway.

Fuck. Where two well-dressed men appeared to be waiting. But wait. Her best chance to get past security would be to accompany someone who had legitimately entered this place. She had no idea what the wrist scan entailed, but she figured it was some high tech ID verification, which she didn't have.

Approaching the men she looked past them, through a

revolving glass door and beyond where dozens of incredibly expensive cars lined up. A suited valet entered from a side door and said to the men, "Sirs, your vehicle is ready."

The gleaming Ferrari was canary yellow. An excellent distraction for any onlookers who might otherwise remember her. Lana hurried forward and walked out with them. Pulse racing, she tapped the man in front of her on the shoulder. "Excuse me, sir," she said in a lilting French accent. He turned around, his hazel eyes widening. A slow smile stole across his lips.

"Well, hello."

"*Bon soir*," she replied coyly. "I am embarrassed to confess that my friend left without me. Would you be so kind to give a girl a ride home?"

His smile widened. "It would be my pleasure." Taking her hand, he tucked it into the bend of his elbow. "Jerod," he called to his friend. "Looks like the party may not be over."

Repulsed by what he seemed to be implying, Lana decided to take her chances with these two would-be studs over one more second with Law. "Please," she breathed, "promise to be gentle with me."

Jerod and the other guy gave each other a silent high five. "My name is Kyle," the one who held her hand said.

"*Enchante*, Kyle." She smiled seductively, "My name is Monique."

As he opened the car door, she moved to slide in. She was almost there. Her nerves taut as a tightrope.

"Ah, there you are, Monique," a deep voice called from the sidewalk.

Whirling around, Lana faced Law's devastating glare. "I'm so glad I didn't miss you." Moving Kyle aside, Law grasped her hand, entwining his fingers through hers.

"Let go of me," she demanded.

"I made that mistake once tonight, I won't make it a second time."

"Hey man, let her go," Jerod called from across the car.

"She's with us," Kyle defended, moving into Law's space.

"I'm afraid, gentlemen, she's with me. I suggest you get into your car and leave."

"Looks to me like she doesn't want to stay with you," Jerod said, coming around his car.

"I don't," Lana said, pulling away from Law's steel grip.

His fingers tightened around hers. She bit back a cry of pain.

In that instant, Jerod made the unfortunate choice to take Law on. The instant Jerod cocked his arm to throw a punch, Law slammed his elbow into Jerod's face, still holding Lana's hand, then turned and elbowed Kyle the same way. Jerod reeled back against his canary yellow Ferrari, and Kyle stumbled backward holding his bloody nose.

"Leave," Law commanded. "Now."

Both men backed away, got into the car and sped off.

Law smirked as the Ferrari disappeared into the night, then looked hard at her. "Nice try."

Stunned by Law's controlled violence, a new fear gripped Lana. She'd known instinctively from the moment their eyes first met that he was capable of destroying another human being. But what she'd just witnessed required virtually no effort for extreme results. He hadn't even broken a sweat, just dealt with the two men as easily as he would tie a tie.

Anger replaced her despair. She had come so close. "Was that necessary?"

"Quite necessary." He pulled her against him. "Try it again, and you'll find out just how violent I can be."

"Are you threatening me?"

"I don't make threats."

Lana dug her nails into his palm. His jaw tightened, giving her the pleasure of turning the pain tables on him. "I'm not an animal that you can cage."

With one swift move, he pulled her into the hardness of his body. "I would never do that. I'm not a cruel man, Brandi," he said softly. Brushing back the black hair of her wig from her shoulder, he whispered, "Unless you give me a reason to be."

Turning her head she bit at his jaw, sinking her teeth into his skin. Law hissed angrily. His large hand grasped her chin. When she refused to let go, he slid his fingers into her mouth and made her stop. The taste of his blood spurred renewed fury in her soul. She tried to bite him again, but his lips crashed down on hers, drawing her breath from her. The hard heat of his mouth scorched hers.

Lana let him kiss her.

CHAPTER SIX

HIS LIPS WERE BRUTALLY POSSESSIVE. Because he desired her? She didn't know. Because she held value? Yes, yes, she did.

She had something he wanted. Badly. He'd risked his men to steal her away from the Dragon as she had heard Anton refer to him. Lana had heard the name. Josef Dragovich was a megalomaniac oligarch. Why had Law brought her here, and revealed his secret world to an outsider?

How far could she push him before he started to crack? She had no way of knowing.

Lana forced herself to relax into the hard body pressed against hers. A low growl worked its way up from Law's chest, his fingers tightened around hers, squeezing them painfully. It didn't come close to the painful ache that ignited at her nipples and flashed its way down her belly to between her legs.

She didn't want to want him, he demanded it and would not take no for an answer. He tortured her with the fantasy of what he could do to her.

Law abruptly released her mouth. The shock of the disconnect left her feeling more vulnerable then she had ever felt before. Shaking her head, she pushed back against his arm holding her against his chest.

"Don't do that again," she whispered, afraid of the desperation in her voice.

His low throaty laughter infiltrated her lust-induced haze. He was laughing at her? Ignoring the valets and handful of people awaiting their vehicles, in a swift turn he moved her backward against the wall next to the glass revolving door.

"Because you liked it?" he taunted.

"I don't kiss," she said honestly. "Don't do it again."

His eyes sparked. "You're going to learn to do a lot of things you wouldn't otherwise do."

"I'm not a whore. I won't be yours."

"I hold your contract. You'll be whatever I want you to be." Stepping back from her, he held out his hand. "Take it."

"No."

That smile again. It was meant to destroy on so many levels. "Take it now or I take you over my shoulder."

"You won't. Not in front of your clients."

Lana screamed with every ounce of energy she had left when Law slung her over his shoulder and proceeded to walk back into wherever the hell they were. She kicked, she dug her nails into rock-hard muscle. She tried to bite the shoulder she was thrown over. Her wig fell off, she lost a sandal, and what was left of her dignity. She raked her nails into his back.

A hard hand came down on her ass. Lana screamed again, this time like a wounded animal. She lost it. And went completely feral on him.

But she was no match for Law. He flung her back to his chest and shook her. "There is no way out for you. Accept it," he hissed.

"I almost made it!" she sobbed.

"Not even close. I knew every step you took and every trick you pulled when you sneaked out."

"You let me think I had a chance?" she screamed.

"You never had a chance. You never will."

"You're cruel. I loathe you." With those last words, she went limp. Spent. The fight gone. Bone-deep exhaustion stole over her. She heard his voice when he replied...but not the words.

What was he saying?

Didn't matter. Nothing mattered...

Lana woke up in a vast bed, feeling vaguely that she was floating on a dark cloud. Which was sort of true. She glimpsed gathering storm clouds, gaining strength and about to break, outside a wall of windows. She guessed she was in a penthouse or something like it.

The space was unnervingly quiet. She concentrated on coming back to reality. She was on her back, still dressed, lying across an immense bed covered in something infinitely soft. Her fingers clenched in it. Sable? Maybe. Everything she saw looked expensive, custom-made and hellishly dark. She turned her head to the side.

And saw Law, sitting on the edge of a chair. Watching her.

"Where am I?" The murmured question was almost involuntary.

Law sat forward. "In my bed."

She looked away, scanning the rest of the enormous room through half-closed eyes. There had to be a way out. There was always a way out. She didn't see one. She stiffened at the noiseless sound of him rising.

He loomed over her, as if he was about to pounce. "Not what you signed up for?"

She flinched at his words. "Let me go. I won't talk. Nothing's happened yet."

His green eyes bored into her when she finally looked him full in the face. "But something will," he said softly.

"I can get you money. Pay you whatever you want," she lied. Not a single soul on earth would so much as flip a quarter her way.

"I don't need money."

"Then why did you steal me from Carson? What are you going to do to me?"

Ignoring her questions, he stepped closer and scowled down at her. "I don't think you want to hear the answer to that question."

He strode past her to a nearly invisible door. Pressing his hand against a concealed sensor panel was enough to open it.

"Don't leave me!" she cried. She didn't want to be alone.

He turned and stared at her. "I'm not." He strode through the door but left it open.

Remembering that she'd taken Treva's knife, she dug into her bodice for it. Gone. Her eyes had adjusted to the darkness, and to her relief she saw a set of katana swords of varying lengths and a matching dagger displayed on a red-lacquered Japanese tans.

Valuable antiques, for sure. But the dagger would do. Quietly, she slid from the bed, and on shaky knees, moved to the dresser and grabbed it. Untrained in the nuances of knife fighting, she slid it into the side pocket of her dress biding her time to strike.

Feeling like she had a chance this time, Lana inhaled a deep breath then exhaled slowly. Stepping through the doorway she stopped and gazed in awe at the large open living space before her.

No one could accuse Law of not liking creature comforts. The room, despite its masculine theme, spoke to her every feminine sense. It was hyper virile, like the man who inhabited it. Sophisticated power oozed from the leather walls and ancient weapons. Wild wanton images flashed in her mind of alpha-male dominant sex on the fur throws on the floor before the fireplace.

It struck Lana at that moment that this was not a place Law shared with others. This place, his lair, was a secure sanctuary. The lion's den where, away from the pride, he could, for a few brief moments, just be.

In the center of the room a floor to ceiling polished slate fireplace crackled with warmth. Above the flames was another blade collection of what looked like medieval weaponry. Fur throws hung over slick leather furniture. Crystal decanters filled with varying shades of amber liquid caught the flicker of the fire, casting a rainbow of colors on the mirror. The scent of leather, musk and jasmine enticed her further into the stunning room. Thick animal skins covered the polished black hardwood floors.

Metallic shades rolled down, covering the high windows, preventing even a sliver of light from peeking through. Did Law control them remotely? He undoubtedly did. So much for going out the windows.

Low light from the lamps cast a quiet glow on the room. There were no light switches or controls on the walls. She ran her hand over the nearest wall to be sure and felt nothing.

Just like the rest of the building, there was no escaping this place.

"You're wasting brain power on something that doesn't exist," Law said, returning with a bottle of water in his hand.

"You're a mind reader too?"

"One of my many talents."

Lana crossed her arms over her chest, resting one hand over the hidden dagger at her side.

"Oh. So…about wasting my time. What doesn't exist?"

"A way out."

She shrugged. "Maybe I don't want to escape."

Law's brows rose. "I gave you more credit than that, Brandi."

She looked at him warily. "What do you mean?"

"I didn't expect you to pretend that all of a sudden you were warming to the idea of staying here."

"A girl can change her mind."

He set the bottle of water on an end table and sauntered toward her like a powerful cat. "Really?" he purred. "What brought that around?"

Swallowing hard, Lana grasped the dagger's hilt. She had never intentionally hurt another human being in her life. But then, she had never been enslaved to the devil either. She had one shot at freedom right now.

Her hand trembled. She'd have to kill him. Wounding him would do her no good. But it might be all she could manage to do. And he'd fight to the death. His. Or hers.

If she wanted to live, she would have to kill. How could this be her life?

Could she do it? Kill to survive?

"Don't—come any closer," she warned.

Law slowed his stride but continued toward her. "Stop!" she screamed.

"What are you hiding? Show me your hands, Brandi," he said, stalking her now.

"I swear, if you come another step closer, I'll kill you."

He continued toward her. "Really? Give it your best shot. It'll be the last one you get."

Backing away from him, she shook her head. Tears stung her eyes. "Please, just let me go."

"Impossible."

Her spine stiffened and she lifted her chin so that she met him eye to eye. "Then you leave me no choice."

A slow smile stole across his lips. "You always have a choice." He extended his hand. "Give me the dagger."

"How—?"

He looked up past her head. "Mirror."

She made the colossal mistake of turning to see for herself, when instantly, he grabbed her arm and wrist, swinging her around to face the mirror.

The dagger slipped from her fingers into his hand. Expertly, he flung it across the room where it landed with a solid thwack in the wide molding around the bedroom door. "You're going to pay for that," he purred against her ear.

"Let me go!" she screamed, bucking against his arms. "Let me go!"

"Look in the mirror, Brandi," he commanded, taking her chin in his hand, so she had no recourse but to look up. His big powerful body overshadowed hers. "Look hard and look long." His eyes captured her reflected gaze. "I am lord and master here. Nothing and no one, not even the most insignificant detail escapes my eye." His inescapable grip tightened, forcing her to arch backward, submissive against her will. "I own everything in my dominion. Including you."

"You don't own me," she sobbed.

The sensation of his fingers tracing across her bare shoulder proved otherwise. She squeezed her eyes shut, clenching her jaw when her nipples hardened.

"See how your body already craves my touch?"

"It's cold."

His low laugh made her blood race. "But you're hot."

"You're vile, Law."

"You won't think so for long."

He released her. "The bathroom is that way. Go clean your-self up."

"I want to go to the white room."

"You'll have to earn the right to your privacy."

Knowing if she stayed and argued he'd touch her again, Lana hurried through his bedroom to the wide door he'd indicated. There was no handle, how was she supposed to get in? On cue, it silently slid open revealing a magnificent space. Dark, masculine and luxurious. Worthy of the man who owned it. Her captor. Lord and master. Controller of her world.

For long minutes Lana stood at the threshold. If she cleaned up as he commanded, what was next? If she obeyed his commands in the big bed, then what? When he'd finished with her would he send her down to the pleasure palace?

No, she wouldn't do it.

Hopelessness suffocated her. Stepping over the threshold, she waved her hand. The sliding door closed behind her, giving her much needed privacy.

Placing her hands on the edges of the black marble sink, she closed her eyes and hung her head. She was tired. Hungry. Terri-fied. That wasn't all.

By now she craved a fix so bad she could feel the sting of a needle slip beneath her skin. Imagined the euphoria that only heroin could give her, engulfing every cell of her body. It had been perfect that first time. God, how she loved the warm place. What she would give for a permanent fix.

Out of habit, she looked into the medicine cabinet, concealed by the mirror. Nothing there but a glass and a bottle of ibuprofen, not worth stealing because it couldn't get her high.

Raising her head, she looked into her own eyes. The loneliness there caused her heart to stop beating for a brief moment.

She had lost herself a long time ago. Given up pieces of herself until she stopped caring about what was left.

No one was going to rescue her. She had no one to call. Nowhere to go. No one who gave a damn what happened to her.

She couldn't even beg for help. Her lips twitched. "Fuck all of you."

Fifteen minutes later, she sank into warm bathwater. Closing her eyes with a long sigh, Lana settled back into the deep tub. The water buoyed her small body upward. Pressing the soles of her feet against the end of the tub, she was able to stay submerged to the neck. It felt good. The warmth soothed her frayed nerves, burning stomach, and achy bones.

Allowing the tension to seep from her body, she lifted the jagged rim from the drinking glass she'd found—and deliberately broken.

Carefully, looking for a vein, she slid it lengthwise along a phrase tattooed on the inside of her forearm.

...it's all a lie...

No truer words ever written.

The sting of the initial cut was barely noticeable. By the time she cut up her arm enough to slice the words in half, the tub was pink. When the glass slipped from her fingers, it was red.

CHAPTER SEVEN

THE SHARP PAIN radiating through her arm roused Lana from the sweet oblivion of unconsciousness. She moaned as it intensified.

"Hold her still," a concerned voice commanded.

Powerful hands pressed against her shoulders. "Don't move." Law kept her pinned.

Slowly, she surfaced from the depths of nothingness to groggy awareness. Too weak to fight.

Her eyes fluttered open to meet Law's angry green gaze. She stared back, unable to speak, feeling a surge of mute fury. He looked away and up as another face moved into her line of vision. Dark brown eyes, compassionate. "I need you to stay completely still, miss. You've done a lot of damage to yourself."

Damage?

"Fixed. Halfway." Law answered her silent question as if he'd read her mind. She winced when he pressed down harder. "Don't fucking move. Do what the doctor says."

Moving her head slightly to the left, Lana cringed. Her forearm was half sutured. The rest of it was flayed open and bloody. There was no escape. She had landed in hell—and tried to take the only sure way out. Hadn't worked.

A sob tore from her chest. "I hate you," she murmured. "Hate you." Her arm screamed in pain. She was alive. For what it was worth.

"Give her something," Law muttered.

The other man's blue-gloved hands held up a tiny vial of clear fluid and a syringe, expertly withdrawing its contents with a gleaming needle. Her eyes rolled back into her head the minute the morphine slid into her bloodstream. A long sigh escaped her before she mumbled, "Thank you," and drifted off to the lovely place.

Where she drifted in and out of a drug-induced haze, not knowing if time passed or stood still. The one constant was Law. His voice, and his hands on her brow or on her arm. When she was cold, he covered her; when she was sweating bullets, he pressed cool compresses to her sweltering body.

Always there. Pacing. Or watching.

"She's whiter than the sheet, Doc. What's wrong with her?"

"Should be obvious," the doctor snapped. "You found her in time but she still has lost a lot of blood."

"So give her some."

"I don't have the equipment to cross-type her. Unless you know someone who is O negative, I need to get her to a hospital or we'll lose her."

"I'm O neg. Take mine."

Lana moaned, but trying to speak through the sedative was impossible.

She heard small noises. Clicks. Rips. Law moved away, sat somewhere. Lana fought the enveloping fog, registering what she could, unable to protest.

A whiff of disinfectant stung her nose. A soaked gauze pad

scrubbed her unhurt arm. Gloved fingers sought a vein. Stroking. Pressing. Taping down a thin tube that snaked away. She barely felt the needle pop through her skin.

The thin tube jerked against her wrist. Rich crimson blood flowed into her. She was helpless to prevent it.

The doctor exhaled almost inaudibly. "Almost done." He leaned over her, looking into her eyes. No compassion. Her illusion. He pressed two fingers against her neck, assessing the strength of her pulse. Totally professional. Examining her for signs of shock.

Heartless bastard. If he insisted on getting her to a hospital, she could escape. She was still a prisoner. With the blood of her jailer circulating in her veins.

"I'm going to give you another sedative. When you wake up, you'll feel better."

"No," she managed to say. "No blood. Just…let me…go."

CHAPTER EIGHT

"AM I ALIVE?"

Her teeth chattered the words, her body shaking from the cold emanating from the steady green gaze that transfixed her. With chilling clarity, all at once, she remembered everything that had happened.

Law.

Her kidnapping. The introduction to his mysterious world: Chimera. Her failed escape and epically failed suicide.

She would have succumbed, but the devil had other plans.

A snaking ribbon of crimson had pulled her back from the edge of death. How could such a black heart bleed such a life-giving red? The vision of his blood flowing from his vein into hers would be etched in her mind until she died. The gift of life. Why had he done it?

The very thought of this all-powerful man's blood coursing through her body infused her with a sudden burst of renewed strength. Power. She could feel the hot shimmer of it sluice through her.

How far would Law go for what he wanted? Intuitively, she

understood he would go all the way. Law acted. He was not a bystander. Like the sleek, powerful panther he reminded her of, he would be on constant prowl. Moving through the jungle in search of his next conquest, whether it be friend, foe, or—her heart slammed against her chest—meal. He was the ultimate predator.

She scooted up against the mountain of pillows behind her. The linens slid down her chest to her lap. She was in his bed. Again.

He sat across from her in a black leather chair. She squirmed under the weight of his stare.

Damn him. She craved the feel of the hot heat of his body covering hers. His teeth at her neck, his arms possessively holding her down as he thrust powerfully into her.

This couldn't be real. She had to be imagining it. And yet... Her eyes widened as a soft gasp of breath escaped her parted lips. The primal vision aroused her beyond belief.

Her eyes narrowed as his lips lifted into a self-satisfied smile. Did he know what she was thinking? How could he? Was it because they were now inexorably connected?

Law was a mix of extremes. His power absolute. Yet, he was a sensualist. Everything he surrounded himself with screamed it. And naturally dominant. She knew instinctively that he could inflict extreme pain with one hand and punishing pleasure with the other.

She, Alana Monroe Conti, had tremendous value to this man. In that, she wielded some power even though she resented his blood pulsing through her veins. Heat shot from her belly to her nipples when the vision of her naked on this bed, awaiting the torture of his touch, flashed through her mind's eye.

Law's gaze dropped to her chest. Her nipples tightened.

"You owe me. Twice now," he drawled.

"I don't owe you what I didn't ask for."

"Really, Brandi?" he purred her name. She hated the way he said it. She despised the alias and all it represented. But she would never tell him who she was.

Didn't matter, she told herself. He most likely knew everything about her by now. The files and pictures of her on the computer screen in his secret command center proved otherwise. How long had he been watching her?

Stiffening, she looked down at the cornflower blue camisole nightshirt and matching panties.

Heat stung her cheeks. "Who dressed me?"

Those lazy green eyes sparked as a sly smile curved his lips. "I did." She could hear the deep thrum of satisfaction in his voice.

"What else did you do to me while I was unconscious?" Vague memories slowly surfaced, one by one. Endless tossing and turning. The inability to sleep but not being awake. The bone chilling cold, the sweats and nausea. He'd helped her to the bathroom, made her sip soup and …what else? Her heart thudded. He'd soothed her through her night terrors. Gently. So gently.

"Your body was very receptive to my touch, Brandi."

She snapped out of it. "You're disgusting."

Law shook his head. "You misunderstand. I alone cared for you. I fed you, I bathed you, I dressed you." He gave her a long look. "And each time I touched you, you begged me to touch you more. You don't remember?"

"No! I would never want that! Never with you."

"Methinks the lady doth protest too much."

She wished she had the strength to slug him. "Did you—?"

"Did I what, Brandi?"

"Have sex with me?"

"That depends on your definition of having sex."

"Did you fuck me?"

His reply was instantaneous. "No. And not only did I not fuck you, I didn't suck you, finger you, or touch either one of those eager nipples of yours."

Lana sighed. "Thank you for not being a complete asshole."

So her fantasy had never happened. He never crossed the line the way she'd imagined.

Of course, now that she was lucid enough to remember everything, she understood that for a man like Law there would be serious consequences for what she'd done to herself.

She was in no rush to find out what those consequences were.

For now, she was still a prisoner in his domain. At least now the metal shades that were closed when she first awoke had slowly opened, allowing the afternoon sun to filter through.

Feet propped up on an ottoman, leaning back in the leather chair, Law didn't blink when he said, "And by the way, if you ever pull a stunt like that again, I'll fucking kill you myself."

"Fine with me. Save us both the effort and just get it over with," she countered. Why hadn't he just let her die? What plans did he have for her? He was a criminal. He'd stolen her from a terrible man who had paid over two hundred thousand dollars for her. Who did that? And why?

She used her uninjured arm to push herself back against the headboard and touched metal. Lana looked down and saw a short chain attached to—oh hell. A nervous buzz began in her belly.

"Handcuffs? Really?"

CHAPTER NINE

"SOLID GOLD."

"I'm honored. Or should I be?" He made no reply as she looked at the gauze dressing over the inside of her elbow, a souvenir of his blood donation that she desperately wanted to rip off. That arm was cradled in an open sheepskin-lined cast. The other was free. Maybe if she got him to come closer, she could land a blow. At the very least it would get that smug expression off his face.

She circled her wrist with the open cuff—and locked it. "Look at that. It really works," she said mockingly. "And I thought it was a sex toy."

Law sighed. He reached into his front jeans pocket and withdrew a small gold key.

"Letting me go?"

"Not really."

When she focused on Law, finally seeing him clearly, he looked like he hadn't slept for a week. "Nice of you."

He stood up and shrugged. "Today is your eighth day."

When he touched her hand to unlock the handcuff, his warmth penetrated her cold. Exhaling rapidly, Lana collected herself. Anxiety shimmered through her when he leaned across her. Despite his obvious lack of sleep, he smelled clean. Balsam with a hint of leather.

Stepping back, he held out a hand to her.

"I don't need your help," she said, stubbornly.

"You've lost blood, eaten almost nothing, and barely moved in eight days. Take my hand or I'll carry you to the bathroom."

Not wanting him to touch her any more than needed, Lana reluctantly extended her hands. He slid an arm beneath her back and took her right hand. Gently, he lifted her to a sitting position. The room whirled around her.

Lana swallowed hard. That old anxious feeling that slowly began to build when she needed a fix began to creep up on her. Fighting it back, she raised her chin, catching then holding Law's gaze. Dozens of questions with answers only he could provide swirled in her head. Time to ask them. Before her voice failed her.

"Are you going to tell me why you're keeping me here?"

"I have my reasons. Is that enough of an answer?"

"No. But I can guess." She took the bull by the horns. "For starters, how do you know who my father is?"

Law hoisted her up into his arms like she weighed nothing. "It's my job to know everything about every person who sets foot in my world."

He strode toward the luxurious bathroom and set her down on the closed toilet seat.

"Everything you need, with the exception of a replacement drinking glass, you'll find in the closet, including the robe. Leave the door open, do what you need to do, then call me."

"What I need is something to take the edge off!" she yelled at his retreating back.

"Suck it up."

Lana sat for a long time, shivering in the bathroom, rationalizing away the feeling. It was December in California, and despite the temperate year-round climate, it still got cold.

Not in a climate-controlled man cave with invisible doors, she told herself, knowing exactly why she was shivering. She needed another shot from that doctor. Who was nowhere around, apparently. Law really was in charge.

Her loosely braided hair smelled like shampoo. Her nails were filed smooth and polish free, her body clean. Rolling her eyes back, she leaned into the side of the marble vanity. He had bathed her. Touched her in her most intimate areas, and she had been powerless to stop him. What he'd done wasn't entirely her fantasy. But she knew he wasn't the kind of man to take advantage of an unconscious woman. He had too much ego for that. No—Law liked his women hyper aware and begging for it.

She could get embarrassed, but then Lana reminded herself she had stripped for months.

What had started off as a cocktailing job for some quick cash had turned into a heroin-fueled horror show. She had done things she never thought she would do. Things she had *sworn* she would never do.

Lana could be the poster child for the Never Say Never club.

But there was one never that would stand. She would never fall in love. Not that she could. She didn't believe in it. Lust? Sure, she'd witnessed it first hand in her own home. It had torn her family apart.

Lust—not love—was dangerous. No one was immune. Least of all her.

For the first time in her life she felt vulnerable to it. Law was virile, compellingly so. And now that potent blood pulsed though her veins.

He was literally inside her—just not in the usual way. Alive, taunting, and oh so tempting. She could easily forget everything she had ever learned or felt about sex, and trust it to take her to a new exciting universe.

If she made the jump? She trembled all over as she stood. She would fall longer and harder than she ever had coming off a heroin high. She wasn't cut out for the roller coaster ride that was Law.

No. She had to get away. Her drive to escape exploded inside her with redoubled intensity. She would do whatever was necessary to disappear before anyone knew she was gone.

To that end, it would be imperative to convince Law that she was intrigued by his secret world and more than willing to be part of it. Let him think he held sway over her emotions, her body even, when it was she who was pulling the strings.

A renewed determination swelled within her. She would do it this time. She would stay clean, focused, committed to escape.

She almost didn't recognize the woman staring back at her in the mirror. Despite the soul sucking fatigue that gripped her, she actually looked—normal. Her natural honey blonde hair shone with health. Her eyes were clear and blue, no hint of bruising or redness. Her skin clean and smooth, no hollowed cheeks or cracked lips.

Finding a toothbrush and toothpaste, she quickly brushed her teeth and washed her hands after she peed.

As she reached for the short robe, a tall shadow fell across the threshold. Law. Shoulders exaggerated by the light pouring over them and his powerful arms. The dark outline of his hand seemed to cup her between her thighs. Lana stepped back as if he had actually touched her there.

"Don't."

"I already did, Brandi."

Angry, she tightened the sash around her waist. "What right do you have to do that?"

"I own the rights to every inch of you."

"You stole the rights!"

"Would you like me to return you?"

"Yeah. And I don't care to who. Anyone would be better than you," she said, knowing he wouldn't call her bluff. His man True had shot Carson twice for her contract. He wasn't giving her back.

The documents she'd pulled up on one of the computers in his control room suddenly made sense.

"Did you kidnap me to get to my father? 'Cause if you did, I hate to break it to you, but he thinks I'm dead and he's damn happy about it. So, that's a strikeout. Can I go now?"

Law crossed his arms over his chest before he answered. Like he was protecting himself. Why?

"I kidnapped you to get to the man who purchased your contract. But first I needed to know how valuable you were to him." His eyes twinkled as his full lips lifted into a sly smile. "Now I know."

"Dragovich?" She'd not only heard the name mentioned by Carson and True, but whispered now and then by some of the wilder girls at the Ultimate. And once she overheard Anton having a violent argument with him on the phone in his club office.

"Do you know the identity of the man who purchased you?" Law asked.

"N-no. Not personally."

"Let me tell you a little about him. He's a modern day

barbarian. No one who defies him lives to brag about it. He maims and kills for sport. "

"Let me guess. You do it for a reason."

He nodded.

Lana threw him a contemptuous look. "Do you know him, this Dragovich?"

"Really well."

Lana swallowed. "Isn't he going to be angry that you stole me?"

"He's beyond angry. He still thinks he owns you. And he doesn't like to share. Which could work to my advantage."

Frissons of panic assailed her.

"Does that mean you're going to force me to have sex with you?" she blurted.

Law threw his head back and laughed. If she didn't hate him so much she'd admit how the gesture changed everything about him.

"What's so funny about that?" she demanded.

Shaking his head, he reached out to her. She only took his hand because she seriously didn't think she had the strength to walk back to the bed by herself.

"I have never forced myself on a woman in my life." He grinned, the action devastatingly handsome. She should be afraid. For some reason she wasn't.

When they moved toward his bed, she stopped. "I don't want to be here. Let me go back to the white room."

"Currently not an option."

Not strong enough to argue, she continued into the large room. When she got to the bed, she pushed off him and sat on the edge.

"How did you take care of me?"

"Very carefully."

"Seriously. If I've been down for eight days like you said, how is it that I don't have bed sores or remember much of anything?"

"Doc kept you slightly sedated. Not enough that I couldn't walk you to and from the bathroom or get a little food into you."

"Why sedate me?"

"You were going through withdrawal. You were combative and uncooperative. Sedating you allowed me to tend you."

"I'm a junkie and you sedated me? Kind of defeats the purpose."

"Not with opioids."

"Who else other than you and the doctor knows what happened?"

"Just Monty." His eyes narrowed. "You remember Monty, don't you?"

The baby-faced guy in the stairway. Her cheeks warmed. "Did I get him in trouble?"

"No, Monty isn't capable of doing anything to anger me, but you certainly hurt his feelings. When you see him you will apologize."

"For what? Trying to escape a psycho kidnapper who thinks he can do whatever he wants to me or with me? Monty was in the way. And I'm not going to apologize to him." She jabbed at Law's rock-hard chest. He barely seemed to notice. "Or you."

Law was silent. Not even looking at her. Lana kind of lost it and jabbed his chest again. "And don't give me any crap about that contract!"

He pushed her hand away. "It exists. Deal with it."

"How? What kind of man are you to enforce it?"

"A man on a mission."

"Never mind that kidnapping and keeping me against my will is against the fucking law!"

"When I have what I want, you will be free to walk out the door."

"With what strings?"

"None at all."

"I don't believe you."

"You don't have to."

She studied his impassive expression for a long moment, thinking.

Truth be told, playing along might well be the fastest way to get away. In the meantime, she was safer here than outside. And being able, however unwillingly, to permanently kick her habit in his luxurious private suite certainly beat the hell out of a grungy rehab center.

Could work. Had to work. She didn't see any other fucking options. Lana slowly leaned back onto the cool sheets.

Law's penthouse invited the senses to indulge in opulent sights, textures, smells and sounds. Every inch of her surroundings provided extraordinary visual pleasure.

Looking at him did too.

Her nipples tingled as her mind ran wild with wanton images of his undoubted prowess in this big bed. He said he wasn't attracted to her. She lifted her eyes to his intense green gaze and caught her breath.

"I want your promise you won't try to escape again," he commanded.

Cocking her head to the side as if contemplating his request, she sat up straighter. Holding his gaze, she pulled the sash, allowing her robe to fall open. Then, nonchalantly, she shrugged it off.

His eyes dilated, his nostrils flared. For a man who flaunted his self-control, Law looked decidedly like a mortal who wanted something from her...

Settling into the mountain of pillows, she lifted her hips and slowly drew her panties down her thighs, to her knees, then her toes, revealing her smooth body inch by slow inch. Handing them to him, she murmured, "These are scratchy."

Smiling softly, she rolled over onto her belly, careful not to put pressure on her wound, allowing Law plenty of time to take a long, hot look at her dancer's ass. Holding her wrists suggestively over her head, she said, "I'm afraid I can't guarantee I won't try to escape."

Law smacked her bare bottom. "I'm afraid that won't do."

Rolling over, she grabbed the headboard with her good arm and challenged him. "So what are you going to do about it?"

In a flash he grabbed her up against him and smacked her ass again. The sharp heat of his palm on her skin sent warm ripples through her. Her very core unexpectedly tightened with desire.

"What do you want me to do, *Alana*?" Sliding his hands down her back to her bottom, he dug his fingers into her tender flesh. Oh good god, the way he just owned it. Pressing his lips to her ear, he whispered, "I don't have to ask."

"Then just do it," she whispered back, tense with anticipation. She had never let anyone do this to her. As of this moment she wanted it. Intensely. How had he known?

He spanked her. She yipped in pained pleasure.

His hand on her skin struck like a live wire to her core. The stimulation so intense, tears stung her eyes. She reveled in his sexual audacity, and the unexpected cravings he evoked. She'd never given a man control over her like she did now. She liked to be controlled by *this* man. By Law. Her deep desire to be disciplined—and protected—by him overwhelmed her.

"You can tell me to stop." Before she could speak, he delivered a few more stinging slaps, expertly placed. Followed by soothing strokes rounding up and down her behind that made her want to beg for more. And more.

"I don't want you to stop." It was all she could do to answer. And he didn't stop. Lana said nothing more, pressing herself against him. Because if she spoke, she would cry.

CHAPTER TEN

ABRUPTLY, Law released her. Falling back into the pillows, Lana lay stunned. Her body jerked toward him as he stalked from the room closing the door behind him.

What the hell just happened? Had he cast some spell on her? Or just this place?

The heat Law had so easily generated was slow to leave her. She pulled the sheet up to her chin. Squeezing her eyes closed, she didn't try to make sense of what just happened. Maybe tomorrow she'd pick at it and figure it out. But right now, her fight was gone. Exhaustion overtook her. Giving in to it, Lana dug deep into the big bed, and closed her eyes.

It was hours later when he returned to her. It was dark now. The quiet startling. He stood over her, his expression unreadable. But that slight curve to his lips gave her hope. Until she silently reminded herself that she didn't believe in hope.

He's not your friend. Good for sex, yes. Anything else, no. Don't trust him.

Hot almost-sex followed by a long sleep had her feeling somewhat stronger. But she knew despite her will to curb it, her body would continue to crave a fix. Savoring the warmth of Law's colossal bed, she was still aware that it wouldn't be long before she was cold, achy, and exhausted again.

"Sleep well?"

The offhand question had to be answered.

"Yes." She left it at that, uncomfortable under his steady gaze. What would he do if she told him to go away? More importantly, what would she do?

She was on her own, with just the devil to guide her. Her past existed only in nightmares. Her future was unimaginable.

In the present, there was only Law. Who'd done everything he could to keep her alive. Why?

Something in the way he was looking at her kept her from asking that crucial question. Those dark green eyes shielded his soul.

Days later Lana woke blinking against sunshine. Not looking around, somehow she knew Law was not in the bedroom. His massive energy had disappeared. She was alone. But he—or someone he'd put in charge—had still been taking care of her.

And sedating her to do it. An IV methodically dripped fluids into her through a small port near her wrist. Glancing at her left arm, she gasped. The open-sided cast was gone. The bandages were too and so were the stitches. The only thing left as a reminder of her suicide attempt was a swollen, ugly six-inch red scar, distorting her tattoo.

...it's all a lie...

The words were a testament to her failure at death. She couldn't even get that right.

Seagulls called outside of the window. Straining to look, she collapsed back into the sheets. Waiting for the craving to bite.

It didn't.

Was she clean?

"Welcome back," Law said from the doorway of the bathroom.

Warmth fizzled through her veins, much like the beginning of a high. But instead of being cocooned in a floaty sense of well-being, she felt nervous and afraid.

Law was…hot. Hotter than she'd realized. Unfucking-believably hot. Holy-fuck-shit hot. Touch-that-and-go-down-in-flames hot.

If she was clean, he was sure to become her new addiction. The thought of it terrified her. But she had to take him in.

His jet black hair was wet, slicked back. Water dappled his skin across the expanse of his bare shoulders. His long muscular arms were roped, defined by sinew, thick veins pronounced beneath the intricate detail of his tattoos. His chest was wide, with a dusting of coarse black hair. So fine. Oh yes. She felt a little dizzy, even lying down.

Her eyes followed the dark trail down to his navel to the top of the grey towel he'd wrapped around his lean hips. Then her gaze drifted lower.

She didn't need x-ray vision to alert her to the presence of what made him a man. The thick outline of his penis was clearly defined beneath the damp fabric. He held the towel with one hand as he patiently waited for her to respond.

"Ah, um, what did you say?" Her brain kicked in—sort of.

"I said, welcome back."

"Oh. Yeah. But I'm not sure I want to be back." Her muscles ached from disuse. "I need to get out of this bed."

He nodded, but didn't move.

She raised her eyebrows. "Like now."

He continued to stare at her.

"Please," she forced herself to say.

He tucked the end of the towel into the other side, securing it, then helped her sit up.

"First things first." He removed the IV needle from the port and checked the point of entry. Reaching past her to the end table, he unwrapped a small bandage and applied it.

"How do you feel?" he asked, straightening.

"I'm not sure yet."

She had been weak and unsteady before, now she felt depleted. "I don't think I—" Before she finished her sentence he whisked her up into his arms and strode into the bathroom with her. Lifting the toilet lid, he set her down on the seat, and pulled her panties down to her knees. She didn't have the strength to fight him.

Lana did her thing. When she flushed the toilet he hoisted her up with one arm and pulled her panties up with the other. The friction of her body against his loosened his towel.

"I need to wash my hands," she protested.

Securing his towel again, Law remained close, his body a steadying force behind her.

Her hands shook as she rinsed them. Law's nearness made her nervous. Power swirled around him, wrapping her in its intense grip. She was a fool to think she could ever escape this man.

Law reached past her to a towel. Lana gasped, surprised at her intense reaction to the heat of his skin as he pressed into her. Their eyes clashed in the mirror.

"Please," she whispered. "I can't do this."

His lips quirked as he handed her the towel. "You mean dry your hands?"

She managed it.

He handed her a glass of cold water. After she drained it, she felt better.

"Can you make it back to the bed?"

"I think so."

Kind of amazing that she felt better going back to the bed than she had leaving it. Perching on the edge, she stretched. Law glowered down at her.

She supposed he had reason to. Lana was aware by now of just how much she'd upended his carefully controlled life. He seemed to be a true loner. His well-dressed guests or whatever they were—friends?—were kept at a distance on the lower floors. He was literally above them in every way, all by himself.

"Why do you live alone?" she asked.

His swift reply was blunt. "I don't like people."

"How can you say that? From what I've seen outside of here, you're surrounded by them."

"And I control every one of them."

"You're an egomaniac."

"Just careful."

"Why? Who's plotting against you?"

"Good question." Law threw his head back and laughed. "Could be the guy who threw you into that van and dropped you off here. Not quite the special delivery I was expecting."

The smart-ass comment nettled her. Not that she was about to admit that to him.

Laughing or not, he had a dangerous gleam in his eye. The distorting scar that ran the length of the left side of his face only served to emphasize it. This man was not to be fucked with. By anyone on any level. He would always win.

She went quiet. If she let him do the talking, she might learn something she needed to know.

"Any further questions?" he asked.

She shook her head.

"Good, because I don't plan to answer them. Now, I want your word you will not leave the penthouse unless you're with me. You won't try any more attention-getting tricks like you did in the bathtub. And you'll eat."

The mention of food suddenly had her ravenous. She would agree to his terms. Until she found a way out.

She glanced down at the yellow bruise at the bend of her right arm where the transfusion needle had been inserted, reminding herself that he'd given his blood to save her life.

And that he'd probably never let her forget it. Slowly she tilted her head back to look at him.

"Should I thank you for saving my life when you have no intention of respecting it?"

He shrugged. "Do whatever you want, Alana."

"Are you going to kill Dragovich?"

"Eventually."

"In the meantime?"

"I'm going to fuck with him."

"By that you mean dangle me in front of him like a worm on a hook?"

"I would never be so crass. I have much subtler ways of drawing him out."

"I don't want to play your game."

"You don't have a choice."

It occurred to her his name was Law for a reason: He *was* the law. At least here. Oh but the irony of it stung. Law was anything but law abiding. And he had her locked up in his opulent jail of creature comforts. None of it mattered without her freedom.

There had to be another way to win this potentially deadly game of cat and mouse she was being forced to play. Strong as he was, he had to have a weak spot. No doubt he was just a whole hell of a lot better at hiding it than ordinary men. But even so. There had to be one thing in his perfect fucking life that he didn't have.

In a flash of insight, it came to her: someone who didn't bow down to him. For that reason alone—and others she didn't fully understand—she was what he wanted, right here and right now.

His desire for her was his weak spot and she intended to exploit it to the max. She would have to become the one thing Law couldn't live without. A warm flush cascaded through her.

He was no one's fool, though.

This wasn't going to be easy. To become the one thing he couldn't live without, she'd have to be the elusive thing he couldn't possess. Lana wasn't so sure she had the fortitude to tempt him without tempting herself.

"You're awfully quiet," he said suspiciously.

"Just thinking."

"Yeah? Then think about this, Alana. I don't want to hurt you, but I will use whatever force is required to prevent you from injuring yourself again or running away."

Lana opened her mouth to debate that, but the steely resolve in his eyes told her she would lose.

Law rubbed the scar tissue on his neck. It was an absent gesture. Something she noticed he did when he was miles away.

"What happened to your neck?"

"It was burned."

"Why?"

"To remove what was there."

"What was there?"

"You're nosy."

"It's not like I have anything else to do. What was burned off?"

"A brand."

"Oh my God, why would you do that?"

"Long story. Never mind why. But that mark was no longer of value to me," he explained. "Not after Chimera was born." He flexed his right bicep, showing off a striking raised design of a flaming circle with a lion, snake and goat head.

"You know Chimera is a girl, right?" Lana scoffed.

"I also know the female of the species is the strongest."

"It takes a real man to acknowledge that."

His lips quirked. "You know I'm a real man too."

Ignoring the obvious, Lana asked, "So why a girl that's part goat?"

"When you think of a male lion, what do think?"

"Powerful, protective. Aggressive. Polyamorous. Lazy. Hunter. Loyal to his pride."

"A goat?"

"Stubborn. Agile. Adaptable. Stinky."

"A snake?"

Lana shivered. She didn't like snakes. "Stealth. Sneaky. Constrictor. Patient. Deadly."

"That's Chimera."

The hair on the nape of her neck spiked. There was no doubt in her mind that Chimera was all of those things and more.

"It's a real brand?" she asked, reaching her fingertip to it. Running her finger slowly around the design, she shivered. "That must have hurt like hell."

"Like a mother."

Not thinking, she reached to the burn scar on his neck. "What kind of society are you to do such things?"

He grabbed her hand, his gaze piercing her. "The kind that girls like you should stay away from."

A curious fear—mingled with excitement—coursed through her. "What if I don't want to?"

"You will." He dropped her hand like it burned too, then strode to the bathroom. Without closing the door, he finally let go of that damn towel and stepped into his briefs. Female that she was, she bit her bottom lip when his fine ass flexed.

Make that *very* fine ass. Serious muscle. Made for driving down and hard into a willing woman.

But not her.

CHAPTER ELEVEN

"STOP STARING AT MY ASS."

Heat flushed her cheeks when he looked over his shoulder at her. With a wink.

"I wasn't looking."

"Liar."

Fine, she was a liar. There was no other way with Law. Honesty would be used against her.

A moment later he strode from the bathroom through the door to the right of it, reemerging several moments later fully dressed.

Heat swirled low within her. She'd have to be made of stone not to be affected by the way he moved. He had the graceful stealth of a wild beast. His body thrummed with leashed power, his gaze everywhere, all-seeing. Nothing slipped past this man.

Swallowing hard, Lana suddenly understood she'd have to outsmart him at every turn if she were going to get out of here alive.

It seemed hopeless.

"Instead of thinking about how you're going to one-up me and escape, why don't you focus on getting well?"

Her jaw dropped. How the hell did he know what she was thinking?

He grinned at her as he buckled his leather belt. "Yeah. I can read minds."

His dark brows rose as he pondered the question. "Your freedom aside, what do you want from me, Lana?"

Posing prettily on the edge of the bed took serious effort. "What do you want from me—Law?" As he moved toward her she slid backward on the bed.

"Are you offering yourself to me?"

"Wouldn't dream of it."

He leaned over her. "Don't play with me, Lana. I don't play by the rules."

Holding his hot stare, Lana deliberately licked her lips and purred, "Neither do I."

His lips turned up into a taunting smile that made her insides overheat. "Game on."

Long sizzling seconds held them both captive before the soft chiming of a doorbell infiltrated their spell.

Reluctantly, Law drew back, extending his hand to Lana after she donned her robe. Slipping her hand into his much larger one sent ripples of pleasure coursing through her. She shouldn't feel this way. She never had. Why with him?

Unfortunately, she'd have plenty of time to figure that out. Lana followed Law to a wide metal door that led into a foyer with an elevator at one end. The noiseless double doors slid open.

The woman who exited, pushing a gleaming brass cart piled with upscale shopping bags and boxes, whisked past Lana as if she didn't exist. They all had the same label: Neiman Marcus.

Setting everything on and around an end table, she pointed to them and said, "It's all there, Law. You owe me."

She ran a hand through her spiky black hair and turned deep-set, dark hazel eyes on Lana, giving her a dismissive glance before turning back to Law.

"You know I always pay," he answered with an amused smile. The suggestive tone of his deep voice irked Lana. Was this his girlfriend?

The woman smiled back, revealing two dimples that changed her from badass to angelic. "You know how much I love payday."

"You're greedy, Jhett."

She zinged him back. "Like the pussy that can't get stroked enough."

Oh *please*. Not exactly subtle. Lana frowned.

He was teasing her and the woman seemed to be lapping it up—and not remotely caring that Lana was right there, forced to listen to their annoying banter. With Jhett's attention fully focused on Law, Lana gave her a covert onceover. Who was this slick, leather-clad dynamo?

More importantly, who was she to Law? Their familiarity irritated Lana. The sense of being an outsider, overwhelming.

Jhett was tall and lithe. Her energy intense. And the physical opposite of Lana in every other way to boot: black-haired and dark-eyed with copper colored skin.

Her movements were quick, sure and strong. Aside from the piercings that laced her ears, the one thing that stood out like a flare at midnight was the black leather and silver chain choker.

Lana's stomach did a slow whirl. The meaning of the collar wasn't lost on Lana. Was Law her master? Lana didn't want to care about that, but she did.

The room began to swim. Lana hugged herself tighter, as if

the gesture would keep her standing. Wearing only the skimpy pajama set and robe, she felt shaky and exposed.

"I need to sit dow—" She didn't finish the word. Her knees buckled and she collapsed.

Ninja quick, Jhett slid her body beneath Lana's before she hit the floor, cradling her in her arms.

The act startled Lana back to hyper awareness. "Don't touch me," Lana hissed, trying to push out of the woman's arms. The harder she pushed, the tighter Jhett's embrace became.

"Easy does it, Jhett," Law said. "She needs time."

Needs time? She needed time? For what?

"Please, just help me up," Lana muttered.

Jhett stood, gently bringing Lana with her. She led Lana to the sofa and held her steady as both of them sat down.

"I'm fine," Lana said, edging away from her.

Jhett and Law exchanged looks, which Lana noticed with renewed annoyance.

"Hey, I almost forgot," Jhett said to Law, shifting into business mode. "True has some info for you and he wants to meet with you asap."

Nodding, Law strode to the kitchen. "Give me thirty, then tell him to come up."

Jhett looked over her shoulder at Lana. "With her here?"

Law glanced at Lana, then back to Jhett. "Last time I checked, my doors close."

Which didn't mean they were totally soundproof, Lana thought. She was *so* going to eavesdrop

"Have Monty keep an eye on her," Jhett advised.

It was Law's turn to be annoyed. "Thank you, Jhett, for telling me how to run my life."

"Sorry, Law, it's just that—" Rising from the sofa, Jhett lowered her voice. "Everyone's on edge."

"Nothing to be on edge about. Everything's under control."

"I know, I just—"

Law took Jhett's chin in his hand and cocked her head back. He lowered his lips to her ear and whispered something. Warm shivers broke in slow waves across Lana's skin. Imagining the warmth of his breath and the brush of his lips on her skin.

Jhett nodded, glancing again at Lana before she exited the room.

Not trusting her voice to sound steady or her confusing emotions, Lana sat silent.

"Lunch is on the way," Law called from the depths of the kitchen.

Her appetite had waned. And now that they were alone, there was the question she hadn't had a chance to ask. "What do I need time for?"

Law appeared with a bottle of mineral water and a glass of ice. Pouring as he came toward her, he handed her the glass. "You need to hydrate."

She set it on the end table and looked pointedly up at him. "I need to find out what the hush-hush plans are."

"There aren't any. Drink up."

"That's bullshit and you know it, Law. What are you going to do with me?"

"Right now? Feed you. After that, make sure you get a shower and put you back to bed."

"Stop talking around my question. Are you expecting me to engage in sex acts with that woman or other women?"

There. She'd said it. Nagging suspicion of Jhett won out over reticence. Normally, Lana wasn't the jealous type. But there was nothing normal about what went on in Law's domain.

Law's green eyes sparkled mischievously. "Don't you like women?"

"I tried once. Not my roll."

His lips broke into a wide grin. "Every man's fantasy."

"Really? You'd like to watch two women sixty-nine?" Like he would shudder and go *oh my goodness, no no no*. Men never said no to that scenario. Women faking it was nearly as good.

"Only if that's what they wanted. I don't like performances."

Lana took a long sip of her water. The cold helped cool her fire.

"And what would you do while they were going down on each other?"

He smiled again. "Anything they wanted me to do."

The image of Law fucking a beautiful woman from behind as she sucked and licked another woman was unexpectedly erotic. Why? Because he was part of the fantasy, that was why. She squirmed in her seat.

"Would you like to be part of that party, Alana?"

"No!"

Law laughed. "Liar."

The awkward moment was interrupted by Monty's entrance. He maneuvered a serving cart through the door—and not just any serving cart. The domes over the platters were sterling silver and so was the cutlery. Damask napkins, folded with a flourish. The gleaming domes promised gourmet fare, no doubt prepared by Law's personal chef. Lana's stomach growled. Not wanting to face Monty, Lana stared at her toes.

"Is she okay now, Law?" Monty asked, with genuine concern.

Squeezing her eyes tightly closed, Lana wished she could disappear. Instead, she slowly opened them and stared into the worried gaze of a man-child. "I'm fine," she said before gazing toward the window.

When Monty left the room, Law rolled the cart toward Lana.

As he uncovered the dishes of soups, fresh baked bread and fruit, he said, "Do not mess with Monty. Do not entice him. Do not engage him in any way other than hello and good-bye."

Spreading a cloth napkin across her lap, Law bent down to face her. "Do you understand?"

"Yes." *And you can go fuck yourself,* she added mentally. *Or go fuck Jhett in her pierced ear.*

"Good. Now eat. And when you're done, go through the bags Jhett brought. You should find enough girl things and clothing to keep you happy for awhile."

Lana did as she was told. She ate. She showered. She changed into fresh pajamas she'd pulled from one of the bags. She slid between the smooth cool sheets. Fatigue stole over her as Law closed the bedroom door behind him.

Fighting sleep, she listened for the sound of the penthouse door opening. After what seemed like an hour, she heard True's deep voice, then Law's.

Slipping from the big bed, she tiptoed to the bedroom door, and carefully opened it just a crack.

In the light of the day she was able to get a clear unobstructed view of True. Whereas Law was dark and moody, True was bright and open. His thick blond hair was cut in a choppy side part pompadour. Clear sky blue eyes sparkled. His naturally tan skin with a hint of golden stubble set them off like shiny aquamarines on the beach.

He was dressed for the road. Black leather pants clung to his long legs. A long-sleeved black Henley shirt molded to his defined torso. A gold chain hung around his corded neck, a chunky cross hanging from it.

His golden aura didn't fool Lana. He had to be as deadly as Law.

A hard shiver shook her from head to toe. Not in fear—in

awe. She was a girl in the presence of two extraordinary men. Powerful men. Intelligent, highly skilled men who played for high stakes and never lost.

Law was the architect. True executed the plans.

The deadly Russians who frequented the club had nothing on these two. They would just as soon put a bullet between her eyes for shits and giggles. Law and True were highly evolved predators who would never be so gauche. Their methods would be slow and deliberate. Excruciatingly effective.

"The contract just went up to five million," True said.

"By the end of the week it'll be twice that."

"The body count is climbing."

"By the time this is over, there won't be a thug left on the streets."

She craned her neck, trying to keep True in her line of vision as he moved from door. "There is that."

"Now," Law drawled. "What do you suggest we do with the senator's daughter in the meantime?"

CHAPTER TWELVE

LANA FROZE, her ear glued to the crack in the door. True's answer was lost on her as the men moved further into the vast penthouse. All she could make out was deep muffled voices.

Weren't contracts for killing people? Who put up the contract? Was it for her? Shaking uncontrollably, Lana wrapped her arms around her waist. What *was* Law going to do with her? Put her to work in his sex club?

She wouldn't do it. That is, if she had a chance in hell against all those big mean men Law was able to summon at the snap of a finger. Which she didn't. So...maybe she could bartend or serve. The irony of it, despite all of her fuckedupness, was that she had a degree in international banking. She'd picked that degree to get her out of the country where her chances of staying dead were higher than in this country. Hah, and what had she done for a living? Stripped. And now? Would she be forced to earn her keep on her back?

That was what happened to Ultimate girls who were about to be kicked out for drug abuse or stealing. Eventually they checked out of life forever, one way or another.

Panic swelled. Law's voice was close. He was coming straight toward her. Quickly stepping back from the door, she stumbled, barely catching herself when the door opened.

"Eavesdropping?" Law asked.

"Is there a contract out on me? Who wants me dead? My father? He knows I'm alive! Is my father trying to have me killed?" she shrieked.

Grabbing her hands, Law drew her toward the bed. "Get some sleep."

"No! Tell me, tell me now! Is he trying to kill me?"

Pushing her onto the edge of the bed, Law smoothed her hair back from her face. "Why did you make your father think you're dead?"

Shaking uncontrollably, Lana fought for words.

"Because," she softly said, "It was the only way to escape them."

"Them?"

"My parents. The world."

Raising her eyes to him, she fought back the terrifying images of that night. The argument with her mother. The threats. The guilt. The ultimatum...

"Why?"

He wouldn't understand. No one would. "I—" she whispered, "couldn't stand the pressure of being their daughter," she lied. "At my high school graduation party, I jumped off the yacht they had rented to celebrate. They thought I fell overboard. I swam as far away from that boat as I could. I never looked back."

Law's thoughtful gaze unnerved her. "I think your parents would be thrilled to know you were alive."

"No—he knows. He wants me to stay dead." Grabbing his

shirt with both hands, she twisted the fabric and pleaded, "Promise me you won't tell them I'm here."

"I promise," he softly said. "How do you know your father wants you dead?"

"He instructed Anton to sell me off."

"And how do you know that?"

"Anton told me. It's why I finally signed the contract." Tears began to stream down her cheeks. "I—I just didn't care anymore. If my father knew what was happening and encouraged it, what was there left for me?"

Drawn into his arms, Lana dropped the floodgates and cried a river.

"The contract isn't on you, Lana."

"Who then?"

"Me."

"What?" she cried, choking on her tears. "Why? Who wants you dead?"

He smiled that dangerous smile and let her go. "If I told you—"

"What are you going to do?"

"Do everything I can to drive up the price."

"Why?"

"It will serve several purposes."

"But—"

"No more questions. I have work to do. Get to sleep."

"I'm wide awake now!"

He tapped several icons on his cellphone and the blinds magically turned until the room had completely darkened. A soft glow emanated in the farthest corner, giving just enough light that she could watch Law stride toward the bedroom door, then disappear behind it.

Long, drawn-out minutes turned into hours. Lana lay wide-awake in the big bed, her mind racing with one chilling scenario after another. So strange, that she was probably safest here under Law's protection than any other place on the planet.

Tossing and turning every time she closed her eyes, she couldn't rest, bedeviled by haunting images. Her efforts to push the past out of her present were futile.

Unable to sleep, Lana padded to the living room, disappointed to find the penthouse empty.

Drawn to the city lights, she gazed out the window. A fine mist swirled over the water, shimmering like fairy lights. Exhaling a long sigh, Lana climbed up into the deep windowsill. Pulling her knees to her chest, she wrapped her arms around them, pressed her cheek to her kneecaps and gazed upon the night.

An odd sense of calm infused her. For the first time since the night that changed everything thirteen years ago, she felt safe.

Mother couldn't get her. Nor could her father. Oddly, it wasn't him that she feared. It was her mother. Elizabeth Marie Seton-Conti. The coldest bitch in the land. Classic wire-monkey mom.

Thank God for Mamita. Tears welled in her eyes then spilled down her cheeks. Brushing them away, she leaned into the cool glass. It seemed a lifetime ago. It was. She'd royally fucked up. Hurt the person she loved the most. Nothing was the same.

Everything had changed. If only she could turn back the clock…

"Why are you crying?" Law's deep voice asked from several feet away.

Startled, Lana cried out in alarm. Embarrassed he'd caught her at such a raw moment, she pushed up from the windowsill and moved past him. Gently he reached out and stopped her. "Why are you crying?"

Sniffing her runny nose, Lana swept her hair off her damp cheeks. "If I thought you gave a fuck, I'd tell you."

He didn't counter, and let her pass. She wanted to whirl around, pound her fists on his chest and demand he push harder. Tell her he *did* give a fuck. Tell her he would protect her. Tell her she was going to be OK. Instead, she continued toward the bedroom and slammed the door shut behind her.

Lana was awakened by a deep moan of pain.

At first she thought she was dreaming until she realized the anguished sound emanating from the bed came from Law.

He was lying next to her, on fire, damp to the touch. His fisted hands clenched hard, as if he were fighting.

"Law," she murmured.

Agitated, he growled, the sound so feral she recoiled in fear.

His breathing became labored. "Law," she said, louder. "You're having a dream."

He flung the covers from him. The dark hair on his chest glistened with sweat. Scooting closer, Lana pressed her hand to his chest. His heart thudded wildly beneath her palm. "It's okay," she crooned.

"Aria?" he said, his voice a desperate whisper.

"No, it's Lana."

He moved so quickly, Lana didn't see it coming. He grabbed her neck with his big hand and squeezed. Shaking her, he demanded, "Where is she? *Where is she?"*

Air cut off, she couldn't cough, much less scream for him to release her. Clawing at his hands, kicking at him with her bare feet, Lana fought for her life. Muted, desperate sounds escaped her throat. Instantly he let her go.

Law rolled over, turned on the nightstand lamp. Disoriented, he stared at her, a shocked look in his eyes. Coughing, Lana moved away from him.

"Christ. Lana, I'm sorry. Oh, Christ." He reached for her but she backed away. "Did I hurt you?" The concern for her was real. So was her pain and fear.

Lana shook her head and hung onto the far side of the bed away from him. When he approached her from the other side, she cried out for him to stop.

Law stopped in his tracks and muttered another apology. He hurried from the room, closing the door soundly behind him.

She didn't go back to sleep. She paced. She wept. She prayed.

She damned her mother, her father and God. She damned Anton, and Law, and finally, as she stood in front of the mirror tracing her fingertips along the budding bruises on her neck, she cursed herself.

The windows lightened as dawn debuted. It began like a typical dreary winter day in not-so-sunny California. Thick fog repelled the rising sun's attempt to cast warmth on the churning bay.

The room was cold. Lana was cold. Angry. Frustrated.

She retreated to the only room in the penthouse with no windows—and a limitless supply of hot water. Standing under the pounding spray, palms against the shower wall, the anger morphed into rage. She wasn't a fucking punching bag! She might not have value to anyone on the planet, but her pity party was officially over. Damn every man in her life who thought he could control her with sex, drugs or shame.

And worst of all, violence. Just because they lost control. Just because they could.

Fuck all of them! Today was now Lana Conti Day. Her rebirth day. And God help any man who got in her way.

Lana took her time in the bathroom. Having gone through the bags and boxes Jhett had delivered, she knew there was nothing in them she didn't need. High-end cosmetics and toiletries. Beautiful lingerie, trendy jeans, skirts, dresses and shirts mixed in with couture pieces. Boots, shoes, slippers and sandals, jewelry even.

The only thing missing was her freedom. And that, she decided, would come much sooner than later.

Dressed in artfully ripped skinny jeans and an Aegean-blue off the shoulder silk blouse held together by a single mother-of-pearl button, Lana smirked. She'd decided against panties and bra. The smooth silk outlined the curve of her breasts and tips of her nipples. Perfect.

Her aim was to subtly seduce Law. Starting with acting as if he didn't matter in the least to her. Which would be easy, since he didn't. Once she had his complete attention, she'd eventually gain his trust. With that accomplished, freedom was inevitable. His vigilance would diminish. Given an effective distraction—to be invented—he could be caught off-guard like anyone else. And the day that happened, she'd be gone before he knew it.

Releasing a long breath, she glanced up at the mirror. Lana didn't recognize the woman staring back. It had been a long time since she'd looked so healthy. Thin, yes. She could use a few more pounds for sure but the dullness in her eyes was gone. There was a determined set to her jaw. A spark of defiance in her eyes. Tossing her long hair over her shoulders, Lana smiled.

She looked really good, and she knew it. She'd use it to her advantage. On her terms and no one else's.

Going to the bedroom door, Lana pulled it open and strode into the living room.

Law was nowhere to be found. She heard the elevator in the foyer ding and waited for the inner doors to open. Seconds later, Monty arrived with a serving cart. Same deal as before. Domed platters and deluxe tableware.

"Law told me you'd be hungry," he said amiably. "There's food in the fridge too. I already restocked it."

"Thanks." Lana's tone was curt. "That wasn't necessary. But maybe you can help me with something else."

"Uh, I guess so. I mean, sure."

"Don't look so damn scared," Lana snapped. "I just want to know something. Who is Aria?"

CHAPTER THIRTEEN

MONTY BLINKED THEN QUICKLY LOOKED AWAY. "I don't know."

Lana circled him like a cat zeroing in on a mouse. "And who's Jhett?"

Monty smiled with obvious adoration for the aforementioned. "She's—Law's—main girl."

Air whooshed from her chest. Damn it, why did that bother her? Rationalizing that it was actually good news, Lana swept the reasons why it wasn't from her mind. At least now she knew where she stood with Law. The "main girl" information saved her from making a fool of herself. Lana wasn't a poacher but more than that, she refused to play the one-up game for a man. Any man. The degradation the girls at the club subjected themselves to for high rollers disgusted her. But she wasn't any better than they were. The things she'd done for a fix were as degrading.

She wasn't going there. Never again. There were other ways out of here.

The gatekeeper stood before her. And if that puppy dog look

on his face was any indicator of his willingness to please, this was going to be as easy.

"I asked Henri to make you something special," Monty said proudly. "I hope you like eggs."

The aroma wafting from the tray suddenly had her salivating. "I do. Thank you."

With a flourish, Monty removed the domed lids from the dishes. The eggs benedict looked divine. "There's fruit, toast and yogurt too."

There was enough food to feed five of her.

"I brought coffee and tea and hot chocolate. I wasn't sure..." he looked at her, wanting desperately to please.

"I like them all, but I prefer coffee in the morning."

He grinned. "And regular cream and vanilla cream."

Lana sat down at the sleek glass dining table. One by one, and ever so carefully, Monty set the plates in a half circle before her. "If you need anything, Miss Lana, I'll be right in the kitchen."

Lana nodded, digging into the scrumptious meal. Her taste buds happily danced, her belly greedily accepted each delicious bite, panting for more. She'd lost a lot of weight over the last year. Time to reverse that.

Unable to take another bite, Lana sat back in the chair, satiated.

"That was really good, Monty. Thank you."

He smiled sheepishly. "I'll tell Henri."

"Who is Henri?"

"Law's chef. Law takes care of us."

"He kidnapped me, Monty. I don't think that's taking very good care of *me*." She didn't feel the slightest twinge of guilt for disobeying Law's order to not talk to Monty at all besides hello and goodbye.

"He must have a good reason. Law doesn't do anything without a good reason."

Lana sat back in the chair, doubtful she could stand she was so full. "Law isn't his real name, is it?"

Monty suddenly found the floor quite interesting.

"You can tell me the truth, Monty. I can keep a secret," she said in a low conspiring tone.

Lana ignored the twinge of guilt that sparked with her question. She instinctively knew that the damage to Monty's head had something to do with how he processed things. While she was respectful of his condition, she was also trying to survive in a hostile environment. Patiently, Lana just let her comment sit there for him to contemplate.

"No one here has a real name."

"Why?"

"We're ghosts."

"Can you tell me what you mean by that?"

Monty shrugged, offering no further explanation. The hidden story of this mysterious organization and the man at the top was way too intriguing to let go. She wanted to know every nitty-gritty detail about all of them. Especially Law.

"Is Law called Law because he's the boss? Is that the reason?"

Monty's cheeks paled a few shades. "No."

Cocking her head, she studied him for a long moment. "Then why?"

Monty's face tightened as he grabbed empty plates and stacked them. "Because he killed a cop."

CHAPTER FOURTEEN

THE BLOOD DRAINED from Lana's face. *Law killed a cop?* Stunned, she didn't move. Didn't know what to say. How? Why? If he was capable of cold-blooded murder, would he kill her too?

"Wh-why isn't he in prison?"

Ignoring her, Monty continued to vigorously remove the dishes from the table.

"Please, Monty. I need to know." Would the reason even matter?

"It was a long time ago. Back in the Legion days."

"Legion?"

"I'm not supposed to talk about what went on then."

"Are you talking about Lucifer's Legion?" she nearly shrieked. The Legion was not unknown to her. They were a vicious motorcycle gang that hung out at the strip club. They were a rough bunch. For reasons unknown to her, Anton allowed them into the Ultimate. She'd heard that the girls who'd left with them never came back.

"Look, I have to know. Why did he kill a cop?"

Monty finally stopped his agitated cleaning up and stood

straight. Looking her in the eye, he said, "You're not going to get Law in trouble, are you?"

"No—I—how could I? He's holding me prisoner here!"

Monty covered the stacked tray with a cloth. "I have to go."

"Please stay," she softly pleaded. "I promise I won't ask more questions."

"What did I tell you about leaving Monty alone?" Law's deep voice asked from the opposite side of the penthouse. She hadn't heard the elevator. Where had he come from?

Nervously, she stood as he moved toward her, his piercing green eyes riveted on her. He epitomized the devil in both character and dress. Shining black hair. Custom black suit. Black shoes, black shirt, and onyx cufflinks.

The Law who'd stayed by her side night and day, watchful and caring, was gone. In his place, the dark predator she had met two weeks ago.

"I'm not bothering him, we're just having casual conversation." Had he heard Monty's stunning revelation?

"Monty, you can come back in about an hour," Law stated. The tenor of his voice was calm when he spoke to his man.

Leaving the cart behind, Monty hurried out of the penthouse. When the elevator door closed behind him, Law turned his full attention on Lana. Every instinct told her to run and hide. But where? And when had she ever bothered to pay attention to instinct? Wordlessly, he came closer. Balling her hands into fists to keep them from shaking, Lana stood defiant.

Her heightened awareness of his capacity to kill renewed her desire to escape. Despite it, she was angry he had committed an unforgivable crime.

When he reached toward her, she flinched. But all he did was sweep the hair from her shoulder. Then feather light, he touched —just barely—the bruises on her neck.

Her skin warmed, her nipples tightened. Jesus. What was wrong with her?

"Did I hurt you?" he asked huskily.

Oh, let her count the ways. "Bruises don't usually pop up without contact." His nightmare had somehow triggered his violent outburst. It was highly likely that she'd have to defend herself against more—and worse.

"I'm sorry," he said, tracing her collarbone.

Biting her bottom lip, Lana tilted her head back and looked up at him. Without blinking she asked, "Who's Aria?"

Lightning flashed in his eyes. Fingers tightened against her flesh. Lana stood rigid, forcing herself not to shrink away in fear. Thunder rumbled deep in his chest.

"Where did you hear that name?" he bit through clenched teeth.

"You—last night—before you hurt me."

He stepped back from her. For a long few seconds he wrestled with an explanation. Instead of giving her one, he strode to the tall bank of windows that overlooked the Oakland estuary. The dark swirling clouds gathering in the sky rivaled the storm brewing in the penthouse.

Hands clasped behind his back, legs spread, chin high, Law stood motionless.

"She's someone I used to know."

"Did you love her?"

"Yes."

"Do you still love her?"

"Yes."

Lana's body shivered. The profound sadness in his voice moved her. What kind of woman was Aria to be loved so deeply by a man like Law? He didn't give any of himself to anyone. He was a complicated puzzle with damaged pieces. Lana's feminine urge to soothe his hurt away and make him whole again was strong.

Lunacy, she told herself. He was a cop killer.

"What happened?"

"I don't discuss Aria." He turned those lethal green eyes on her. "With anyone. Don't ask me about her again."

"Well, I'm glad she's gone. You would have hurt her just like you hurt me!"

Color drained from his face as unleashed emotions contorted his features. Pain. Terror, if that was possible, and lastly, anger. At her.

"You're a vicious little bitch. Now I know why your father sold you off."

Law shoved past her to the bedroom, leaving her speechless in the middle of the living room. His sharp words hurt. The urge to hurt back harder swept through her. Rage whipped into a furious frenzy.

She hadn't asked for any of this. Yes, he had helped her, undoubtedly only because it suited some nefarious purpose he had yet to reveal. And he had no right to hold her here against her will. Fuck him. Spurred by hurt, frustration and biting jealousy she couldn't rationalize, Lana nearly ran to the bedroom.

Law looked up from his phone just as she lunged at him.

Flinging out a long arm, Law caught Lana around the waist and tossed her onto the bed. When he turned his back to her, Lana screeched and jumped on his back. Law shrugged her off. Lana jumped at him again. He turned as she hit him square in the chest.

Law's arm locked around her waist, forcing the breath from her. "Stop it! Right now!"

She answered his snarl with a shriek. "No!"

CHAPTER FIFTEEN

LAW LET her go and stepped back. Long seconds ticked by. With each one, Lana's heart beat higher in her throat.

"What's your fucking problem?" he asked.

"My *fucking* problem is *you*."

"I'm not your problem, I'm just a manifestation of it." He shook his head.

"That's cold. *You're* cold."

"As ice."

"Is that an excuse? Seriously lame, Law."

"It is what it is. And I'm not accountable to you."

"Bullshit. You kidnapped me. You're holding me hostage. There are consequences."

He snorted. "I'm not sure you know the meaning of that word."

"What are you talking about?"

"You owed Anton almost twenty large for that nasty little habit of yours. As payment, you signed a contract agreeing to give the person in possession of it control of you. I hold the contract. I want you here. That's what I call consequences."

Smug fucker. She wanted to hit him. "I signed under—duress. I was strung out. Desperate. Hopeless."

He seemed unimpressed. "Are you still desperate and hopeless?"

"Yes—I—hate being forced to do anything against my will."

"No one likes it, princess. But this is the real world. The sooner you accept it, the sooner you'll feel better about it."

"Wonderful. I totally want to feel better," she snapped. "I just have to learn to wait, right?"

Law shrugged. "Am I supposed to feel sorry for the poor little rich girl?"

Tears stung her eyes. He had no idea what she had endured. Witnessed. Lived in constant fear of. "You haven't walked in my shoes. You don't get to judge me."

"Touché."

With that one word, he sucked the life out of her fight. He was right. And just as he had not one clue as to her demons, she was clueless about his.

Gently, Law reached out to her cheek and caught a teardrop on his fingertip. "I'm not that difficult to get along with."

Lana rolled her eyes. "You're impossible."

"Impossibly amazing." He grinned. Her heart thudded. She didn't know what to do with this Law. Tenderness was foreign to her. It knocked her off balance. Made her suspicious.

It was crystal clear to her that she was a means to an end for him, and it had to do with Dragovich. An old score to settle? A super secret deal? It didn't matter. What did matter, if she admitted to it, was that she was caught off guard by Law's kindness and in fact actually craved it. That wasn't something she accepted easily.

A sob escaped her tight lips. Lana couldn't help it.

"Tears don't work on me," Law drawled.

Anger flashed again. "You're such an asshole!"

Pushing away from him, not wanting to look at him another second, she went to the bedroom window. Crossing her arms, she gazed at the tempestuous bay. The dark water rolled and dipped, whitecaps curling on the troubled surface beneath the slanted rain.

"I don't like to be used as someone's tool of vengeance."

Law's big body shadowed her much smaller one. Heat emanated from him, a stark contrast to the chill she could almost feel rising from the water below.

"I don't blame you."

Lana exhaled and turned slowly. Looking at his shadowed face, she found his dark gaze staring past her to the bay behind her. "No apology? Just business as usual?"

Finally he lowered his gaze to hers. "Do you want me to lie to you? Invent some gallant bullshit?"

"It would be nice to know that you're not a complete monster."

"I think I've proven to you that I'm not."

"You're fattening me up. I'm your sacrificial lamb. What's not monstrous about that?" Lana shook her head frustrated with so many things none of which she had control. "You're no better than Dragovich."

Law's jaw tightened. "Don't forget it." He headed for his cave, brushing by her, shutting the door soundly behind him.

When he emerged from the secret room sometime later, Lana still stood at the window. The rain had stopped and the distant city glittered like a Christmas tree, casting speckled streams of light on the water far away.

"What day is it?"

"December twenty-first." When Lana turned around she caught her breath. Law was barefoot and dressed down in worn jeans and a black T-shirt that made her heart go pitter-patter. If she didn't get out of here soon, she'd end up in bed with him. Consciously.

"I want to leave."

He shrugged. "I'm not having this conversation with you again."

Hands on hips, Lana calmly began, "As your kidnapped victim, just how much of my life am I obliged to give you?"

He shrugged again. "Your contract doesn't include an expiration date."

"My contract with Anton was simply that I'd give a private dance at his residence in exchange for drugs. I *never* agreed to be sold off."

Law moved past her into the living room. She hurried behind him, hot on his heels, ready to press her point when he stopped at his desk. Pressing his hand to the top right corner, a drawer popped open on the other side. Taking a sheet of paper from the open drawer he handed it to her. "Your contract is very specific."

Lana snatched it from his hand and quickly read the words. Her hand began to shake when she got to the end where she'd signed and dated the document below Anton's signature, noting that the bill of sale gave the bearer of the contract full access to her body for eternity.

"This isn't legal. Therefore it's not binding or enforceable."

Before Law could stop her, she balled it up and threw it into the fireplace.

"There. No contract. Let me go."

Law laughed, shutting the drawer. "That was a copy. The original is safe from you and the rest of the world."

Lana stared at the balled paper burning in the fireplace, quickly devoured by red flame before it crumbled into ashes.

So much for that dramatic gesture.

Of course he wouldn't give her the original. Of course they both knew it wasn't legal. Why did he insist on enforcing it? And why for the love of God was she always so damned irrational around him? Panicked even. He knocked her off balance. Made her face things about herself she had pushed away, refusing to acknowledge. She had been safe in her drug-induced cocoon. Here, she was raw, exposed.

And afraid.

The problem with Law, she suddenly realized, was that he made her *feel*. She didn't want to feel! She wanted to remain comfortably numb. No pain. No stress. Just sheltered inside that warm place that asked nothing of her.

But he didn't give up. She looked over at him.

At least he wasn't laughing. With a panther's grace, he strode into the kitchen, yanked the fridge door open and grabbed a beer. Using the bottle opener on the wall, he removed the cap and raised the bottle to his lips, taking a long swallow.

Lana watched, mesmerized as the muscles in the long column of his throat moved up and down. He had more in common with a panther than his powerfully sensual physicality. For starters, he had never been tamed and by her guess, he couldn't be tamed. His considerable intelligence was dangerous.

Her female intuition kicked in. There had to be other, even more dangerous hidden layers to this dominant male. She had to try harder to escape again. In the meantime, she'd act casual.

"OK. So the real contract is safe. Then what's the plan?"

Lowering the bottle, he cocked his head in question. "Keeping you safe."

"From the others here?" Let him fill in the blanks. She might learn something she could use.

He didn't say yes or no to that. "Some are asking questions about you."

That told her nothing. She'd have to coax more out of him somehow. "You're not like them." The voices she vaguely remembered when she was dragged out blindfolded and half naked sounded a lot rougher than his, for sure. How odd that she remembered her sense of relief the moment he'd had her extracted her from the van and the man who drove it.

On the inside, drifting in disguise among his privileged guests at that weird party, it was super clear to her that they were all about designer clothes and designer drugs meant to heighten discreet sexual experimentation. Law wasn't like them either.

His face tightened at her statement. He finished the beer and faced her. "You don't know that. Or anything else about me. Let's keep it that way."

Sounded like an order. Which she ignored, pleased that she could get under his skin. Finding out more was a risk she was willing to take. "Is your friend, the one who kidnapped me, like you?"

Law's scowl deepened. "Forget about him."

"Can't. He saved me from being raped by Carson."

"Did he touch you?"

"Your friend?"

Law shook his head. "No. Carson. Did he touch you?"

"Would it matter?"

"Yeah, it would."

"Why?"

"Because if he did, the next time I run into him, I'll run into him hard."

Lana shivered when she remembered how close she had come to being assaulted. "He tried, but Val stopped him."

"The Giant, Anton's man?"

Her head snapped back. "How do you know that?"

"It's my job to know."

"Who are you? I mean, in real life?"

"Fuck real life. And you know the damn answer. My name is Law," he said, as if he was talking to a small child. "I run the Chimera syndicate."

"Aren't syndicates organized crime?"

"A syndicate is a business group, whose members pool their assets

"What is Chimera's common interest?"

He wagged his finger at her. "You get one guess. Go ahead."

Lana felt sick to her stomach. She knew he was a criminal. He'd kidnapped her from another criminal. What did she expect?

"I'm not going to guess," she muttered. "But just so you know, I'm not cut out for a life of crime."

"You'd be surprised what you're cut out for when pushed hard enough."

She opened her mouth to ask him what he meant by that but the elevator pinged. They had a visitor.

CHAPTER SIXTEEN

LAW SLID his cellphone from his pocket and glanced at it, then hit an icon. Striding toward the door, he spoke into the phone, "Give me a minute."

As he hit the end icon, Lana heard a throaty voice say, "Don't keep me waiting."

Low, but definitely female. Didn't sound like Jhett.

Not to be ignored, Lana followed Law to the penthouse door. Scowling at her, Law opened the door. The redhead cooling her heels on the other side smiled up at Law, completely ignoring Lana who stood next to him.

"Hello, handsome," she purred.

Lana made a funny scrunchy face just when Law glanced down at her. His green eyes sparkled mischievously.

"Hello, beautiful," he responded. The deep timbre of his voice caused both women to tremble almost imperceptibly. The man was sin personified.

He didn't seem to notice their simultaneous reaction, but the women did, glaring at each other with mutual contempt. Lana wanted to rip the redhead's hair out by the roots.

Undeterred by Lana's presence, the woman smiled up at Law. She was a knockout. Thick natural red hair in a short stylish cut accentuated her creamy skin, gigantic brown eyes, and chiseled features. Her cultured voice exuded confidence and sexual promise. And she had impeccable style.

Biscotti-colored riding pants and a hunter-green velvet jacket hugged her curves like a second skin. That wasn't all. Black leather stiletto boots raised her to eye level with Law.

The subtle cinnamon scent of her fragrance topped it all off into a killer-bitch package.

Lana instantly disliked the woman. Having nothing better to do, she leaned against the doorjamb and watched their interaction.

"It's good to see you, Sienna." Taking the woman's hand, Law drew her into the penthouse. Eagerly she allowed him, glancing around discreetly, much to Lana's annoyance. If the redhead was expecting to see any signs of wild lovemaking, she was out of luck.

"Just thought I'd stop by, Law," she said airily. "I waited as long as could before coming up here."

"Sorry for not responding sooner. I've been busy. You know how it is."

Yes. Busy with me, bitch. Lana wished Sienna could read her mind.

"So I heard," the redhead said casually. "I'd like you to come to my place a little later."

Lana had to give the woman props. She wasn't begging Law for attention; she expected it.

"Time?"

"Hmm. I do like being accommodated, Law," she said softly, smiling at him.

Law grinned. "Anything for you."

She gave a silvery laugh as Lana fumed.

"Let me think," Sienna said archly. "Shall we say six? Come hungry," she added, heading for the door.

And not a minute too soon, Lana thought, wondering all the same about the reason for such a swift exit after that show-stopper entrance. Maybe her presence was a deterrent.

Sienna stopped and finally acknowledged Lana—for Law's benefit—by giving her a long once-over. Then she stalked past her, seeing herself out with a honey-voiced command. "And by the way, Law—don't be late."

The door closed behind her perfect ass. Lana mimicked her. "Law. Don't be late."

"Jealous?"

"Shut up. And hit the brakes on that ego of yours."

Before Law could answer, the doorbell rang again.

Lana raised her brows. "I think Sienna came back for your balls."

Law glanced at his cell and smiled. "Nope."

A moment later True entered, coming to a quick halt in front of Lana and whistling. "Damn. You clean up nice."

Lana straightened up to her full five foot four inch height. No, she wasn't runway-model tall like Sienna, but she didn't need to be. Lana was a showstopper in her own right. When Law's brows drew together disapprovingly, Lana smiled at True and pushed off the wall. "So do you."

True grinned.

Lana played along. "I didn't get a chance to thank you for saving my life. I'm forever in your debt."

True's blue eyes twinkled. Bowing slightly, as if she were the Queen of England, he said, "It was my pleasure. So. Is Law being nice to you?"

"He's an ogre." As she said the words, she shook her hair

back over her shoulder, and moved past them both to the bedroom. Not quickly.

True's eyes narrowed as he caught sight of the bruises on her neck.

"What the fuck, man?" he asked, giving Law a hard look.

"It was unintentional."

Lana flipped them the bird as she went into the bedroom and closed the door just enough to eavesdrop.

"What's going on, Law? It's not like you to manhandle a woman." True asked.

"I had a nightmare. When she tried to wake me up, instinct kicked in and—"

"You're sleeping with her?" True asked incredulously.

"Fuck no! She's a train wreck."

True wasn't buying it. "Not any more. I almost didn't recognize her. Has she calmed down any?"

"Yes. No. She's complicated. Woman's body. Woman's brain. But emotionally, she's a child."

Really? Infuriated, Lana peeked through the crack in the door, ready to storm back in. Which would prove Law's point. She hesitated.

True seemed skeptical. "You sure you got this?"

"The woman part is distracting," Law admitted.

"No shit. Anything else?"

"She's smart. Too damn smart for her own good." There was a long pause. "I'd bet Chimera she's never been fucked properly."

True cleared his throat, like he was trying to think of something tactful to say. "Uh—are you wanting to remedy that?"

"I'd be a damn fool to get involved with her. The child part throws temper tantrums, and cries if I look at her wrong. The woman part of her tries every male part of me."

True laughed. "Better you than me, brother!"

"Thanks," Law said, his tone not grateful.

"Mind if I change the subject?" True didn't wait for an answer. "Good. I bumped into Sienna. Is everything okay between you two?"

"I think so. We're having dinner later tonight. I'm sure she's going to rip me a new one for being unavailable."

"You have been for a couple of weeks, yeah. Is she really that high-maintenance?"

"Yes."

Lana smirked behind the door. Served Law right if the redhead had him on a chain.

"Could we get back to business?" Law added, sounding noticeably irritated.

"Yeah, sure," True said quickly. "So here's the deal. I've got new intel that could be a game-changer. Which is why I'm here in person and didn't call you. You're never going to believe it."

"I'm all ears."

"The Riyadh papers have surfaced."

Startled by True's unexpected answer, Lana drew in a sharp breath. Not that she knew exactly what was in the Riyadh papers or why they were such a big deal—only that they were important to very important men.

Among them, Anton, the club owner, who'd been contracted by a shady Russian Mafioso to procure them for the almighty Dragovich.

Just one of the many tidbits Lana had picked up during private dances. Stupid Anton, he had no idea Lana spoke Russian.

"Where?"

"On an unidentified container ship that's scheduled to dock here in Oakland by the New Year."

So True didn't know which ship. But Lana had an inkling of what it might be—no more than that. She swore silently, trying to think, and realized she couldn't quite hear what Law and True were saying now. She looked through the crack in the door to see them moving away from the bedroom, deep in conversation.

Lana stepped back and sat on the bed, pressing her fingers to her temples, forcing herself to remember her last days at the club...before she'd been auctioned off by Anton...

There had been men coming and going in the private suite where he kept her a virtual prisoner, strung out on the sofa. Not customers. His thugs.

She'd overheard more cryptic Russian conversations during that time than she had the entire time she worked at the Ultimate.

"The Karabo *is sailing to America for the New Year,"* Anton *had informed his nephew.*

Maksim. Known as Maks. Kind of a loser, but useful to Anton now and again. What had he said?

"I will need you to retrieve an article from one of the containers. If you fuck this up, I'm sending you back to my sister."

"I won't fuck it up, Uncle."

Anton looked pointedly at Maks as Lana lay strung out on the sofa and asked him if he remembered the year when his mother was born.

"Yes. Nineteen—"

"Shhz. Just don't forget it."

"Do we have the container number?"

"I'm working on it," Anton snapped.

A pause.

"Who else knows?"

Had Maks even asked that question? Lana's mind went blank. She couldn't remember anything after that.

The *Karabo*. That could be the one.

She wondered how she could use the remembered information to buy her freedom. If she was wrong about the name of the ship carrying the Riyadh papers, whoever she sold the info to would be likely to kill her, just for knowing too much. The significance of the rest—Maksim's mother's date of birth?—hell, she had no idea what that meant.

In ten days the *Karabo* would be docking. She had that much time to figure it out.

Flopping onto the bed, Lana closed her eyes and pulled up the fur throw, so weary she dozed off for a little while, without dreaming.

Noise, undefined, outside the bedroom door, woke her up again. She just lay there, thinking for a while longer. She needed to be patient. Strategic. Smarter than Law.

Yeah. How to do that was the big question. She had one advantage: if he was preoccupied by something ominous about to happen on the Oakland docks, that would get in the way of his vigilance over her.

Then she heard heavy footsteps and True's voice saying good-bye.

Good riddance. For a minute there, he'd seemed to care about her, had even chided Law for the bruises on her neck. Then...nothing. Business as usual, between crime brothers. Sitting up in bed, Lana tossed the fur throw from her.

If Law planned to force her to stay here, she'd make him regret it. If True was complicit, then forget him. She was on her own.

Lana checked her makeup and hair, then headed out to the living room.

Law looked at her from across the room. He was dressed in a classic black suit. He hadn't come into the bedroom to change as far as she knew. Unless he'd entered when she dozed off.

"Lucky you," she said acidly. "Going out?" She knew the answer. Sienna was expecting him.

"Yes, but later." He refastened a cufflink. "I have a little work to do first. Did you have a nice nap?"

Nice nap? Was he serious? She hadn't forgotten his comment about her acting like a child.

"No. And how is it that you're dressed in different clothes all of a sudden?"

"I have a shower and wardrobe in my office."

"Do you have a futon to fuck on, too?"

"None of your business."

"Speaking of that—" Lana moved toward him. "Just what *is* your business? Seeing as I'm a hostage here, I think I'm entitled to know *something*."

"When the time is right, you'll be briefed."

"Right now is good for me."

Law looked at her warily. "You'll have to wait."

"When, Law? Damn it, I have a right to some answers!"

Calm as a heart surgeon, he said, "Maybe you do."

She was outraged. "*Maybe* I do? Listen, I'm not some worthless piece of—"

He interrupted her. "You're not worthless. Not at all. Didn't you ever wonder why the bids on you were so much higher, when the other girls were in better shape?"

"I—what do you mean in better shape?"

"They weren't strung out on heroin."

"Right. I was half dead. But getting back to what you were just saying—I'm worth more because my father paid Anton a lot to make me disappear."

"You really think that?"

"I don't think it, I know it. Anton told me."

"Anton Koslov specializes in misdirection."

"Are you suggesting he was lying?"

"I'm suggesting it's highly improbable your father gave his blessing."

"Why do you think that?"

His answer was blunt. "Because it would be political suicide."

"As opposed to making sure his cringe-worthy daughter permanently disappeared to never smear his good name?" Lana had no reason not to believe Anton. Her father had no problem with assuming she was dead for the last six years—why wouldn't he make it permanent?

"The man who bought your contract isn't interested in using you for anything other than getting under your father's skin."

"Daddy dearest wouldn't pay a dollar for my safe return."

"I'm not talking about a ransom. You, dead, he's the poor grieving father all over again. Alive, you cause the good senator significant embarrassment."

"Thanks." Story of her life. *Go away, Lana. Be quiet, Lana. We don't want you here, Lana. Tell my secret and I'll kill you too, Lana.* She shivered hard as the hateful whispered words spoken so many years ago haunted her still.

Law didn't seem to notice. Just kept talking. "Dragovich would generate a scandal."

"Why? What would he do?"

"Keep you rigged for public consumption. Threaten to expose you in all your strung out glory. Social-media-splash you all over the place. A simple set-up to control the senator."

"So you didn't save me from Dragovich because you're the hero, you stole me because you want to use my father?"

"Dragovich has vital information I need. You're the key to my obtaining it."

"You-you're going to hand me over to him in trade?"

He thought a moment before answering. "I deal in high stakes information, Lana. People pay me a lot of money for what I know."

"So, I'm just a means to an end, and my wishes be damned?"

Law looked past her to some object across the room and said, "I'll be entertaining here tomorrow evening. I'll instruct Monty to move your things into the white room so as not to bother you."

"You're just going to stick me in another room so I won't embarrass you either."

He seemed a little annoyed. "You said you wanted to stay in the white room. Permission granted."

"Maybe I don't want to now."

"You'll be more comfortable there."

"While you fuck away here?"

That question really annoyed him. "What I do here or anywhere else is none of your business."

"Well, fuck you very much. But being stuck behind closed doors whenever you feel the need is not where I want to be."

"Look on the bright side," he said blandly. "It could do you good. Your only job is to get healthy."

"I feel much better. I can't sit around and twiddle my thumbs while you party. As your brother in crime would say, what the fuck, Law?"

"He's not in charge here. And you have no place here."

If he had struck her with his fist, it would have hurt less. Hot tears stung her eyes. "I hate you."

Pouring a drink from a decanter on the gleaming bar, he took a sip, and then said, "Hate is safer than love."

Then as if she had simply disappeared, he moved past her to his desk, cracked open his laptop and began to type.

Fighting the tears, Lana stood rooted to the floor. Anger at his dismissal of her battled with her need for self-control. She didn't want Law's attention. Yet she craved it for unknown reasons that made no sense to her. But there it was.

And there he was, staring into the laptop, his stern face illuminated by a strange glow.

A dark iridescence, like nothing she'd ever seen, rolled across the glass. As if he'd been instantly aware of her curiosity and switched to software that would block her gaze.

Lana realized that he probably had. The laptop was larger than most, sleek and black, like practically everything else in the penthouse. No brand name that she could see. Okay. Custom cyber ware. Maybe that was his business. She wasn't going to ask him about that.

A new wave of anger swept through her. How could he sit there as if she didn't exist and expect her to be okay with it? The urge to lash out physically had never been so strong. Fisting her hands, Lana dug her nails into her palms until it hurt, not minding the pain.

His worst enemy wanted her, apparently. And Law didn't, except as a bargaining chip. That pain almost stopped her heart.

CHAPTER SEVENTEEN

LANA LEFT him to his work, changed into a pair of pajama shorts and matching tank and climbed back into the big bed. For a long time she stared at the ceiling, fighting sleep. She was trapped. But there had to be a way out....

Hours later, she woke to darkness. Anxiety scraped at her nerves.

Quietly she slipped from the bed and eased open the door. Low lights illuminated the living room, and rain beat against the windows.

Barefoot, she padded across the wood floor to the rug before the low burning fireplace, digging her toes into the luxuriant fur. She was alone. Of course she was. Law was elsewhere, free to come and go. And no doubt at this very moment fucking the pretty redhead.

Lana envisioned herself in Sienna's place. Heat shimmered to her core. Sex with Law would be epic. She knew it as sure as she knew the sun would rise the next morning.

She could still feel the hard strength of his hand on her ass. Lana started as if his hand just landed on her bottom. Without thinking, she ran her fingers down her right cheek just as his long fingers had when they stroked the heat away.

She'd enjoyed every second of his unexpected spanking. Why? Because she did. And maybe because he'd shredded her ability to think straight. What the hell was wrong with her?

She was losing her mind. She seriously needed a drink.

Lana helped herself to a glass of excellent scotch, and then moseyed back to the bedroom she'd slept in and dug through Law's medicine cabinet. Just in case he'd stashed something stronger than aspirin in there since the last time she'd looked. Nothing but toothpaste.

The door to his personal cave was locked. Refilling her glass, Lana headed for the door to the white room. Propping it open with a chair to keep an ear out for Law, she rifled through the cabinets in there.

Aha.

Tossing back the second scotch, she set her glass down and smiled as she opened a vial of Soma.

Her body had already eagerly accepted the alcohol. Throwing back two of the four muscle relaxers, she closed her eyes and sat down on the toilet. The combination didn't take long to infiltrate her body.

Fuck Law. He wasn't the boss of her. If she wanted to drink and pop pills she was free to do so!

Instead of pouring more deliciousness into her glass, Lana grabbed the bottle of Macallan, and drank straight from it.

Hours later, she was happily stoned on the sofa when Law returned.

"Hey," she slurred raising the half empty bottle his way. "Wanna party?"

He scowled. She burped.

"Oops. Forgot I'm not good enough for the king of the world."

He didn't argue that point.

Lana stood, swaying, but he didn't move toward her.

"Well, King," she said, attempting to sound polite but failing. "I'm a fucking princess who wouldn't give the likes of you the time of day in my kingdom."

Taking a last swig from the bottle, she set it down on an end table, then got her siren strut on. When Law's scowl darkened, her rancor rose. "You think you're so badass."

Silence from him.

"Looking at me like I'm not fit to wipe your shoes on." Swaying, she grabbed the edge of the wall. "You're the worst of the worst. You're a cop killer!"

When he refused to react, Lana's drunken rage mushroomed. "Cop killer!" she screamed, pointing her finger at him. "Cop killer!"

She saw it in his eyes before he moved a muscle. Something snapped. *Oh shit.*

Law grabbed her wrists and shook her hard. "Who do you despise more, Lana? Me for killing a cop or yourself for selling yourself for a fix?"

His harsh words penetrated her drug-fogged brain. Because he held her wrists, she couldn't slap him. Rising up on her toes, she head-butted him. Or tried to. Instead of his head she only managed to reach his breastbone.

Spinning her around, he pressed her body flush against the wall. "If I thought it would do any good, I'd take you over my knee and spank you so hard you wouldn't be able to sit down for a week."

She remembered the first one. Hell yes. "Take your hands off me! Let me go!" she screamed. To her utter surprise he did.

Turning, she swayed. He reached out and grabbed her forearm to steady her. Yanking it from his grasp, Lana fought back the hot sting of tears, humiliated and confused.

Shaking his head, Law quietly said, "If I let you go, you'd be on your knees servicing Dragovich's thugs in less than an hour." His eyes narrowed. "Is that where you'd rather be?"

"Any place would be better than here!"

He towered over her. "Be careful what you ask for, Alana Conti. You might get it."

"What's that supposed to mean?"

"It means if you turn into more trouble than you're worth, your life could drastically change. And not for the better."

Lana blinked, feeling queasy. The room began to tilt a little. Grabbing at air to steady herself, she stumbled into the wall. Law didn't move an inch to help her this time.

Tears blurred her vision. When she stared up at him, his big body seemed far away. "I—need help—" she murmured as her knees buckled.

Strong arms caught her just before she hit the floor. Hauling her up, Law got her into his bedroom.

Where he began to undress her. Easing her to the floor and undressing himself.

Interesting, she thought woozily. Because he didn't seem aroused. But even so. He was still a sex god, every inch of him, whether that thing was up or down.

Lana didn't fight. He'd seen her naked before.

He didn't seem to have any ulterior motives, in fact. Once she was undressed, he hoisted her up in his arms and walked into the shower with her, turning on the taps. A stream of instantly warm water drenched her.

"What are you doing?" she asked softly.

"Sobering you up a little."

He turned the shower knob to waterfall mode. Nice. Felt good. She imagined a tropical island for two. He soaped her back and butt, then turned her around and soaped everything in front. Better than good. Like being...loved.

Finally, the fight gone, her body spent, Lana closed her eyes and cried silent tears as a big warm towel was wrapped around her. Setting her on the bed, Law vigorously rubbed her down, all over.

Once she was dry, he left her naked on the bed. On her belly, she watched him move around the room. His movements quick and precise. A man on a mission. Coming back to the bed, he rolled her over onto her back. Her damp hair stuck to her cheek, chest and ribs.

He stopped for a brief moment and looked down at her. His eyes darkened to jade. Quickly he pulled a T-shirt over her head and down her torso, then pulled her damp hair away from her neck.

"Thank you," she whispered as he walked away.

He stopped and turned. "Until you respect yourself, Lana, don't expect any from me or anyone else."

He left her, in his bed, with those words echoing in her brain.

CHAPTER EIGHTEEN

LIGHT SPEARED HER CORNEAS. The pounding in her head vibrated through her entire body. The unexpected aroma of bacon puzzled her for a minute. Where was she?

The night came rushing back to her.

She pressed her fingertips to her throbbing temples, sensing a migraine coming on. Well, that was nobody's fault but hers.

"Miss Lana?" Monty called from outside the bedroom. "Are you okay?"

Even though he couldn't see her, Lana nodded. "Yes."

"I brought you some breakfast."

She had to smile. Monty's kindness meant more to her at that moment then she could explain. "Thank you. I'll be out in a few minutes."

"Okay," he said.

Fifteen minutes later, face washed, teeth brushed, dressed in a pair of yoga pants and a sweater, Lana moved slowly from the bedroom to the kitchen table, which was laden with enough food to feed an army.

Monty smiled. "I helped Henri with the cooking this morning. I hope you like everything."

As Lana sat down, she fought the rumbling in her stomach.

"I'm sure I will. And hey—I owe you an apology. I'm sorry for tricking you that night in the hallway," Lana softly said, raising her eyes to Monty's patient gaze.

Monty's face lit up when he smiled. "No harm, no foul. That's what Law tells me when I make a mistake."

She teared up a little. That was so sweet of Law to be so patient with Monty. Head injury or not, Lana knew Monty was a gentle soul who was loyal to a fault and wouldn't hurt a fly—or a spider.

Taking the cup of coffee Monty offered, she slowly sipped it. "Ah. This is heaven."

Monty smiled again. "I'm going to go make the bed while you eat."

"I can make the bed."

"Just eat. Law said you need some, um, meat on your bones and I was supposed to make sure you ate so much you couldn't move."

Lana frowned. "Law thinks I'm scrawny?"

"He didn't say that, just that you needed to eat."

Choosing a fresh-baked croissant, Lana tore off a piece and popped it into her mouth. Yummy. "If I ate all of this, Monty, you'd have to roll me out of here."

He smiled sheepishly, dropped his head and headed for the bedroom.

Food was what she needed. And a lot of it. She polished off two croissants, four pieces of bacon, a ginormous scoop of Italian omelet and the two vanilla crepes.

Literally, she couldn't move.

When Monty came back into the kitchen, he nodded with approval. "That wasn't so hard, was it?"

"It was delicious. Which part did you make?"

"The omelet."

Lana smiled and sat back, patting her belly. "I thought so. It was my favorite."

His cheeks flushed at the compliment.

Busily he began to clear the table. Lana watched him. His movements were quick, efficient, like he had done this for a long time.

"How did you meet Law?"

A plate shook in his hand. Quickly he stacked it. "I—" His brows scrunched together. "Well, he rescued me."

"From what?"

"Some bad guys. They were beating me up." He blinked, then rubbed the damaged area of his forehead. "I don't remember much—I woke up in the hospital and Law said I was coming home with him."

"I'm sorry that happened to you."

He nodded. "Law saved my life. He saved Sienna's too. They tried to get her first."

"Oh, I didn't know that. I believe Law had dinner with her last night."

Monty continued to clear the table, not saying anything to that.

Her curiosity got the better of her. "I thought you said Jhett was Law's main girl."

"She is. But so is Sienna."

"Oh. So he has them both here, at the same time?"

Monty looked confused by her question but he answered it. "Sometimes. And True comes up."

Lana stopped herself from gasping. A foursome?

"I didn't know they all got together like that."

"Not too much. Law prefers his privacy here." Monty wiped down the table. "He must like you a lot to let you stay here. All of the other ladies stay in the other room."

"Even Jhett and Sienna?"

"No, they don't ever go in there."

So he didn't like her *that* much. Whatever.

"Monty, is there anywhere inside the building I can work out or do a little jogging? Something instead of sitting around here waiting for Law to come back?"

"Come here," he said, motioning her up. Following him through the dining room to a wide hallway, she saw there were three doors. One she already knew led to the white room. She just now noticed the other tucked in a corner and the third next to it on the right. Monty opened the one in the corner, turned on the light and stood back while Lana walked into the mother of all home gyms.

It had everything from a heavy bag to an elliptical machine—and yes, a small indoor track around the perimeter. Racks of free weights lined one mirrored wall. Benches, barbells and weight plates occupied a corner near a row of medicine balls. There was a treadmill, a leg press, and a rowing machine along with several arm and back machines.

Except for the track and matted floor, the entire room was mirrored, ceiling included.

"Wow."

Monty smiled and pressed a mirrored panel beside him. It opened to a lighted hydration center. "There's mineral water, spring water, sports drinks. If you want, I can make you a protein shake." He pressed another panel, which revealed a stack of neatly folded white towels with the Chimera logo.

"There's another bathroom right outside the hall here if you need it, right next to the steam room and sauna. And there's a pool on the roof."

"A rooftop pool? It must be freezing this time of year."

Monty smiled, shaking his head. "Law keeps it warm."

She was a strong swimmer. She'd be happy to check it out. "Thank you, Monty. I'm going to work off some of that amazing breakfast."

Lana hurried back to the bedroom, hearing Monty retreat, and one of those doors closing behind him.

Excellent. She was sure there was workout clothing in one of the bags of clothing Law had provided for her. She hadn't bothered putting anything away. If she did, that meant she accepted her fate here. Since she didn't…

Ten minutes later she was dressed in workout clothes, including sneakers.

As she warmed up on the treadmill, Lana made a decision. She was going to get as strong physically and mentally as she could. If she found herself in Drago's lap, she needed to be able to fend him off. No man was going to force her to do anything she didn't want to do, ever again.

Twenty minutes later, Lana hopped from the treadmill and over to the heavy bag. The gloves were enormous. Triple wrapping the straps, she started hopping and punching the bag like she had seen in the movies.

Once she had warmed up her arms, she started to kick the bag. Leaning back, kicking good and high. Then higher. The more she kicked, the angrier she became.

Punching the bag again, she swore, "Fuck you, Anton!" Round house kick. "Fuck you, Daddy Dearest!" Another punch. "I hate you, mother!" she shrieked. When she turned to kick the bag, she missed. Her momentum landed her flat on her back.

Tears she wasn't aware she'd been crying stung her eyes,

blurring her vision. "I hate all of you," she wailed, her voice raw from screaming.

Moments later, she felt Law's presence. She looked directly up into his inquisitive green eyes. Heat rushed through her body. He was so fucking hot in those black jeans and white fitted shirt. The fabric hugged each and every plane of his wide chest, contoured abs and thick biceps. The dominating sight of him above her caught her off guard.

When his lips turned up into a knowing smile, she scowled. Could he read her mind? She refused the hand he offered, springing to her feet unaided.

"I don't need your help. It's your fault I'm even here."

"Is that mouth of yours good at anything other than complaining?"

Her eyebrows went up. "Wouldn't you like to know."

"You have a dirty mind, Lana Conti."

She smiled a smile only a female toying with a male could conjure. "You have no idea."

Law's grin widened. "Well, give me an idea then. Make it hot."

Shocked he'd go there, she shook her head. "I heard what you said to True about me. Don't pretend you're interested in anything other than using me for your crime lord schemes."

"I never pretend."

"Then don't lie."

"I'm not lying."

"Well, either you lied to True or you're lying to me. More like messing with me, actually. So stop."

"I said I'd be a fool to get involved with you, not that I didn't want to fuck you."

His words went straight to her pussy. "Really. So what'll happen if we fuck?"

His grin nearly split his face. "We both get off."

"I don't do that."

He laughed. "Sounds like a challenge." He took her gloved hand into his. "And I never back away from a challenge."

"I don't want to have sex with you, Law."

"Why not?"

"Do you want the truth?"

"Always."

"If we fuck, I suspect I'll like it too much. Since I happen to have an addictive personality, I'd want more. You might not and that will frustrate me."

"I see your dilemma."

"Please respect my space."

"Of course." Dropping her hand, he stepped back and pointed to the bag. "Why were you kicking the shit out of my heavy bag?"

"I'm buffing up for anyone who might need an ass kicking."

"Like who?" He seemed amused.

"You."

Law's thick eyebrows went up. "Is that right? But I've never touched a woman who didn't want to be touched by me."

"Except me." She stepped back a few feet. He *was* tempting. She needed a little distance.

"Right. To be fair, though, it was for your own good."

"So you keep saying." She took another step back and got to the crux of why she needed to be physically strong. "Do you plan to trade me for something important that your enemies own or control?"

"Hmm. No, probably not. Any other questions?"

Probably not? His casual tone was infuriating. But since he was taking questions, she went all in. "Can you give me even the slightest hint of when I can leave here?"

"If I could, I would." He looked her up and down. "Now, if you're training, I have a few tips. For starters, you're going at the bag all wrong."

She put her hands on her hips, indignant. "How do you know?"

"I was watching you. If you want to have an impact, you need to know how and where to strike."

"Show me."

He moved closer. "Now?"

"Yes, Law. Right fucking now."

CHAPTER NINETEEN

"IT WILL REQUIRE TOUCHING YOU."

Lana thought it over, not taking her eyes off him, half-expecting a surprise move she'd have to fend off. He stayed put and she relaxed a little.

"So long as you don't touch the goodies, I don't have a problem with that."

Law grinned. "I'll do my best. Now take the gloves off."

"But—"

"If you ever get attacked, you probably won't be wearing boxing gloves," he pointed out with irritating superiority. "But you can practice hitting later."

"Gee, thanks. On you?"

He ignored the jab. "Right now you're going to learn how to temporarily immobilize an attacker so that you can run."

"But—"

"Your safety depends on you getting away, not beating the snot out of your attacker. Now take the gloves off."

When she did, he stepped behind her, put her in a light chokehold and said, "How do you get away?"

"I—"

"Don't tell me, show me."

Grabbing his forearm with both hands, she dug her nails into his skin and tried to twist out of his grip. His hold tightened. Kicking backward, she squirmed in his grasp. He dodged her kicks with ease. His hold tightened more. She started to feel lightheaded. Ramping up her defense, Lana panicked and started to flail in his grasp.

Releasing the chokehold a second before he pushed her down to the floor, Law rested his body just above hers. Lana gasped for air as he spoke into her ear. "You missed your chance to stop me the moment you dug your nails into my arm."

Rolling over, she was chest to chest with Law, breathless. His green eyes burned brightly. "You're too big!" She got the words out somehow. "I couldn't have stopped you."

"You're wrong." He stood up and brought her with him. He turned around, presenting his back and looking over his shoulder. "Come at me from behind like I just did to you."

"I'll need a ladder!"

Law dropped to his knees. "There."

Lana smiled and jumped him from behind, locking her right arm around his neck in a chokehold. He grasped her forearm with his right hand, distracting her for a critical split second. His left hand flew up so quickly she didn't see it but she sure as hell felt it when he pressed his thumb against her left eye. She cried out and released him.

He stood and turned on her. "If I'd made that move for real, you'd be screaming on the floor. When you strike, do it hard. Make it hurt—a lot. You might not get a second chance."

Nodding she said, "Let's try again."

This time, she grabbed his arm around her neck with her right hand and with her left hand, turned it out palm up, and pressed her thumb into his eye socket just enough to show him she could gouge it out if she had to. She moved so quickly and with such confidence, she rocked Law back on his heels. She released him and ran for the door. "Yes!" she yelled throwing her arms up in victory.

"Good. Again," he said.

They repeated the move a dozen times. Once she felt confident she could and would do it, he showed her a few other moves.

Almost an hour later, sweating and out of breath, Lana put her hand up. She needed to hydrate and to catch her breath. Law hadn't broken a sweat.

Grabbing two bottles of water from the fridge, she handed Law one. Draining her bottle, she leaned against the wall and said, "Thanks for the workout. Maybe I'll use my cool new moves on you for real someday."

"Save yourself the embarrassment."

"Of what?"

"Losing."

"Say what?" She hadn't worked off all her angry frustration, after all. It surged right back, boiling hot. "It's your fault I'm even here having to learn to fight for my life!"

He didn't visibly react. Just asked a calm question. "Whose fault is it that you stripped for heroin?"

She came right back at him. "Anton for getting me hooked on that shit. My parents for being awful. Myself for not getting straight."

He seemed almost bored. "You can blame me for now, Lana. I kidnapped you from a megalomaniac who paid two hundred thousand dollars to use and abuse you as leverage against your father. But blaming everyone else before you got here is the easy way out."

"Shut up! Just shut *up*. You know nothing about me."

Law sighed. "I know more than you think I do. But I won't get into it. Let's just say that you've made a lot of bad choices."

"Yeah, I did!" She caught her breath, willing herself to calm down. Didn't work. One last jab burst out of her. "But I'm not a criminal like you!"

He gazed at her for a long minute and finally spoke. "If it means anything to you, I don't like this situation. But I didn't create it. And I can't undo what you did but I can keep you safe. For now."

"Buy out my contract and I'll pay you back."

"It's not about the money. Dragovich would have paid five times what he paid to have your father in his pocket." Law leaned against the corner of the wall a secret smile playing on his lips. "But *if*, I paid off your contract, how would you repay me?"

Lana straightened. "Not sex."

"I would never take sex as payment for anything."

"Of course not. I'm sure the women throw themselves at you."

Law shrugged.

"Oh! Now I get it," Lana gasped just as something occurred to her. "You have no problem letting those women I saw in your club take money for sex because you're a pimp!"

Law laughed. "Don't be so sure."

"I'm not blind."

"Blind or not, I'm not going to divulge the secrets of Chimera."

"You don't trust me?"

"No, I don't. Even if I did, the less you know about me and Chimera, the safer you'll stay."

"Safe from who?"

"Dragovich."

"Let's say he's out of the picture. Who else?"

"Every other man or woman who bid on you. The cat's out of the bag, Lana. The bad guys know you're the key to controlling your father. If they knew you were here? They'd push hard for information about me and Chimera."

He opened his mouth to say something else. When he didn't, she pushed. "Tell me what you were going to say."

Finally Law spoke. "OK. Listen carefully because I'm only going to say it once. My reasons for bringing you here aside, right now this is the only place where you're safe. You walk out the door, you'll end up dead or wishing you were."

"As opposed to being here with you. A man with the morals of a pit viper."

That didn't seem to bother him. "Snakes do what they have to do," he said calmly. "And so do I."

"You're cold-hearted."

"It keeps me alive."

"Do have feelings for anyone?"

Shaking his head slowly, he answered, "Emotions get you killed. I'm not ready to die."

"That's sad and scary at the same time."

"Lana, you have nothing to fear from me."

"Except that you're cold-hearted *and* dangerous."

"I'm as dangerous as the threat."

"What does that mean?"

"It means I'm not dangerous unless I have to be."

Lana's heart thudded. He was dangerous, period. And on so many levels. She knew he had a hair trigger On/Off switch. Watching him in action would be exhilarating.

Thinking of him in that mode, she realized the last thing she wanted to be doing tonight was stare at the ceiling in her room while he was 'entertaining' in his swanky digs. He'd said something about doing that before, and she hadn't really listened.

She'd be shut away, forced to do nothing.

"Can I hang out at the club while you, uh, entertain tonight?"

"Actually, I'd like to talk to you about that."

Her eyes widened. Oh no, what did he want her to do?

"The guests I mentioned the other day that I was expecting are still in transit and asked that I postpone our dinner until they get here."

"Whatever."

Her dismissive reply made him smile slightly. "They're important people, Lana. Or I wouldn't have invited them up to my lair."

"So? What does any of that have to do with me?"

"A lot, actually. I'd like you to act as hostess."

"*What?*"

"I would like you to act as my hostess during dinner, here in my penthouse."

"Why?" she asked suspiciously.

"You weren't raised by wolves, Lana. This is a chance to show off your expensive education and beautiful manners."

"Fuck you!"

He grinned. "And you're gorgeous, which doesn't hurt. And as for the clothes, Jhett's handling that."

Lana narrowed her eyes at him. "There must be a catch."

He winked. "Only one. Wear something elegant and sexy. You'll give me the opportunity to observe them as they observe you."

"Sienna is all of those things, why not her?"

"Because I asked you."

"Do I have to pretend I like you?"

"Romantically, no. But no plate throwing or temper tantrums."

"I'll think about it."

"You do that. Just remember that these guys are treacherous. If you try to enlist their aid, you'll find yourself on your back faster than you can slip on those Louboutins Jhett mentioned.

Lana smiled. "Okay. I'll do it. Not for you. For me. Otherwise I'll go crazy."

"Can't have that."

She couldn't figure out if he was teasing her. But a little sarcasm in return wouldn't kill him. "No, of course not. Anyway, I'm kind of excited to meet your super secret dangerous friends."

"They aren't my friends."

"Whoever they are, I'm sure they'll be nicer to me than you have been."

"I can always change my mind."

"Why don't you show me the pool instead?" The sudden thought was a godsend. Anything to get out of her luxurious prison for a little while and put an end to this ominous conversation. And she was curious, though not because she thought the rooftop pool would be an escape route. "I just want to see it," she added.

"Up to you."

Law walked to the back side of the slate fireplace. He pressed his hand against the nearest wall there and magically, a hidden door silently opened. How about that. Another elevator, a small one. He pressed a button inside to keep it there when she hesitated.

"Super sneaky," she murmured.

"Fastest way up. After you," Law said.

"Ah—can I change first?" Her workout wear was damp. "I'm kind of sweaty."

"Sure."

"What a view," she said, gazing across the bay to the San Francisco skyline.

Law stood at her side. An immense infinity pool with subtle underwater lighting sparkled at their feet. Several cabanas with padded lounges, chairs and tables framed two sides. Potted plants dotted the enclosed oasis. She didn't doubt there was more to the vast rooftop oasis, but most of the area was darkened. Only the pool was illuminated.

"It's heated," Law said.

"Great." She'd wrapped herself up in an oversized hoodie that went down nearly to her knees, expecting it to be cold up here. It was, but high glass walls surrounded the space.

The entire bay glittered below, a spectacularly beautiful sight. Her imagination conjured up a summer soiree here, where fine champagne accompanied gourmet food, and international magnates both criminal and legit rubbed elbows vying for Law's attention.

Turning, she caught her breath. Law had moved away from her—all she saw of him was his shadow. He didn't speak. She wondered if he preferred the darkness.

He was a criminal—she was sure of it, despite his enigmatic answers to her questions. But a criminal of the highest order. Could she live that life?

Lana realized she could exist in any world so long as she was sober—and with Law. A sudden yearning for him consumed her when she looked again at his motionless shadow. The dark outline was even taller than he was, slanting toward her across the pool surround. Lana shivered.

She didn't want to leave here. No, that wasn't true— she didn't want to leave Law. When had that happened?

He took a step forward. Catching his gaze in the darkness, Lana slowly opened the hoodie, revealing the tight, stretchy boy shorts and cami she'd changed into after hunting for swimwear and not finding any. He came toward her.

What the hell. She wanted him. Lana let the hoodie drop and lifted the cami, baring her breasts. A warm sensation swept the cold away as Law's gaze moved over her. She slid her thumbs into the waistband of the boy shorts. As she slowly pulled them down, she held Law's intense stare.

Stripper moves meant to drive anonymous men crazy. Done for him alone.

Standing naked and proud before him, allowing him to take as much of her in as he wanted, Lana stilled her pounding heart.

She didn't feel vulnerable, afraid or ashamed. The boldness of Law's gaze empowered her. He wanted her. More than that, he wanted to possess her. Own her. Not contractually but physically. Because she wanted that too.

Turning slowly, Lana dove into the pool. Warm water sluiced across her sultry body, the tension tugging at her sensitive nipples and swollen pussy. Yeah, just by looking at her, Law did something no other man ever had: aroused her deeply. In every way.

When she surfaced at the opposite end of the pool, she turned to look at Law. He was gone.

Quickly she turned full circle, frowning, aware that he'd disappeared.

To ease the tension from her tired muscles and tumultuous heart, Lana started swimming laps. She didn't know how long she swam. It felt good to stretch and move with no resistance but the water. No thoughts, just movement.

The sensation that she was being watched came over her. Not slowing, she covertly looked beyond the pool.

Law was observing her, his body in silhouette, a shadow guardian.

"Why are you watching me?" she called to him.

Stepping from the shadows, he said, "I like the way you move."

As deftly as a dolphin, Lana corkscrewed and floated on her back. Her wet nipples gleamed and water pooled in her navel. She ran a hand over her belly, then moved her hand lower as she arched her back. Letting her hips rise.

"What are you doing?" Law asked, his voice rough.

"Swimming."

"You're attempting to seduce me. Why?"

She didn't have to give him a reason. "Is it working?"

No answer.

Sensing he was going to keep his distance, Lana stayed in the water, ignoring him.

Until she heard a huge splash. Law had shucked his clothes and jumped into the pool. Lana cried out and swam away from him.

Catching her ankle with his big hand, Law pulled her back against him. The hard length of his fully engaged cock pressed against the small of her back. Law swam forward with her to the edge of the pool that overlooked the bay.

Letting her go, he planted his hands on either side of her on the pool's edge. The only way she could move was a few inches forward. Or backward into his hard cock.

"Are you suggesting sport fucking?" Law asked.

"No!"

He turned her positioning her back against the pool wall. "Then just tell me exactly what it is you want."

His hot gaze drilled into her. The sensation of powerful male desire buzzing straight to her pussy rattled her. She'd never felt so sexually aware of herself.

What she wanted was Law buried deep inside of her. Breath rushed from her lungs. Oh my, it would feel amazing. Once would not be enough for her.

"I thought you didn't touch women who didn't want be touched," she taunted him.

"Yeah. I don't. So what do you have in mind?" He moved closer, dragging his cock along her belly down to her pussy.

"I—Law, I want you to—" Squeezing her eyes closed, Lana tried to think. She wanted everything.

Spreading her legs, she cocked her head and gave an order. "Make me come."

Sweeping her into his arms, Law brought her lips to his but didn't kiss her. "Not yet," he whispered.

Arching against him, Lana brought her legs up to wrap around his waist so that she could slide down on him.

He suddenly turned sideways, holding her off. "Stop."

"What?"

"You heard me, Lana."

Mortified by his rejection, she pushed past him and swam to the edge of the pool where she got out and wrapped herself in the oversized hoodie, stuffing the cami and shorts into a pocket.

He stood in the pool staring at her. "You did us both a big favor," she flung at him.

"I know I did." With long, strong strokes, Law swam to her, stepping from the water looking hotter than Jason Momoa in *Aquaman.* Water sluiced down his broad chest splashing onto his erection.

Lana swallowed hard. Good God, she wasn't made of stone. He was awesome. A real-life sex god.

As Law yanked on his clothes, he gave her a side-eyed glare. "No more games, Alana."

"I wasn't—I mean—" Shaking her head, she copped to it. "Look, I really want to fuck you. And yes, I was trying to seduce you."

His eyes widened.

Had she said too much or not enough? She decided to put some spin on her confession, and throw in a smile to make it all seem like no big deal.

"I just don't know if it's because I'm bored, which isn't a good reason, or if I'm like totally intrigued by your badness. Also not a good reason. So—I'm confused. Leave it at that."

"Deal. But what happens next?"

Lana shrugged. "Stay in your lane, Law and I'll stay in mine."

CHAPTER TWENTY

LAW DIDN'T FOLLOW her into the penthouse from the elevator. Instead, he let her off, then hit the magic button to the door. Silently it closed, leaving her standing alone staring at the wall. Forgotten, and pissed off about it.

The soft chime of the main penthouse doorbell startled her. Knowing that Law had security feeds streaming on his all-seeing smart phone didn't check her curiosity.

She made her way to the door and pressed her ear to it, wondering for a couple of seconds if the dangerous dudes who'd bailed on him had unexpectedly arrived. If so, she'd have to somehow contact—

"Law?" a woman's voice called. "Are you there?"

Lana scowled.

"Law?"

"Go away!" Lana yelled. The sudden silence made her smile. "He's just using you for sex!" she yelled louder. The click of heels hurrying away from the door told her all she needed to know.

Rolling her eyes at her immaturity, Lana leaned against the

wall. She had a lot of nerve calling the woman out for craving Law, when she'd done the same damn thing. She'd literally thrown herself at him and he rejected her.

So much for sexual healing. And to think she'd gotten through withdrawal hoping that would save her. Not happening.

Pushing off the wall, Lana strode angrily toward the bedroom. Law had made himself plenty clear. He didn't want her, except as a hostage. That didn't mean she had to sink into the depths of pointless despair.

Sulk, yes. Suicide, no. No fucking way was she going there again. The healed wound throbbed faintly as if to remind her. Peeling off her damp clothes Lana flung them to the bathroom floor.

Turning on the taps, she stepped into the instant warm spray. She wasn't going backward for anyone. Including her fragile ego.

She felt better afterward, all warmed up and toweled off.

Dressed again and leaving her room, she wasn't surprised to find Monty wheeling in a laden cart of food. If she kept eating the way she was being fed, she was going to have to be wheeled into the gym.

"Miss Lana, Law said he wouldn't be back until later and not to wait up for him."

"How funny that he would assume I would care."

Monty blinked.

"I'm sorry," she started, "I—I'm just frustrated."

Bobbing his head in understanding, Monty went about setting the table.

"Thank you," she absently said.

Just as she took her first bite the front doorbell chimed again. Lana looked over at Monty in the kitchen. He smiled then headed for the door. Unable to curb her curiosity, she quietly rose and peeked around the corner of the dining room wall.

A gorgeous brunette, decked out in a skintight yellow mini-dress and skyscraper heels peeked past Monty as she asked, "Is Law here?"

Different voice than the one earlier. Higher. The fake boobs had to be pressing on her vocal cords.

"No, Miss Chloe," Monty said. "He's gone for the night."

As she slid past him, she looked around. Lana ducked back into the dining room. It wasn't that she cared, she just didn't want to look like she did by eavesdropping.

"I don't mind waiting for him," the brunette said, moving deeper into the living room.

"I'm sorry, Miss Chloe, but no one is allowed here when Law is gone."

"Welll," she drawled. "I think he wouldn't mind *me* waiting for him."

"But—"

"But what? I'm not going anywhere," the brunette snapped.

Monty coughed, flustered. Lana wrestled with helping him out or not.

"I think you should go," Monty said.

"I think *you* shouldn't think. Oh, wait, how can you with half a brain?" Brianna said sweetly.

Aaand that was it.

Seething, Lana strode into the living room, sizing up the yellow-clad bitch. "Leave, Chloe. Right now. Before I kick you out."

Lana put herself between the intruder and Monty, who looked like he didn't know what to do.

Chloe gave Lana the stink-eye and unfortunately for her, stayed put.

Lana didn't think twice as she stepped into the woman's space and popped her in the nose with her fist.

Chloe screamed. Grabbed her bloody nose and wailed. "My nose! You broke it!"

"Nothing a good plastic surgeon can't fix. I'm sure you know one." Lana opened the door and held it. "Out, before I break something else."

Holding her nose with both hands now, she glared at Lana. "Law is going to make you pay for this."

"Not when I tell him how you treated Monty."

Chloe's big brown eyes widened before she hurried through the door.

Slamming it hard, Lana turned to find Monty cleaning up the blood drops on the floor. She kneeled down and took the damp cloth from him. "Let me, Monty."

When he looked at her his eyes shimmered with unshed tears. Lana's heart hurt for him. "She's not worth one tear, Monty. Not one."

Leaving him his dignity, she didn't comment further. Instead she cleaned up the floor. Tossed out the bloody towel, washed her hands and sat back down at the table. Though she hadn't been hungry before, now she ate with gusto.

Clearing the dishes herself, she asked Monty, who was finding things to do in the kitchen, "Do you run all of Law's computers?"

"Yes," he said absently, neatening up the silverware drawer. Making order out of chaos. She understood.

"What happens if one gets a virus or hacked?"

"They can't be hacked."

"How come?" she asked, trying to sound casual.

"Because I programmed the firewalls to hack back. Anyone

who tries to get into our systems can kiss their hard drive good-bye, Law says."

"Wow. That's genius." She opened the fridge and grabbed a bottled water. Beaming at him, she twisted off the cap and drank.

Not saying another word, she headed for the bedroom. As she closed the door she called to him, "Good night, Monty."

"Good night, Miss Lana," he cheerfully called back.

Smiling, Lana closed the door.

She was up early the next morning. Monty confirmed that Law had okayed her use of the pool and went with her up to the rooftop. It was raining, but that was all. No thunder, no lightning. She rather enjoyed swimming laps in the heated pool with the cold drizzle.

Several times she felt eyes on her but each time she looked toward the elevator shaft enclosure, expecting to find Law, she found the door closed and the space empty.

In the daylight, there was so much more to see. A helipad at the farthest point from the pool, for one thing. Large solar panels took up an entire side of the massive roof. There was a garden area, with a full bar and comfortable outdoor seating around a chimneyed open fireplace.

Once again she imagined Law holding court, greeting international magnates and other guests—with her at his side.

But it wasn't a day for a daydream. Chilled through, Lana thought about getting out of the water and turned around. Law stood at the edge of the pool, his dark hair whipping around the hard planes of his handsome face. His hand-tailored suit fitted his muscular chest and thighs to perfection.

He reminded her at that moment of a modern day Heathcliff.

The dark tortured lord of the rugged English moors. His heart twisted by love and loss.

"Hey," he said flatly. "Forecast says there's a storm rolling in. Lightning and all that. You need to get out of the pool."

"I was just going to." But she didn't. His tone bugged her.

"Then do it." His dark brows dove together. "C'mon. Out."

Not feeling much like fighting a battle she would lose, she saved her ammo for a later skirmish.

When he leaned down and extended his hand to her, she took it, letting him pull her up and draw her close. He didn't seem to mind that she was dripping wet. She fought the urge to press into his warmth. Grabbing the towel she'd left on a lounge chair, he wrapped it around her. When he didn't let go of her, she sensed something was wrong.

Tilting her head back, she looked up into his deep green eyes. "What?"

"Thank you for having Monty's back."

"It was the least I could do."

"Why is that?"

"Umm, he takes care of me."

"At my command."

Pushing out of his arms, Lana shook her head. "You sound like an egotistical jerk. Oh wait, you are!"

"I didn't mean it like that, Lana. I was just trying to say that you did the right thing—"

She wouldn't let him finish. "You don't mean to do a lot of things, but—" she threw her hands up— "that stunk."

"Can we talk about this when Monty's not around?"

Forgetting for a moment that Monty hadn't returned to the penthouse but discreetly busied himself tidying up the cabana area, Lana dropped her voice to a whisper. "You may *command* him to take care of me, but you don't command the fact that he actually cares about me. And you sure as fuck can't command me to care about him too, because I did that all on my own!"

Frustrated again, Lana stepped back and said, "Maybe you should tell your *ladies* not to come sniffing around your door."

"Jealous?"

"Not even close." Striding past him she said over her shoulder, "I'm going to shower and then I would like for you to show me how to work all of those remotes to the living room TV."

Wordlessly, Law followed her to the elevator. Pressing his hand to the invisible sensor panel, the door opened. Once they were back in the penthouse, Lana headed for the bedroom.

"Why are you going to my room?" he asked when she headed in the opposite direction to the white room.

"Because my stuff is still in there."

"Damn it, I forgot to ask Monty to prepare the white room."

Lana stopped and turned around. "I don't want to go in that room."

"Why not?"

"Because it—feels like the virgin offering room."

Law laughed. "I promise, there has never been a virgin in that room."

"Then who?"

"Ladies who accept my invitation for the evening."

"To fuck?"

He nodded. "To fuck."

"You fuck in the white room, they sleep there, and do their walk of shame the next morning while you cut and run here?"

"Pretty much."

"Well, you haven't invited me to fuck, and since I kind of live here," she said, motioning to the living areas, "for the moment, and I hate the color white. I've decided to stay where I am."

"Let me understand what you're saying: You don't want your own room. You want to sleep in my bed with me?"

"I—" Ugh, what was she supposed to say, yes? Ego told her to run not walk to the white room. A copulation of emotions begged her to dig in her heels and refuse to move. She liked being near Law. Felt safe beside him in the big bed when he was there. Intimacy was crucial to her ever escaping.

In the white room she wouldn't have the same interaction with Law as she would in his bed. Her chances of gaining his trust were higher the more familiar they became with each other. What better place for that then in the same bed?

It dawned on her as the thoughts and emotions knocked around in her head, that she did want Law's trust, but not for the original reason. She wanted his trust because he respected her not a means to an end. "Yes," she answered.

"I hurt you the other night. In my sleep. It could have been worse. You're safer in the white room."

Lana smiled slowly as she sauntered over to him. "Well, I guess you're just going to have to think of happy things when you close your eyes each night instead of bad things."

"I don't do happy."

"Is that so?" Her tone was sharp as a needle. "Then we're two of a kind, Law."

CHAPTER TWENTY-ONE

LATER, after she had showered, Lana got busy digging through more deluxe shopping bags from upscale stores, gob smacked by the price tags. Law could afford it, though. Everything had been purchased with his money and he had enough of that for nine lifetimes. She tried on some things, experimented with different combinations. Jhett's cutting-edge fashion sense made a real difference.

The sound of a woman's voice drifted into the bedroom. Lana moved silently to the cracked door.

"The word's out, Law. When do you think Drago will make his move?" Jhett asked.

"Any time now. And he'll go for broke. He's been waiting too long for what we have."

"I hope Tamayo has his shit together."

Lana wondered who Tamayo was, and listened harder.

"He does."

That terse reply told Lana exactly nothing. Oh well.

Jhett changed the subject. "So how's your guest? Still the same hot mess I saw the other day?"

"I wouldn't go that far," Law drawled. "Let's just say she's in recovery."

"Seriously? But why here? You should send her down to Nikki. She can go crazy and no one will care."

So who the hell was Nikki? Listening in was only making Lana more confused.

Law took his time about answering Jhett. "I might," he finally said.

"You might send her to Nikki or you might care if she goes crazy?"

There was a long pause before Law answered. "She's been through a lot."

"We've all been to hell and back, some of us more times then others. None of us whined about it or threw temper tantrums. We sucked it up and got on with our lives, however different that life became."

Lana frowned. Apparently she wasn't the only one. What exactly was going on here? Rehab for runaways? She pressed her ear to the door to hear better.

"You're not doing her any favors keeping her locked away in this gilded cage."

Lana nodded. *Preach it, sister.*

"I'll deal with her my way," Law said.

"Hello? What happened to ice-for-blood Law? Are you his good twin?"

"My plans haven't changed."

"Are you going to put her to work?"

"I'm considering it."

Jhett sighed loudly. "Sienna is always saying she needs good translators. Didn't you tell me your girl spoke French at that fancy boarding school in Maryland? And Spanish?"

"Yes."

"Okay. Then give her headphones and have her translate for Sienna."

"Take care of that for me, would you? And don't get Sienna worked up again like you did last week."

"What do you mean?"

"You two broke up. If you can't control your temper, at least fight someplace else. Not at Chimera."

"For the record, we're just taking some time to figure things out. And you know damn well I've never allowed my personal stuff to get in the way of Chimera operations."

"Keep it that way."

Jhett and Sienna were a thing? Lana shrugged. Whatever. The implication was that Sienna and Law—and also Jhett and Law—weren't lovers. Or maybe they were. Did the girls swing both ways?

An interesting question, and the answer to it might involve her. Deciding it was time she made her presence known, Lana opened the door and walked into the living room.

Jhett and Law's conversation abruptly ended. Jhett's curious gaze swept her from head to toe. Her dark eyes brightened.

"Sorry to disappoint, Jhett, but I don't play for your team."

"Guess you were listening." Jhett's lips curved into a smile. "Hey, if you gave it a shot, you might change your mind."

"I did once. Not my thing."

"Maybe it wasn't the right woman."

Lana played along. "Maybe."

Glancing up at Law, who regarded Lana with a similar glint in his eyes, Jhett said, "I'm not opposed to sharing with Law."

Law coughed. "I don't share, Jhett."

"Thank you both for talking about me like I was a piece of meat." Lana sauntered into the kitchen and took out a granola bar from a snack canister. She wasn't going to eat the icky-sticky thing. Just needed a reason to exit the convo, that was all. And, hmm, distract them enough to maybe change the subject.

"What's up with you? Don't you like sex?" Jhett called.

"I don't consider it a sport."

That'd give them something to talk about, and the time to do the talking, Lana thought, crackling the intact wrapper for effect. But the other two were quiet. Until Jhett taunted her again, from a safe distance.

"Oh, yeah, right, your type has to be in *luuuuv*."

Lana set down the granola bar and went back into the living room. "My type?"

"Yeah. Rich, spoiled, stuck up."

Lana laughed. "Rich? I don't own a damn thing except my thoughts. Spoiled? My parents tore me away from everything I loved and sent me away to boarding school three thousand miles away when I was eleven. They thought I was dead and want to keep me that way. Stuck up? For the last six months, I fucking stripped for a living."

"My mistake." Jhett looked like she was about to laugh.

Irked, Lana got closer, invading Jhett's personal space.

"Yes. And by the way, since you seem to be so interested, I don't have to be in love to fuck. But I do have to be in lust. And it has to be *my* choice."

Lana reached up, slid her fingers deep into Jhett's spiked hair and pulled her head down, brushing her lips across Jhett's.

The room got awfully quiet. A rush of adrenaline tingled through Lana's veins. Not for the woman but for the man watching intently.

"I don't drop like a trained bitch for just anyone." Lana nipped at Jhett's bottom lip. "But I'll give you a whistle if I decide to give you a shot." She stepped back from Jhett. "And you'll come."

Jhett grinned so wide, Lana thought her face would tear in half. "Oh, baby girl, I am *so* there." Turning to Law, she teased him. "You don't mind if I do her, right?"

Lana glanced at Law, whose arms were folded over his chest. Trying to control himself—or angry? Lana couldn't really tell.

"You leaving?" he asked Jhett coolly.

Translation: *leave.* It was a command, not a question, Lana thought.

Jhett literally skipped to the door. Before she opened it, she looked over her shoulder at Lana and winked. Laughing, she opened it and exited.

As much as Lana would like to deny it, Jhett intrigued her. Not sexually, although Lana was sure Jhett knew her way around a woman's body better than most men. Jhett was everything Lana wanted to be. Confident, fierce and clearly multi-talented. How to develop that skill set, Lana wasn't sure but she knew it was dope.

Glancing up at Law, her blood warmed. He made that happen —there was no doubt about it. No other man she'd ever known triggered such instinctive desire in her. She wanted him. Physically.

Law's moody stare only intensified the feeling. Lana looked down, breaking away from him, moving to the high windows. The predicted thunderstorm was still rumbling through, wreaking havoc. She gazed out at the tumultuous bay. Dark and angry, it was beautiful in its frothy fit.

She had a lot to think about. Starting with Jhett asking Law whether he'd mind if she did Lana. His response intrigued her. The image of him fighting off a strap-on-wearing Jhett over her made her smile.

Laughter bubbled up from her chest. Before she knew it she was laughing loudly.

"What's so funny?" Law asked, coming up behind her.

Chuckling, Lana shook her head and said, "I doubt you want to know."

"Try me." He stopped less than an inch away from her back, almost touching her but not quite, radiating heat.

Turning around, Lana caught her breath as her breasts slid across the hardness of Law's torso. Her amusement dissolved into instant sexual excitement.

Glancing up at him, she caught her breath. His green eyes had darkened. His scar pulled tight. "What's so funny? I, ah— don't remember."

Law drew her even closer, lowering his lips to hers. She closed her eyes, hot all over, eagerly anticipating his kiss.

"Try to remember," he whispered, lifting his head. Pulling away from her. Leaving her standing there looking like a fool.

Lana gasped. "That wasn't nice!"

Law stood back. "No? Should I apologize for not kissing you? Don't hold your breath, Lana."

"What?"

"For a second there, I almost forgot how often you've told me not to touch."

"I—"

"Change your mind? So which is it? Yes, I can touch you or no, I can't?"

"I—I don't want you to hurt me."

His full lips turned up into a suggestive smile. "Sometimes, Lana, the hurt feels good."

"I'm not into pain." Except the good pain—when he spanked her.

"I'm talking about the pain of wanting something so badly it hurts."

"There are some things we shouldn't want."

"And how does that apply to you?" he asked softly.

She answered without hesitation. "I don't want you to become something I can't have."

Law's green eyes gleamed. "You can have me any time."

"You pushed me away, said you didn't want me."

"I lied."

"Good to know," Lana retorted. "What else have you lied to me about?"

"Just that."

"Why?" She had to know.

"Because I don't want *you* to become something *I* can't have."

"Oh." Lana stiffened as Law moved past her to the window. "Sounds like we're both out of luck, then."

For long moments, side by side but not touching, they stared out at the storm.

CHAPTER TWENTY-TWO

"TELL me more about your time in boarding school," Law asked casually.

Lana knew he had a reason to ask. Just not what it was. She stalled. "What is there to tell that you don't already know?"

"Why boarding school in Maryland and not California? Why did you run away from that school?"

"How do you know about that?"

"I told you I deal in information. Some information is harder to come by than others. Enlighten me."

"Why?"

"Call me curious."

"You'll use it against me."

"Never. Only to understand you better."

She turned to him. "Why is that important?"

He brushed her hair from her shoulders and traced a finger along the fading bruises on her neck. "I honestly don't know, but it is important."

Lana shook her head. "If you understand me, then you'll

really like me. Then you'll be following me around like a puppy. I don't like to be followed around."

Law sighed. "Did you notice when you worked at Ultimate that you were followed sometimes?"

She looked at him suspiciously. "Yes. Are you saying you had something to do with that?"

Law nodded. "You've been on my radar for a long time, Lana."

"How, when the world thought I was dead? And why?"

"I got a tip awhile back that you staged your death." He cocked a brow. "You weren't as smart as you thought you were. Pawning that Rolex sent up a few flags for anyone who was interested."

Oh yeah. The Rolex. Never accept a super-expensive gift with a serial number if you planned to disappear and might need to sell it, because you'd be tracked. But she hadn't known that when her father had given her the damn thing for her graduation. And then there was the diamond bracelet from her mother on the same day. Both were keep quiet bribes, as far as she was concerned.

"That Rolex bought me a new identity and the diamond bracelet I pawned set me up for a couple of years while I worked my way through college."

Looking pointedly at him she said, "If you figured it out, how come the cops never could?"

Law shrugged. "Maybe they were paid off not to."

Her jaw dropped. "But why?"

"Your death gave your father a nice bump in the polls that election cycle."

"I had a brother. He was born before me. He was six months old when he died. Father won his first term two months later."

"An unfortunate pattern."

"I know."

Sadness for the big brother she would never know engulfed her. He would have been twenty-six this year. Many nights she had lain awake thinking of him. Wondering if he would love her as much as she loved him even though they had never met.

"Mamita said Robby was perfect." Swiping at a tear, Lana looked up at Law's patient eyes. "It was after Robby died that Mamita and father—got together. I have a half sister, Miranda. We're three months apart."

Law's eyes widened slightly. Lana managed a smile. "I guess you don't know everything, information man."

"True enough. I never came across anything about you having a half sister. Where is she?"

"I don't know. Mother sent her away—" Closing her eyes, forcing the memories from her brain, Lana rushed her words. "After—Mamita died."

She was silent for a long moment. Law didn't press her. "I don't want to talk about the past," she finally said. "Or anything else right now. Your turn. Tell me why you were watching me at the Ultimate."

"Because of the company you kept. It was just a matter of time before someone figured out who you were. When Anton finally did, he didn't waste a minute generating interest in you. To the highest bidder you would go."

"Those men hanging around—the ones who didn't want bottle service or lap dances—they were yours?"

"Mostly."

"There was a guy one day I couldn't seem to shake. What about him?"

"He was following the man following you."

"And I thought it was Anton keeping an eye on me."

Law looked at her wearily. "You had no idea then how much danger you were in. Here you're protected."

"Right," she scoffed, "until you decide you don't need me anymore. Then what? You cut me loose and I have to fend for myself?"

"It's more complicated than that."

"It's my life!" Lana wailed. "I have a right to know what you plan to do with it!"

"For now, I'm going to keep you safe. And just so you don't get bored—"

He went to the end table next to the sofa and pressed the lid of an ebony box there.

It slowly opened, revealing several remotes. He took one, and then closed the box. "This is the universal remote. Use it for the TV." Motioning her over, he said, "It's easy."

"Skip the tutorial, Law. I know how to work a frickin' remote. I want to know what you know."

"I can't tell you any more right now."

Lana crossed her arms over her chest. There was no prodding, pushing or temper tantrum that was going to budge him at the moment. Mentally, she conceded the point. For the moment.

Wanting to lighten the mood, she pointed to the flat screen and asked, "How big is that thing?"

"Eighty-five inches."

"My psych professor said that men compensate for small penises with large televisions, big trucks and fast cars."

Law grinned down at her. Her heart did a giddy-up. "Would you like proof to dispel that philosophy?"

"Um, no." She didn't need proof. Not after seeing him naked and fully aroused in the pool.

Law let it pass.

"Okay. Then you get a tutorial." He pointed the remote toward the television. "Green button turns it on, red turns it off. The volume is here, the channel selector here. On Demand, you can figure it out. Buttons and arrows are for fast forward, pause and rewind."

"Seems too simple," she said mockingly. "I thought guys liked it complicated?"

Setting the remote on the end table, Law said, "Not me. I don't like complications."

"Or head cases."

"Some of those are more interesting then others." He winked and handed her the gizmo. "See you later. I have work to do." He turned and left the penthouse.

Annoyed at his casual dismissal of her, Lana stood staring at the large flat screen. She wasn't interested in watching TV. Never had been. Her smartphone had been her lifeline to the world and that was long gone. Turning to the black box she took out the three remaining remotes and set them on a couch cushion.

One of them might connect the TV to the Internet. Using the universal remote first, she turned the television on and clicked on the menu, scrolling through the options.

Bingo! All kinds of email icons populated the screen. Clicking Gmail, she smiled when it opened. Quickly she input her addy and password and hit Log In.

Your ID did not match your password.

"What?" she said, exasperated.

She tried again. Four times. Slowly. Got the same error message four more times.

She wasn't mistaken. She'd had the same ID and password since she created her Gmail account eight years ago.

Had she been hacked?

Clicking on every icon that might link to the Internet proved futile. Law had shut her out.

Tossing the remotes onto the sofa, she paced the living room. Each time she stepped past Law's desk, she eyed the laptop sitting on it. With the highly specialized cyber ware Law no doubt had installed, the laptop would probably self-destruct if she touched it.

Finally, she tried to open it. The lid didn't budge. Of course it didn't. Pressing her hand where she had watched Law press his, she tried to get into his desk. Maybe he had a burner cell or two stashed away. No go. The desk, no matter how hard she tried, stayed shut.

Methodically, Lana dug through every drawer and cabinet in the penthouse she could access hoping to find something, anything that could link her to the outside world. Not a damn thing.

Maybe the white room had a hidden treasure or two. Making a beeline there, she almost screamed when the door wouldn't open. Locked.

The security keypad to the right of the door required a code to open it. If she tried too many times, it would probably alert Law.

"Damn him!"

The only door open to her was the gym room door. Jerking it open, she attacked the heavy bag barehanded, smacking it. She yelled Law's name each time she kicked it.

Little by little, her sudden fury and frustration turned into resolution. To continue to get healthier. Stronger. To never go back to where she had been. She was in a fight for her emotional life and physical life. She would win, damn it!

No one but Lana was in charge of her destiny. That damned

contract didn't bind her to anyone. Never mind his smooth words—
Law was basically using fear to keep her here. What he said about
her being safer here with him than outside on her own was bullshit.

Like she didn't understand it was a jungle out there? She was
clean at last. Which made her stronger. Smarter. More determined then ever to find her way in the world.

In a weirdly twisted way, she had Law to thank for that. He
had saved her from someone who would've exploited her ruth-
lessly before discarding her or passing her along to the next man
when she no longer served his purpose. She wouldn't have had a
chance.

In a very short time, Law had begun to rebuild her. Above
all, first of all, he'd brought her back to life when she had done
her best to end it.

She would find a way out of here. Find a safe place to start
over. To reinvent herself. And thrive.

Sweaty and sore as hell, her body protesting, Lana gave in to
her fatigue. Two workouts in the same day were too much for her
right now. For the second time that day she jumped in the
shower.

Done with that, dried off and dressed, Lana grabbed the
remote from the sofa and plopped down. As she flipped through
the channels, Lana realized that even though Law drove her
crazy, she enjoyed his company. He was highly intelligent. He
challenged her. Made her think harder. Expected more of her
than anyone close to her ever had.

She found herself not wanting to disappoint him. And then
there was the sexual attraction. Like lightning in a bottle. She
couldn't control it. Truth be told, neither could he.

It pumped her confidence knowing that a powerful man like
Law was that interested in her. Yeah, yeah, she told herself, he'd
made it clear, enough that he was a hit-it-and-quit-it kind of guy.

However, judging by the hotness quotient of the women forever knocking on his damn door for more, more, more, he was doing something right.

She decided then she would tell him about her time in boarding school and why she was sent there. Even now, the memory made her skin crawl. But she didn't have to tell him all of the truth. That, she had never shared with a living soul.

But she'd only share if he told her why he killed the cop. Not remotely an equal *quid pro quo*, but she was going for it. And it was how she was going to handle him going forward.

If he wanted something from her, he had to give her something in return. Every time. With each piece of information gathered, she'd tuck it away until she could put them all together and make a clean break.

CHAPTER TWENTY-THREE

HOURS LATER, having eaten another unbelievably good meal —delivered from some fancy restaurant for a change—happily ensconced in a food coma, Lana snuggled deeply into a fur throw. Its warm sleekness and masculine scent reminded her of Law. Closing her eyes, she imagined the two of them lying naked on the throw in front of the roaring fireplace, as the rain pelted the windows.

An even hotter fantasy of their bodies writhing in the throes of passion invaded her senses. How would his warm skin and taut muscles feel pressed to her body? Her nipples tightened when she thought of his hands stroking her, his lips pressed to every intimate curve of her body. Of his thick cock inside her.

She moaned out loud, liquefying as she imagined how good it would feel each time he thrust deeply into her.

Slow, sensuous, sublime.

Intuitively, Lana understood that sex with Law would ruin sex with other men. Not that she had ever enjoyed sex with any man. It was painful mostly. Something she had never emotionally committed to.

She'd been only fourteen the first time. She'd seduced her roommate Polina's twenty-year-old cousin.

The seduction had been easy. What came after was not. He had a possessive streak a mile wide. He wanted marriage. Thought he could persuade her to move to Mother Russia when she graduated. She had been young—hell, underage at fourteen —and wild and reckless but she wasn't stupid. Marriage to a man like that would have been a lifelong prison sentence.

The shrill sound of an Emergency Alert startled her. Sitting up, turning down the volume, she read the information on the flat screen TV. *Five-year-old Miguel Tamayo was abducted at 10:05 p.m. from his mother's Union City home A silver economy car with a dented rear bumper was seen leaving the area, heading west on Decoto Road toward Interstate 880. No license plate available at this time.* A list of surrounding counties followed.

"Poor kid," she sighed. Glancing at the clock, Lana noted the time was almost eleven. What took the cops so long to release the info? The little boy could be far away by now.

Feeling sick at heart, Lana still knew there was nothing she could do. She folded and replaced the fur throw on the sofa back where it had been. Turning off the television, she padded back to the bedroom and brushed her teeth. Her nightly routine didn't have to change, and she went through the motions same as always. Finished, giving herself no more than a glance in the mirror, she let her mind wander. To Law, of course. There was no escaping him, literally and psychologically.

What would it be like to be his? A powerful man like Law, an all-out alpha, driven by iron determination, would drive her truly crazy. Would he behave differently just because she wanted him? Not a chance.

Law wasn't hard-wired to ever stand back, beaming proudly, as his woman took off without him.

Could he if he wanted to? No. Not in his oh-so-mysterious business where it was nonetheless clear that everyone was jockeying for power. And not in his love life. Although he didn't seem to think much of love, when it came right down to it. Or maybe it was that he defined it differently from the rest of the world. Whatever. He would likely be so overprotective and paranoid, he'd smother her to death.

Slipping on a sheer lavender nightie, Lana smiled smugly. Law could eat his heart out. She had no intention of playing nice. Making him so damn uncomfortable he'd be forced to remove her from his penthouse seemed like a much more intelligent plan and definitely less difficult than being one of his girls. He had too damn many. Practically every time she turned around, one was banging on the door for him.

They knew him better than she did. And he wasn't as indifferent to them—or to her—as he pretended to be. There had to be a way to use all of that to her advantage.

As she lay down in the big bed, Lana heard the penthouse door open, and smiled.

Unmoving, she listened to Law enter the bedroom, then the bathroom. The shower ran for twenty minutes before it turned off. Long minutes later, Law slid between the sheets, stretching out but staying as far away from her as possible.

On purpose, she'd snuggled dead center in the bed. Even from where he lay, she could smell his clean scent. Feel the warmth of his body.

"I know you're awake," he said, his voice low.

"No I'm not."

He rolled over to face her. "Why aren't you on your side of the bed?"

Opening her eyes, she caught her breath. His was bare-chested, his hair damp. His hot gaze bored into her. "I like it in the middle."

"You're too close."

She pulled down the nightie as far as it would go. Which wasn't very far. And he seemed to have noticed that it was sheer. "Afraid you might get burned?"

"I'm immune to pain, Lana."

"So am I." Not true, but he might fall for it.

"That's a lie."

She pretended to be upset. "How can you say that?"

"You're hurting. I can tell, even though you cry in secret."

"And when do I do that? Since you're so fucking observant, I mean."

"When you can't take it or fake it another second."

Lana was taken aback by the accuracy of that statement. He was right. "That's because you frustrate me."

Reaching out, he took a strand of her hair and twirled it around his finger. "If you were immune to pain, you would be immune to frustration."

Not wanting to discuss her feelings, she changed the subject. "Let's talk about you. Truth or Dare."

"Not my game," he muttered. "But go ahead."

Lana went for it. "I would like to know why you killed a cop."

He fisted her hair. It hurt but she didn't shy away. Instead she inched closer. "I'm not being bitchy this time. I'm asking because I don't want to think the worst of you."

"It would better for you if you did."

"That's not for you to say."

"I give up." Law released her hair and rolled over onto his back. "You first," he said.

Scooting closer to him, she shook her head. "Oh no. *You* first."

"It happened years ago. I was riding with rough trade at the time. We'd stopped in Paradise for a few days on business, with a guy named Ace. His old lady and their daughter lived there. Kid was twelve or so."

She stroked his chest. "And?"

"We weren't looking for trouble—that day or any day. And when we rolled through, most of the cops in Butte County were happy to look the other way for a few bucks. But one of them figured he had a right to whatever the hell he wanted since my crew owed him for some damn thing or another."

Law stopped.

"Go on," Lana coaxed him. This was better than TV.

"Ace and his old lady took off one night, leaving the kid behind. I told him I'd check in on her. When I got there a deputy's cruiser was parked out front and the door was locked. I heard the screams, kicked it in, pulled my gun. The motherfucker had his pants halfway down—"

Law squeezed his eyes shut. "I dragged him off her. He drew on me, but I shot first."

"Oh my God, that's horrible!" Lana moved closer. The pain in Law's eyes undid her.

"He was dirty. It wasn't his first offense."

"Is the little girl okay?"

"She grew up fast after that," was all he said at first.

The laconic answer wasn't enough for Lana. "Did she get help? You know what I mean."

"I do, and the answer is yes," he said. "She's holding her own now."

"Did you kill him?"

"Yes."

"Were you arrested?"

"No."

"What happened to the deputy—his body?"

"Disappeared without a trace."

"I can't believe the department didn't flip the entire state looking for him."

Law shrugged. "In my line of work we have people that take care of things like that."

Lana lay on her back and closed her eyes. "You live in a violent world."

"We all do. Most people just don't realize it."

That terrified her.

"So. How do you feel about me now?" His flat question was barely audible.

Slowly she opened her eyes. How *did* she feel? Turning to look at him, she said, "I'd have done the same thing." Swallowing, she added, "At least I would have wanted to."

His reply was calm enough. "I have no regrets."

Law's phone vibrated on the nightstand, startling her.

He picked it up and checked the screen. "Yeah," he said.

In the quiet, the male voice on the other end, speaking rapid Spanish, had Law sitting up.

"¿Porque me llamas?" Law asked, his voice alert. *Why are you calling me?*

So he spoke Spanish. Probably other languages too.

"Meet me on the dock in twenty."

He hung up, shot off a quick text and bounced from the bed to his cave closet. This time he left the door open as he dressed.

"Is everything okay?" she called.

"It will be," he said.

Lana slipped from the bed and padded over to the open door. When she peeked in, she had to say a silent wow.

Rows of suits and shoes and shirts and slacks lined two walls. A large island in the center held several glass-topped wooden boxes. Standing on her tiptoes, she could just make out the glitter of precious metals. Probably a collection of watches and cufflinks.

Sliding metal doors along the back wall were half open, revealing an arsenal of guns, knives, ammo boxes and all kinds of accompanying paraphernalia.

To her right stood an enormous safe. Shut tight. Keypad blinking a warning light.

This was more than the ultimate gentleman's closet. It was a freakin' armory.

Law dressed himself head to toe in black. Not a tux, not fancy. More like rugged and sinister. Glancing over at her, he scowled, then slid a black nylon holster over his right shoulder, selecting a big pistol and sliding it in. He clasped a neoprene sheath to his belt and slipped a wicked-looking knife into it.

Done. Heading out.

When he grabbed a black duffel bag from the floor and heaved it over his other shoulder, he strode toward her. Lana backed up as he shut the door behind him. She knew it automatically locked.

Transfixed, Lana stood rooted to the floor. Law was the embodiment of deadly force.

"Are you going to kill someone?"

"Not if they stay out of my way."

The penthouse doorbell softly chimed. Law headed for the door. Lana wrapped herself in a robe so big she realized too late that it was his, and hurried behind him.

Jhett stood on the other side of the threshold, giving Lana no more than a glance before she looked at Law. She was dressed completely in black, like him. Gun, knife, sinister vibe —everything.

"You ready?"

Law nodded.

CHAPTER TWENTY-FOUR

"TRUE'S BRINGING THE BOAT AROUND," Jhett said.

That explained exactly nothing to Lana. She stayed in the background, just listening for a few minutes.

Eventually Law remembered she was there and turned to her, pointing to the keypad by the front door. "If you need anything, hit the pound key on the intercom and Monty will be right up."

That was all he said. Before she could respond, they walked around to the other side of the slate fireplace column and disappeared. Lana hurried around just as the hidden elevator to the roof door slid closed.

Stepping back from it, Lana turned off all of the lights and ran to the windowsill for an unobstructed view of dark doings in plain sight.

Sure enough, a few minutes later, Law exited the building, heading straight for the closest dock. Several minutes passed before a powerboat approached, its wake slicing a white vee through the dark water until the dark-clad man at the wheel cut the engines and steered in slowly.

Law waited, catching the line that was cast toward him, using it to pull the boat alongside the dock before looping the line around a piling. Jhett tossed several duffel bags to the man who'd thrown the line, who quickly stowed them in the back of the boat.

Lana figured the man was True, and confirmed it when he reached out a hand to help Jhett board, then hopped from the boat to the dock. Jhett got busy with the bags, unzipping them for a final check of gear Lana couldn't see, while Law and True stood together no more than a foot apart, their heads bent in deep conversation.

The stormy weather was getting worse—she could tell by the whitecaps. She spotted another boat out on the rough water, zeroing in on the dock, barely slowing, shoved along by the force of the wind.

True and Law didn't seem to hear it. The boat came in and tied up fast. They looked over their shoulders when a man jumped from it to the dock.

The man seemed agitated, gesturing wildly, growing angry by her guess. But his vibe told Lana he was more than angry. Afraid? Desperate? He seemed to be pleading with Law.

Was he begging for forgiveness or a favor?

Law placed his hand on the man's shoulder as if reassuring him. True took over the conversation as Law turned away and made several calls. In between the calls he appeared to be texting. At one point, the unknown man took out his phone for Law to look at. He glanced at the screen and nodded. That was all. The meeting ended abruptly.

One after the other, both boats sped off into the night. Lana's mind raced with scenarios. What the hell was going on? She couldn't figure it out from what she'd seen.

Closing her eyes against the morning sun filtering through the high windows, Lana snuggled deeper into the blankets, aware that Law hadn't come home. The warmth his body added to the bed was absent. So were his deep breaths and the protected feeling of knowing he was near.

What if Law was hurt or worse? She didn't want to think about that.

Rolling over onto her back, Lana rubbed her eyes, making herself wake up all the way. Law would come back, she was sure of that. No one and nothing could take him down.

After she cleaned up, she grabbed a robe and headed to the kitchen. She was famished. Digging into the ridiculous breakfast Monty brought in some time earlier, Lana turned on the TV to catch the news.

She missed her smartphone and all of her social media feeds.

Settling on a local channel, she poured another cup of coffee.

"This update just in on the abduction of little Miguel Tamayo," the anchor began. "Union City police have confirmed that five-year-old Miguel, who's been identified as the son of notorious outlaw Jamie Tamayo, biker boss of the San Francisco-based Coyotes, was boldly taken from his mother's bed while the two slept." The anchor stared into the camera, did a dramatic pause. "His captors are demanding ten million dollars, to be delivered by ten o'clock this morning. And they are threatening to kill the boy if the ransom is not paid."

Lana gasped.

A glance at the clock told her that little Miguel had less than half an hour.

"A tip hotline, posted at the bottom of your screen, has been set up. Authorities are asking for confidential information that could assist in the safe return of the boy."

The next segment showed the mother, Lucia, hysterically begging for the return of her son. Sinking into the sofa, Lana trembled. How terrible for that poor family.

Glued to the set, hoping for further updates on little Miguel, Lana prayed for his safe return to his mother.

The secret elevator slid open with a soft whoosh. Lana's heart kicked up a notch. Law was back. Unmoving, she waited for him to come around to where she was.

When he didn't, she stood up and moved toward the kitchen and stopped in her tracks. With his back to her, Law stood at the high kitchen bar.

Head dropped, he massaged his neck, rolling his shoulders, as if he were working out muscle kinks. Shrugging off his shoulder holster, he tossed it on the counter.

Just doing that much made him wince with pain.

Lana knew instantly that he'd been in a major fight. His dark clothes were torn and blood soaked. He slumped, bracing himself against the counter with both hands, exhausted.

Concern rose but she quickly tamped it down. He was alive. Quietly she moved back to the sofa and sat down.

"Rough night?" she called from where she sat.

Law moved into her view. "I've had worse."

"Looks like it." Pointing behind him, she said, "Monty brought breakfast. There's enough in the warmer to feed you and the guy who did that to you."

"Guys." Running his fingers through his tousled hair, he shook his head. "I'm good on the food."

Shrugging, she turned her attention back to the news. Law went past her to the bedroom, emerging after a little while showered and dressed in pajama bottoms and a ribbed black tank top that clung to his chest. His bare, heavily muscled arms showed signs of bruising, and deep scrapes. Padding into the kitchen, he grabbed a bottle of water from the fridge and chugged it.

Lana sat still, enthralled by him. The morning light outlined his powerful body. The urge to soothe his hurts was strong. A vision of him picking her up in those strong arms, laying her down on the big bed, the morning sunlight warming their naked bodies as they made love, had her squirming. The evidence of his power was a total turn-on. She was dying to ask him what happened.

For almost a minute, he just stood there, staring past her to the windows, blinking a little at the sunlight reflected brightly off the bay.

"You okay?" she asked.

Her question brought him back from wherever he had gone. "I'm good. Just beat." Rubbing the back of his neck, he said, "Wake me up in three hours," and disappeared back into the bedroom, closing the door behind him.

Lana stuck her tongue out and turned back to the television, leaning in when little Miguel's face flashed on the screen.

"We have breaking news on the Tamayo abduction," the anchor intoned as the visual switched to the studio set. "Miguel Tamayo has been found unharmed, asleep in the doorway of his paternal grandmother's house in Oakland. Stay tuned for more details and a live report after the break—"

Lana muted the volume with the remote.

"Thank God," she breathed, falling back into the big sofa. Swiping at tears, she wondered why she cared so much. All her sympathy went out to the mom, and the little boy, though she couldn't help a small twinge of envy that he had a mother that cared.

Maybe something she'd long forgotten was coming back to life—raw, engaged life. Like emotions. Well…fuck that. She'd bagged that whole business long ago.

And yet, the tears continued. Not self-pitying tears, happy tears for the Tamayo family.

CHAPTER TWENTY-FIVE

THREE HOURS later to the minute, holding a cold damp towel in her hand, Lana stood over Law's big body. He probably hadn't moved from the moment he'd sprawled out on the huge bed, and wasn't moving now, not even when his phone vibrated with an incoming call for the fifth time. She tried to see who it was, scowling when the caller ID didn't show. Of course the mysterious Law kept his phone settings hidden.

Everything about him was private. Even here in his personal space, he was private. Everything that could possibly define him was locked behind closed doors.

Including her. An interesting thought.

Taking advantage of the quiet and his sleep state, Lana started to look him over. Long legs, the hard muscle showing under the thin material of his pajamas. Defined abs, oh yes. And wide chest. More hard muscle roped his powerful arms, the intricate tattoos upping the ante to seriously hot. Besides the raw scrapes, his right hand was slightly swollen, angry bruises bright red over his split knuckles.

A purpling bruise ran along his right collarbone. Her gaze

moved up, admiring the dark hair that tumbled over the pillow, away from his handsome face. Straight blunt chin, full lips that she imagined would be irresistible to any woman, despite the severe scar at the crease at the right side.

That scar intrigued her. She would bet her freedom he hadn't come by it accidentally. It had been inflicted on purpose, intended to maim. Dark stubble shaded his chin and cheeks, giving him an even more predatory look. His nose was straight, his lashes as black as his hair, his dark brows slashes above green eyes that at the moment didn't laugh at her.

Because they were closed. But she couldn't shake the odd sensation that he was looking at her.

For the first time in her life, Lana understood the feminine urge to tame a man who could never be tamed. Which didn't mean, not for one second, that she would ever give into it. In fact, standing here with the towel, she realized she was annoyed with herself for obeying his order and waiting like a good little wifey to wake him up.

Angry with herself because the thought of escaping Law didn't hold the urgency it had previously held. Right now, she would just as soon punch him for making her want to stay. Not fight for her freedom. Who the hell did he think he was, kidnapping her and holding her hostage?

She was losing her mind. There was no other explanation for her wildly mixed feelings for Law.

Raising her hand with the sodden towel, she dropped it onto Law's chest. "Get up—"

She screamed when he yanked her down to him, rolling over onto her, his fist cocked, as if he were about to hit her.

"Law! No!" His green eyes looked crazed, unfocused. "Law, please," she sobbed. "Don't hurt me."

Slowly he lowered his fist. Shaking his head, he rolled off her. "I'm sorry," he muttered, not moving.

Despite his drowsiness, the coiled power of his big body was very evident. She lay still, not wanting to antagonize him further.

The mattress moved slightly when he stretched, still not fully awake. Lana slowly sat up in the bed. Pulling her knees to her chest, she wrapped her arms around them. Law opened his eyes and stared at her.

"Did I hurt you?"

"No, just scared me."

Looking past her to the wet towel on the bed, he scowled. "Next time you pull a stunt like that, I'm turning you over my knee."

"You would," she pffted. But she just might do it again, just for the thrill of disrupting his control over her.

Law yawned and picked up his phone to check his messages and send a few texts, then stretched again.

"You're ignoring me." Lana added a fake pout. Like he would give a fuck.

Mid-stretch, he studied her for several long seconds. The intensity of his gaze unnerved her to the point where she got out of the bed.

"Seems safest." He tossed the phone aside, thought better of it, and stuck it in his pajama pocket as he rose.

Lana stood silent and watched the sleepy, beat-up gladiator stalk from the room, supremely annoyed with herself by this point for her inability to stop staring at him.

Cabinet doors banged. A plate rang against dark gray marble. Knives rattled and silver clinked. The beast needed to feed.

Ignoring the racket, Lana tidied the bed before returning to the living room.

TV time. She turned up the volume.

"Turn it down." An order, followed by an afterthought. "Please."

She wasn't impressed. "I'm following this story."

Clink clank. Cutlery hit the plate. She had his attention.

"What story?"

"Kidnappers abducted a little boy last night and demanded ten million dollars in ransom or they'd kill him. This morning he showed up at his grandmother's house. I guess the family paid."

"Huh."

Law's monosyllabic reply held no emotion. If that was some sort of veiled warning that she should stop talking and change the channel, she got it. And ignored it.

The anchor continued. "Authorities have released no details on how the boy arrived at his grandmother's house."

"Why would they?" Lana muttered.

"Do you always talk back to the TV?" Law inquired. "Or do you just talk back, period?"

"Yes to both questions." She wondered why he wanted to know.

"At this time there is also no information on the ransom payment, if any," the anchor went on, fiddling with his earpiece and listening—or pretending to—for a couple of seconds. "Or who the kidnappers are or where they may be. CeeCee has more."

The blond female co-anchor, a weird vision in pink, stretched out a smile. "In other developments…"

"They must've paid. I'd do anything to get my child back," Lana said.

"The boy's father," CeeCee continued, "is reported to be the leader of the Coyotes, an outlaw motorcycle club. It's not known if the abduction was connected to the gang."

Law said nothing. And it wasn't because he'd resumed

eating. Lana faced him. The blank stare he favored her with flipped a switch inside her. She could connect the dots without asking him a whole lot of questions he clearly would never answer. Her instincts kicked in, big time. "You know something about this, don't you?"

Lana pointed the remote at the TV to mute the commercial and looked at Law. "Is Jaime Tamayo the same Tamayo that Jhett mentioned to you?"

Shrugging, he said, "I don't know what you're talking about."

"Yes, you do. Why did you just lie to me?"

"I didn't."

Setting the remote down, Lana pounced on the bland answer. He *was* lying. Why?

"Jhett asked if Tamayo had his shit in order, or something to that effect. True asked you when you thought Drago would strike."

By the way he avoided a simple yes or no answer, Lana knew he was involved. "Monty told me you used to ride with Lucifer's Legion. And a Legion member named Ace used to hang out at The Ultimate. Don't tell me you don't know some outlaw bikers." She moved in closer. "Is little Miguel's father the same guy as your Tamayo?"

Law speared her with an intense glare. It wasn't enough to warn her off and she was sure he wouldn't hurt her. She swallowed hard. Make that reasonably sure.

"You have quite the imagination," he said, pushing his mug away from him.

"I didn't imagine what I heard last night," she said heatedly. "I speak Spanish and you know it. That call you got? The man was desperate. I could hear it. He spoke Spanish and you answered him in Spanish. 'Why are you calling *me*?' That's exactly what you asked him, Law. Why, when you're enemies?"

Law just looked at her, his expression implacable. The mask of a man hiding something. "What have you been smoking while I was gone?"

"Nothing. "

"Nice to know you can stay clean without a babysitter."

The sarcastic comment angered her.

"Fuck you, Law. And don't try to distract me."

"Why would I do that?"

He was stalling. She just knew it. He couldn't totally hide that he was somehow connected.

"Because you don't want to answer any questions. Getting back to what I was saying, you must be that guy's friend. Or protector."

Law shrugged.

"Okay, don't tell me. But I watched you from the window afterward. I saw True and Jhett with the duffel bags she brought down and I saw the other man on the second boat."

"You're cute when you think."

Infuriated, Lana practically spat in reply. "*Double* fuck you. And I saw all of you leave. Guess you got to wherever you were going. To do…what?"

Reaching for his bruised hand, she held his gaze, waiting for him to scowl and pull it away. When he didn't, she carefully took it into hers. His skin was warm. His hand, easily twice the size of hers. Long strong fingers, the veins pronounced on his tan skin. A hand that could kill as easily as it could give pleasure, judging from the fucking harem he kept around.

Holding it up, she said, "You fight hard, don't you?"

He pulled his hand back without a word.

Lana traced her finger along his scraped collarbone. "Don't tell me you weren't involved."

Brushing her hand away, he picked up his mug and raised it to his lips. "You're tripping," he said, taking a sip of coffee.

No, she wasn't. *He* was tripping if he thought she was going to drop this. The pieces suddenly fell into place. "Oh, my God," she hissed.

Law scowled.

"It *was* Tamayo who called." Lana's heart slammed against her rib cage. "He called you to find his son!" Blood drained from her cheeks. "The bad guy called the badder guy to do what he couldn't."

Law *was* bad. She hadn't understood just how bad until now. If she was smart, she would shut up. But Lana wasn't renowned for making good decisions. Especially not when she was angry. "How many kidnappers were there?"

"Google it."

"Why, when you were there?"

"Stay out of my business," he warned. His tone made it clear that his patience had been tried to its breaking point. She didn't have a damn thing to lose.

"Who kidnapped that little boy? Why? Did his father pay you to save his son or in your criminal world, does he owe you now?"

Law shoved the mug across the counter and stood. Her jaw dropped when he took a step toward her. She turned to flee.

His big body blocked her. He had her cornered. Now what?

The intimacy of the moment wasn't lost on her. She hadn't dressed, choosing to stay in her comfy pj's. Law's hard thighs were pressed to her butt, his groin against her back. His shoulders enfolded her upper body. If she turned her head, her nose would be in his armpit. Closing her eyes, Lana leaned into him and inhaled deeply, trying to control her racing pulse. When she did, she got a big whiff of musky clean male with a hint of leather. He smelled potent. Strong. Powerfully arousing. Seriously sexual.

"Oh, wow," she murmured, her lips brushing the inside of his bicep.

His entire body stiffened behind her.

Stumbling back against the counter, Lana tried to collect herself. What just happened? Slightly dazed, she looked up at him. She couldn't tell if he was angry or aroused.

"You have quite a mouth," he whispered.

"Kiss me," she blurted.

Law's dark brows shot up to his hairline. She didn't take it back. She'd misunderstood. He was a bad ass who had done what the *cops* couldn't do. Hunted down vicious kidnappers, saved the boy, returned him to his family, then came home like he'd just run out for groceries.

She was seriously turned on at the moment.

Lowering his lips to hers, Law slid his hands beneath her pajama top. His skin was warm, his fingers strong.

Lana moaned at the contact. Her breasts suddenly felt heavy, her sensitive nipples tingled.

"If I kiss you," Law said softly against her lips, "I won't be able to stop."

"Then don't."

CHAPTER TWENTY-SIX

HE OBEYED HER ORDER. That was a switch.

Sliding his mouth to the edge of hers, he nibbled her lower lip.

"Then I'm going to want to do other things to you."

Lana exhaled. "Mmm?"

"Bad things." She didn't need words to understand his meaning. His lips traveled along her jaw and down to her neck, pressing against the sensitive cord on the side.

"Law," she panted, arching when his hands slid around her waist. He slid them up and cupped her breasts. Lana made a small squeaky sound of surprise.

"Really, really bad things." His thumbs teased her hard nipples.

Oh, oh, that felt so good. Swallowing hard, rising on tiptoes, she pressed hotly into his hard body. He was as aroused as she. The hard thickness of him dug into her belly. Never had a man made her feel so alive or so desperate for more.

But this was just—wrong. She should pull away. Move her things into the white room, and not come out.

Sex with Law would make her want more. And more. She shouldn't start with him.

"Law," she breathed. "Stop."

He released her so quickly; he had to steady her because she was off balance.

Unable to look at him, she ran to the bedroom.

She wasn't angry with him. She wasn't even angry with herself. She was frustrated. She really wanted to have sex with Law, damn it! And she wanted to mean something to him too, wanted to matter, and not just as a chess piece. She was losing her shit. It had to stop.

Groaning, Lana changed into workout clothes. Tried to let it all go with a long, cleansing breath. She strolled into the living room like nothing had happened.

Law had his nose buried in his laptop. The breakfast dishes were gone.

"What did you do to the bad guys?" she asked.

Without looking up at her he said, "What I had to do."

"And who kidnapped the little boy?"

Law's answer was curt. "Drago."

"Why? What did Tamayo do? Steal? Betray him?

"I've told you too much already. Stop pushing for more."

"Hey." The deep voice startled her.

Lana was working off her nervous tension on the treadmill when Law came in. Might as well watch him, she thought, stepping down and mopping her neck with one of his monogrammed towels. He started off with a series of stretches. If she got lucky, he'd drop and give her fifty. A girl could dream.

The bruises looked worse, but he was limber. And for

someone who'd been in a badass fight last night and was going on only three of hours sleep, he looked fine.

She took her time about stretching her quads. Left, right. And her hamstrings. Right, left. Any excuse to keep looking at him.

Law donned the gloves and loosened up on the heavy bag. The power behind his punches was something. Mesmerized, she watched him circle the bag, hitting it, kicking it, shouldering it, pushing off from it.

The play of muscle on Law's arms, back and shoulders was amazing. She realized she was gawking at him when Law stood back from the bag, breathing hard.

He unstrapped his gloves and tossed them to the floor, opening the hydration station for a cold drink. Refreshed, he pulled a smaller pair of gloves from one of the drawers and handed them to her.

"These should fit you."

"Okay." He helped her put them on and secure them.

He swung the bag hard, right at her. She wasn't quick enough to get out of the way. It slammed into her. She went flying and landed on her back.

"Always be prepared. Your assailant isn't going to ask your permission to attack."

"You didn't either." She got up and dusted herself off. As she bent to retie her sneaker, the bag hit her again, on the side of her face this time, knocking her over.

"Stop it!"

"Make me," he said, pushing the bag toward her again. Side-stepping it, she came at Law and slapped him. Or tried to. He blocked her. Quickly she turned and tried with her other hand. He blocked her again. Grunting, she swung low, attempting a hook that didn't land.

He gave her a little shot back and said, "Clear your head. Focus. No emotion."

Lana was too angry. She yelled and charged him. Law deflected both her hands. Backing up slightly, she moved in again. He took her down with a quick leg sweep. Humiliation swamped her pride. Blindly she kicked up at him. "You're a bully."

"Knock it off, Lana." Law stepped forward, his hand extended. Lana whipped around and took him out with a leg sweep of her own.

Law landed with a thud, surprised as hell. Springing up to pounce on him, she lost a few seconds. He rolled and she missed.

Dropping to hands and knees, Lana attempted to donkey-kick him. Law jammed up her kick and flipped her onto her back. In a quick maneuver, Law landed in a push-up position and immediately leaped sideways on top of her.

Face to face. Lips to lips. Law held her down, fitting his body to hers.

Desperately, Lana tried to catch her breath. He pressed deeper with his hips, then, leaning in, he licked her nose. He chuckled when he rolled off her and pushed up to a stand.

"You've really got to work on that temper of yours, Lana. It's going to get you killed."

Standing, huffing and puffing, Lana motioned him closer. "Teach me more."

An hour later, Lana stood sweaty, breathless and feeling damn proud of herself.

Law was full of surprises. He was a jiu-jitsu black belt. He'd introduced her to several takedown moves. He was in superb shape. So quick, and so powerful, it was scary to imagine the damage he was capable of.

Sitting on the mats, backs against the wall, they chugged bottled water.

"That was crazy," Lana breathlessly said. "Like off the hook crazy!"

"You did good," Law said.

Nodding, Lana smiled. She did do good. She was stronger than she thought. She'd always been active. Dancing kept her toned.

"Thanks," she said, feeling weird accepting the compliment. She couldn't remember the last time she had received one.

Except from Mamita, who, as she'd braided Lana's hair, told her how smart she was. That she could be anyone she wanted to be, she just needed to believe in herself as much as Mamita did. She was eleven years old. A month later their worlds fell apart.

Fucking tears. She scrubbed at her eyes.

"Why are you crying?"

"I'm not crying."

"Okay, what did you get in both eyes that made you tear and sniffle?"

Lana leaned her head back and thought how insignificant her problems would seem to a man like Law.

Rolling her head against the wall to look at him, she honestly said, "I was thinking how simpler life was when I was eleven."

"What changed?"

Crushing the bottle in her hand, Lana laughed. "Everything."

"*Every*thing?"

She nodded. "Everything."

"Tell me."

She shrugged, staring at the air vent in the ceiling rather than look at him. "I found out my father was fucking the nanny.

Turned out that the daughter of said nanny just happened to be his, making her my half sister."

"And?"

"And what? My mother went ballistic. Tried to kick Mamita and Miranda out." Lana laughed caustically. "The only time I ever saw my father sack up was when he put his foot down. Told mother that Mamita and Miranda were staying."

"Did they?"

Squeezing her eyes shut, Lana nodded. "Until Mamita died. Then mother sent Miranda away."

"Then what?"

"I ran away," she lamely said.

"What happened when they found you?"

"I ran away again. Then they shipped me off to Miss Emily Pratt's Academy for Girls," she said in hoity-toity voice.

Law whistled. "Sounds fancy."

"As elite boarding schools go, it wasn't too bad, I guess. But I hated it."

"It could have been worse."

Her head snapped back again. "You're right, Law, it could have been. But for me, having had my world ripped apart, then getting packed off three thousand miles away from home that seventy-five-grand a year tuition couldn't buy a drop of compassion, and I didn't know anyone—yeah, it was traumatic."

"Then what?"

Losing some of her steam, she shrugged. "I did what every fucked up, unloved, little rich girl does. I acted out."

When Law made no retort, she smirked. "I know what you're thinking, and I don't care."

"You have no idea what I'm thinking." He smiled. "And you do care."

"I did some stupid stuff, Law. Stuff I'm not proud of, that

could have gotten me killed or locked up. I was hurting so much then. Doing crazy shit blocked out the pain of feeling like I had no place to go and no one to turn to."

"What kind of stupid stuff?"

"There was a guy—I hung out with him only to get back at my parents. Of course, the only person I hurt was myself. But— that guy, he was really intense. Scary intense. I was afraid of him. Really afraid. I knew if I wanted to live, I'd have to go dark."

"Got it."

She laughed harshly. "Want more?"

"Go ahead."

"My roommate Polina's overindulgent dad was a Russian art dealer. We took off with enough cash to backpack to California. It was cool until we got caught. But it was worth it. Best six months of my life."

"You're lucky you didn't run into trouble."

"I was running from bigger trouble."

Law nodded. "Who was the guy?"

"No one I want to talk about." Those months on the run had taught Lana that despite her best efforts to screw things up, she was a survivor. Glancing up at Law, she said, "We got in big trouble after that. Lockdown for a year."

"What did you want to be when you grew up?"

She blinked. No one had ever asked her that question. "I—" She was about to say all she wanted to be was normal but she didn't. "I never gave it much thought."

"What did your parents want you to do?"

"Be invisible."

"What about your half-sister?"

Lana stood and wiped her face with her towel. "I haven't spoken to my sister in thirteen years."

"Why not?"

"Because she didn't care enough to reach out to me. I have no idea where she was sent. For all I know my parents changed her name and sent her overseas. Pisses me off."

"What if she wasn't able to reach out? What if she thinks you didn't care enough to do the same thing?"

"I—" Lana rubbed her temples. "That never occurred to me," she said, feeling ashamed. She'd only thought about herself and her pain.

"I'm sorry."

"Don't be." Lana's head snapped back as she came to the stunning revelation that she didn't need anyone. Including Law. It was time to put the past in the past and some serious space between them. Time to laser focus on herself.

Which still required that she get the hell out of here, a fact she kept avoiding. She couldn't let herself get used to this odd life of luxurious isolation. And she would. Hell, she already was halfway there.

Tossing the towel into the hamper, she extended her hand to Law. He took it. Pulling him up was easy since he did all of the work.

"So that's the story."

Looking up at Law, she added "I've survived my darkest times alone. I don't need anyone, including you, Law. So don't start acting like you think you matter to me because you don't."

His eyes narrowed before he gave a nod. "You're preaching to the choir."

Ten minutes ago that statement would have hurt her feelings. Now? It bounced off. "I'm glad we're clear on that."

She edged past him, done with explaining.

CHAPTER TWENTY-SEVEN

LANA OPENED drawers and started to remove the clothing she had put away the day before. Law strode in. "What are you doing?"

"I'm moving my things to the white room."

"Why?"

"Because."

"That's not a reason."

Turning to him, hands on her hips, she told him the truth. "Because you're a distraction. Because I don't want to get comfortable, only for you to pull the rug out from under me. Because, if I sleep in that bed with you night after night, I'll eventually do something I won't be able to take back."

"Like have sex?"

She nodded.

"The problem isn't the sex, Lana. The problem is that you want an emotional commitment to go with it."

"That's where you're wrong. I don't want anything from you except for you to let me walk out of here and not look back."

"After everything you know about Drago and how violent he is, you still want to leave here?"

"At the very least, I want the option."

"That's not possible."

"Try and stop me." She turned back to the dresser and grabbed a stack of folded shirts and sweaters.

Moving past him, she got as far as the door of the white room. This time it opened. Setting her clothing on the bed, she emptied everything from the armoire and drawers and cleaned the bathroom of all former fuck-girl things.

Law followed with several more armloads of clothing. Lana spent the rest of the day arranging her room, constantly reminding herself this was the right thing to do.

Dinner was delivered. Sitting across the table from Law, Lana dug into the orange glazed Cornish hens and roasted winter veggies. Law's mood was dark and noncommittal. He drank more whiskey than he ate. As the meal progressed his mood soured.

Sliding his empty glass away from him, he studied Lana for a few moments and then asked, "What would you say was your darkest hour?"

She set down her fork and looked directly into his eyes. "The night Mamita died."

Clenching her jaw, Lana fought back tears as she remembered more. She'd suppressed so much.

"Tell me what happened."

Panic stampeded through her. "I'm not allowed to talk about it."

"Says who?"

"My mother."

"You're a grown-ass woman. You can talk about whatever the hell you want."

Suddenly having difficulty breathing, Lana shook her head, unable to steady her shaking hands. "I don't want to."

"You don't have to then. Tell me about Miss Emily Pratt's Academy for Girls."

Much easier subject. "Em Pratt is where rich uninvolved parents send their daughters to get an education and get rid of them. You know, a two-for-one special. Rich people like bargains too. And Mother insisted I enroll after we heard that—Mamita died. Like two minutes after."

"Your mother is a cold-hearted bitch."

She gave him a curt nod, not wanting to say that they didn't come any colder or bitchier until Law told her how he knew that. "You've met her?"

"Not formally."

"How do you know of her then?"

"I have colleagues who've had dealings with her."

"Your colleagues are thugs."

Law snorted. "Don't think your mother got your father to where he is by doing good deeds and hosting bake sales."

"Are you saying she's a criminal?" The irony was, Lana knew damned well she was but not for the same reasons as Law. If he knew the half of what her mother was capable of...

"Yes."

Lana sat back in her chair. "Does my father know?"

Law shrugged. "They're still married."

Lana exhaled loudly. He had no idea. "I've never gotten her. She was the classic wire-monkey mom. The only reason I'm not a complete psycho is because of Mamita's kindness. She treated me like I was her own daughter. And I let her down." She looked up at Law. "I miss my sister."

"I was getting around to her," he mused. "Your half sister

—illegitimate half sister—is a loose end the wife of a senator with an eye on the White House can't afford."

"Is she still alive?" She wanted so desperately to know. If anyone could find out Law could.

"I'm working on finding that out."

Lana searched his impassive face. "You've known about Miranda all along?"

"Not until you told me today. I made inquiries while you were in the shower. I'll have information soon."

A little piece of her heart thawed for the proud man sitting across the glass table from her. "If you find her, promise me you won't let anything happen to her."

"What do I get for that promise?"

Lana swallowed hard. "My gratitude."

Law harrumphed and poured himself another glass of whiskey.

Wanting to know about him, Lana quietly asked, "How did you get the scar on your face?"

Law stiffened. His jaw clenched so tight she though he might break his teeth. "I was cut."

"I figured that much out on my own, Law. How, why, who?"

Throwing back the glass of whiskey he poured another and drank it fast, then looked pointedly at her. "I attacked the man who slit my father's throat, raped and bludgeoned my mother and kidnapped my sister. He cut me with the same knife he killed my parents with."

Lana said nothing at first. Just stared at Law. Her response, when it came, was almost inaudible. "Oh my god, Law. I'm sorry, I had no idea."

"I swore I'd get him one day. And I'd cut him up piece by piece and feed them to a pack of wild dogs while he watched."

"How—old were you?"

"Just a kid," he bit out.

She was literally speechless. The second it looked like she was going to move toward him to offer comfort, he stiffened. She checked the urge with difficulty. He would only push her away.

Holy hell, what he just told her trumped every awful thing that had ever happened in her life. Downing her glass of water, Lana helped herself to Law's bottle of Angel's Envy. The slow burn felt good going down.

She chose her next words carefully. "Law—I can't change my past. And you can't change yours. But maybe the future can be better."

"You sound like a damn greeting card."

Breathing fire, Lana thought. The whiskey was getting to him. As much as she was dying to learn more about him, Lana redirected the conversation to something that Law would be most eager to hear.

"I know what ship the Riyadh papers are coming in on."

He glared at her. "What did you say?"

"The papers you and True were talking about when he came to see you."

"How do you know?"

"The week before the auction I heard Anton talking about it with one of his associates. He wanted them because he heard Drago was willing to pay a fortune for them."

His eyes narrowed. "What ship?"

"The *Karabo* out of Cape Town."

"I have that information."

"Then why did you ask me for the name of the ship?"

"To find out if you knew what I already know. She's due to dock at the Port of Oakland New Year's Eve."

"Do you know which container the papers are hidden in?"

"Not yet," he said grudgingly.

"I know which it is."

Law's gaze sharpened. He pushed the whisky bottle aside.

"Well, I think I do. Most likely the container number is the same year that Anton's sister was born."

Law stood up and swooped Lana into his arms, sharing the rush.

Lana put a hand to his chest. His heart was racing. "I hope I'm right. And if I am, you have to make sure that good people don't get hurt."

He eased her down and got her on her feet before he replied. "You should know by now that's how I roll. If Drago gets his hands on them, people will die."

"Did he kill your family?"

The fury in his eyes was answer enough.

Irrationally, Lana felt almost afraid of him for a moment. She went back to the table and started to clear it, needing something to do. "I want to help you get him."

"No."

"Then let me go."

"No." He strode past her to the secret elevator door and disappeared.

Lana threw her glass at the wall, where it shattered into a thousand pieces.

CHAPTER TWENTY-EIGHT

STARING UP AT THE CEILING, Lana raged in silent frustration. She hated the white room. Hated that she was weak when it came to Law and that her plan to create space between them only made her want him more.

Law. Law. Law. The more she learned about him the more mysterious he became to her.

Her heart ached for him when she thought of him as a little boy, a terrified witness to the cold-blooded murder of his family, powerless to save them.

It made sense to her now. His thirst for vengeance had driven him to become the cold, emotionless criminal he'd become.

They were similar yet polar opposites. Whereas adversity had hardened Law, she'd been so determined to destroy herself, little by little and all at once. No one had ever been able to stop her. Not with force, not with love.

Throwing the covers aside, Lana grabbed her robe and slid from the bed. Restlessness drove her from her room into the darkened penthouse. Law's bedroom door was open. Had he come back?

She peeked in to find the room empty, the only clue that he'd been there, his strong masculine scent.

Inhaling it deeply, Lana leaned against the doorjamb. The urge to run gripped her again. It just wasn't right that Law and his associates could come and go while Lana was forced to stay here and twiddle her thumbs.

He insisted he was protecting her. But trusting him could be the worst mistake she ever made. No matter what, all she knew about him was what he chose to tell her.

Did Law plan to put her on a hook, and taunt Drago with the promise of her? Her awakened sympathy for him might be no more than sympathy for the devil.

She ought to know better by now than to let her heart—and her sex drive—overrule her common sense. Enough was enough.

Dear Brain. She began an imaginary letter to that underused part of her body. *Please don't let me down.*

Looking out the window, Lana absorbed the view. The night was still young, at least by Law's standards. Only a little past midnight. The bay shimmered darkly in the aftermath of the recent storms. The glass-enclosed extension of the club built out over the water was lit up in a kaleidoscope of gem tones, the guarded doors open only to the beautiful people with deep pockets.

She bet the club would be *the* place to bring in the New Year. Not for her, though. She'd be locked away, supposedly safe.

There was an upside, though. Right now, she was where she needed to be. Alone. Focusing on herself. Not partying in a VIP suite where expensive champagne would be flowing, the tiny pipes all aglow and ecstasy pills getting passed around like candy.

Climbing up into the deep windowsill, she got comfortable,

her gaze rising to the glittering vertical cables of the bridge over the bay.

So beautiful. She longed to cross it again and see it with new eyes.

Lana leaned against the cool glass of the window, letting her mind go where it would. Law's revelation made her think of her own family.

How many times had she wished she had been strong enough to stand up to her mother, tell her father off and find her sister? Miranda was strong. She never would have slid into the gutter, trading her body for drugs because it was too hard to be her.

But Miranda had never been held back by a terrible secret like Lana held. Miranda didn't live in fear for her life. And wherever she was now, Miranda was better off not associating in any way with Lana or their father.

Tears blurred her vision, the bridge lights sparkling like stars in her eyes. Law was right about a lot of things. She was trying hard, exercising harder, but she was still a hot mess.

Two yachts slowly coming in to the dock below caught Lana's attention. She straightened up when she spotted Law, dressed in a dark suit, stride down the dock, calling to the first yacht's uniformed crew, and giving orders to his dockhands. Moored quickly, the seventy-footer bumped gently against the dock as the gangway was lowered.

Lana's heart beat hard as Law walked up it and extended his hand to a tall brunette wrapped in a full-length dark fur coat. Probably sable. There was something familiar about her. Even squinting, Lana couldn't get a clear enough look at her face.

Law pulled the woman to him. She melted into him like butter on a hot grill. He kissed each cheek, but she hung on, evidently wanting more. He slid his arm around her waist, guiding her carefully down the gangway.

Pain stung her bottom lip before Lana realized she was biting it. As the couple turned toward the club, she could see Law's face under the brilliant dock lights. He was laughing, and his date was—Lana craned her neck to see better—was fucking gorgeous.

A memory started to kick in. She knew that face—she'd seen the woman at the Ultimate with a Legion honcho.

Squeezing her eyes shut, Lana saw more. The biker hadn't been like the others. He'd been super well-groomed, for one thing, and older, maybe in his early forties. And high up in the hierarchy—his patch declared his rank. The woman, who'd strutted her stuff in skintight designer leather then, looked like a Victoria's Secret model tonight.

What was she doing here without her biker boyfriend? Lana knew from the girls she'd worked with that once you were marked by the Legion, there was no way out.

Law happened to glance up at the penthouse. Fuck. Caught spying.

Lana pushed away from the window, and tumbled backward onto the floor.

Stifling a scream when she hit the hardwood, she lay still, mentally checking each body part to make sure nothing was broken. The only thing she realized that hurt was her feelings.

Here she was, flat on her back, miserable and trapped in the tower, while Law entertained a beautiful woman down in his notorious club. Why that should matter was beyond her. She didn't care about who Law fucked.

"He's just a man, like every other man. He'll use you, abuse you then forget about you," she said out loud. Just to hear a human voice, even if it was only hers.

In a weird way, it was good he left her alone. She needed to be locked away from the world. She needed the solitude to heal, to remain sober. To get stronger.

So she could escape.

She hoped that happened before Law slid her on a hook and went fishing with her.

CHAPTER TWENTY-NINE

HOURS LATER, Lana was thinking hard—maybe obsessing was a better word. There was no easy explanation for her conflicting feelings about Law.

She sure as hell didn't love him. And lust wasn't the driving force that kept him at the center of her thoughts. It was the man himself.

Lana got up to hunt for pencil and paper, and sat down again, making a list.

Rescue/medical care.

Shelter/clothes/food.

Exercise/fight training.

He'd done everything for her. So why didn't she feel grateful? Viciously, she scratched a big fat X over the list and stabbed it with the pencil. He'd done all that because he was going to use her for bait.

But, he hadn't denied that she was an integral part of his revenge scheme. They both knew that.

All the more reason for him to insist she stay here, in his

penthouse, his sanctuary from the rest of the world. He hadn't been happy when she moved into this cold room.

While it offered every creature comfort imaginable, it was impersonal.

Lana sighed. She got it. Keep it clean, keep it simple, keep emotions out of it. *Emotions are weakness. Relationships get you killed.*

In Law's line of work, those words were gospel.

She needed to make them hers as well.

So much easier said than done.

The sound of footsteps outside of her room from the hallway piqued her curiosity. Slowly she sat up.

Low voices, male and female, infiltrated the thick door to the outside hall, locked on her side—she'd checked.

Slipping from the bed, Lana moved to the door and pressed her ear against it.

The deep timbre of Law's voice sent warm shivers through her. But she couldn't make out the woman's voice. They moved away.

Lana hurried to her bedroom door, the one to the penthouse. When she opened it, she gasped. Law stood staring at her.

"I—heard voices."

"Why aren't you asleep?"

Her answer was fast. "The bed is really uncomfortable."

"I'll order a new mattress for you tomorrow."

"No—I—it's fine. I just need to get used to it." Lana struggled with her body's reaction to him. Looking up at Law made her heart beat faster. His hungry eyes pinned her to the spot.

He wanted what she wanted. Lana's skin tingled all over. She took a tentative step back into her room. He followed. It was cold where they stood, but heat sizzled through her veins. Her traitorous pussy clenched. She couldn't control it. Did he have any idea what his presence did to her? His words? His touch?

Just the smell of him lit up her senses. He was bigger than life. The most dynamic, frustrating, ultra-hot guy she had ever come across. His sway over her was terrifying. Exhilarating. Deadly. If she let herself be swayed by his potent allure, she wouldn't be strong enough to let him go.

His eyes darkened when his hand caressed her hair. "I'm going to tell you something right now, and I don't want you to read anything into it other than what it means."

"What?" she breathed.

"I'm a bad guy. I've killed people with my bare hands. I've broken the law so many different ways, so many different times, there aren't enough years in ten lifetimes to make me pay behind bars." His thumb rubbed along her bottom lip.

"I don't care," she whispered.

"You should. Because I'd rather spend time with you. Tonight, for starters." He brushed his lips along the curve of her cheek. And then—for some reason he hesitated.

"Don't stop." Her plea was barely audible.

"I have to, Lana. Because eventually it'll be over and you're going to be hurt. And bad as I am, I don't want to hurt you."

"I still don't care."

Raising her mouth to his, he made a small pained sound before his lips touched hers. Desire flooded every cell in her body.

"You're beautiful, Lana," he whispered against her lips. "Too smart for your own good." He nipped her bottom lip, then trailed kisses down her neck. The cropped cami she wore was designed to entice. The deep plunging V barely covered her nipples.

She arched her back as his lips slid down between her breasts. Oh, God, that felt so good. Gently he sucked a nipple into his hot mouth. *Finally.* As she pressed into him, he released it with a pop.

"No," she gasped, gazing up at him.

His eyes blazed with enough heat to melt a glacier. Lana could barely breathe.

He slid his hand down her belly to her soft mound. She was so wet for him. "I want to fuck you so bad, right now."

"Do it," she breathed. Did she just say that? Yeah, she did. She wanted him, body and soul.

Moving back from her, he pointed to the bed. "Get back in bed and roll over onto your stomach."

"But—"

"Do as I say."

"I don't want it that way," she said, embarrassed by how pathetic she sounded. No surrender. She had some say in this. She wanted Law face to face.

"I'm not going to fuck you. I'm going to put you to sleep."

Disappointment so profound she wanted to cry overwhelmed her. But, too proud to beg for what her body so desperately wanted, she complied.

Law's deep, even breathing was the only sound in the room. Lying on his back on top of the blankets, still dressed in his suit minus his jacket, he seemed impervious to the cold. Lana snuggled deep into the blankets.

Why had he stayed?

The room was so dark she could barely make out the silhouette of Law's profile. Even so, everything about him was distracting. His leather-and-balsam scent infused her nostrils. His body warmth heated the bedcovers. And her.

Even asleep, he radiated intense energy that pulsed around her. Or was that her nerves? He made her aware of things she'd never cared about. Things that could get her hurt. Things she had sworn never to explore.

He wrecked her resolve. The more he resisted her, the more she was willing to throw her better judgment out the window for a taste of what he could give her.

Lust, hot and potent, ran through her in thrilling waves. She didn't know what to make of him. What to do with him. How to react to him. He was Law, the self-admitted criminal.

But there was the other side. The man who had nursed her back to health. The man who forced her to work out harder, do her best, want more out of life—and on some level, want him.

The man who, earlier, had commanded her to roll over. She'd felt ashamed and heartbroken all at once, thinking he wanted to take her from behind. Once upon a time, she'd demanded that position from other men, avoiding eye contact. No faces, just fucking.

That wasn't what he was after. Instead, he put his big warm hands on her back and began to massage her. She'd liquefied. His bold hands didn't skip parts. His fingers dug into her muscles, caressed her butt cheeks, stroked along her sides, between her thighs. Her body had caught fire. He'd massaged her from the tip of her head to her toes, then back again. He never spoke.

She'd moaned with pleasure, fighting the urge to roll over onto her back and invite him into her body. It was a first for her, actually wanting a man to touch her so intimately. Not fuck. No, no, she wanted him to hold her in his arms, caress her cheek, tell her she was beautiful, that she meant something to him, and then, make slow sweet love to her. It was crazy. But then, so was she.

She exhaled, and tension she didn't realize she'd been holding on to eased from her body.

Even though she couldn't trust him. She just couldn't, not with her feelings. However, whether she liked it or not, she did know where she stood. He'd told her she would get hurt. That was honest.

Maybe she should be grateful that a criminal with a conscience was holding her captive. But she wasn't. The doubt came from within her, not him. She wasn't beautiful enough. Smart enough. She wasn't worth the trouble she caused.

Pressing her thighs tightly together to quell the throb there, she found it had the opposite effect. A soft whimper slipped past her lips. Rolling over onto her belly, Lana glided her hand between her skin and the sheet. When she touched herself, desire shimmered through her. Squeezing her eyes tightly, she moaned into the pillow. She was wet. Swollen. And hungry.

A stranger to her newly healthy body, she let instinct fueled by intense need take over. This time, it was for her. Not a vindictive act. Not a means for a fix. Not a cry for help. Just pure pleasure.

As one tension slipped from her body, another filled it. Lips parted, she gasped for breath as she imagined Law spreading her out on the bar in the luxury club where he was master. Pushing her skirt up to her waist, exposing her wanton sex to everyone.

Telling everyone that what they saw was his. That *she* was his. Cupping her pussy.

Moaning, she pressed the heel of her hand against her mound, grinding against it.

"Ahhh," she breathed. "My God..." It felt so good.

In her fantasy, his eyes burned possessively into hers. Holding her with their power, branding her. Law ruled. Leaving no question to anyone that she belonged to him. As he slid a thick fingertip along her swollen seam, she caught her breath, pressing into him, not caring that they had an audience.

"Please," she begged. "Please." Sliding her finger along her swollen seam, then into herself, Lana moaned.

"Deeper," he commanded.

When she slid a second finger into herself, she imagined it was Law. Her eyes flew open to look at him. It wasn't a dream. His intense green gaze burned holes into her.

"Law," she breathed, his name a desperate plea. "Help me. I don't know what to do."

He didn't say a word. He just held her with that dominant gaze.

"Come closer," he said, his voice nearly a growl.

Closing her eyes, she obeyed.

"Now look at me," he rasped.

Slowly she did. On her back again, she turned her head to face him, desperate for a connection. She didn't break contact with herself. It felt too good. She was warm, wet, and tight.

"Let it go, baby. Let it all go, and fly," he commanded. *Baby.* She liked the way he said it, like he meant it.

Fingers inside—then out. Inside again. Lana released the incandescent sensuality rising within her. And took flight.

His face inched closer to hers. His warm breath came in quick shallow bursts in cadence to her heartbeat.

"Faster," he encouraged.

Dreamy-eyed and shameless, Lana gyrated against her hand.

"You should see your face. So fucking hot right now."

Breath burst from her lungs.

He slid his hand along the curve of her cheek to her jaw, letting his fingers trail down her throat as he moved closer, was almost over her, the intensity in his expression terrifyingly powerful. A maelstrom of desire flared in his stormy eyes.

He slid his thumb along her bottom lip. Lana bit it, sucked it into her mouth, licking the tip.

"You're going to be the death of me, Lana," he hoarsely said, pressing his thumb deeper into her mouth.

A sound like a wounded animal escaped her lips. Delicious spasms coursed through her body, sparkling with sublime intensity.

As she rode each erotic wave, Law moved with the thrust of her hips. He slid another finger into her mouth. She sucked hard as each beat of rapture throbbed through her.

It was incredible. Masturbation had always been a private thing for her. Not that great either. It was amazing shared. As lofty a pleasure as it was, the void in her, the one he had exposed, ached to be filled in only the way his body could.

As she drifted downward, recovering, he disengaged.

She tried to focus. Working hard to gather her wits. "Law," she breathed. "I—" She sobbed, because what she needed was for him to break his promise to himself.

Throwing the covers from her steamy body, her hips caught the side of his leg. "I can't stand this," she cried.

Law was holding back. The withdrawal was unbearable.

Smoothing her damp hair from her face, he said softly, "Go back to sleep. We have a big day today."

"We do?"

"Yes," he said. "I'll tell you more later."

When he rolled over, the hard ridge of his erection slid along her hipbone, groaning under his breath with pleasure. And pain. There was no question that he was as aroused as she. A small smile tipped her lips. His suffering turned her on as much as his touch just had.

Still smiling, she fell asleep.

CHAPTER THIRTY

LANA SHOT UP IN BED. Bright sunlight streamed through the high window. Momentarily disoriented, she didn't know where she was. Then last night slowly came back in bits and pieces. Heat rose in her cheeks. She'd given in to her craving for Law. Tossed her newfound self-control right out the window.

How was she going to escape when she allowed herself to be so shameless? She would have gone a lot farther last night if Law hadn't been so resolute.

She wished to God they could just go for it. Law would be amazing. He *was* amazing already. His hands on her body had been pure bliss. Last night when he sucked her nipple into his warm mouth, she thought she would orgasm. When both her nipples tightened, she *had* orgasmed.

The knock on her door startled her. Reaching for her robe at the foot of the bed, she slipped it on. "Come in."

Monty's happy face popped in from behind the half open door. "Miss Lana, it's almost lunch time. Are you hungry?"

"*What?*"

He nodded toward the window, where sunlight poured through the clear glass. "The sun's been up for hours. You missed breakfast. But I kept it warm for you."

"I can't believe I slept so long."

"Law told me not to wake you."

Alarmed, she tried to look past Monty, without success. "Is he here?"

"No. He said he'd be gone most of the day. And that you should be ready for a night out by eight tonight."

Big news. He was taking her out? Like on a date? She didn't know what to say.

"Come on in the kitchen," Monty coaxed.

Ten minutes later, dressed in workout clothes, she almost ran there, she was so hungry.

As Monty busied himself preparing her plate, Lana thoughtfully munched on a piece of raspberry-crème-stuffed brioche. "Monty, did Law save True too?"

Without looking at her, he said, "No, True was in the army with Law."

Hmmm, that actually explained a lot. "What about Jhett?"

Monty turned around and smiled. "He saved her from a bad cop. When her mom died later, he brought her here."

Lana stopped mid-chew. "Jhett is the little girl who was—" she broke off, reluctant to give away violent details that Monty might not know "—who was hurt? And Law shot the cop that was trying to hurt her?"

"Yes."

"How did her mom die?"

Monty pursed his lips, thinking over his answer carefully. "Law might not like me telling you."

"Who am I going to tell, Monty?" She smiled. "Besides, I don't know if you've noticed or not, but Law likes me. *A lot.*"

"Oh?" His brows scrunched together. "He seems to be angry a lot."

"That's because he doesn't want to like me so much."

Monty smiled again. "Maybe. I've never seen him spend so much time up here. He usually stays down in his office. He has a whole bedroom and bathroom down there."

"Does he take ladies there?" Ugh, why did she care? Because Lana had discovered that when it came to Law, she was capable of jealousy.

"No. Except Jhett and Sienna, oh and Treva, but they just talk."

"Would you please tell me about Jhett's mom?"

Just as the words left her mouth, the front door elevator softly chimed. Monty hurried to the panel and pressed a sequence of numbers. The door opened and Jhett walked in like she owned the place.

Monty smiled and said to Lana, "Ask Jhett, she'll tell you about—what did you want to know, Miss Lana?"

Lana felt horribly self-conscious. And embarrassed.

"Ask me what?" Jhett snatched a piece of bacon from the silver platter. Popping it into her mouth, she munched it as she leaned against the counter and looked silently at Lana.

For the first time since they'd met, Jhett wasn't wearing black. She had on a pair of torn acid-wash jeans, knee-high military-style boots and a pink jersey shirt. Her spiked hair was somewhat less spiky today and her makeup more subtle. Fewer piercings too. She was pretty, actually, with great expressive eyes and flawless skin. The casualness belied the tiger lurking beneath.

"Oh, nothing," Lana said, not wanting to tangle with the baby beastie.

"She wanted to know more about you," Monty offered.

Jhett straightened away from the counter, wiping her fingertips with the napkin he handed to her, and stared at Lana. "What makes you think my life is an open book?"

"I'm sorry, I was just curious."

"Don't be. That's a bad habit in our business. Change it."

"Is that an order?" Lana asked. Dabbing at her mouth with her own napkin, Lana set it on the counter and stood.

"What if it is?"

Lana moved into the spacious kitchen. "I intend to ignore it."

Jhett's big eyes brightened and she laughed. An uproarious, you're-an-idiot laugh. "But Law would agree with me. You're not the boss around here."

Lana fisted her hands, her anger rising, thinking for a few seconds how satisfying it would be to run right into the woman and punch her hard.

Lana took a different approach and told herself to stay calm —and speak in a neutral tone. "I think you'd better leave."

Jhett stopped laughing and got serious fast. "Make me. Or try to, anyway. I'll break your arm."

Lana glanced at Monty, sensing his nervousness. It was hard to tell if Jhett meant it or was just pushing her buttons. Maybe a little of both.

"Like, how would you do that?"

"Huh? You want to know? Are you fucking kidding me?"

"Yes and no."

Jhett eyed her warily and Lana heard Monty's sigh of relief. "What I mean is, Law's been working out with me, demonstrating self-defense techniques. Maybe you know some moves he doesn't."

The sly appeal to Jhett's vanity and the reminder of Law seemed to be working. Lana watched Jhett think it over for a bit.

"No," she muttered.

"Why not? Afraid I'll kick your ass?" Now it was Jhett's turn to figure out if Lana was kidding.

Jhett said nothing more, only looked up and away·from Lana, thinking.

Or maybe she was just being annoying and making Lana wait. Lana tapped her on the shoulder. In less than a second, Jhett made her move, pinning Lana up against the refrigerator.

"You have a long way to go, *chiquita,* before you can get me."

"Maybe so." Stay calm, Lana reminded herself. Monty seemed disinclined to step between them, disappearing into the bedroom instead.

Jhett let her go, throwing her a contemptuous look, which Lana ignored, pouring herself a cup of coffee. She set it on the counter and looked directly at Jhett. "I'm a quick learner. Please."

Jhett grabbed another piece of bacon and munched it as she gave Lana a long up and down appraisal. "Why should I?"

"Because Law would want you to."

"I don't do everything Law tells me to do."

"Yes you do," Monty said to Jhett as he came out from the white room with Lana's damp towels.

"Hey." Jhett was clearly irked. "Mind your own business, Monty."

"You are my business."

"Since when?"

"Since Law told me to keep an eye on his girl. You're his girl."

Envy jabbed at Lana. Jhett's cheeks turned pinker than her shirt. "I think he meant her." She pointed to Lana.

Vehemently, Monty shook his head. "No, Miss Lana sleeps with him and makes him angry. You don't do those things."

Lana coughed on the coffee she'd just sipped. Jhett hooted with laughter. "Monty, you call them like you see them, don't you?"

"I'm always honest."

"You cannot tell a lie."

Monty smiled, shaking his head as he headed toward Law's bedroom.

Jhett turned her attention on Lana. "Listen, I know you're here because you're crucial to Chimera. What I can't understand is why Law hasn't relegated you to the residence."

"What's the residence?"

"That's where most of us live." Which didn't tell Lana anything about where it was. She let it go.

"Who is most of you?"

"Chimera."

"How many in the—?" Lana didn't know how to define it. Tribe? Group?

"Dozens."

"Were you all rescued by Law?"

Jhett's eyes narrowed but she nodded. "He's a regular Outlaw Josey Wales."

"Who is that?"

Jhett glanced at Monty. "He knows what I'm talking about. The old Clint Eastwood movie."

"Haven't seen it."

"Okay, well, Clint plays a Missouri farmer after the Civil War, when rogue Union soldiers kill his family but not him. He gets revenge and saves a bunch of down-on-their-luck misfits while he's at it." Jhett rattled all that off and paused. "The hunted becomes the hunter, basically."

"Sounds…interesting." Lana couldn't think of anything more intelligent to say.

Jhett wasn't finished. "The misfits all have one thing in common. Their unshakable loyalty to Josey Wales. They'd die for him."

"And Law would die for us," Monty added. "He almost did when he saved most of us."

"Sounds like he's a regular saint," Lana said, and instantly regretted it.

"Hey!" Jhett backed Lana into the wall. "You have no fucking clue what that man has sacrificed for all of us. Mock him, you mock all of us." She stood too close to Lana, like she was going to escalate, but thought better of it when Lana stared her down, stepping away but getting in the last word. "Hurt him, you hurt us."

Lana really, really hated being intimidated by the likes of Jhett. Lashing out at the man she and Monty seemed to idolize was risky, but at the moment Lana didn't care. "Law isn't capable of feeling pain."

"Oh yeah? He bleeds like the rest of us."

"Are you sure he isn't a god? Because you seem to think he can do no wrong."

Jhett snarled. "There you go again. You're a bitch, you know that?"

"It's kept me alive."

Jhett gave Lana another one of her long up and down glares. "What's kept you alive is your tits. Hot girls like you use sex to get what you want."

Lana slapped Jhett. "You're the bitch!"

Jhett rubbed her fingertips across her swelling cheek. "Ooh. I guess the truth hurts."

"Please don't fight," Monty said, wringing his hands. "Law will be mad at me."

"Mind your own business, Monty!" Lana and Jhett said the same thing at the same time, but both of them dialed the anger way down.

As pissed as they were at each other, Monty wasn't to blame and his feelings trumped their spat. Lana smiled and patted Monty on the shoulder. "I'm sorry."

Jhett play-punched him on the other shoulder. "Me too."

Eying the remaining bacon, but exercising self-restraint, Jhett said, "Monty, can you find a couple of plastic spatulas for me, please?"

He didn't even question Jhett's strange request. A moment later he handed her the items. Jhett stuck one in her boot, rubber end down, and handed the other to Lana. "Slide this down the small of your back and follow me."

Jhett hit the gym lights and spun around, pressing the spatula so quickly against Lana's jugular, she almost peed herself.

"Slice, slice. You're dead."

"Teach me," Lana said breathlessly.

"I never leave home without a blade. Came in handy more times than I can count."

"Like when you and Law rescued little Miguel?"

Jhett's eyes popped open wide. "Law told you about that?"

"Yes. But not everything. He came home pretty beat up."

Jhett snorted. "You should have seen the four guys who jumped him."

Lana swallowed hard. "Are they dead?"

Jhett gave Lana a long look before she answered. "Take a guess."

"You live in such a violent world."

Jhett tossed the spatula back and forth between her hands. "Just like any other environment, if you're prepared and expect the unexpected, you'll survive."

"Do you ever just want peace?"

Jhett shrugged and slid the spatula back down the inside of her boot. "I owe Law more than I can ever repay."

"That's not an answer."

"I like the action. And I like giving piece-of-shit assholes what they deserve." Jhett jerked her chin up. "Okay. Take your spatula out as quickly as you can and try to stab—"

Before she finished her instructions, Lana whipped the spatula from her back, swiftly closing in on Jhett, and trapping her arms before she could blink. She pressed the rubber end into Jhett's chest. "Slice, slice, you're dead."

"Someone's a fast learner."

Jhett grabbed Lana's wrist, bent it back, forcing her to drop the spatula.

"That's not fair," Lana cried. Her wrist fucking *hurt.*

"Do you think a bad guy's going to play fair?"

"No, but—"

Lightning quick, Jhett grabbed her spatula from her boot and jabbed Lana in the gut with it. Lana cried out. "What do I do now? I'm bleeding out!"

"Defend yourself."

Lana dropped to the mat, desperately clutching her ridiculous weapon. As Jhett stepped over her to stab her again, Lana took her out with a leg sweep and pounced.

Jhett laughed and pushed Lana off. "Not bad."

"Got you at last."

Jhett extended her hand and pulled Lana up. "Baby girl, I'm going slow-mo. If we were in a real fight you'd already be mincemeat."

For the next hour, Jhett put Lana through more moves, repeating and varying until she got the hang of it.

"You don't carry a blade until you're confident in its use. I recommend a short blade for close quarter defense."

It made sense. Lana wielding a big knife would be suicide.

"Like Law taught you, you fight to run, not to the death."

Breathing heavily, Lana nodded. "Do you fight to run?"

"Fuck no. Someone comes at me, one of us is going down and not getting up." Jhett cracked her knuckles and tilted her head. "I'm still standing, so you figure it out."

"Did you kill one of the kidnappers?"

"Unfortunately, I didn't get the chance to."

"Law?"

Jhett shrugged her shoulders. "They didn't walk away."

Lana took two bottles of water from the hydration bar and handed one to Jhett. "What happened to Monty? I mean long ago. I know something did. But Law wouldn't tell me."

Jhett made a weird growling sound and squeezed her bottle so hard, water spewed. "Fucking Bulgarian gangsters nabbed him."

"Why?"

"Monty was a world-class hacker before they tried to kill him. And despite the brain damage he suffered at their hands, he still is." Jhett drained what was left in her bottle and tossed it into the trashcan.

Lana was shocked into silence.

"I don't know the exact details," Jhett went on, "but once Monty hacked the information they wanted, they thought it would be funny to dig a hole and bury him with just his head sticking out—and then go bowling. Nothing but strikes."

Lana gasped. That he had survived such cruelty was a miracle.

"Sienna—back then she was a girlfriend of one of the Bulgarians—begged them to stop. They raped her, then dug another hole." Jhett studied Lana for a moment. "Are you going to be sick?"

"N-no," Lana managed to whisper.

"Good. Toughen up."

"What happened?" She was compelled to ask. She had to know. Had to.

"Law showed up on other business and from what Sienna told me, he tore them apart." Jhett coughed, her voice raw despite all that water. "Law dug Monty and Sienna out. Law called a doctor with a private clinic—friend of his—and got them there alive. Barely."

"Oh my God," Lana gasped. No wonder Law was so protective. Sitting down on a nearby bench, she glanced up at Jhett, who looked like she wanted to kill their enemies all over again. "I know there isn't a happy ending."

Jhett's steady gaze held fiery rage. "Sienna will never have kids, and Monty won't either."

"What—?"

"Sienna was brutalized. Severe internal injuries. Those fucks nearly killed her. And Monty was castrated."

The horror of it began to sink in.

"So Law took care of them and gave them a safe place?"

"All of the above, yeah. That's who he is and what he does."

"The others I met the night I came here. Treva and Tyrus too?"

Jhett nodded. "Everyone here is loyal to Law." She added

some advice. "Don't try anything. Law comes first, second and last."

"I just want to go home."

"Where is that?"

"Ah—" Suddenly, Lana realized she had no home. There was not one person on earth who gave a damn about her. "It'll be wherever I land."

"Stay here and earn your keep."

"I don't have a choice at the moment."

"You have more choices than you realize."

Lana pulled herself together, choosing her words carefully. "Law kidnapped me as a means to getting Dragovich. He'll use me as a piece of bait to dangle in front of that homicidal freak. I think my options are pretty limited."

"Law won't let anything happen to you."

"How can you be so sure?"

"Because it's not like him." Jhett leaned against the wall, pressing her shoulders against it, suddenly weary. "Anyway, I'm not sure what his plans are. Law doesn't divulge more than he has to."

"I noticed that," Lana muttered.

"Look, if we get kidnapped, the less we know and the less we can tell."

"Makes sense. Still and all—"

"Lana, if you step outside of the compound you're going to end up dead or wishing you were."

"I'll keep that in mind. But I wasn't planning to leave," Lana said. *Yet.*

Jhett didn't call her out on the lie, for some reason.

"Give Law some room," Jhett advised, "and when he's done, he can create an entire new identity for you. You can go wherever you want. Be whoever you want."

"Oh boy." But Lana wasn't feeling it.

Jhett kicked her boot backward against the wall and straightened up like a soldier. "I've said too much."

Lana didn't know whether to agree or disagree. It didn't matter. Jhett had the spatula against her throat before she opened her mouth. The pressure made her gag slightly.

"Got the message? Always be vigilant. It will save your life one day." With that she was gone.

CHAPTER THIRTY-ONE

FOR A LONG TIME Lana stood in the shower allowing the hot water to massage her tight muscles. It was impossible for her to wrap her head around the violence of Law's secret world. She knew he was bad. Baddest of the bad. What Jhett had told her was all Lana needed to know about the barbarity of the company he kept. She just didn't want to know it.

Turning off the water, Lana wrapped a towel around her head and another around her body. And then there was Law. He'd suffered too—and still done everything he could for the others.

Her woes didn't measure up to what she'd just learned. But even so… Squeezing her eyes shut, Lana forced the image of Mamita's twisted broken body from her brain.

How could she think the loss of her beloved nanny didn't compare? What happened that terrible night would be burned in her brain until she took her last breath.

Most of what followed was a little girl's inability to deal with the trauma of it. Lana's self-induced attempts at dulling the pain had spiraled out of control. Yes, she was a child too when unthinkable tragedy struck. There had been no one there to hold her and tell her everything was going to be okay. No one who stood up for her.

Until Law. Shaking her head free of the towel and slinging it over a chromed bar, Lana looked into the foggy mirror. How fucking twisted was that?

The only person who ever had her back was an underworld mogul who had kidnapped her and held her hostage in his secret world.

Lana forced herself to set aside all of the emotional baggage she seemed to drag everywhere. She intended to enjoy tonight.

───

An hour later, Lana stepped back from the mirror and smiled. Law was definitely going to like this smoldering sex kitten look. Her thick blonde hair was swept into a tousled updo showing off her neck. She'd chosen a pair of gold and diamond chandelier earrings to add sparkle to her understated makeup: smoky eyes and nude lips with just a touch of gold gloss.

The sexy crimson dress she'd picked out from the designer bags clung to her curves. It was anything but modest despite the long sleeves. The plunging V-neck and belly cutout showed plenty of skin.

Gold-soled stilettos, fastened around her ankles with thin gold clasps, were the final touch.

For the first time in a very, very long time, Lana looked at herself in the mirror with pride. Smoothing the skirt of the dress to where it ended at her knees, Lana straightened. She could do this. She was dressed to thrill.

Lana sauntered out to the living room like a runway model. Working at his laptop, Law looked up.

She stopped and posed. "Well? What do you think?"

He pushed the laptop away and stood. "You look amazing. And you know it, Alana."

But he didn't smile.

Maybe he just needed encouragement. She strutted up to him and pouted sensually then traced her finger along the scar on his face. "And you know you want me."

Grasping her hand, he nipped the tip of her finger but didn't let it go. "That's neither here nor there. I want you to behave tonight. That means my guests are off-limits. You don't get to lead them on."

Apparently her glamorous entrance had completely back-fired. She yanked her hand away.-Why did he have to be such a jerk? "I'm not a slut, Law."

"I didn't say you were."

"You implied it. I have no intention of leading anyone on." Glaring up at him, she said, "Least of all you."

"I'll survive. And all I'm asking is that you follow a few simple rules. Here's another one. Don't speak unless you're spoken to."

"I don't do rules." She flipped him off. "You're living in the stone age."

"These men live in my world. Under no circumstances are you to so much as flirt with them or anyone else tonight."

"Where exactly do you draw the line?" Her mocking tone seemed to annoy him. Good. Served him right. "And how will I know when I've stepped over it?"

He grinned. The promise of what he was capable of went straight to her pussy. "How about a safe word?" he asked.

The question hung between them like a big juicy steak in front of a ravenous dog. Was he serious? Did his safe word mean what she knew it to mean or was he fucking with her again?

"If you really feel you need one, be my guest."

He threw his head back and laughed hard. A—genuinely amused, I'm-not-laughing-at-you-but-with-you laugh.

The tension between them dissolved and Lana found herself smiling.

"Woman, if you weren't you and I wasn't me, I would sweep you off those thousand-dollar stilettos throw you over my shoulder, toss you onto my bed and fuck you into next week."

"You're assuming I'd let you."

Lowering his head just an inch, he moved into her space. "You want to let me right now."

"Your ego is showing."

"Not the case." He traced a finger along her cheek and jaw as she had done to him. "You make me want to forget everything and everyone, Alana."

He nudged her chin up with his fingers. "All I dream about is kissing you."

"Really? Show me," she said, without thinking. Too late.

"If I show you, you'll want me to show you more, and then some more after that."

"Go for it."

"Now?"

Lana nodded.

"You're going to look seriously kissed. And we have a party to attend." He lowered his lips to hers. "They'll ask if we're a couple."

"I'll say, no, I'm your hostage."

"Simply say you're a guest."

"Why don't you want them to think we're a couple?"

"Romantic involvements are seen as a weakness that can be exploited. If my guests and I can't come to an agreement tonight, they will strike me where it hurts most." His lips brushed across hers. It took every bit of willpower Lana possessed at that moment not to melt into him.

"Ah, so what? You're not allowed to feel?"

"I choose not to. There's a difference."

"That must be a miserable way to live."

Law's expression was unreadable. "It's healthier for everyone. And much less risky."

"If you say so." She was done arguing. For now, she just wanted to stay close to him a little while longer.

Law raised his head. His warm breath caressed her face when he spoke. "Anyway, there's always risk in things that matter. I manage the risks. It's kept me alive in a highly competitive world."

Demurely, Lana pulled away from him. "Believe it or not, I get it."

An awkward silence hung between them.

"Okay. Well, I'll be ready to go in twenty minutes," Law said, heading for his bedroom.

She smoothed the crimson dress he'd rumpled. "Should I change?"

"Hell fucking no."

CHAPTER THIRTY-TWO

LANA PACED THE LIVING ROOM. Nerves got the better of her. Deciding a small glass of wine wouldn't hurt, she grabbed the first bottle she saw in the wine fridge and opened it. Sipping the lovely elixir, she sighed.

When Law came back into the living room, Lana took another sip of her wine. A big sip. Wearing tailored black slacks, black leather shoes and belt, and fitted black shirt, he looked fucking hot. It wasn't the cut of the cloth that set Law off from other men. The man who wore them made those ordinary clothes look amazing on that extraordinary body.

She raised her glass to him. "Would you like a drink?"

"I never drink during business." He eyed her nearly empty glass. "Go easy on that tonight."

"I'm not a child."

"No, you're a recovering addict who is feeling anxious." He glanced at his watch. "We'll meet them downstairs for drinks in the club, then come back here for dinner."

Lana's heart thudded against her rib cage. "The sex club?"

"It's not a sex club."

"Law, I saw—okay, *heard*—women and men hooking up." She set down the wine glass.

He smiled. "You saw and heard correctly. But there was a lot more going on than that. "

"Someone is paying someone for sex."

"What consenting adults do in my club is between them so long as no one is intentionally hurt."

"Why do you have to be so vague? Why not just say it's a pay-for-sex club?"

"Because it isn't."

Lana threw her hands up. "What is the name of your not-sex club?"

"Myth."

It took a minute for Lana to process that bit of information. "*The* Myth?"

He nodded.

"Holy shit, Law! Myth is the hottest ticket in the state. I heard you have to be invited to apply for the golden entrance ticket—"

He interrupted her. "Only after being referred by several members and passing an initial screening."

"But wait—I thought Myth was a nightclub, not a sex club."

"Myth *is* a night club. The area you discovered is known as the Forum."

"I've never heard of it."

"As it is intended."

"So the Forum is a super-secret sex club?"

"For someone who professes not to be interested in sex, you sure bring it up a lot."

"It's hard not to think about it when everything around here reminds me of it!"

"Try harder."

"Wait," she said, picking up her bejeweled evening bag. "What name do I use?"

"Your given name."

"But—I thought you said people would pay a lot of money to know I was alive and here."

"True, but keeping you a secret no longer serves my purpose. You're here, you're my guest." He extended his hand. "Let's go."

"But—I don't understand." She took his hand anyway.

"You don't need to," Law assured her.

"I want to know what your plans are for me."

"To keep you safe."

"You keep saying that. So…that's accomplished by exposing me tonight?"

"It's all part of the plan, Lana. Try to trust me." He stopped and looked meaningfully into her eyes. "I won't let anything happen to you."

"But what happens when you're done with me? You said I'm toast on the street. So long as my father is a powerful senator my life could be threatened."

"I have connections all over the world. Creating a new identity for you is easy. Even with the advances in technology, you can be whoever you want to be, go wherever you would like."

"I don't want to be someone else." Her words shocked her. For how long had she wanted to snap her fingers and reinvent everything about herself?

But if she were someone else, she wouldn't be here. The realization that she had feelings for Law hit her with the impact of a sledgehammer. Being in lust was one thing. It passed, but she— oh fuck. She had to get out of here—and far away from his compelling presence as well—before she lost herself to him completely.

Guiding her around the other side of the slate fireplace, Law pressed a panel. Noiselessly the door slid aside, revealing the secret elevator. They went in side by side—he was still holding her hand, which shook a little in his. For the first time in six months she would be entering a room full of strangers, stone cold sober.

"You okay?" Law asked.

"Yes. Just nervous. I don't know why."

Smiling, Law brought her hand to his lips and gallantly kissed it. "My money's on you, Lana."

Her heart sank, even though Law's confidence in her bolstered hers. Everything about him made her feel better. It was time to run, girl. *Figure it out, and haul ass!*

The elevator car effortlessly descended several floors, coming to a soft stop. The gleaming door opened, revealing an anteroom of sorts. Percussive music permeated the space. Law pressed his palm against a panel. Yet another hidden door slid aside, granting them access to a VIP suite overlooking the dance floor. Immediately a uniformed server greeted them and showed them to a table. Not just any table. An ice sculpture of a mermaid in the center was surrounded by crystal dishes filled with caviar and other expensive nibbles. Imported, zillion-proof vodka was chilling in ice next to frosted crystal shot glasses. And Law had worried about her glass of wine? Lana almost wanted to laugh.

Sienna entered the suite from the club side, looking beyond fabulous clad from head to toe in translucent gossamer gold. Like a Greek goddess.

A horrific scene flashed in Lana's mind's eye. Of Sienna battered and brutalized, buried up to her chin in dirt. Good God.

Sienna looked calmly at Lana, and then she saw it. The haunted look of a soul so damaged they would never recover. She'd seen it one time before at the Ultimate, when Asia, a petite little dancer, staggered from one of the private rooms, badly beaten and begging for help. Lana had been so strung out that night she thought she had imagined it. But now, with chilling clarity she knew it had been real. She never saw Asia again after that night.

Giving Lana an acknowledging smile, Sienna said to Law, "Your guests have arrived, shall I bring them up?"

"I think we'll go down and meet them."

Lana swallowed. "Do you want me to stay here?"

"Of course not." He offered her his arm.

An attendant at the door opened it and a wave of loud music hit her like a wall. Her heart thumped hard against her chest. Gazing down at the beautiful people, Lana couldn't contain her excitement. She recognized the world-renowned DJ and the starlet at his side, wearing headphones and dancing in place. The low lights, shining glass, polished railings and bars were outer-space-glam in style, sleek and upscale.

As the three of them moved down the catwalk, Lana couldn't stop looking across the dance floor. It was no wonder everyone wanted in. Half of the people dancing, she recognized from TMZ or had read about in *People*.

As they came to the ground floor, Lana glanced toward the bar, suddenly aware that two men in dark suits stood intently watching them.

She felt a prickle of unease. Wait. She knew one of them… from years ago. He had changed, though. A lot.

"Ilya, Pyotr," Law greeted them, extending his hand.

Lana stopped in her tracks. Ilya Markov! He—

Ignoring Law for the moment, Ilya's stunned look of recognition flashed across his handsome face before he quickly concealed it. Like a fox, he moved in closer.

Back off. Law didn't actually say the words, but made a low sound of warning that was lost on Ilya. So was Sienna's cool look at him.

Law just about growled. Lana could feel the vibration. She smiled before Law lost his shit in his own club, and pretended to be Miss Congeniality. What the hell else could she do?

"Oh—hello. Do we know each other? My name is Alana."

Ilya's eyes glittered as he pressed his lips to her hand. "How could I forget?"

Gone was the gawky but serious twenty-year old young man she had met at her roommate's birthday party in boarding school.

Ilya had matured into a man to be reckoned with since she last saw him. His tall athletic build combined with his chiseled Slavic features and striking ice blue eyes had caught her attention for all the wrong reasons when she was younger. Now? Apparently she now preferred the dark brooding type.

How she wished she could forget him. Lana drew her hand back.

Pyotr extended his hand. "We are honored, Law," he said, giving Ilya the stink eye. Ilya stepped back, still focused on Lana. So creepy.

"You're going to get us killed," Pyotr muttered to Ilya in Russian.

"What did he say?" Law asked.

"That if I didn't mind my manners, you were going to kill me."

Law slapped Pyotr on the back. "An excellent observation."

Lana slid her hand down Law's arm to his hand. He refused to take it. Embarrassed, she glanced up to see who'd noticed. Pyotr and Sienna avoided her glance but not Ilya. He smiled slowly.

The DJ abruptly slowed the music down. Ilya

took her free hand and gently pulled her toward the dance floor. "Come, Alana, dance with me."

"I—" She looked at Law, daring her with his eyes to do it. Her pride rebelled. If he couldn't hold her hand, then she could dance with Ilya. Setting her evening bag on the nearest unoccupied table she followed the Russian Romeo.

Selena Gomez crooned *Good For You*, the sultry beat enticing Lana to the dance floor.

Closing her eyes, Lana pretended that it wasn't Ilya who danced so close. She pretended she was just out with her friends, doing what anyone would do in the most fabulous nightclub on the west coast.

Losing herself in the sensuous beat, she swayed with the music. When she opened them, she smiled a slow, sexy smile. Law wasn't far away. His hot gaze burned into her. Ilya slipped his arm around her waist and swept her fluidly around, catching her in his other arm.

Smooth move. He didn't scare her. Not anymore. She wasn't a confused fourteen-year-old girl. She was a woman on a mission.

"I thought you were dead," he breathed, gazing intently at her.

"As you can see, I'm alive and well."

"It gives me great pleasure to see you, Lani. I have thought of you every day for the last ten years. Why did you run away from me?" Ilya asked.

Lana swung her body away then came toward him. "Because I didn't want to be your slave."

"Is that why you staged your death? Because of me?"

Lana threw her head back and laughed. "You give yourself too much credit, Ilya."

"I would have given you the world. I still would. Leave with me tonight."

Lana laughed as if she were having the time of her life. Law had seemingly given up in the blink of an eye. He was nowhere in sight. So much for him giving a shit.

"You laugh when I am serious?"

"Ilya, I choose to stay here with Law."

"I knew he held a contract on a politician's daughter. I didn't know it was you."

He pulled her close. "I will pay ten times what he paid for it."

"How do you know about it?"

"It's the biggest secret in our world."

"Your world? In the real world that contract is meaningless, Ilya. Even if it was, I signed it under extreme duress. It would not hold up in any legitimate court."

"In our world it's binding."

"You and your world can go fuck yourselves. No man owns me."

"You have changed, Lani."

"That's for damn sure. I'm not a needy, insecure teenager anymore."

"I can see that."

"Then respect it."

"Why stay, Lani, when Law will throw you away the minute he is done with you? I would give you whatever you want."

"Ilya, we haven't seen each other for ten years. You act like we're long-lost lovers."

"I never stopped wanting you, even when I thought you were dead."

The music shifted to a blast of hip-hop. The volume made it hard to hear.

Ilya took her hand and led her back to the high-top where Pyotr stood with Sienna.

Pyotr spoke to Ilya in Russian. Ilya smiled as he handed Lana a shot of vodka. "Do you remember the Russian I taught you?"

"After a decade? Not much more than a few words," she lied.

He raised his shot glass. "To new beginnings," he said in Russian.

"In English, Ilya," she said.

"To new beginnings, Lani," he said and threw the vodka back. Lana barely sipped hers. It was ice-cold and smooth. Just like Ilya.

CHAPTER THIRTY-THREE

SETTING her shot glass on the table, Lana covertly looked for Law. He had vanished into thin air. Was he watching her from an unobstructed vantage point? Testing her? Expecting her to act out or betray him some way?

Lana knew enough about Law to understand that he made no move unless it was part of a greater move.

Deciding not to hang out and wait for him to call the shots, Lana grabbed her purse from the table top. She gave a little wave to Pyotr and Sienna, who seemed to be engrossed in a deep conversation, then spoke to Ilya. "If you'll excuse me, I'd like to powder my nose."

Taking her elbow, Ilya smiled and said, "Allow me to escort you."

He was pushing his luck—and she could have made a scene. Wanted to, in fact, but more than that, she wanted to annoy Law enough to get him off guard, and in the process, glean as much information from Ilya as possible.

Her hasty rationale: information-gathering would help her

understand Law from an outsider's point of view. But she knew there was more to it. In reality, Lana's budding loyalty to him trumped everything, despite the fact that he was the most frustrating man on the planet.

Law inadvertently pushed her to be better. Stronger. Wiser. He was something like a teacher to her, his very unwilling student in the weirdest finishing school ever. After fighting him every step of the way, only now was she beginning to appreciate the compelling lessons he taught.

And Lana didn't shy away from the fact that Law intrigued her. She had accepted—finally—that she wanted to please him. Even make him proud of how far she had come in such a short amount of time.

Fuck. She was going down the rabbit hole again. Time for an unromantic reality check: she desperately wanted to please a man who was emotionally unavailable.

As they walked toward the restrooms, Ilya slid his hand around her waist. Lana tried to shimmy out of his hold but he tightened it.

"There is sadness in your eyes, Lani."

"It's a sad world we live in."

"You are not happy." It wasn't an observation on Ilya's part but a stated fact. Okay. So she wasn't happy, at least not in the tra-la-la sense, but there was a part of her that had never been more glad to be alive. She'd kicked her drug habit. Was getting mentally and physically stronger by the minute. And to be honest, if only to herself, the challenge that Law presented excited her in more ways than one.

"Why would you say that?"

"Because it's the truth. You are pretending. Although you are not the only one. No one here is really who they are, *lubimaya*."

"That isn't true. Look around you." Lana gestured to the crowded dance floor. Celebrities and glambots glittered and grinded in a perverse frenzy to the urban beats of a local rapper. With shivering realization, she knew that Ilya was right. Every person in sight, including herself, wore a mask. Concealing their vulnerability behind a sleek, sophisticated veneer. It was so much easier to hide than to face one's naked truths.

Ilya dismissed the whole scene with a gesture of contempt. "Myth is a legendary escape for those who wish to be invisible. One must sign a nondisclosure agreement before setting foot on the property. Cell phones are not permitted. Not even a smart watch."

Wow, Law really had a lock on this place. "I had no idea."

"For one so intelligent, you appear to be remarkably uninformed. Perhaps—it is Law's intention to keep you ignorant?"

"My life is none of your business, Ilya."

He maneuvered her into a small alcove that offered privacy, exactly what Ilya wanted.

"I can make it my business, *lubimaya*," he softly said, using his chilly fingers to lift up her chin and gaze into her eyes. Lana allowed it only because she wanted to gain his trust and extract potentially useful information.

"How?"

"By taking you out of this place."

"What if I want to stay?"

"I think that is a lie."

"It doesn't matter what you think."

"You would be surprised how much it does matter," he said in Russian.

The dark undertone of his words was not lost on Lana. Nor the fact that his attempts to trick her into responding when he spoke in Russian told her he didn't trust her. "Ilya, please, in English."

"Forgive me," he said in English, "When I am excited, I sometimes forget." He smiled tightly, then cleared his throat. "Whatever Law has promised you, I will promise as well, in every detail. And I will deliver."

Cocking her head she asked, "Why are you so determined for me to leave here with you?"

"You are a beautiful, brilliant woman who needs to be shown off. Law hides you here. Why, I ask?"

She sidestepped that question. "Law doesn't own me."

"No? He watches you like a hawk." He leaned more intimately into her, so intimately she felt the hard ridge of his erection. Ugh.

He took her hand and continued to plead his case. "I am an international businessman. With you by my side, I would conquer the world. You would want for nothing."

"You only want me because I belong to Law."

"No, *lubimaya*. You are just a passing interest for him. Law has many women. All over the world."

Ilya's words stung. "What guarantees do I have that you wouldn't do the same thing?"

"I give you my word."

"Really?" she drawled. Her tone insinuated she might believe him...or might not.

"I'm very serious." He moved in closer. "I was your first. I will be your last."

Lana's lips twitched. She'd encountered enough ambitious Russians at Ultimate to know that emotions took a back seat to acquisitions, which is exactly what she was to Ilya. "I see you haven't changed."

"Why should I? I see what I want and I take it."

"This girl likes to be asked."

The cacophonous music blared in her head as she tried to push the day she lost her virginity to Ilya deep into her forget-it-ever-happened storage bin.

Looking past him to the beautiful people who glided past them in both directions, she struggled for composure. Her mind refused to let go of the memory.

Forlorn. Afraid. For all intents and purposes, banished from her former life, she'd just turned fourteen when she met the dashing Russian.

All she had wanted was the simple human comfort of being held. Loved. Cherished.

Ilya, her roommate Polina's cousin, was visiting the US with his family and took an instant shine to Lana. Honing in on her insecurities, he turned on his charm, and well, she hadn't resisted.

The pain of the sex paled in comparison to her shame afterward. She didn't feel loved and cherished. She felt cheap. Damaged.

Ilya wanted more. She refused him and in so doing created a raging, jealous monster. Two weeks later she ran away from her boarding school and spent the next six months backpacking across the country.

Bringing her hand to his lips, he kissed her there. "You are the one for me." When Lana pulled her hand away his grip tightened. He pulled her closer to him. "I will not be leaving without you this evening. I'll leave the choice of how you'd like to go up to you."

The sharp glint in his glacial eyes and hard edge to his words sent chills through her.

"What does that mean?"

"It means I would remove any obstacle that stands in my way."

"Including me?"

"You are the prize, Alana. I would not harm a hair on your head—unless seriously provoked."

Lana pushed off his chest and smoothed the fabric of her dress. "Leave me alone, Ilya."

Pressing his cool lips to the base of her throat, Lana stiffened. "Impossible," he softly said.

"Knock off the suave bullshit, Markov. Unless you're looking for a fight." Law's barely controlled voice, low and rough, came from behind them. "You won't win."

The moment Law spoke, Lana pushed Ilya off her. Catching Law's furious gaze, Lana's first thought was to reassure him. Which she squelched. His interruption wasn't about chivalry, it was about his ego. The reality of how little she mattered to him kicked in.

Catching Law's accusing glare, she stiffened then swept past him, and down the hall to the ladies' room. Before she entered the automatic opening door, she glanced over her shoulder. The two men stood facing each other like gladiators before Caesar.

Lana's heart rate accelerated. He refused to take her hand earlier. The humiliation still stung. He disappeared when she danced with Ilya, obviously not caring that another man touched her. Why all of the sudden was he breathing fire? Maybe she mattered a little to Law after all?

Hurrying into a large posh lounge with two attendants, Lana managed a gracious smile before continuing toward a set of large glass doors. One of the attendants opened it for her. Thanking her, Lana moved past yet another attendant stationed inside, between lavish mirrored counters displaying every feminine necessity one could possibly require.

Heading for an empty chaise in the corner, Lana sat down and checked her appearance in the mirrored wall tile. Flushed. Disheveled. Both fixable in seconds. She chewed nervously on her lower lip, trying to think. Her pumped-up ego aside, Law's barely controlled fury terrified her. She'd never seen him so angry. Not with Ilya—the Russian was obviously no threat to him—but angry with her! Desperately, she didn't want to care what Law thought of her. And right now she was sure he thought she was playing Ilya, which she was, but not like Law thought.

She opened her evening bag for her lip gloss

A phone! How and when had someone put it there? Think, Lana. She had left her bag on the high-top table when she danced with Ilya. Had Pyotr slipped it in? Had Law? Was he testing her? She took it out gingerly, wondering if it was password-protected. It booted right up when she pressed the power button. And some more buttons, and icons, to find out more. There was only one number in the contacts. No name, just a number. Ilya's?

Her heart raced. If it was and she used him to escape Law, could she ultimately escape Ilya? Swallowing hard, she turned the phone off and slid it back into her purse.

When Lana emerged from the bathroom, she wasn't surprised that Ilya wasn't waiting for her. Law could be very persuasive. Walking slowly toward the end of the hall back to the dance floor, she overheard angry voices, speaking in Russian. Slowing, Lana moved toward another small alcove just ahead of her.

"Leave the girl alone, Ilya!" Pyotr snapped in Russian.

"I will not be leaving without Alana."

"Law will kill you."

"My friend," Ilya cajoled, "When have you known me not to be two steps ahead of the competition?"

"What are you talking about?"

"Chimera will find out tonight that loyalty can be bought. And rather cheaply."

Lana's heart thudded. Someone sold Law out?

Pyotr was having none of it. "He will kill you, Ilya. Not here, not now. In his own time and his own way. With no witnesses."

CHAPTER THIRTY-FOUR

"YOU FORGOT OUR LITTLE INSURANCE POLICY?"

"For all you know it has been discovered! Think, man, *think*. Dragovich will destroy us both and everything we have worked for if you proceed this way," Pyotr hissed.

Ilya laughed at his doubtful friend. "He will be forced to come ashore to personally handle the arrogant American. When he does, we make our move."

"You will get us both killed!"

"I've kept us alive so far. With the case and the drive, we'll own every Pacific Rim drug route," Ilya assured his comrade.

"I hope you are right."

"Am I ever wrong?" Ilya boasted.

"*Nyet.*"

Lana approached cautiously after their conversation ended.

"Lani," Ilya breathed in Russian. "Your beauty is blinding."

"Please speak English." She deliberately kept her tone pleasant, not wanting either man to think she'd understood a single word they'd said, other than *nyet*.

"Of course," Pyotr agreed quickly. "And allow me to translate. He was saying that there is no effective weapon against feminine beauty."

Ilya nodded, smiling widely. If Lana didn't know the cold-blooded Russian better, she'd say he was actually smitten.

That was good for her. Over hearing what she just heard scared her. She was scared for Law. For Monty and Jhett. True and Sienna. For Chimera. What was Ilya up to? She was going to find out then warn Law.

Taking a decidedly more affable approach to Ilya, Lana smiled turning her head slightly up at him. "Flattery will only get you so far, Ilya."

"It is not flattery if it is the truth." He bowed and extended his arm. Apparently, Ilya didn't respect Law enough to heed his earlier warning. Pyotr slipped past them into the surrounding crowd. Forcing herself to appear calm and interested, Lana gazed up into Ilya's smiling face and took his arm.

Instead of following his friend, Ilya smoothly maneuvered Lana down the hall past the restrooms where it was quieter, and more private. Lana glided easily along, as if she didn't have a care in the world.

Ilya wasn't a fool. She walked a fine tightrope between plausible I-changed-my-mind-about-you and I'm-faking-it-until-I-make-it.

As they moved into a dimly lit area that Lana realized was created expressly for stolen moments, Ilya softly said, "The number in the phone is mine. It is the only one that can be called from the phone."

"I was under the impression cell phones had to be checked in at the door."

Tracing a finger along her high cheekbone, Ilya leaned against the wall pinning her against it.

"As with everything, my love, there are ways around the rules."

Lana dropped her lids, and then looked slyly up at him. "How did you get it in?"

He smiled. The image of a shark crossed her mind. She held steady.

"I am willing to give you everything, Alana, but you give me nothing in return."

"What do you want?" she asked softly.

"A kiss."

"Don't you remember? I don't kiss."

"I remember everything, Lani. You were beautiful then. You are stunning tonight."

"That was a long time ago," she said trying to keep the emotion out of her voice and the painful memories from her mind.

"A kiss and I will tell you how I slipped the phone beneath Law's almighty nose."

Kissing Ilya she decided wouldn't be difficult. She would do what she had to do to protect the people who had cared for her. For Law who had saved her life. Twice.

Leaning into him, Lana pressed her hands, palms open against the hard plane of Ilya's chest. His heart thudded against her hand. Smiling, she pressed her lips to his. She didn't linger. Doing so would make him suspect.

Breaking the kiss, Lana moved back glad it was over. "Now tell me."

His ice blue eyes held hers for a long moment, as if he was trying to see her truth. Steadfastly she held his gaze, not backing down.

"Tell me, Ilya."

"It was delivered in pieces over the course of the last week. I collected them and then assembled the device."

"Is that why you postponed the meeting? So that all of the pieces could be delivered?"

His lips tightened into a smile. "Very astute of you."

"Why, when you didn't know I was alive much less here?"

"The phone wasn't for you. It is a simple precaution under these circumstances to use as I saw fit." Sliding his fingers into her hair, he said, "I saw fit to give it to you."

"What else did you have smuggled in here?"

"Let us see what the night brings us. You will see for yourself how cheaply the price of loyalty sells for at Chimera."

Lana stiffened. "Are you implying that one of Law's trusted people sold him out?"

"More than one. Several."

"What are you going to do?"

"If I told you it would spoil all of the fun." He grabbed her chin and brought her lips to his. Cruelly he kissed her. Twisting out of his grasp Lana shoved him. He pushed her hard against the wall.

"That right there, Ilya is why I will never be yours."

"You already are. You just haven't accepted it yet."

"Never." She shoved him hard. This time he let her pass.

Hurrying down the hallway, Lana steered around the overflowing dance floor, almost colliding with a rapper she'd heard was running with one of the Jenner sisters.

Hastily she smoothed her hair back. Ilya's sudden cold presence behind her unnerved her. She looked up at the VIP lounge and caught her breath. Law's hot glare bored into her. She knew exactly what he was thinking. Would he believe the truth?

Sienna tapped her on the shoulder. "Law would like to bypass drinks in the lounge and go straight to the penthouse."

Lana nodded and looked up again to find Law gone.

Sienna showed Pyotr, Ilya and Lana to a private elevator that took them to the penthouse front door. It wasn't, Lana noted, the secret elevator. Did Sienna know about it?

By the time they arrived at the penthouse door, Lana had regained most of her composure. She'd act normal as if nothing had happened.

As they entered the penthouse, Lana was surprised at the transformation to a lovely wonderland. The dining room was exquisitely set with brilliant cut crystal, gleaming sterling silver and white orchids.

CHAPTER THIRTY-FIVE

THEY WERE GREETED by a handsome dark-suited man she didn't recognize, who introduced himself as Montrose and explained that he would see to their needs that evening.

He directed them into the living room where the lord and master had already arrived, Lana noticed. Law sat in his leather chair, a glass of what she assumed was vodka in his hand and a darkly brooding look on his face.

"Law," Ilya said from behind her, "Come join me for a toast."

Law rose, his eyes riveted on Lana. A small muscle twitched along his scar. Holding his gaze she refused to feel bad for what she did.

A moment later, Montrose reappeared with a tray of frozen shot glasses filled with vodka. Ilya handed one to Lana, then to Pyotr, Sienna and took one for himself.

Raising it, he said, "To new beginnings." He smiled at Lana, adding "With old friends," and then spoke to Law. "And new friends."

He threw back his glass. Lana sipped hers. Law scowled.

Montrose served excellent chilled caviar and champagne as they stood at the vast windows looking across the clear bay.

"Your country is beautiful, Lani." Ilya smiled down at her and said, "Mine is as well. Perhaps one day you will visit and I can show you my favorite places?"

"Perhaps," she murmured not wanting to draw more attention to herself or provoke a situation that could quickly get out of control. She was treading deep water here, not sure what Ilya planned but wanting to warn Law, who from his sunny disposition wanted nothing to do with her at the moment.

"Have you been, Law?" Ilya casually asked over his shoulder.

"Where?"

"Russia."

"Yes," Law boorishly answered.

Despite Ilya's casual conversation, tension snapped around them.

Foreboding loomed heavy. Nerves got the better of her. Biting at her bottom lip, Lana excused herself to the restroom off the dining room.

Exhaling, she leaned against the vanity and stared at herself in the mirror. Her mussed hair and smudged lipstick left little to Law's over active imagination. Quickly she fixed her hair then slipped out and into her bedroom for fresh lipstick.

Pinching her cheeks, Lana psyched herself back up. She was going to go back out there and dive into her role as Law's guest, not a scared little girl.

As she passed the kitchen a fussy Frenchman gave orders in a low voice—Henri, no doubt. Two assistants and one black tie server nodded a greeting as they deftly went about their work. The mouth-watering aromas floating from the kitchen reminded Lana she hadn't eaten in hours.

Law hadn't moved. Ilya stood at the window next to Pyotr and Sienna who pointed out several different landmarks.

Lana smiled at Law, which elicited a scowl. Gliding toward him, she perched on the edge of his chair. Leaning down she whispered in his ear, "I don't know what, but Ilya has something planned. Please be careful." Moving away, she laughed a soft seductive laugh. Ilya turned and scowled as he looked between them. Law smiled widely, like she had just told him she was going to give him the mother of all blowjobs.

Giving him a wink for affect, Lana picked up her full shot glass of vodka, raised it to him and drained it.

"Diner is served in the dining room," the black tie server announced.

Ilya grasped her hand and tucked it into the bend of his arm. "I would be honored if you sat with me tonight, Lani."

"As our guest this evening, it would be my pleasure," Lana sweetly responded. Not glancing at Law, she allowed Ilya to show her to the table. Slyly he seated them across from Pyotr, Sienna and Law.

Lana shivered as she caught Law's glacial gaze. Such a moody man. But could she blame him? Ilya all but flaunted their past under Law's nose. It occurred to Lana that it was intentional. Ilya's way of gauging Law's interest in her to ultimately use it against him?

Law was unflappable when it came to his emotions. Why the angry vibe when he reminded her regularly that emotions were bad for business? Law, wasn't, she realized, made of stone. He was a living, breathing, human being with feelings despite his best efforts to hide them.

With that realization, she lost a little bit more of her heart to him. The strain of his solitary life must be overwhelming. But here he was, sitting at the top of his powerful world, untouchable.

Quietly, Lana observed Law observe their guests.

The vodka flowed. Sienna's serene smile and sultry voice as she chatted with Pyotr and Ilya about Russia kept the mood light, despite the tension that swirled around them all.

"Sienna," Pyotr said, "Have you been to Russia?"

"No, I've actually never left California."

"How is it possible you know so much about my country?"

"I used to work for a Bulgarian."

"Why did you stop working for him?" Ilya asked, pouring himself another shot of vodka.

Sienna's hand shook as she set her wine glass down. "He was killed."

Pyotr slid his hand over Sienna's. "I'm sorry for your loss." He brought her hand to his lips and kissed it. "For the record, I specialize in vengeance."

"Pyotr is not as docile as he appears," Ilya said. His lips twisted into a cunning smile. "Nor am I."

Sienna withdrew her hand from Pyotr's. Picking up her wine glass, Sienna said, "He deserved to die."

Leaning into her, Pyotr raised his glass of vodka and whispered loud enough for them all to hear, "You must tell me all about it."

"Maybe one day I will." They clinked glasses and drank.

Lana looked up to find not only Law's brooding gaze on her but Ilya's too. One warmed her from the inside out and the other chilled her to the bone.

Breaking the morbid silence, Henri swept into the dinning room and stood by as the suited servers lavishly presented a whole smoked salmon, raw oysters and caviar croquettes.

Ilya sampled the food and smiled. "All the flavors of Russia. Thank you, chef."

More courses followed. Lamb kebabs, herbed potatoes in sour cream, sturgeon *en croute*, rustic bread, and an array of brined vegetables and pickled apples. The conversation bounced from geopolitics to the weather to forgettable small talk.

"Henri," Lana said, "This is amazing."

Henri stood by beaming while Law moved food around on his plate.

Once the table was cleared, espresso and liqueurs were served. And more vodka.

Law had returned to his leather chair, and the guests followed. Lana chose a seat close to Law where she could see everyone but still be on the sidelines. Listen and learn, she thought.

Montrose brought out Law's humidor. Cigars were selected, cut and lit. The aromatic, heavy blue smoke was instantly drawn into the recessed ventilation system, as far as Lana could tell. Which was fine with her.

Lana glanced over at Law, studying him covertly for a few moments. Unlike Ilya who had a distinct tell of twitching his left upper lip when he was anxious or lying, Law's tell was that he had no tell. His hooded gaze didn't fool her. She knew only too well that he was aware of every breath each one of them took. This was the deadly don't-fuck-with-me-or-I'll-cut-you-down Law.

Discreetly, Sienna ushered Henri and his staff from the penthouse before she returned to her seat beside Pyotr.

Nervously, Lana waited for what she knew was going to be showdown between two masters.

"Tell me, Ilya," Law drawled, "What do you hear out of Riyadh these days?"

Setting his cigar in an ashtray, Ilya threw down a shot of vodka before he answered. Liquid courage, Lana thought.

Looking straight at Law, Ilya answered. "Oil production is lagging, the conflict in Yemen is escalating and the king is weary."

Law leaned forward, his eyes glacial.

"I invited you up here so we could talk. Don't waste my time with bullshit from the Al-Jazeera newsfeed."

Quietly Pyotr said in Russian to his partner, "Do not taunt the lion."

Ignoring him, Ilya replied again to Law's initial query. "About Riyadh—yes, there is more to be said. But I cannot *give* away valuable information."

"Get to the point, Ilya. What the hell do you want?"

Puffing his cigar again, with a flourish of his hand, Ilya said, "This conversation would be easier if you and I spoke in Russian."

"I speak several languages, but Russian isn't one of them. Get to the point."

Ilya didn't seem intimidated in the least. "Very well. I represent a client with specific requirements, which you are highly qualified to fulfill."

Law nodded. "Go on."

"My particular client has a large sum of cash he would like —legitimized."

"How much?"

"Twenty million." Languid blue smoke swirled around Ilya's head. "Each month."

Lana set her espresso down and glanced at Law, who didn't blink. That was a hell of a lot of money. From drugs or illegal arms deals, most likely.

"Does that interest you?" Ilya asked casually.

Law took a few seconds to reply. "I'm willing to consider it —on my terms. My fee is fifty percent per month, twelve month minimum contract."

That got Ilya's attention. He sat up straight. "That's outrageous, Law. Even for you!"

Law stayed calm. "Twenty million is an outrageous amount to move every thirty days." He refilled his shot glass with his personal bottle of vodka. "And I have to know more before I decide to work with your client."

"Ten percent." Ilya scowled. "That's standard for you. Or so I have heard."

"Why would I charge my standard fee for nonstandard sums?"

"Fifteen."

Law scoffed at that, tossing back the vodka he'd poured for himself and setting down the shot glass. "Not enough."

"Twenty percent. That is my final offer."

"Then we don't have a deal."

"My client has also instructed me to propose a partnership in his expansion project in Peru."

"I'm not interested in the drug business."

"Are you interested in precious metals?"

"Always."

"Gold?"

"Possibly."

"The mining industry in South America is destroying the rain forests," Lana interjected.

All eyes turned to her. "It's devastating the flora and fauna there," she defended. "Deforestation is terrible for the environment. Trees absorb carbon dioxide. Each tree that is destroyed contributes to global warming."

"There are other rainforests, Lani," Ilya muttered.

"Not as vital as the Amazon."

Ilya cleared his throat and looked at Law, who seemed almost bored.

"I'll pass," Law said.

Lana smiled.

Pyotr looked panicked. "There is also a lithium mine start-up in Chile," he volunteered. He winked at Lana and added, "In the desert."

"Hm. Well, first I'd have to study the mineral reports, the engineering, the production tallies and projected estimates—everything—before I committed." Law looked to Lana, "That is, unless the local scorpions are endangered."

Ilya cleared his throat. "The Atacama desert is the driest desert in the world. There are no creatures that exist there."

"If there are, she'll tell me about them." Law gestured toward Lana, who didn't argue with that statement, just smiled inwardly. And took the cue.

Ilya looked at Law like he couldn't believe that the big bad wolf was allowing *her* to drive their negotiations. Tough luck.

"Desert mining requires a water source—meaning the lithium has to be separated from sand. So how does this start-up you're talking about plan to do that?" Lana asked.

Perplexed, Ilya and Pyotr glanced at each other.

"Surely they're not going to truck it in," Lana said.

"I—" Ilya had no answer.

"Let me explain. They'd have to drill for it at the site," Lana explained. "There's a huge aquifer beneath that desert."

The two Russians avoided Law's steady gaze as Lana continued. "Other mining companies have had a huge negative impact on the water table, which prompted the Chilean government to place a moratorium on drilling." She looked at Law. "So this new mine just isn't a sound venture."

"Law," Pyotr said, "Forty-eight million for the year is generous. As you Americans say, throw us a bone."

Law shook his head. "I'm out. But I know some other investors who'd be more than happy to discuss these golden opportunities."

"*Nyet*. Our client was specific. Only you."

Law sat back in his chair, his body language casual and open. "Then accept my terms."

Ilya threw back a shot of vodka before he said, "I will waive my five percent broker fee for the first year."

"You're willing to give up twelve million to seal the deal?"

"Yes, on one condition."

In Russian Pyotr said to Ilya, "We are not authorized to offer more."

"And that condition is?" Law drawled.

"Lani's contract."

Law stiffened. Lana's stomach lurched.

Pyotr said to Ilya in Russian, "You are a fool."

"The contract is not for sale." Law's tone was suddenly menacing.

"Ten million."

"For any price."

Ilya was visibly agitated. "You do realize there's a five million dollar bounty on her head."

"Which begs the question, why would you offer ten to lose five?"

"I have my reasons."

"Unlike you, Markov, I don't buy or sell humans."

"You hold her contract."

"Ms. Conti is not open for discussion."

"Hello," Lana interjected. "I'm sitting right here while the two of you discuss me like I'm a sack of flour up for sale."

"I would set you free," Ilya stated.

Wide-eyed, Lana looked over at Law. He shrugged.

Part of her wanted to challenge him to let her go with Ilya. The other part was afraid he would do it.

Lana glanced at the determined Russian. Even if she was given one, there was no choice. If she were going to be a prisoner, and she would be again, if she left with Ilya, she would rather be a prisoner to Law. With him, she had a chance to wheedle her way out of here and disappear.

In an attempt to defuse the tension, Lana smiled at Ilya. "I appreciate your offer, but my place is here."

Ilya glared at Law. "You accept a man who does not value you?"

"At the moment, I accept no man, Ilya."

There was no doubt to anyone in the room that he was furious. Ilya visibly wrestled with his ego and what was best if he wanted to walk out of the penthouse alive. Throwing back a last glass of vodka, he stood and said, "If you would provide me with a burner so that I may call my client, I will contact him for permission to up his offer."

Law pointed to the end table. Ilya opened the drawer. Lana leaned forward and caught her gasp of surprise. There were at least four cell phones that she could see. When she had gone through the penthouse looking for a phone that drawer was empty. Had Law planted them there for this express reason tonight?

Ilya grabbed one then strode to the dining room. A moment later she heard the restroom door open and close.

Minutes slowly ticked by before Ilya returned and sat down. "I have been instructed to offer you thirty percent, with a two year guarantee."

"Fifty percent."

Ilya visibly steamed.

Law let him.

"Law," Pyotr began, "Is there something else we can throw in to sweeten the pot?"

"Perhaps."

"What would that be?" Pyotr asked.

"I want the date, vessel and container number the Riyadh papers are coming in on."

The Russians exchanged looks. Ilya nodded. "If I give you this information, you will reduce your rate to thirty-five percent with a two year term."

"Agreed."

CHAPTER THIRTY-SIX

FOR THE LIFE OF HER, Lana couldn't begin to figure out why Law would give away the fifteen percent for information he had. Apparently, he was in a generous mood, despite his obvious anger. Seething inwardly, Lana forced herself to stay outwardly calm.

Ilya audibly exhaled. "On New Year's Eve, the *Gorky* is scheduled to dock at Long Beach. The container number is 2019. I will provide a map of its precise location among the stacks— it's accessible, of course. It is filled with sacks of grain. There is one marked with a dragon hanging by the back, which can be seen when the container is opened. It contains the flash drive."

"How do you know this?" Law asked.

"I personally arranged the logistics," Ilya said.

"Did you now?" Law said.

Pyotr's eyes narrowed. Ilya chose not to notice the suspicious undertone in Law's voice and poured vodka for everyone at the table.

"Now that we have a deal,"—he raised his glass—"I propose a toast—to America!"

Law didn't bother to pick up his glass. "I want your client's name and information first. Or the deal's off."

Ilya stopped mid-drink. "Law, one of the services I offer all of my clients is anonymity."

"I don't do business with ghosts."

Pyotr set his glass down. "Perhaps once you have possession of the drive and discover the information it contains, you will see the value in dealing with our client anonymously."

Law stood up and slid his phone from his pocket. Tapping an icon, he smiled tightly and set the phone, screen up, on the coffee table. The Russians stood and peered at the shadowy video, while Lana squinted at what seemed to be special ops guys opening a shipping container by force. Once it was breached, several men with guns moved in while several others stayed outside. The one with the body cam went directly to the only piece of cargo in the container: a box screwed to a pallet strapped to the inner walls.

"What is this?" Ilya demanded.

The box was opened, followed by the smaller box inside. Tucked into a foam bed was a flash drive. The guy with the body cam grabbed it and held it up in front of his face. "Got it," he said, then stuffed it into his vest and turned off the camera.

Took her a second, but Lana recognized the voice. *True.* He was there and he had the flash drive.

Law slid his phone back into his pocket and sat back down in his chair.

"You lied to me, Markov. I don't do business with liars."

"I don't understand what I just watched," Ilya said, trying to play dumb.

"My team intercepted the *Karabo* off the coast of Baja earlier this evening and retrieved the authentic Riyadh papers. Is the drive hidden on the *Gorky* a different Riyadh drive?"

"I don't know what was on the *Karabo*! I only know what is on the *Gorky*."

Law leaned back in his chair, crossing his arms behind his head. "The *Gorky* drive is a red herring. But the information on the *Karabo* drive? That's the real prize." He straightened in the chair, then stood, his gaze fixed on Ilya. "Tell me who wants it and I might reconsider your original deal."

Pyotr shook his head. Ilya stood silent as he contemplated the request, taking precious seconds to think.

Finally, he looked at Law and said, "Dragovich."

Law smiled slowly. "I suspect he is also your client?"

"Yes."

"Okay." He paced toward the window, glancing outside without seeming to see anything. "I will agree to all of your terms as well as negotiate a price for the *Karabo* drive—"

"But—"

Law turned around. "Listen to me. You don't set the terms, Ilya. I do. Dragovich has to agree to meet me here to discuss the details."

"He will never leave his fortress."

"As his agent, you will just have to convince him of the benefit of coming ashore," Law said dryly.

Pyotr got his two cents in. "Ilya is telling you the truth. Drago will never do that. You are asking the impossible."

Law strode to Lana and she rose to meet him. He took her hand in his and softly said, "He would for her."

Lana gasped. His audacious assertion and the closeness of his body made her nervous. Damn it.

There was a flash of anger in Ilya's eyes. "Oh? You would trade Lani to the Dragon for—what?"

"What I do with my guest is none of your concern, Ilya. Arrange the meeting."

Signaling that the negotiations were concluded, Law stepped away from Lana and went into the dining room, leaving the four of them staring incredulously at each other.

Despite the ambient warmth, Lana's blood chilled. So, this was it. Law's plans revealed at last. Dangling her like a worm on a hook to get Drago here so that Law could kill him.

"I am afraid, Law," Ilya said loud enough to be heard in the dining room, "Alana will be unavailable for that meeting."

Ilya slid his arm around her waist pulling her against his chest, the hard nudge of metal between her shoulder blades stopped Lana from turning around.

Before she processed what was happening, Ilya positioned her between himself, the front door and Law.

"What are you doing?" Pyotr hissed in Russian.

"Taking what is mine."

Right under Law's nose. The gun. It must have been hidden it the bathroom. Who had access? Who would betray Law?

Shaking, fear swept through her. Not for herself but for Law. Panic mushroomed. No way in hell would he allow Ilya to walk out of here with her. He'd fight. Ilya had a gun. He'd use it. She didn't want Law to die. Couldn't imagine his life force leaving this earth. No, not Law.

"Let go of me," she demanded twisting away from the barrel. Ilya grasped her tighter around the waist.

"Stop before you get hurt," Ilya commanded.

"Have you lost your mind, Ilya? Let go of me!"

Law stepped around from the dining room, cool as an iceberg, stopping at the edge of the wall. They would have to get through him to the door.

"Let her go, Markov," he said his voice deadly calm.

"Give me her contract. The *original* contract and we'll go."

Law's lips tightened, his angry gaze held Ilya's. "If you don't let her go right now, you won't leave this room alive."

"I have a loaded Glock dug into her back. I pull the trigger and you both die."

"Pull the trigger and you die."

"Law," Lana said softly. "Give him the contract. Let us go."

Law's eyes sharpened as he lowered his gaze to her. "Is that what you want? To go with him?"

"Yes," she forced herself to say. "But," she looked up at Ilya, "only if you promise to leave everyone here alive, Ilya. No exceptions."

"I agree to your terms, *lubimaya*."

"Please," Lana begged turning back to Law, "Just let us go."

Pyotr, who stood several feet to her left, took a step toward Law.

"Don't move," Sienna smoothly said pressing the tip of her switchblade to his throat.

Pyotr slowly raised his hands. "I wish you no harm," he said.

"If you blink too hard, Pyotr, I'll give you a nice Russian bow tie to go home with."

He kept silent.

"I don't agree to your terms." Law strode directly toward Lana and Ilya. Ilya spun Lana away, leveled the gun at Law and pulled the trigger. Lana screamed and bolted for Law. Ilya grabbed her by the hair yanking her back. Law kept coming. Ilya pulled the trigger again. Law grabbed the gun by the barrel from a stunned Ilya and struck him hard with the butt across the face with it.

Ilya fell back against the high window ledge. Head down he rushed Law catching him in the gut. They went down hard.

Law slammed his right elbow into the side of Ilya's face. The Russian grunted, grabbing Law's face, digging his thumbs into

Law's eyes. Law head butted him and rolled off. As Ilya got to his knees, Law, sprawled on his back, twisted his legs around Ilya's waist and arm around his neck and like a human constrictor he slowly squeezed the life out of him. Transfixed by Law's unorthodox moves, she watched Ilya slowly suffocate. His bugged eyes turned to her in a silent plea to intervene.

She despised him. In every way possible she despised him. But she wouldn't be a silent party to murder. Not again.

Visions flashed before her eyes. Screams. Blood. Squeezing her eyes closed, Lana fought to drive the terrible memories from her mind.

Ilya's gags for oxygen pulled her back to the present.

Ilya slammed his hand on the floor. Tapping out. Law continued to tighten his grip. Ilya's body flailed.

"Law!" Lana cried dropping to her knees. "Stop. You're going to kill him."

"Please, Law," Pyotr, pleaded still under the watchful eye of Sienna, "I give you my word, I will get Dragovich here. Into Chimera if I have to kidnap him myself. Let Ilya go."

Pyotr's plea fell on deaf ears. There was no getting to Law. He was in the red zone.

"Law, please," she begged grabbing his arm. Hard as steel, she couldn't budge him. "Please," she sobbed. "Don't do it. For me don't do it."

Unbelievably, the muscles in his arm loosened. Sanity slowly dawned in his dark green eyes. Law fully released Ilya then stood up. Ilya coughed, gasping for air. As Pyotr helped him to a sitting position, Lana moved toward Law, silently checking him for damage. Aside from his disheveled hair and torn cuff, he looked unhurt.

"Ilya, can you hear me?" Pyotr said in Russian.

Ilya nodded, inhaling great gulps of air. Though he quickly

regained his arrogance. Glaring up at Lana then at Law, Ilya bared his teeth.

Law bent down and picked up the gun he had dropped and threw it at Ilya. It hit his chest before it landed in his lap.

"A gun is no good without a firing pin."

"How did you know?" Ilya rasped.

"Chimera can't be bought, Markov." Law said. "I should kill you now. You can thank your girlfriend for your life."

Law stepped back and waved them away. Pyotr helped Ilya stand. Once he was steady, they walked slowly toward the door. When they reached it, Law said, "Three days. Dragovich here. Alive."

"I will need more time." Pyotr asked.

"Your time runs out on the fourth day."

Lana rubbed her hands up and down her arms, the chill of Law's words cutting to her bones.

Sienna gave Law an understood look, then opened the penthouse door to the hulking giant, Tyrus, Lana remembered from the night she was brought here along with two other equality intimidating giants.

Hugging herself in an attempt to still her shaking body, Lana struggled to rationalize what just happened. God god. Ilya had set Law up to die tonight and Law had nearly killed him!

The doors closed silently, leaving Lana and Law. Alone.

"Law," she said rushing toward him. "Are you OK?"

He walked past her to the door and locked it. Turning around, he leaned against the doorjamb and casually regarded her. "That was an interesting get-together. Did you enjoy it?"

"*What*? Of course not. That was awful! We could have been killed!"

A nasty smile twisted his lips. A sudden realization hit her. "Are you blaming me for what happened?" She demanded aghast that he would think she—Moving toward him, anger swarmed her. "You proposed to toss me to Dragovich!"

Fury shimmered through her. She'd had too much vodka. She was too emotional. Had fucking nearly died and he was—what, turning on her? She wanted to hurt Law back. Shred his smug face to pieces.

Somehow she tempered the violence swirling inside of her.

"I think you set me up," she accused.

He laughed. "Set you up how?"

"You used me to get Ilya riled up."

"It worked."

"Fuck you, Law." Lana tossed her hair over her shoulders. There was no reasoning with him. She'd be damned if she'd apologize for something she didn't do. "I'm going to bed."

"Don't forget your evening bag," he crooned. Picking it up from where she had left it on the hall table he handed it to her.

Before he let go, he opened it and slid the cell phone out of it.

"What is this?" he asked.

Refusing to rise to the bait, she simply said, "What does it look like?"

"Did you fuck him?" Law quietly asked.

"*What*?"

"Did. You. *FUCK*. Markov?"

He was angry. She was angry. They had stared death in the face less than thirty minutes ago. Adrenaline continued to pump through her. It didn't give him the right to question her past. "My life is none of your business," she said.

"*Did you fuck him*." he grit out.

"Yes!"

Shoving the cell phone back into the purse, he surprised her by handing it to her. "When this is all over, give him a call."

"You're an ass." Taking it, she set it back on the table. "It happened a long time ago." That was all the explanation she would give him. Even though he didn't deserve it.

Law visibly shook with anger. "I'm a goddamn fool." His raw voice dropped to a growl. *"You* set *me* up!"

Incredulous, she shook her head. "What are you talking about? I was auctioned off to Dragovich, then you kidnapped me."

Law started to laugh. "Why didn't I see this coming?" He looked at her equally incredulous. "You pulled off the ultimate double cross." He bowed. "And you win the Most Conniving Bitch of the Year award."

"I hate you," she seethed. How dare he turn this around on her? *She* was the victim, not him!

He came closer. "That's the first thing coming out of your mouth that I believe."

Lana backed up against the wall. She wasn't sure what was happening. Law was furious. She'd never seen such deadly anger in her life. But why? Was he—jealous? Adrenaline spiked. The very thought that Law was capable of the emotion terrified her. Not that he would hurt her. No, no, he was a man who never lost control. He held his feelings, few as they were, in check.

"How far are you prepared to go to convince me you're not a mole?"

"What?" He was crazy.

"Why didn't you leave with your lover when I gave you the chance?"

"He's not my lover," she breathed. Law had moved in so close the heat of his body pulsed angrily against hers.

"Answer me."

"I didn't want to."

"So you could stay here and pretend to be the poor little rich girl?" Law swept her hair from her shoulders. "So you could play me?"

"N—no," she gasped as his fingers dug into her hair. Lowering his nose to her neck, he inhaled her scent.

"Your heart is beating like a drum." He raised his head and looked into her eyes. "Are you afraid of me?"

"No," she breathlessly answered. Despite his anger, she wasn't afraid he would harm her. Law had too much respect for women and self-control for that. Her fear stemmed from her intense reaction to his nearness.

"Good. Because I have no intention of hurting you, Alana," he crooned.

Lana inhaled deeply as her tingling nipples pressed against Law's hard chest. A low moan escaped her lips. The air between them intensified.

"Such a pretty, needy girl," he softly taunted.

"Shut up," she breathed.

"I didn't realize how needy you were for cock until tonight."

"Shut up."

"Just tell me something. Is it *my* cock you want?"

"Yes."

"Not Ilya?"

"No," she said in a rushed breath.

"What do you want me to do with it, Alana?" he purred as his fingers traced the bow of her lip.

"Make it stop," she whispered.

"Make what stop?"

"The ache."

He laughed low, taunting her, his lips just inches from hers. "You're on."

Rising up on her toes, she reached his mouth and kissed him hard. He moaned—and moved back. Pinned her against the wall.

Because he had to be in charge, Lana knew that in an instant. They would play this game his way or not at all.

His unwavering green gaze met hers. She couldn't tell what he was thinking. But she could guess.

"You don't want to want me," she breathlessly challenged. "But you can't help it—just like I can't."

CHAPTER THIRTY-SEVEN

LAW STOOD STILL, his eyes blazing hungrily.

Pressing her hands against his hard chest, standing up on her tiptoes, Lana raised her lips to his. All-out seduction, coming up.

"One of us has to crack," she whispered. It started before they touched. She could see it in his eyes, the way he wanted her. Hot breath pulsed between them. Anticipation tightened their bodies. She pressed fully into him. "It can be me."

When their lips met, a low moan of arousal escaped her. Lust, hot and burning, shot through her veins like fireworks on the Fourth of July, the sensation so powerful, she pulled away.

Sliding his arms around her waist, Law pulled her back. "Now it can be me," he said hoarsely and then caught her lips with an urgent claiming.

The physical rush of his command was liberating. In that perfect moment, Lana understood the power of desire.

Her fingers slid around his neck, into his hair, caressed his face. Wildly, she kissed him. His big body pushed her flush against the wall, his jaw moving as he deepened the kiss. It was rough, ragged and intoxicating. When his tongue thrust in and out of her mouth, like he was fucking it, her knees buckled.

Law pulled away. Breathless, she moaned, craving more.

"You look so fucking turned on right now," he said as he dropped his lips to her neck. "Such a beautiful actress." He nipped her jugular.

"I'm not acting and you fucking know it." Lana braced herself for his angry seduction. His big hands cupped her breasts. She wanted him. All of him. She had never been more desperate for anything in her life.

The sensual storm in his eyes sent hot waves of desire through her. She wanted to touch every inch of him, discover what he liked and hold that power over him. The sweet pain of wanting something forbidden overwhelmed her, making it extremely difficult to remember why having sex with this man was a bad idea.

Sliding his big hand down her red dress to her bare belly down her thigh, then beneath her skirt, set her on fire. Lana's breath hitched, her heart thudded against her chest. The anticipation of him touching her hurt. When he slid a fingertip between her legs and along her wet seam Lana cried out and bit her bottom lip to keep from making a fool out of herself. His skillful touching felt so fucking good.

She wanted to climb on top of him, slide down his glorious cock and fuck. Another moan slipped from her lips. Her hips undulated hotly against his hand. "Law," she breathlessly said. "I —need—" she couldn't say the words, *I need you inside of me.* The fear of rejection was too strong. If he laughed at her and walked away, she would never have the guts to go there with him again.

He slid his finger into her mouth and pressed her bottom lip against her teeth. The intensity of his gaze unnerved her. "Tell me what you need." He bit her neck.

Lana nearly lost it—she wanted him so badly.

Releasing her, he stepped back and with both hands ripped her dress in half allowing it to slide to the floor. She was bare-assed naked beneath. Law growled his pleasure at the sight.

"Do you need me to touch you here," he asked, sliding his finger along the swell of her breast.

"Yes" she breathed.

"Here?" he asked, brushing a thumb across her straining nipple.

"Yes," she gasped.

Dipping a finger into her soaking pussy, he softly said, "Do you need me here, Alana?"

"Yes."

He slid his finger deeper into her hungry body. She liquefied around him.

"So fucking tight," he whispered against her sultry skin. "I'm going to make your pussy purr, Alana."

Gasping for breath, she could only nod. Afraid if she spoke the neediness in her voice would betray her weakness for him.

Dropping to his knees, his lips burned a hot trail between her breasts, down her belly before hovering above her sultry mound. Wantonly, she spread her legs for him and dug her fingers deeply into his thick hair. Never had she felt so raw or exposed. Never had she wanted anything more than she wanted his mouth on her.

Slick with her wetness, his thumbs slid between her lips, opening them. "So pink and lush," he rasped. The percussion of his hot breath on her clitoris nearly launched her.

She glanced down just as his fingertips slid across the hood of her clit, gently pushing it back. His tongue lashed out, curling around the stiffened organ. Lana mewed like a cat. The rush of her excitement slicked his lips. "Fucking beautiful," he growled before he sucked her into his ravenous mouth. Digging her nails into his scalp, she snapped. Lightening struck between her legs, the hot jolt of it shocked her in its intensity.

Bucking hard against his mouth, Lana lost what little control she had left. Law's big hands steadied her as wave after wave of an intense orgasm slammed through her.

His lips suckled, his tongue lapped and swirled, riding the orgasm out.

Her knees buckled no longer able to support her body. Law, held her up. When he disengaged his mouth from her she whimpered wanting his cock to go where his tongue had just been.

"Is that what you needed, Angel?"

Shaking hard, as the ripples of the orgasm continued to stun her, Lana licked her dry lips trying to catch her breath. "Yes."

Standing, he slid his fingers into her disheveled hair, Law brought her lips up to his. Her sex scent swirled between them. Licking his bottom lip, Lana sucked it onto her mouth liking the taste of her.

Law's body pushed hard into hers. Grasping her hands from his hair, he pushed them down to her sides. Breaking the kiss, his eyes glittered passionately. "I swore I wouldn't touch you like this."

"Why?"

"Because it's wrong of me when you're at such a disadvantage."

Stepping back from her, he raked his fingers through his hair.

"What is that supposed to mean?" she demanded realizing she was butt naked, except for the heels and earrings she wore. Chin high, she held his stare. No way was she going to allow him to reduce what just happened. It was amazing. "You can stop the martyr bullshit, Law. You didn't do anything to me that I didn't want you to do."

Hand on hip, she shook her hair and tilted her head. "And you're a fucking liar if you say you didn't like making me come like that." Her gaze dropped to his tented trousers. "You want me."

"Yeah, I want you. And that's a problem for us both."

He stepped away and stalked out of the penthouse, leaving her naked and still horny as fuck for him.

"Fuck you, Law!" she yelled at the door. "You don't get to make me come and then walk away like it doesn't matter!"

Lana was done being told what she could and couldn't do. He didn't have the right to make her wait for anything. Least of all, his precious dick.

Running to his bedroom, she yanked open the door and grabbed a katana from the sword rack. Unsheathing it, she jumped on his bed and started hacking away at his pillows, his fur throw, his gazillion dollar sheets and his huge custom mattress. Fur, foam and fabric flew into the air, as she slashed and gouged, screaming and yelling. She swore like a whore, damned him, hexed him and voodoo cursed him.

Everything, everyone, every shitty decision she had ever made, she blamed on Law, cursing him over and over. He was the devil. And she hated him.

"*Alana!*"

She turned on the bed, sword held high over her head, her hair and feathers swirling around her, her bare breasts heaving.

Law reached out, squeezing her hand so hard she had no choice but to release the sword. As she did, she grabbed his shirt and ripped it open, panting.

He tossed her onto the destroyed bed. Bouncing back, she lunged at him again. This time, Law pinned her flat against the shredded mattress. Wildly she kicked, screamed, pulled at his shirt until there was nothing left to pull.

"Calm down."

"Make me!"

"Okay. I will." He yanked his trousers open and slid them down his hips. Grabbing her hands, he pushed them over her head into the tattered sheets. Skin to skin, her body drawn taut, her breasts poked his chest, his thighs pressed hotly into her. His hard cock throbbed against her thigh.

Swallowing hard, a small moan escaped her when his lips swept softly across one bare nipple. Then the other. Lana's pussy literally clenched and unclenched as it tried to grasp his cock and draw him deep inside of her.

When he looked up at her, she nearly came. But she wasn't going to tell him that.

"Is all of this your way of telling me you want me balls deep inside of you?"

Reckless abandon seized her. There was no escaping the desire he triggered. Yes, goddamn it! She wanted him balls deep inside of her.

"Yes," she breathed.

Before she could take another breath, he slid deeply inside of her.

"Law," she sobbed as he filled her. There were not words to describe what he felt like inside of her. The way her body desperately clenched around him, refusing to give him up. She was wet and hot, her body on fire, submitting to a masterful sensuality beyond her wildest expectations. There was no fantasy that could top her reality.

He was nearly all the way in—no more than an inch of his long, thick shaft still showed—and then—

Law moved back and thrust into her, all the way. All the man she'd ever wanted, for all time. She would never be able to let go of Law. What he did to her. Made her feel. There was nothing like it.

He thrust again. Good god.

She wanted him harder. Deeper, damn it. She wanted him to tear her apart, put her back together, then do it again and again until she couldn't stand it.

Wild, wanton emotions overtook her. Thrust for thrust, her body met his, driven by pure passion.

Feral moans escaped his lips. Sweat slickened their bodies. Their anger and passion battering them into an erotic frenzy.

He dug his fingers into her palms. She dug her nails into his knuckles. Their combined pleasure skyrocketed until an orgasm ripped through Lana at white-hot intensity. Law cursed as his hips ground into hers and he came in a wild, blazing flourish.

Before they recovered, Lana shoved him away, about to leap from the bed. He grabbed her and pulled her back and under him. "You're not going anywhere."

No tenderness. No easing into sleep in powerful arms. Back to square-fucking-one and the inescapable facts she had to face about who Law really was—and her own vulnerability to him. "I don't want to sleep here with you."

"You're not leaving this room until you clean it up."

"Fuck you," she said, pushing him away. Knowing he was letting her do it was even more irksome. She rolled over away from him. Damned if she was going to clean anything up.

A faint sensation tickled her skin. Lana brushed it away—and looked at her hand. Tiny feathers. Bits of foam. He was sprinkling them on her.

"Like I said…"

"You do it."

"We can clean up together," Law suggested. She could hear the amusement in his voice, which was even more irritating.

"No."

"Okay. I'll call the housekeepers. And say that my pet gorilla did it."

She rolled over, pummeling him, half angry and half not.

"They won't bat an eye. Wouldn't be the first time a woman went wild on me."

She hit him harder.

Law caught her wrist and laughed. "Good thing we have more than one bedroom. Ready for Round Two?"

Surrender was inevitable. She was still tense and the man who held her captive was just too hot to waste.

She nodded.

He was warm, naked, and—after a big-cat nap sprawled on the destroyed bed, leaving her almost no room—hard again. Lana slid over him and before she could tell herself no, or ask permission, she sheathed herself on his thick cock.

Law groaned, his hips bucking into her. "Christ, Lana," he groaned.

Entwining her fingers with his, she raised their hands over his head as he had done just hours before. With slow, deep undulations—and no regrets, she fucked him.

He hit her hard, he hit her deep, he hit her passionately. The orgasm built deep inside of her. Each time the wide head of his cock went to the limit, Lana caught her breath fighting back tears. Tears of wonder. Tears of joy. Tears of sublime torture.

Grinding down hard on him, her thighs quaked as she began to come. Law broke her hold. Grabbing her hips, he pushed her down harder on him as he thrust deeper into her. She screamed. Literally screamed as the orgasm fully released, shaking her to her core.

Law thrust high into her as he came.

Long minutes later, still straddling him, Lana looked down at where they were joined. The pronounced vein at the thick root of his cock pulsed. Her smooth pussy glistened around him. Erotic visions of them in the throes of torrid passion flashed before her eyes.

The afterglow faded out soon after she collapsed beside him. It always did. Other thoughts, cold and stark, took over. Of him tiring of her and moving on to the next willing woman.

Moving off the bed, she said, "We're even now. Don't touch me again." She walked out without looking back.

This time, he didn't stop her. Under no circumstances would she ever allow him to touch her again.

He was already what she wanted most in the world. And she didn't have to ask him to know that he didn't care.

CHAPTER THIRTY-EIGHT

TWO DAYS PASSED with no Law in sight. It drove Lana crazy that he hadn't been rocked about what had happened between them. Each time she closed her eyes she caught her breath as the vision of their entwined bodies came back to her. The memory of his mouth and hands on her, inside of her. Her explosive orgasm was nearly unbearable.

Neither hours in the gym nor hundreds of laps in the rooftop pool lessened the ache in her heart or the need that pulsed through her body. She couldn't sleep, couldn't stay in bed. She wandered through the quiet penthouse in the wee hours, hoping that Law had returned.

And if he did, then what? Beg him for more? Demand it? Old Lana wrestled with new Lana. The only thing they could agree on was their desperate need for Law.

On the third morning as she came out of the gym, Lana abruptly stopped. Law stood at the threshold. His brooding gaze looked her over thoroughly. Determined to be indifferent to him, she said, "What do you want?"

He tried to hand her a flash drive. Nothing doing. Lana folded her arms across her chest. Law seemed annoyed. "I need your help, Alana. I speak Russian, but I can't read it. Do you?"

"You told Ilya you don't speak Russian," she pointed out.

"I lied." Law held the drive up. "The names on this are worth millions of dollars to the wrong people."

"Are you one of the wrong people, Law?"

"No."

"Why not ask Monty or use one of those translation sites?"

"Because I'm asking you."

Did he trust her with his business? If this was some kind of test she had to pass she was willing to take it. Trust was a commodity Law didn't deal in. She wanted to prove to him he could trust her. Staring at him for a very long time, she extended her hand, palm up.

He dropped it into her hand. "Thank you." Following him into the living room, he pointed to his desk, and said, "There's a laptop there for you to use."

Sitting down at his desk, she inserted the drive. Once the information was pulled up, she asked, "Do you want the names handwritten or in a doc file?"

"Handwritten." He handed her a legal pad and pen.

As she scrolled through the names, Law stood over her. She began to write them down.

"By the way—how did you know about the lithium mines?" Law asked.

Lana stopped writing and looked up at him. "My college lab partner was the daughter of the Chilean Minister of Agriculture. Lithium has been a hot topic in Chile for years."

"Oh. And did someone else's daughter, say, a South American dictator, school you on global warming?"

"No. That's called giving a shit about the world's environment."

"I wonder how the conservative senator would feel knowing *his* daughter is a tree hugger?"

"I'm sure my father wouldn't give a fuck what my political leanings are."

"How many languages do you speak?"

"Four."

"How many lovers have you had?"

The question came out nowhere catching her off guard. "None of your business."

"Too many to count?"

She stood and slapped him hard across the face. He didn't flinch. The imprint of her fingers were a startling contrast to his tan skin.

"I deserved that," he said.

"You deserve worse. And more."

"You're probably right on both counts."

"Damn straight."

Sitting back down, Lana leashed her rising anger.

"I'm sorry, Lana."

Could have knocked her over with a feather. Nodding her acceptance of his apology, she turned back to the list of names, she wrote the last one down. But instead of closing the drive, she took a deeper look. There was another file hidden in the last name. Opening it, she scrunched her brows. "There's more here than just names, Law," she said, looking up at him.

Pulling up a chair beside her, he asked, "Like what?"

"Like..." She scrolled up and down. "Swiss bank account numbers."

"To be expected. Anything else?"

It was hard to tell if he was being obnoxious or what. Lana jotted down info. "Let's see. Those are tagged as Cayman Islands account numbers and...there are several more accounts in an offshore Belize bank."

He scowled. "What's the name of that bank?"

"The Belize bank?"

"Yes."

"Belize LTD. Designated A Class."

"Fuck," Law hissed. "What are the Belize account numbers?"

Quickly she wrote them down and handed him the separate sheet of paper. His jaw tightened. "Double fuck."

"It's an offshore unrestricted institution," Lana said.

"I know exactly what it is."

"Excuse me, for attempting to enlighten you."

"Does it list any names associated with the account numbers?"

Scrolling through the lists, she shook her head. "No cross reference that I can see. But there are names. Hmm. I recognize a bunch of them. It's a virtual Who's Who of Hollywood and DC." Her eyes widened. "My father and grandfather are listed as owners on Panamanian shell companies!" She frowned, and kept staring into the screen, not wanting to meet Law's eyes.

"They're hiding assets."

"Noted," she said dryly. "I majored in international finance. What I want to know is who compiled this list and how they intend to use it."

"The who I'm unsure of, the why is obvious. Extortion." Law set the sheet of paper down.

"Are those your Belize accounts?

"It's my bank."

"Oh." How about that. "I had no idea you were so—funded."

"What else is in there?"

"There's one more file—titled duplicate." She clicked on it. As her eyes scrolled through the intricate sequence of letters, numbers and characters, each cross-referenced to a designator.

She turned the laptop toward him and pointed to the long sequences. "These are codes." Then she pointed to the referenced acronyms. "And those are country designations. DPRK and IRP. " Lana thought hard. "Wait—I remember. Democratic People's Republic of Korea and Islamic Republic of Pakistan."

"They're missile codes."

"*What?*"

"Missile launch codes."

"*Nuclear* missiles?"

"Highly probable."

"Oh my God!"

"The codes don't mean a damn thing unless the black box is accessed."

"Law, I overheard Ilya and Pyotr mention a black case that Dragovich possessed. They said if they had it, they'd own the Pacific Rim."

"Fuck."

Quickly he picked up his phone and hit a number. A deep voice answered. "It's me," Law said. "Last month when the consulate in Islamabad was breached, were the computers compromised in any way?

"Officially, no."

"Unofficially?"

"Hacked. Actors unknown but the trail is pointing east."

"Was anything else missing?"

"Rumor on the streets has it that a little black box is on its way to a new home. Working on the location, as we speak."

"Dragovich has the black box," Law pointed out.

"And the codes?"

"I've got them."

"If they're nuke codes, only the Joint Chiefs can reset them."

"What are the chances of that?"

"Depends," the deep voice said after a few seconds. "If the Pakistani government informs the UN Council they've misplaced their box they permanently lose their nukes. I'm betting they're currently in intense negotiations with Drago's agents for its return."

Law glanced at Lana. Her blood warmed despite the fact she didn't want it to. "Those guys were here three nights ago," he told the man on the other end of the call.

"You mean Markov and his lap dog? What did they want?"

"Dirty money of theirs needed cleaning." His eyes narrowed. "And they wanted my guest."

Dark laughter echoed from the phone. "No pussy is worth those nuke codes, brother."

Lana straightened. Maybe that was the case, but the comment was still ugly.

a small smile twitched along Law's lips. "You haven't met her," he said.

"Don't need to. True gave me the heads up. Stay away from the crack, man. It'll kill you."

Law took the call to the other side of the room, lowered his voice and got down to business with the man on the other side.

Several moments later, conversation over, he rejoined her.

"Your friend is crude."

"My brother."

"I didn't know you had living relatives."

"There's a lot about me you don't know."

Wanting to push for answers, Lana chose not to. She was battle weary. Questioning Law always led to an argument.

Looking over what she'd jotted down, Lana glanced up into Law's brooding face. "I don't think Anton knew the importance of the drive," Lana said. "He just had instructions to secure it for Dragovich. I suspect Ilya does."

Just hearing the name made Law tense up. "Bet you could find out."

Lana ignored his implication. "If it helps you to find out if Ilya knows what's in this drive, I'll find out."

"No need. But it's nice to know you'd take one for the team."

For sure, he was being obnoxious. "You don't think much of me, do you?"

He shrugged. "I just thought you were different."

"Different how, Law? Like I didn't have a past?"

Law dodged both questions. "You played me."

"I didn't play you. You never gave me a chance to explain, you just assumed." Leaning toward him, she said, "I didn't agree to leave with Ilya because I wanted him, I agreed because I didn't want you to die."

She saw it, barely perceptible, the spark of shock in his eyes followed by a softening before they returned to their implacable green. Her confession hit Law hard. He didn't expect that and he knew, despite whatever he wanted to think to make his life easier, she told the truth.

"It doesn't matter. It's better this way."

Lana was taken aback. "Better for who, Law? You? Because you're a fucking emotional coward? You decide to think the worst of me so you can walk away like there wasn't something starting here. Fuck you."

He answered calmly. "Better, meaning you don't get hurt."

"Seriously?" Lana had to laugh. "That's rich. So *I* don't get hurt?"

She moved in on him. "Listen, *I* can handle getting hurt. It wouldn't be the first time. But *you* can't." She'd never been more certain that she was right. "And I know why. You're afraid."

CHAPTER THIRTY-NINE

"DON'T TRY and make me your Psych 101 project."

"You're so perfectly fucked up, Law."

"Then we're bookends."

"Not even close. I have abandonment issues. Your problem is you're afraid to feel anything except anger and hate."

"I have feelings just like the next person."

"You're an emotional zombie."

"Okay, so that's been established. You win. I lose."

"It's not about winning or losing, Law. It's about honesty."

"I just agreed with you. How honest do you want me to be?"

Lana blew out a breath releasing some of her frustration with this stubborn man. "You were traumatized early in life." Her voice softened, when he stiffened. "I can't imagine the horror of that day." She reached out to touch Law but he moved away. An injured creature, fearing deeper wounds.

Undeterred, she moved closer to him and placed her hand on his forearm. "I'm sorry."

"For what?"

"For your loss. For how it's affected you."

She knew it took everything he had to stand there and allow her that comforting touch. It made her more determined to keep the contact.

"I don't need your pity."

"I don't pity you. And despite your macho bullshit, I'm kind of in awe of you."

"Hm. I wasn't picking that up. But whatever you say." Law tried to move away from her but she tightened her grip on his forearm.

"Law—I'm going to tell you a secret, but you have to promise not to use it against me."

"What is it?"

"I'm a little more fucked up than I may have lead you to believe."

His brows shot up to his hairline.

"I should have said *was* fucked up. Because I really was far-gone when I was dragged here kicking and screaming. Now, not as much. And I have you to thank for that."

"How is that?" he roughly asked.

"I was in boarding school when I lost my virginity at four-teen, to Ilya."

Law looked extremely uncomfortable.

"Not because I had a schoolgirl crush on him. But because—after Mamita died, father refused to allow me to return home. They just cut me out of their lives. Permanently."

"That's shitty."

"I ran away after that. From Ilya, the parents who threw me away, myself. It didn't help. I didn't have sex again until I was eighteen. It was terrible." She laughed a little. "I thought maybe I wasn't meant to be with men so I tried the other way." His brows rose.

Lana turned around. Leaning against the high sill, she

shrugged. "It actually was better but not much. Better because it didn't hurt."

Emotion played across his face. Anger. Compassion. "Look I get lousy sex isn't a tragedy, for me it was a way I tried to connect and just couldn't. Not with anyone.

"Not even when I tried to force myself to open up. Which never worked. It was like I was watching everything that happened to me through thick glass. Nothing got through."

"Why are you telling me this?"

"Because...even though it got weird, when you and I hooked up the other day, it was the first time in my life when sex ever felt that good. It felt right—crazy right. Like we connected on some surreal plain. I realized that I *could* feel. I *wanted* to feel."

She came back to where he was sitting. Touched his hand. "It was like—I don't know how to say this." She stopped for a few seconds to collect her thoughts. "Like so physical the emotions didn't matter. Fucking like wild animals—wow. I liked it, Law. I liked it a lot."

"Good."

Lana's answering smile faded under his intense stare. No telling what he was thinking. Law was an expert at only allowing her to see what he wanted her to see.

"So. What happens next?"

"We save the world from nuclear meltdown and go back to bed."

He laughed out loud. "You're on."

"I'm willing to do whatever is necessary to bring Drago down," she said.

Reaching to her cheek, he lightly caressed it. "There's been a change of plans. I won't need you after all."

He left it at that and got up, going past her to his bedroom.
Click.

Speechless, Lana stared at the closed door. Did that mean he was releasing her? How crazy was it that she didn't want to go?

When Law reemerged an hour later dressed completely in black, Lana's heart lurched in her chest. His custom tailored suit accentuated every inch of what made him such an impressive male.

"I'd like to take you out to dinner later this evening," he said.

"Like a date?" The minute she said the words she regretted them.

Law shook his head. "Just dinner."

"Oh." Leaning back against the couch cushions, she contemplated his request. "Dinner here in Chimera or outside?"

"Outside."

"Seriously?"

"Yes. But I have one condition. Don't leave my side."

"Meaning…don't try to escape?"

He nodded.

"I agree." And she meant it. Escaping was still on top of her priority list, but not tonight. Tonight she was going to relax and enjoy her sobriety with the hottest man in town.

"I'll be back at six," Law said then left the penthouse.

Hours later, rested, showered, shampooed and painstakingly coiffed and made up, Lana stepped back from the full-length mirror and smiled. Her thick blonde hair hung in long, luxurious waves around her shoulders. Once again she'd gone for smoky eyes and nearly nude glossed lips.

The Versace she wore tonight was a showstopper. The neon blue silk mini dress with a supple leather collar clung to her curves, stopping only a few inches above the matching thigh high suede stiletto boots. This time she'd slipped on a pair of panties. Why not.

The final touch: a grey cashmere wrap trimmed in faux silver fox along with a small silver clutch.

Emerging from her room, she tossed her wrap and purse onto the entry table and then walked into the large living room to find Law admiring the San Francisco skyline. The lights leading the way along the Bay Bridge glowed brightly beneath the moonless sky.

Law turned slightly, his gaze traveling slowly over her.

"What are you thinking?"

He gave her a wry look. "If I told you that you were the most beautiful woman I've ever laid eyes on, it might go to your head."

"Would that be such a bad thing?" Her vanity actually seemed to amuse him. That was a start. "Just go ahead and say it. Repeat after me." She paused and took a deep breath. "I. Am. The. Most. Beautiful. Woman. You. Have. Ever. Seen."

Law's lips twitched.

"Aha. There it is." Pressing her fingers to the edge of his lips, she gently pushed them up. "I know you can really smile, Law."

When he finally did—all the way— his eyes crinkled at the edges and his eyes twinkled. God, what a difference it made. That gorgeous big smile was fleeting, though. So fleeting she wondered if she had imagined it.

"You're a complete mystery to me, Law," she softly said.

"There aren't that many pieces to my puzzle," he answered.

Taking his hand, she pressed it to her cheek, half expecting him to pull away. But he cupped her face, his fingertips caressing her temples. Looking up at his intent stare, she felt something new stir within her, a deeper feeling she couldn't put a name to.

Moving into him, she pressed her lips to the base of his throat, feeling his pulse jump. Desire to soothe this savage beast, to embrace him protectively; to fight his battles for him overcame her.

Then, opening the top two buttons of his shirt, she pressed her lips to his heart. "Nothing breaks as hard as a heart."

Law's strong hands slid down her back to the rise of her butt. Lowering his nose to her hair, he inhaled. "You can't unbreak me, Alana."

"I don't want to fix you, Law."

"What *do* you want?"

"Your trust."

That broke the spell. Lana cocked her head, trying to catch Law's gaze but he refused to look at her. He stepped back and briskly buttoned his shirt. Picking up her silver clutch, he settled the wrap around her shoulders, then extended his arm to her.

Instead of going through the front penthouse door, Law led her around the slate fireplace and pressed his hand to the secret elevator panel.

Standing back, he waited for her to enter and followed.

The doors quietly closed and they were quickly whisked upward.

The car came to an easy stop in less than a minute and the door slid open to the cold swirl of damp December air.

CHAPTER FORTY

THE ROOFTOP at night was stunning to behold. Shimmering lights glowed, silhouetting the infinity pool. The entertainment area with tables, chaises and bar was softly illuminated. Majestic topiaries added texture to the skyline. No one was there. The emptiness seemed odd. But then, this didn't seem to be their destination.

Taking her elbow, he moved her further around. To the helipad. The first time she'd seen it, nothing was there. Now a helicopter stood at the ready.

"Your chariot awaits," Law said, guiding her toward the sleek black chopper.

"We're flying in that?"

"Yup."

Law brought her to the left side of the chopper, opened the door and assisted her into the front seat. "Where's the pilot?" she asked, wondering why she was sitting up front when there were three larger seats behind the two in the cockpit.

"You're looking at him."

Her jaw dropped.

Law grinned, reached over her and strapped her in. Once he came around the other side and climbed in, he handed her a headset, which she put on. Law strapped in and put his on as well. He started flicking switches and pressing buttons. The rotor slowly began to move.

Lana had flown in private jets but nothing like this. The cockpit and what she could see of the cabin was pure designer luxury. Deeply cushioned black leather seats, hidden compartments and recessed consoles. The displays on the dashboard glowed brilliantly in the darkness. A glass partition separated the cockpit and three-seat cabin.

The rain had stopped. The sound of the turning rotor was not nearly as loud as she thought it would be. But they still needed headsets to hear each other.

"This is very cool, Law," she said.

He nodded as he continued to check gauges and flip switches above their heads and on the dashboard. It never occurred to Lana to question Law's competence as a pilot. She doubted there was anything he couldn't do, in fact.

Afraid she might distract him, Lana refrained from asking questions as the engines warmed up.

Ten minutes later, Law said, "Here we go," as they slowly lifted from the roof. In another cool move, Law moved the control stick to the right. Flying at an angle, they powered into the wind and were off. Lana leaned forward, catching her breath for a moment when she looked down through the glass bottom of the cockpit. The bay sped by beneath her feet.

They were heading south. "Where are we going?" she asked.

"That's a surprise."

They continued south, past San Jose, over the foothills to 101. Several times, Lana glanced at Law, to find him completely oblivious to her.

He was, she observed, in deep thought. Thinking about her? Maybe. She guessed Law would not let her go. Not until he had what he wanted: Dragovich.

"What's your new plan for Dragovich?"

"The less you know, the better for you."

"If you don't need me as bait, will you let me go?"

When Law didn't answer, not wanting an argument, she didn't push it.

Twenty minutes later Law expertly landed the chopper on a helipad near what appeared to be a private residence.

Once he shut down the rotor, he unhooked his belts and reached over to unhook her. Taking her headset off, Lana carefully set it on the hook Law had originally taken it from.

When he came around and opened the door for her, she turned to step out. Before she could, he slid his hands beneath her wrap and hoisted her up and out, setting her carefully on the damp asphalt.

A blacked-out Suburban waited for them at the edge of the pad.

Helping her in, Law silently slipped in beside her. They drove off.

It wasn't too long before the SUV rolled to a slow stop. Law slid out and came around, extended his hand to Lana. She took it and smiled hesitantly, realizing where they were: Carmel-by-the-Sea. The last time she was here, her world had collapsed. Long suppressed memories stirred in her heart. Her hands trembled. Suddenly she couldn't breath.

"Are you OK?" Law softly asked.

Nodding, she forced the memories from her mind, out of her heart. Made peace with the fact that they would always be there, lurking in the shadows until she faced them. She realized with clarity and no fear that she would. But tonight was not that night.

She smiled brightly. Intuitively she knew that tonight was a big step for them both. Law had broken his rules repeatedly. She had gotten under his skin.

What did Law have planned? A romantic getaway? An introduction to more of his business associates? Was he finally, officially letting her in?

Taking her hand, Law walked with her into Michel's, a chic peninsula eatery. He was greeted by a grey-haired gentleman, who shook Law's hand and nodded to Lana, taking her wrap. He showed them to a private alcove near a roaring fireplace.

Law held her chair as she sat down. Before she could say a word, a server appeared and poured two glasses of chilled artesian water, placed a lovely charcuterie board on the table.

A sommelier appeared next, presenting wines for her and Law, explaining a little about each one of them before he disappeared.

It was as if the staff understood they were to interact on the barest of levels while offering impeccable service. Including another tray of appetizers that seemed to magically appear, just after the sommelier opened their wine.

Law did the sniffy thing, approved the bottle, and handed Lana a full glass before he lifted his to clink to hers. "Cheers."

Lana sipped her wine. "Mmm, this is good."

"Yes, it is. And don't forget the tray. Eat something."

Daintily, Lana helped herself to the yummy cuts of meat, and imported cheeses. As she nibbled slowly she flushed under Law's considering stare.

"Why are you staring at me like that?"

Law took a sip of wine as he pondered her question. "Just wondering how the beautiful demure girl sitting across from me can switch to the blazing sexpot who frantically fucked me three nights ago."

"You're crude."

"Am I?"

"Yes."

"But you told me exactly what you wanted, Lana. Fucking first." He raised his glass. "And I have to say it was epic fucking."

Setting her fork down, she stared at him. "Why did you bring me here?"

"Don't you want to be out?"

"Of course I do. It just doesn't fit with your hide-me-away-at-all-costs obsession."

"I've given a lot of consideration to many things these last few days," he said.

"Which means...you figured out that keeping me hostage is wrong?"

"Working on that. Right now I have something for you, Lana." Slowly he withdrew a small box from his trouser pocket and set it down on the table. With two fingers he slid it toward her.

"What is it?"

"Open it and find out."

"Oh, okay." Why was she so nervous? But she opened the box. Her brows drew together. A graphite flash drive lay nestled among gold tissue paper.

"What is this?"

"Your key out of here."

"I don't understand."

"Your freedom."

"What are you saying?" she breathed.

"I destroyed your contract, Alana. Your new identity is on that drive. You're free to start your life over wherever you choose."

Her heart sunk. Unexpected pain twisted inside her. Edged with fear. And panic. She wanted her freedom, of course, but she didn't want to leave. Yes, she was fucking crazy. "What am I going to do?"

"Whatever you want to do."

"I'm not ready," she said, hoping to stall the inevitable.

"You've always been ready, Lana."

"But...I don't want to go."

"You need to go," he insisted softly.

"Why?"

"Because if you stay, you'll end up hating me more than you do now."

"I don't hate you, Law!"

"You will."

"You can't predict the future."

"I know that I can't give you what you want."

"Really. So what do you think I want?"

"A man who's all in."

Now she was getting angry. "I never said that. And anyway, you can't be that man."

He took a long sip of wine. "Why not?"

"Because all you ever think about is getting revenge."

"Maybe that's because it's all I have."

"No, it's not. You're hiding behind it, Law. We all have ways of not letting go of our pain. That's yours."

He waved that away. "I'm not going to argue the point. But whatever happens in my life from here on can't involve you. I don't want you to get hurt."

"Because you have feelings for me?"

His jaw tightened. Looking past her, he said, "No."

Lana wanted to scream. She was such a fool to ever think a man as damaged as Law could have feelings for her.

"How can you just let me go? Aren't there bad guys waiting to sink their teeth into me? Or was that all a lie too?"

"True is out front with hard copies of the documents in the flash drive and cash. Disappear, Alana. Become the person you always wanted to be. It's the only way you'll survive."

"For the first time since I was eleven years old I want to be Alana Monroe Conti. I'm not hiding from my life for another minute, Law."

Slamming his fist on the table, he speared her with a glare. "I can't protect Alana Conti in the real world, damn it. I can only protect you if you're locked up in Chimera. I'm not doing that to you."

"I don't need you to protect me."

Law opened his mouth to speak but she shushed him with a wave of her hand. "I need you to teach me how to protect myself, Law. If I can protect myself then you won't have to worry. If you aren't worrying then there is nothing we can't achieve!"

Incredulously he stared at her. He didn't see their future the way she did. Didn't he know that together they were stronger, better, smarter than apart? She wasn't going down without a fight.

"I'm not boyfriend material."

"I don't want a boyfriend, Law. I want a partner."

His eyes narrowed as her words sunk in.

"Equal, no bullshit, straight up trust."

"You've lost your mind."

"We're each others ride or die."

"Don't romanticize what I do."

"I'm not. I know you're a bad guy who does bad stuff. I also know you're a good guy who does good stuff. You can keep doing your bad stuff and I'll pick up the good stuff."

"No."

"Okay fine. I'll do the bad stuff, so long as it's to badder people and you can do all the good stuff."

Law threw back the rest of his wine. "I'm sorry, Lana, but there are no deals to be made here. I work alone."

"What about Drago? How are you going to get him without me as bait?"

"I've made other arrangements."

"Bullshit." Scooting closer to him, she grasped his forearm. The thick cords of his muscles tightened. "I'll call a news conference. Out myself. My parents wouldn't dare touch me once I go public. Dragovich will lose interest in me when he realizes he can't use the former me to get to my father. We can do this damn it! Why can't you see it?"

Leaning into her, he flatly said, "Let me make myself clear: There is nothing between us. There never has been. You served a purpose. That purpose has been served."

She blanched as each word tore into her. "So this is it?" she asked unbelieving that he could mean what he just said and just walk out her life as if she never existed. Was he truly that dead in side?

He nodded. "End of the road for us."

"When does my freedom begin?"

"Now."

Sucker-punched, she blinked back a rush of tears, angry with herself for not wanting to leave him even after his you-mean-nothing-to-me declaration.

"I—don't have—never mind."

Sipping her wine, misty-eyed, she forced a smile. She wasn't going to grovel. She should be good and pissed. Show him she didn't give a fuck. But she did give a fuck. Too many fucks. Setting her glass down, she slowly stood. Law stood as well.

The tactful host appeared with her wrap in an instant. She took it from him, utterly miserable, gazing at Law.

He was unreachable. This big, angry, hurting man would never be hers.

She would have done anything for him, now that the worst was over. But he would never let her.

"Thank you for saving me. Twice." Placing her hand to his cheek, she rose up on her toes and touched her lips to his. "Goodbye, Law."

CHAPTER FORTY-ONE

WHEN SHE EXITED, True emerged from the shadows, startling her. Was it a trick? Part of her wanted it to be — she didn't want to leave Law. But it was for the best. His tragic past had created a lone wolf incapable of loving her the way she wanted to be loved.

Fresh tears welled. True extended his hand to her. She took it, and in an unexpected move, he gathered her into his arms and held her. Fighting back tears, she allowed herself this last bit of comfort.

"I have a passport, funds and other documents for you to start your new life," he said.

She didn't want a new life as someone else. She wanted her life, with Law in it.

Backing out of his embrace, Lana shook her head. "I don't want another life, True."

"You don't have a choice."

"The hell I don't!"

"But—" True tried to take her arm, but Lana yanked it away.

She swiftly moved past him and started walking away. "Where are you going?" True called to her.

"Wherever the hell I want."

Lacking funds, wherever the hell she wanted to go would be limited. That was fine. Lana had a deep bag of tricks to draw from. The determined click of her heels on the cold sidewalk echoed eerily on the quiet street. It was late. A harsh ocean breeze swirled around her bare thighs, up her skirt. Lana pulled her wrap tighter around herself.

She wasn't unfamiliar with Carmel-by-the-Sea.

Anxiety scratched at her. Old nightmares swirled in her mind's eye.

"Remember the love," she whispered. "Remember the love."

There was a house several blocks down the beach. A house where she had spent many summers.

A house where everything good ended and everything bad began. *Remember the love.*

Wistfully she thought back to the good days. Innocence was a lovely thing. She and her sister Miranda, would play for hours in the shallow surf, under Mamita's watchful gaze. Most days her father joined them. It was the only time she could ever remember him smiling.

She could hear his deep laughter as he chased her and Miranda into the surf. Pretending to be a shark. Mamita chastising him in Spanish not to scare the girls. He'd grab them, one in each arm and run back to where Mamita sat beneath a striped beach umbrella. Bright smiles. Carefree happiness.

She saw the past for the first time as a woman with similar feelings. The way Mamita gazed adoringly at Daddy. The way he beamed down at her. Caressed her long dark hair. They had loved each other. Deeply. How had such a loving man become so cold?

They'd spent every day on the beach with no fear of mother joining them. Mother would rather die than allow a ray of sunshine to touch her lily-white skin. Daddy was happy to gaze unabashedly upon Mamita.

She was beautiful. Dark hair, black eyes. Soft almond-hued skin. When Mamita graced you with her loving smile, you felt special. Her touch was warm and gentle. Her voice soft and lilting. Mamita was unconditional love. In hindsight, how could she condemn her father for loving her?

Blinking back salty tears, Lana realized she had so much more to be thankful to Mamita for than she realized.

Mamita encouraged her to take her first toddling steps. Ride her bike and get back on her pony, Montezuma, when he threw her off the first time. It was Mamita who picked her up from school when she was sick. Who made her homemade soup and gave her medicine. Mamita infused Lana with love and warmth. Provided a safe place to heal the many wounds inflicted upon her by her mother.

Her heart ached. For the woman who cared for her as if she were her own biological daughter, for the father who put politics above his daughters, but mostly for the man who refused to love her: Law.

He'd gotten under her skin and into her heart. A sob tore from her chest. How was that even possible?

She'd need serious psychotherapy to answer that question, and yet, she didn't care. It didn't matter why or how, what mattered was how he made her feel.

He made her feel safe. Her body warmed despite the chilly air. She loved how he made her body come alive when he touched her. Craved the hot intensity of his gaze, knowing he wanted her. That despite his fear of feeling, he felt as deeply as she did.

Lana dared to think of what it would be like for Law to give himself over completely. To trust her with his heart. His life. His soul. She would give him all of her in return.

Abruptly she stopped. All her life, all she wanted was to matter enough to someone. Not just anyone. A truly good man who would love and respect her. Someone who would stand by her no matter what, just as she would stand by him. Law was implacable. He reused to heal from his past. The irony of that thought didn't go unnoticed. How could she expect from him what she herself was unwilling to do: Exorcise her demons.

Just thinking about it terrified her.

On the verge of a full-blown anxiety attack, Lana inhaled deeply then slowly exhaled as she had taught herself to do. She wasn't strong enough to face the past. It was ugly. Horrifying. Her fault. *Her* fault Mamita was dead!

How could she face that? How could she forgive herself for causing the death of someone she adored?

"It's not your fault, preciosa*," Mamita's voice softly chastised.* "Te amo mucho. Vas. *Be happy."*

One last time, Lana looked over her shoulder. Her breath hitched high in her throat. The silhouette of a man at the top of the street startled her.

Law.

Every muscle in her body twitched, wanting to run to him. Her heart thumped wildly, wanting to be loved by him. Seconds ticked by. Realizing she was waiting for him to make the move he would never make, Lana stiffened. Slowly, she turned on her heels, and continued to walk.

Her boots weren't made for walking. Lana yanked them off and carried them. It was barefoot or blister city. As she neared the end of Ocean Drive, she glanced left and right. Eerie shadows shrouded the tree-lined beach entrance.

The soothing sound of the waves rushed over her. She loved the beach. The salty air. The feel of the coarse sand squishing between her toes. The sound of the gulls in the morning as they flew overhead, searching for their morning meal. Most of all, she loved her memories of this place.

Lana found herself walking toward her parents' house. Did they still own it?

She had a vague recollection of the argument they had over the house. Mother wanted to sell it. Father wouldn't hear of it.

Why? Why when the woman he loved was murdered there?

She saw the sprawling beach house and memories came flooding back. Good twisted with terrifying.

Her and Miranda, stealing the caretaker's gate key to the beach just before dawn. Mamita screaming. Blood on her hands. Blood on the wall. Blood everywhere.

Happy thoughts, think happy thoughts.

One morning she and Miranda had returned to find the gate locked. Panicking, they tried climbing the high fence and failed. They huddled together knowing they were going to get their butts kicked. Though when the gate was opened, Mr. Stan the caretaker only tsked-tsked at them. Then he showed them where he hid a key beneath a faux rock near an evergreen, draped white fairy lights on a timer, dusk to dawn. Tonight the evergreen was dark. Was anyone home?

The key was still hidden exactly in the same place where Mr. Stan had showed them. Quietly, Lana worked it into the old lock, corroded now from rust and salt. But it unlocked.

Just as she pushed through the gate, the unmistakable sound of a helicopter coming her way overrode the sound of the waves.

The sleek black chopper in the air above belonged to only one person, who couldn't see her.

As she watched the lights disappear into the darkness of the night, Lana froze. The approaching growl of some sort of vehicle slowed. Then judging by the sound, the driver turned onto Ocean Ave, where she had just come from. Hurrying, she slipped through the gate, locking it, just as a blacked-out quad came prowling down the beach.

She ducked down to watch it through the fence slats. The low-slung vehicle rumbled along, the unseen driver flashing a flashlight along the sand. Who was in it? Were they looking for her? As it neared where she had turned toward the house, it slowed to a stop. Light flashed up to the fence.

Crouching as low as she could, Lana quietly made her way through the back yard to Mr. Stan's bungalow. Recessed outdoor lights, undoubtedly on timers, illuminated the small structure as well as the house. Instinctively, Lana knew no one was home.

The shaking of the gate startled her. They were coming for her. Lana glanced down at her damp footprints. Shit. Quickly, she made her way to the bungalow and reached up over the door-frame for a key. Nothing.

Quietly she lifted several planters before she finally found the key. Slipping inside, she went directly to the kitchen and opened the drawer near the sink. Bingo. She scooped up the house keys and the keys to the caretaker's old Range Rover in the front garage.

Slipping back out, she flattened herself against the exterior wall and listened. The sound of the retreating quad was barely audible over the low roar of the waves.

Exhaling a sigh of relief, Lana hurried to the back of the house.

Lana just stood there for a long moment. Twice she turned to leave, twice she turned back to the door.

She couldn't go back on the beach. She couldn't—didn't

want to go inside—but ghosts from the past called to her. She had to face them once and for all.

Slowly she inserted the key. It didn't occur to her until she slipped into the kitchen and locked the door behind her that there might be an alarm. She knew where the panel was. The code...

She stared at the little red light on the panel as it began to flash. On a hunch she punched in 1-3-0-3. Her birthday and month. The red light disappeared, replaced by the solid green.

Lana closed her eyes and took a deep breath in relief. The faint scent of lilies caressed her senses. Mamita's favorite flower.

Lana moved from the kitchen to the dining room, down the back hall, to the last door on the right.

Hand on the knob, she slowly opened it and gasped.

In the full moonlight, a large bouquet of wilted white stargazer lilies dominated the room. Numerous others covered the bedspread, the pillows and floor. They weren't fresh but they weren't dried up either. Someone had lovingly placed them here within the last few weeks.

Fighting back panic Lana told herself to just look. Not react. Not remember. At least not the bad things. Just the good.

The warmth of Mamita's embrace enfolded her. Closing her eyes, Lana swayed, smiling as the remembered feelings stirred.

Flashes of mother's sharp voice dispelled the treasured memory.

Taking a deep cleansing breath, Lana gazed around the room. It was immaculate. No dust or cobwebs. No covered furniture. The opposite. Every piece as Lana remembered it was clean and polished. The faint scent of beeswax mingled with the fragrant lilies.

Who had been here? Who brought the flowers? Who cleaned Mamita's room? Old Mr. Stan, the caretaker?

No, she couldn't see him lovingly place the flowers

throughout the room. Hair spiked along Lana's neck and arms. It could be only one of two people. Miranda or…her father?

Would Miranda dare to after mother sent her away, forbidding her to ever return? Momentary excitement grasped her. Had Law found her sister? She had no way of knowing. But if mother knew Miranda had been here…

A small silver framed picture on the nightstand gleamed faintly, catching her eye. Slowly she walked toward it and gasped. It was of Mamita looking adoringly up at father with Miranda in her arms.

The likeness was undeniable. Miranda was as blonde as their father. Same blue eyes. But she had her mother's creamy almond colored skin.

How furious mother would be if she knew this picture existed.

Reaching for it, Lana stared at the lovers. What was it like, to love so deeply and live with the secret?

Why hadn't father just divorced mother?

Lana set the picture back where it was and picked up another behind it. It was of Mamita and her and Miranda. On the beach. Taken by her father the day Mamita died.

Pressing it to her chest, Lana moved from the room, slowly shutting the door behind her.

Leaning against the wall, stumbling down the hall, Lana tightened her grip on the picture.

She didn't know what to do. Where to go. Who to turn to. Not her parents. She had no clue if her sister was dead or alive. And Law? He'd made it crystal clear he didn't want her in his life.

Tears streamed down her cheeks. A sob caught in her throat when she opened her eyes and realized where she was standing. At the bottom of the stairway—where Mamita died.

Her knees gave. She cried out in anguish.

...blood on the wall... blood on her hands....

"Look what you've done, Alana!" her mother screeched from the top of the wide stairway.

"No!" she screamed. Mamita's dark eyes staring up at her, silently begging for help.

There at the bottom of the stairway, Lana's years of guilt, anguish and heartache surfaced. She sobbed. Screamed. Pounded her thighs, pulled her hair. Dug her nails into her arms demanding why. *"Why? God? Why?"*

Clutching the picture to her chest, sobbing uncontrollably, she dropped to her knees and rocked back and forth.

Curling up into a tight ball, Lana began to hum. Then softly sang, *"A dormer, a dormer, a dormer, mi benito, que tus sueronos sean siempre, de amor, carino y paz a dormir mi bebe—"* Lana still knew the words— *"que los angels van, a cantarte y cuidarte, para que duermas en paz."*

Other memories came back to her. The copper tang of blood. Feeling the sticky wetness as it dried on her hands. Mamita's cold body as Lana shook her, begging her to say something. Anything.

Her father taking her away. The doctor injecting her. Sleep. She woke up alone in a hospital. And ran away. They took her home to Marin. She ran away again. They sent her to Em Pratt. Oddly there she felt safe. Detached.

She didn't know how long she lay there. It was still dark when she was slowly roused by the sound of a door handle being rattled. Opening her swollen eyes, Lana could see the silhouette of a man at the back window across the hall.

The sound of metal on metal, a lock being picked sparked instant fear. Instinct told her it wasn't a random break-in. They were looking for something specific. *Her.*

Lana froze.

Then came to life. As the intruder slipped into the house, Lana moved down the long hallway to the garage door. And inside.

As she quietly closed the door behind her, she realized she didn't have the keys to the Range Rover. She must have dropped them when she collapsed in the hallway.

Fighting back panic, she stood still for a few seconds as her eyes adjusted to the dark.

Praying the Range Rover was unlocked, keys under the mat, Lana looked over her shoulder to see a flash of light through the beveled glass of the door.

Feeling her way toward the car, she found the door handle and pulled. Relief flooded her. It was unlocked. The dome light glowed softly. Thank god. The battery wasn't dead.

The keys had been stashed behind the sun flap. She slipped into the front seat and tried to start the engine. Nothing.

Another flash of light from inside the garage. She ducked down as cautious footsteps slowly approached. Tensing herself to act fast, with all her might, she flung the door open and slammed it hard against the man behind it.

Lana didn't wait to find out who it was or if he was hurt. She ran from the garage through the house back toward the gate and to the beach, spotting the quad, parked but still running. She hopped on it, figured out quick how to put it in gear, opened the throttle and sped down the beach.

A hidden helicopter rose from behind trees separating several homes and the public beach area. Glancing over her shoulder to give Law the finger, she screamed. It wasn't Law's chopper. It didn't sound the same. Lana drove pell-mell beneath the windswept cypresses along the beach. She needed to get out of here. Find a way back to Chimera. It was the only place she would be safe.

Once she could no longer hear the chopper, Lana found her way back by some miracle, pulling over at Michel's. Shivering in the misty rain, she made her way to the alley behind the restaurant.

Quietly, she opened the back door and came face to face with kitchen staffers—and the guy who'd served them.

"I need to get to Oakland," she called into the kitchen. Pushing the door wide open so that the idling quad was visible, she added, "See that? It goes to whoever gets an Uber here first."

CHAPTER FORTY-TWO

TWO HOURS LATER, emotionally raw and physically bedraggled, Lana exited the Uber the quad exchange paid for, made her way to the security gate that lead to the Chimera compound and demanded she be allowed entrance.

The burly guard shook his head. "No entry unless you have a pass or have been cleared."

With what little strength she had left, Lana stepped into the big guy's space. Wide-eyed, he stood his ground. The top of her head barely reached his chin. But she poked him in the chest with her index finger.

"Listen to me. You call Law and tell him Alana Conti is here and if he knows what's good for him, he'll let me in." Crossing her arms over her chest, she nodded toward the state-of-the-art security system behind him. "Now, please. I'm tired, cold and have to pee."

Moments later, instead of Law, Jhett rode up on a tricked-out trike. The heavy gate slowly opened, but Jhett slowed to a stop, looking at Lana.

Lana went over to her. "I want to see Law."

Jhett looked uncomfortable. "Sorry, Lana, he's not here."

"I can see the blades of his helicopter on the roof. Don't lie to me."

"I'm not. He took off in his boat."

"Jhett, if you care about him, even a little bit, you need to let me in."

"He's not reachable, Lana."

"I don't believe that either."

Obviously reluctant to help, Jhett wouldn't meet Lana's eyes. "He'll kick me out if I betray him."

Lana fumed, barely able to control herself. "You're not betraying him!"

"He gave express orders not to let you in if you came back."

"Oh, did he?" Jhett's comment added fuel to her flame. Lana hauled back her fist and punched Jhett so hard on the chin, she knocked her off the trike.

On the ground, Jhett gasped for breath, momentarily unable to fight back. Lana hopped on the trike, throttled it and drove straight for the open gate.

"Let her pass!" Jhett screamed at the guard who leveled his weapon at Lana.

Lana veered to the right, leaving them in the dust as she blasted over a low structure in the way, not giving a shit. The wildly jiggling side mirrors reflected a storm of brilliant sparks as she sped away, coughing from the smoke of burning insulation, realizing that she'd smashed the electrical connection to the guardhouse.

Lucky accident. For the moment, there was no connection to the main compound and no security cams. But they'd come after her soon enough. Fucking Law and his paranoid bullshit protocols.

Lana raced toward the water, searching for the dock she'd

seen from the penthouse. Things looked different down on the ground.

Lana slid off the machine and put it in park, but didn't turn off the ignition. She had to make it disappear. It was just Jhett's tough luck that her expensive toy was going for a swim.

Served her right, Lana thought angrily. Dragging it by the handlebars onto a slipway by the dock, she revved it, then moved to the back and shoved it with all her strength. The trike jerked and rolled down the slipway, sinking fast.

Just like that, it was gone. A few bubbles rose inside widening circles on the surface of the water about five feet out. Good enough.

She had to disappear herself. Lana went toward a tall, shaggy shrub, one of many that served as a windbreak, she figured. Getting scratched, not caring, she squeezed into a hidden opening within its branches.

Hours passed. She heard searchers at first. Held still, held her breath. After a while—Lana didn't know exactly when—there were none.

Her cape was soggy and cold. She couldn't feel her toes. Her hands ached, her face was stiff. From where she was, she could see frost on the planks leading to the bay.

Closing her eyes, she curled up inside the shrub and waited.

Through the haze of utter exhaustion, Lana heard the deep rumble of a boat engine, then movement against the dock. Unable to open her eyes, she tried to call to Law, tell him where she was, but she couldn't. A dark chasm of unconsciousness engulfed her.

The darkness faded.

Strong arms held her. Vital warmth infused her. Angry voices cursed, accused, commanded. She was moving. Slowly coming back, Lana peered up into Law's worried green eyes.

"You can't push me out, Law," she whispered.

"Be quiet," he roughly commanded.

Closing her eyes, Lana smiled. "You know you like me."

When she awoke, she was in her bed. Dry, warm, naked but not afraid. Knowing what she was capable of, what she would tolerate and what she would not, Lana slipped from the warmth of her bed and took a short silk robe from the armoire. Tightening the sash around her waist, she opened the door and went into the penthouse.

Monty looked up from what he was doing in the kitchen and smiled. "I'm so glad you came back."

"So am I."

Awkwardly, he came around from the counter and hugged her. "Law is too. Even though he won't admit it."

Lana smiled and hugged him back. "I hope so."

"I have food for you."

"Thank you, I'm starving. What time is it?" she asked, looking toward the high windows. Fog hovered over the bay.

"Four. You've been asleep all day."

The private elevator door opened. Law exited the car and stopped as Monty hurried into the kitchen. Lana glared at Law, hands on her hips. "How dare you abandon me like that?"

"I didn't abandon you."

"Yes you did! And then you flew off! You left me there, Law, at the mercy of a bad guy you told me you were trying to protect me from."

"You weren't in any danger."

"The hell I wasn't."

"You're microchipped. I knew exactly where you were."

"*What*?!"

He shrugged. "I'm not apologizing for it."

"Where is it?"

"Your arm. Doc implanted it when he sewed you up."

How dare they. Holy fuck—she'd remove it herself if she had to claw it out with her fingernails. Later. "Did you know I was followed?"

Law only scowled.

"Some guy tried to kill me!"

He shook his head. "That was one of my men following you, keeping an eye on you. You banged him up good."

"Following me why?

"To make sure you didn't do something foolish."

"Listen, Law, you can't let me go and then monitor me. I'm either free or I'm not. Which is it?"

"You're free, but until you assume a new identity you're at risk."

Right. He'd better not try to hand her all those counterfeit documents again. If she got caught with those, she'd end up behind bars in a filthy cell. Which could actually be an improvement on Law's gorgeous prison. At least she'd have a right to a lawyer.

At the moment, though, she had other reasons to refuse him. "I don't want a new identity."

"It's the only way you'll have a chance to live a normal life."

"I don't want to live a normal life."

Law stared at her, incredulous. Lana knew she sounded crazy but it was true. "I want to be here, with you, for you."

"Alana," he softly said, "There is no place for you here."

"You're wrong about that, Law. My place *is here*." She punctuated the statement by pointing at the floor beneath their feet.

When he didn't respond she moved closer. "Since you were

five years old, Law, you have lived for one reason and one reason only: Destroy the man who destroyed your family."

His face darkened as she continued. "You act the almighty protector, but have you asked *any* of your people if they're in? If they're willing to sacrifice their lives for your revenge? They should know what they're getting themselves into."

He said nothing.

Monty stepped into the room from the kitchen where he had been readying Lana's meal. "I am," he said and disappeared. Lana's heart swelled.

Taking Law's hand, she said, "I am too. And I choose to stand with you, Law. Let me be part of your plan."

When he didn't answer, she cocked her head to the side and said, "Teamwork makes the dream work."

"You're not cut out for this kind of life."

"You don't get to decide that, Law!"

"I don't want your death on my conscience."

"Why didn't my life matter a month ago but it does now?"

"He likes you too much," Monty said from the kitchen.

"Mind your own business, Monty," Law growled.

"You saved me, Law," Monty said, moving back into the room. "Let Lana save you."

Lana stared at him. That was the last thing she'd ever expect Monty to say. But he'd said it.

"I don't need saving," Law firmly said.

Shaking his head, Monty looked fiercely at Law and said, "I thought you were the smartest man in the world."

For the first time in a very long time, Lana thought, Law was rendered speechless.

"It's not that easy," Law argued.

"Law." Lana took a deep breath and went for it. "We're

simply asking you to allow us in. To stand with you. For you. Because you need us."

"I don't need anyone."

Lana opened her mouth to debate that point but Law put his hand up. "No more arguing. I am who I am. Now, if you'll both excuse me, I have a club to get ready for New Year's Eve." He turned and headed to his bedroom.

"I'm going too!" she called after him.

When he didn't say no, Lana turned to Monty and smiled. For such a shitty beginning, the day was looking up.

An hour later, the fog had thickened into dark clouds. A storm forecast didn't deter Lana.

Dressed in a sexy, gold sequin mini-dress and strappy gladiator heels, Lana strutted her stuff into the living room. As she poured herself and Law a shot each of his favorite scotch, a deafening thud—from the roof?—reverberated through the room. Another noise—rotors, she thought, puzzled, high in the air—faded away. She looked up, scared. A split second later, Law appeared in the living room. "Did you hear that?"

"Yes—what's going on?" She moved to find out but he stopped her with his arm.

"Get away from the windows!" He slid his phone from his pocket, tapped an icon and the metal shutters protectively dropped. Striding toward the elevator, Law tapped another icon on his phone. "Fuck!" He ran to the private elevator. Lana followed him. "Stay here."

"I'm going with you," she insisted. Seconds later they reached the rooftop.

"Keep the door open," Law ordered.

Cold slanted rain hit them as Law ran across the vast roof, out of sight. Long minutes passed. When Law didn't return, Lana leaned out and peeked around the corner.

Her heart nearly stopped at the sight of Law, bent against the wind, carrying the broken body of Sienna. Lana screamed his name, pushing the automatic door back into its slot. "Get in!"

Law didn't rush. "She's dead."

Blood trickled from the corner of her mouth. Nasty bruises along swollen cheeks told the story of her torture.

"Law," Lana cried, encircling Law and Sienna with her arms and body as if she could protect them from the evil that had done this.

Law looked down at her, his deep green eyes filled with tears. Throwing his head back, he howled in pain. The agonized sound tore her apart. There was nothing they could do but go back down.

Ever so gently, Law laid Sienna down onto the dining room table, as if she were only sleeping. The sight was heartbreaking. Lana hurried to her room and pulled the white duvet from her bed to cover Sienna.

Smoothing the dead woman's damp bangs from her face, Lana observed the brutal evidence of Sienna's struggle to survive. She'd been beaten. Savagely. Her torn clothes suggested sexual violation—the blood under her fingernails that she'd fought to the end, still alive. But what had killed her was most likely the impact of being dropped onto the roof. From the helicopter Lana had heard. A sob caught in her throat.

Raising her eyes to Law, she said, "I'm so sorry."

Nodding mutely, he turned away and in minutes the penthouse was full. Jhett, who screamed and fell apart on Sienna's body, True, who stoically held Jhett and then pressed his lips to Sienna's forehead, and Monty, who wrung his hands and cried in silence. Treva—who Lana had not seen in weeks—began to care for Jhett since True, despite his best intentions, was out of his element comforting the heartbroken woman.

Law stood apart, watching, allowing his grief-stricken friends to be with Sienna for the last time. But Lana doubted he saw or heard. The Law she knew was already planning a retaliatory strike.

Quietly, Lana moved toward him. Taking his hand, she squeezed it. "Tell me what to do, Law."

"If you don't want to end up like Sienna, you need to go. Now."

"I'm not leaving."

For a long moment, Law stared at her. Contemplating how he could convince her to leave. She was dug in. No one or nothing could convince her to go. Steering her into the living room, Law slid his hand into his front trouser pocket and withdrew a crumpled piece of paper.

"This was stuffed in Sienna's mouth."

Carefully Lana took it from him and opened it. 'The Dragon travels for no one.'

"Oh my God, Law!"

Her outburst brought True over. "Dragovich?" he asked.

Law shook his head. "Markov."

"Ilya?" Lana gasped. "Are you sure? Why?"

"His time to deliver Dragovich was up last night. We hit him hard this morning. He hit back harder tonight."

"What are you going to do?"

"Kill him."

CHAPTER FORTY-THREE

LAW AND TRUE exited the penthouse. Lana got to work. Helping Treva console Jhett was no small feat. Jhett was hysterical, trying to pull Sienna's body into her lap. Kissing her, petting her, crying uncontrollably, blaming herself for her death.

Lana looked at Treva with the silent question: Do we sedate her?

Treva excused herself but returned a few minutes later. Without Jhett even realizing it, Treva poked her in the arm with a needle and injected her with something. Moments later, Jhett's speech began to slur, then her breathing slowed.

"Let's take her to my room," Lana said. Together they removed Jhett's boots and leather jacket and maneuvered her comfortably onto the bed. Lana covered her and left the door slightly ajar. When they went back into the dining room, Lana said, "What do we do now?"

"Law will take care of Sienna. Are you okay?" Treva asked.

Nodding, Lana said, "I think so."

"Monty," Treva called to him. His head popped around the corner from the living room.

"Yes?" His voice was raspy with emotion.

"Can you get more blankets, please?"

"Yes."

A minute later he was back with a stack of blankets.

"Let's get Sienna cleaned up and wrapped up nice and warm."

Wordlessly the three of them got to work.

Just as they were tucking the blanket around Sienna's body, the private elevator opened. Law, True and a mountain of a man strode from it. Lana wondered how all of that testosterone fit into the small elevator car.

The stranger stopped in his tracks as his gaze settled on Lana. "Your new lady?" he asked Law.

True raised an eyebrow, but Law only nodded. "Alana, this is my brother, Brick."

Brick was a brother from another mother. He was an exceptional mix of African American and Caucasian, his fawn colored skin and intense green eyes a striking contrast. He was older by several years, taller, broader, and instinctively, Lana knew, not much like Law.

Maybe he meant well, but Lana didn't like the way he referred to her. Like there had been so many others. Like the women of Chimera didn't count. But she was willing to give him the benefit of the doubt for Law's sake—just not yet.

Brick smiled slightly, showing straight white teeth. "Nice to meet you."

Lana gave him a nod and let it go at that.

Law guided his brother and True into the room where Sienna's body lay. Lana stayed back, not wanting to interfere with the three men. They had a deep bond that warranted no inference at the moment.

Long moments later, she heard the private elevator open,

then swish closed. Pouring herself a glass of Law's scotch, Lana gazed out at the rain. Beneath the clouds, the city lights across the vast bay sparkled like diamonds. The whoosh of a helicopter dropping down from the rooftop and hovering in front of the window for a second startled her. Lana's heart raced with fear. She took a long sip to calm herself and silently watched it fly south over the water.

Law returned alone. She heard him speak to Treva, then close Lana's bedroom door. Monty quietly left the penthouse. When Law came around the corner, weary and alone, Lana's heart went out to him.

Handing him a fresh drink, she didn't say anything. He threw it back and stared at her. Long moments passed before he said, "I'm sorry about all of this." Then he turned and walked slowly to his bedroom, closing the door behind him. Lana set the half-full glass on the bar. She went to Law's bedroom door and opened it.

The only sound she heard was the spray of water from the shower. As she walked toward the bathroom, she kicked off her heels, then pulled her dress over her head and dropped it onto the floor. Her panties followed.

Lana stood at the threshold of the shower, taking in the sight of Law. Not because she questioned her intention, but because she stood in silent awe of the man. He faced the shower wall, his open hands braced against the slate. His head hung. The long, thick muscles of his arms, back, buttocks and legs rippled beneath the gush of water.

Leashed power emanated in waves from his big body. He was dark, dangerous and powerful. And profoundly alone. The word defined him in every way.

He was, she realized a phantom ship without a harbor.

Law held his world and the lives of everyone in it on his

capable shoulders. But he still needed help—even though he'd never ask for it. Lana stepped into the shower, slipping her arms around Law's waist and held him tightly. Resting her cheek against his back, she closed her eyes, willing to hold him forever.

I'm here. She didn't say it out loud.

She didn't know what to expect. If he was going to break down, she would hold him. If he wanted to pound the slate walls, she'd give him his space. If—then Law turned in her arms. Water trailed down his face, the agony in his gaze almost too much to bear.

"Law," she breathed. "Let me be strong for you. Just for a little while." Raising up on her toes, she melted into him, kissing him deeply. Gathering her into his arms, Law moaned and pressed her back against the wall. Lana opened up for him instantly. Offering herself. Knowing he needed her.

Cupping her face in his hands, Law stared down at her in wonder before he kissed her again. Lana lifted her leg, hitching it around his thigh. Law lifted her, and slowly filled her. In slow, languid, emotional thrusts, he made love to her in the shower.

The intimacy of their sexual healing tapped into the reservoir of emotion Lana had been holding hostage since she was eleven.

It gushed in waves from her heart to Law's. She felt the reciprocal affects when they came at the same perfect moment. Their bodies fully connected. Unshakable and unbreakable.

For long moments, they held each other still coupled, basking in the afterglow of their powerful joining. Law lifted her up into his arms and laid her, wet and supple, onto his bed. Found a towel, dried her tenderly. Pulling him down to her, Lana rolled him over onto his back and pressed him into the sheets.

"Law," she softly said, "When I'm with you, I'm not afraid." She kissed him deeply. "With you I feel brave." She kissed him again. "I'm not going to walk out of your life again."

He was resistant to her words, deeply wary, his muscles tight.

Sliding her naked body along his, Lana ran her tongue along the scar on his face then kissed it tenderly. Running her hands over his muscular chest and belly, Lana marveled at the smooth hardness of his body.

As her lips trailed lower, his hewn thighs tightened beneath her fingertips. The fleshy head of his penis nudged her chin. Law groaned softly. Sliding her hands down the thick length of him, Lana caressed his balls. Warm and heavy. And tightening at her touch. She'd never let foreplay get this intimate. Had never wanted to until now.

"I've never tasted a man before, Law," she whispered, looking up at him. Fierce green eyes gazed down at her. In a long languid swirl she ran her tongue over the wide head. The bead of precome tasted salty. Not bad.

Slowly, Lana licked and lapped his cock, arousing him more and more until he tensed with pleasure.

About to—not yet. The power she held in her hand was barely controlled. Law's virility intrigued her, stoked her, made her crave every inch of him. But she could wait for what she wanted. More than anything, she wanted to make love to him.

Sliding back up his body, Lana slid her fingers between his and raised his arms above his head. Her breasts ached to be touched by him. Her pussy clenched and unclenched as hot desire rose deep within her.

"Law," she breathed, "I'm going to—oh!"

As the last word escaped, his lips caught a tight nipple. Lana arched into his mouth. "Harder, Law," she breathed, "Harder."

Tingling with pleasure, she tipped her bottom back and slid luxuriously down onto his magnificent cock.

"Lana," he groaned.

Lana stilled her body, savoring every glorious inch of him

inside of her. Trying to take control of her pace, Law let go of her hands and reached for her. She braced herself against his chest. Dominating him, she pressed into him. Catching his lips in a deep kiss, she set the pace.

This meeting of bodies transcended their fear, their pain, their longing for something intangible. The truth of it set her free. In this moment in time, with this man, Lana understood everything that had come before was meant to lead her here.

Did he know how good he felt inside of her? How completely he filled her physically and emotionally?

An anguished sound slipped from his lips. Her heart swelled, hurting for him, sharing his pain. Tracing her lips along his face, she tasted the salt of a tear.

Lana wished she could take away his sorrow. But all she could do was reassure him. "Hold on, baby," she whispered. "I got you."

CHAPTER FORTY-FOUR

SOMETHING HAPPENED. Everything changed. Her tenderness had opened something dangerous in him. Law's jaw tightened, his eyes blazed. His body tightened. The predator had returned. Roughly he rolled over on top of her.

As her back hit the mattress, he grabbed her face in his hands, caught her lips in a brutal kiss and sunk deeply into her.

Arching into him, she felt white-hot passion tear through her. She needed him deeper. Raking her nails over his chest, she demanded just that.

Law grasped her hips, digging his fingers into her flesh. Lana cried out as an instantaneous orgasm flashed through her.

"Don't fall in love with me," he groaned. "I'll fuck you up more."

Lana rose up to him. "As long as I'm with you, I don't care how fucked up I am."

Catching her bottom lip in his, Law bit her. The sharp pain of it shocked her. Not because it actually hurt, but because she knew what he was doing and she didn't care. "You can't hurt me, Law." She bit him back. "I know your secrets." She sank her teeth into his shoulder. He grunted painfully, thrusting harder into her. "You can't hurt me," she cried. The hot sting of tears blurred her vision. "Can't hurt me," she sobbed.

Breathing hard, Law lifted her head to his lips. "Alana," he softly said against her hair, "I don't *want* to hurt you."

Catching his lips, she said, "Then don't."

Hungrily, his lips crushed hers. Emotion exploded in her chest. The rough collision of their bodies left her breathless and hungry. But he was a risk she was willing to take. That truth set her free.

"Law," she sobbed as another orgasm ripped through her. "Don't stop."

He'd awakened the primal animal in her. She wanted to scratch him, fight with him, make love to him, just plain all-out fuck him, and then…sleep curled up against him for eternity. She would fight for him. Love him. Protect him.

Higher, deeper—he didn't stop. Delirious with pleasure overload, Lana came again, then again. When Law's body tightened, he gathered her close in his arms. His deep gaze seeing her vulnerable underbelly. When he came, his feral green eyes held hers for thrilling seconds before they closed and he gave a long deep groan of release.

Long minutes passed before either one could speak. What had begun as slow, sensuous lovemaking turned into a wild, torrid battle for survival. Lana's body trembled as rogue waves from her orgasm continued to ripple through her. Law's chest rose and fell beside her. The potent scent of their sex hung heavy between them.

"Did I hurt you?" Law asked.

Rolling over to face him, Lana's gazed raked his naked body. Every scar, every badass tattoo, every inch of his sultry tan skin combined into a deliciously irresistible distraction. "No. Did I hurt you?" She traced a fingertip along a burgeoning scratch over his pecs.

Law shook his head, placing his arm over his head. She caught the slight tremor of his hand. Her intuition told her that he'd revealed more of himself to her in the last twenty-four hours than he had to anyone in his lifetime. Knowing him as she did, she knew it scared the hell out of him.

He stared at the ceiling, a million miles away. Lana scooted closer.

"What are you thinking, Law?"

"You don't want to know."

"Wrong. I really do. So tell me."

He rolled over and faced her. Gently stroking her cheek, he brushed damp tendrils of hair from her eyes. "I was thinking of how I could convince you to leave without either of us regretting it."

"Hmm, that ship has sailed, Law." Scooting closer, she nuzzled his ear. "I'm guessing that you've never made real love to a woman, not like we just did, anyway."

Lazy smile from Law. "You talking about the first round or the second?"

"The first. Although the second round was spectacular. But here's another guess: you've never stayed with a woman after sex longer than it took to toss your condom."

He smiled again. "Maybe."

"Speaking of condoms, we haven't—"

"I got snipped ten years ago. No kids to use against me."

That news saddened her. But she understood. And with that realization she understood that she may very well chose not to have children for the exact reason as Law. The thought of someone like Dragovich or Ilya kidnapping her child like they had little Miguel Tamayo sickened her.

"How are you feeling right now?" she asked.

His answer was blunt. "Scared shitless."

"You, scared? Of what?"

"This thing between us. I don't like it."

"Um, you liked it a whole lot a few minutes ago."

"Lana, I told you upfront, I don't do relationships. Meaning I don't do them for damn good reasons."

Lana threw in a blame-it-on-me question, just for the hell of it. "Is it because of my past?"

"I don't give a fuck about anything that happened before you came to Chimera."

"Why not?"

Sighing, he pulled her close to him. "Because your past doesn't belong to us." He kissed her on the nose. "The here and now is all that matters."

Lana smiled. "That's true."

"This could work for us, you know."

Us. She liked the sound of that. He was off to a good start.

"This, meaning, you know, exclusive," he added. "And, uh... long-term."

She tickled him under his chin, laughing when he lifted his head to let her do it, like a dignified lion enjoying an undignified scratch. "How long?"

He moved over her, his erection pressed demandingly against her belly. "As long as you want," he purred. "Does that work for you, Alana Conti?"

Sliding her thighs open, she welcomed him as she said, "Hell yes. Here and now."

Much later, as they lay in each other's arms, Lana finally had the courage to ask Law about the woman whose name he called out in his nightmares. "Who's Aria?"

Law stiffened. His answer shocked her. "My sister."

Last answer she expected. "What happened to her?"

"Drago took her the day he killed my parents. I have no idea if she's dead or alive. I've been searching for both of them since I was five years old."

"So young to experience such violence," she murmured. "You weren't even in first grade. How on earth did you survive?"

He thought about that. "I just did. Had to. It's what has driven me for twenty-five years. He's going to tell me where she is before I kill him. After what happened to Sienna, I wish there was a way to kill him twice."

"What if—Aria is gone?"

She could feel him tense up. "Then I'll kill him so slowly he'll beg me to end his life."

"Law," she softly said. "I know you might not want to hear this, but just listen, okay?" She patted his chest to reassure him and continued, "If you carry your pain long enough, it prevents you from living. Suffering clouds everything. It's like walking around in a fog." Pressing her body to his, she kissed his lips. "I want to be part of your healing."

"Healing? Healing will begin when Drago is dead."

"I want to be part of that too."

"What are you trying to say?" Law's eyes softened. "You're not a killer and I'm not going to turn you into one. And don't romanticize what I do. Drago and I have a few things in common."

"Name one."

"How about two? I've killed before and I'll kill again."

"But you're nothing like Drago—he kills for sport. Don't

forget he paid two hundred grand for me. I'm lucky to be alive. God only knows what he was going to do to me. I can't imagine what he's done to countless other girls." She kissed him gently. "I want to bring him down for all of the women he's damaged, for you, Law and Sienna. So he'll never hurt anyone again."

"Markov is going to pay for Sienna."

"I don't doubt it. So use me as bait, Law. That was your original intention, wasn't it?"

After a long minute, Law said, "No."

"What do you mean, no?"

"I owed a favor."

Lana moved back a little to better observe his expressions. "Kidnapping me was a favor for someone?"

"Yes."

"You mean someone said, hey Law, since you owe me, would you mind kidnapping the senator's daughter from the evil Drago as payment?"

"Yes."

Moving out of his arms, she shook her hair over her bare shoulders. "Payment to whom?"

"I can't tell you that."

"You don't trust me?"

"It has nothing to do with trust. I'm sworn to secrecy."

"Okay. Then why was I forced to stay here thinking you had a right to me because of that stupid contract? Which we both knew was worthless."

"For your protection."

The conversation was kind of going in circles. But she persisted. "Who was after me?"

"The man I owed the favor to. And Drago."

Shaking her head, Lana bit her bottom lip. "That makes no

sense. How could you protect me from the person who requested that you save me from Drago?"

"It's complicated."

"No one, outside of maybe you, gives a rat's ass if I live or die. I can't imagine anyone asking such a thing of you, for me."

"To be clear, I give several rat's asses if you live or die. I'd bet Monty has a soft spot for you too, and Jhett when she's feeling better."

Was that supposed to reassure her? It didn't. Not coming from the man who'd kidnapped her to serve his own self-interest. Batting her lashes, Lana delivered a jab. "Only Monty and Jhett? What about True and your brother?"

Law's jaw tightened. He moved swiftly over her, pushing her onto her belly. Sliding his arm beneath her, he hoisted her bottom up, slid a knee between her thighs exposing her engorged pussy, and smacked her ass. When she cried out in surprise, he slid a finger deep into her. She about came all over his hand. "Law," she moaned.

"My name is the only name that comes out of your mouth when it comes to sex."

"I was just kidding—" she gasped when he slid a second finger into her.

"I'm not," he ground out, releasing her.

Lana literally crawled over the sheets, rubbing her tits and ass up and down Law's back, arms, chest and thighs, begging him with small purrs and scratches to take her. His steady hand suddenly wasn't so steady and that thrilled her. His want made her hot. He wanted to punish her by withholding what they both desired intensely. Jealous sex.

Sliding up his back, she rubbed her breasts against him. "If you so much as look at another woman like you look at me, I'm going to rip your eyes out." Nipping his shoulder, she slid around him. Lying on her back, she arched before him. Sliding her hand down her belly, she spread her thighs.

Their musky sex scent swirled tantalizingly around them. "This pussy belongs to you, Law." Reaching out, she slowly stroked his thickening erection. "This cock is mine." Leaning in, she swirled her tongue around the wide head. "All. Fucking. Mine." Looking up at his fierce gaze she, said, "Do you understand that?"

Imperceptibly, he nodded. Smiling, she rolled onto her back and spread her legs. "Now come fuck your pussy."

***

Lana woke to Law's deep voice. Who the hell was he talking to? It was still dark outside.

Reaching out to him, she found his skin was damp and hot. He rolled away from her. "Don't," he groaned. Sitting up, Lana's eyes adjusted easily to the semi-darkness. The light across the bay illuminated the room.

Law tossed and turned, struggling against an imaginary foe. He was dreaming. "Aria!" he cried, reaching out for his lost sister. "Come back!"

The anguish in his voice tore at her. The depth of the despair he'd suffered as a five-year-old broke her heart. "Law," she softly said. "You're dreaming."

Unsure if she should touch him, Lana softly soothed him with calming words. "It's Alana, Law. I'm here, baby. You're having a dream. Wake up."

He thrashed on the bed, his moans growing louder, more animal. Sliding from the bed, Lana walked around to his side of it but stood several feet away. She didn't want to get hurt. "Law!" she shouted.

He shot upright, wildly looking for her in the bed. When he turned to see her, he leapt from the bed and grabbed her. "God, Lana, I thought you left me." His voice was harsh, despite the relief in his expression.

She stroked his tousled hair. "I'll never leave you."

Pulling her back to bed, he wrapped his body around hers. She couldn't get away if she wanted to. As she snuggled deeper into him, she said, "We're going to get Drago. Together."

"No," he whispered. "This is my battle. I'm going in alone. I should have a long time ago."

Closing her eyes, Lana didn't argue with him. She had her own plans.

Tracing the curve of her back with his fingertips, Lana liquefied against him. His gentleness with her, coupled with the violence she knew he was capable of fascinated her. "Why aren't you arguing with me?" Law asked suspiciously.

"Because I don't want to upset you."

His green eyes studied her face when he pushed her over onto her back. Ever so slowly, he slid his fingers into her hair and lifted her to his lips, kissing her deeply. A silent homage.

When he released her, his eyes had darkened to jade. "Tell me how Mamita died."

Stiffening, Lana tried to push away from him. He held her gently but possessively. "You wanted my truth. Now I want yours."

Anxiety shivered through her. Calmly he stroked her, the warmth of his hand and the steady beat of his heart against hers gave her courage. "I—" she swallowed hard and said the words "—killed her."

"Not you," Law softly said. "You're not wired that way."

"It was my fault," she stuttered.

Pressing his lips to her forehead, he said, "Tell me."

CHAPTER FORTY-FIVE

"WE SPENT every summer since I can remember at the beach house in Carmel by the Sea. The last time wasn't the same. I didn't know it then, but my mother had found out that my father had a child by Mamita." Lana laughed harshly. "I remember mother demanding that they both had to get the hell out and my father refusing. It's the only time I can remember him standing up to her."

"Did you know before that, that Miranda was your sister?"

"No idea. I didn't understand any of it. I loved Mamita and Miranda. My dad too. He wasn't like he is now. Anyway, we headed down to the beach house without my mother. It was odd that she didn't go with us. I remember it distinctly because I was so happy she wasn't going. We all had such a wonderful drive down. The first few weeks were perfect. Until the day mother arrived."

Lana began to shake. Law pulled her tighter against his strong warmth. "I've got you, Lana."

Hot tears stung her eyes. For so many reasons. Most of them good.

"We were on the beach when she arrived. Didn't know it until we came in laughing, sunburnt and happy. Mother scolded me because I had a rip in my bathing suit. She said I looked like a street kid. Sent me to my room to change." Lana stilled for a long minute while she summoned the courage to tell him what she had blocked out for years.

"I picked out clothes, started getting dressed and heard my mother speaking just outside of my room. It was the first door just past the stairway on the second floor.

"I didn't want to go out and face her, so I stood at the door and listened. She was saying terrible things to Mamita."

Lana hesitated. Law's strong fingers stroked her face. "Take a deep breath, Lana."

She did. Then another. "Mamita wasn't saying anything. She was super quiet around my mother. I opened the door, and saw a hand print on Mamita's cheek where my mother had slapped her. I told my mother I hated her. That I wished Mamita was my mother and not her." Lana pressed her hand to her right cheek.

"What are you remembering?"

"That she slapped me so hard, Law, I couldn't see for a moment. Mamita shoved mother against the wall and told her if she ever touched me again, she would tell the world about Miranda."

"Oh."

"Mother went crazy. Started screeching, kicking and hitting Mamita. I got between them trying to protect Mamita but mother shoved me away and—and I stumbled against Mamita—" Lana sobbed. "She fell down the stairs, Law. I chased after her, tried to catch her but, I couldn't. There was blood on the wall where her head hit."

"How bad was she hurt?"

"I rushed down, she was still alive. I tried to help her up, but she was bleeding. She tried to talk but couldn't. I looked up behind me and my mother just stood there staring at us, with this crazy smile. Told me to go to my room."

"When I refused—" Lana stopped for a few moments.

Law stroked her hair to soothe her. "Go on."

"Mother came down the stairs and slapped me again. She told me if I didn't go, I'd end up like Mamita."

Law just shook his head.

"I ran upstairs but when I got to my room I opened the door and closed it as if I'd gone in and stayed on the landing so I could see. I—I watched my mother kneeling by Mamita, doing something. I didn't realize until it was too late that she had her hands over Mamita's mouth and nose."

"Jesus."

"I screamed at my mother to stop. I ran back down the stairs but it was too late. Mamita was dead. My mother told me if I ever told anyone she'd kill my sister."

Warm and strong Law's protective arms held her as she shook uncontrollably. "She can't get you, Lana, not while I have breath in my body. You're safe."

"Right after, my father came in and he freaked out." Lana closed her eyes as more repressed memories surged up in her mind. She willed them to stop.

Strong hands slid across her shoulders. "I'm sorry, baby. So sorry."

She slumped next to him, weak and still crying. "I can't believe how fucked up everything is. I—I just can't fathom what she did."

"None of it was your fault."

Law gathered her up into his arms and hugged her hard. Then he got up.

"I'll be right back," he said. A minute later he returned with a glass of cold water. She drank it in one long gulp.

Setting the empty glass on the nightstand, she looked up at him—her battle-weary gladiator, still rocked by Sienna's murder, but listening patiently to her shattering account of Mamita's death. In different ways over the years, they'd both been through hell on earth. And understood each other in ways no one else could.

His sad eyes met hers. Held her gaze. She knew they were thinking the same thing. That love might heal both of them in time.

"Does my father know I'm here?"

Law nodded.

"Does my mother?"

"No."

Scooting back in the big bed, Lana made room for Law. He slid down, taking her into his arms. "You're safe with me, Alana."

She felt empty, as if there was nothing left of the life she'd led until this day. Whether that was good or bad, she didn't know. But another feeling slowly filled her as her heart opened for the man holding her. A desire for a vengeance of her own, against the woman who gave birth to her. In Mamita's name, she vowed to destroy her.

But first...she would remove the ghosts that had haunted Law for twenty-five years.

Permanently.

CHAPTER FORTY-SIX

THE SOFT LIGHT of dawn touched the tall bedroom windows as Lana awoke to the comforting sound of Law's deep even breaths beside her.

Though it had only been a handful of hours, Lana hadn't slept so soundly since she was a child. As the thought traced across her memory, the horror of the previous night came crashing back with a vengeance.

Vise-tight emotion constricted her chest. Last night's confession had profoundly changed her. What she'd finally remembered about her mother had forever hardened her. A sad smile twisted her lips.

Oh, how she got Law now. His refusal to give away his emotions. To love and trust. Unlike Law, she was not nearly as patient for revenge. She was hell bent on exacting it now. Before he prevented her. Before she lost her nerve and regretted not acting when she had the chance.

Rolling from the bed, Lana wrapped an oversized bath towel around her and quietly made her way to her bedroom. Jhett was snoring in the bed, Treva curled up on a recliner Monty must have brought in for her.

Digging through the top drawer for Ilya's burner phone, she was glad she kept it. Not that she would ever take him up on his offer. At least not the way he thought. She'd held on to it in case Law needed a direct line to the murdering Russian.

Her stomach roiled as visions of Sienna's broken body flashed before her. Ilya would have to be taken out, and fast. Her lips tightened in a harsh line.

That she could think so coldly was something new for her, but it ran deep. When it came to the people she loved most in the world, she knew she could and would do anything to protect them. Law included. He *was* her world.

Taking out the phone, she went back into the living room and texted Ilya.

Meet me at the Ultimate tonight at ten.

Instantly, he responded: **With pleasure.**

"Lana?" Law called from the dinning room.

Powering the phone off, she slid it back into the drawer then slipped from the white room to the penthouse.

"I'm right here," she softly said not wanting to disturb Jhett or Treva.

"Why did you leave the bed?" he asked fighting back a yawn.

He looked so damn hot. Tousled black hair, sleepy green eyes, flannel pj bottoms hanging off his narrow hips. She was going to have to master Karate or some other martial art just to beat the women away. "I wanted to check on Jhett."

"How is she?"

Sliding her arms around Law's bare waist, she pressed her cheek to his chest. "Sleeping."

His strong arms slipped around her pulling her tightly against him. "I didn't like waking up to find you gone."

"I didn't like waking up and leaving you."

"It's not going to be easy being my—partner."

Lana rubbed her cheek against the coarse hair on his chest. "It's not going to be easy being my—partner, either." Tilting her head back she looked up into his intense gaze. "I'm going to want you all to myself 24/7."

"I'm going to be paranoid every second you're not in my arms."

"That's something we're going to have to work on."

Sliding her hand down his flat belly to the smooth flannel of his pajama bottoms, she gently squeezed his thick erection.

Hoisting her up into his strong arms, he said, "Let's discuss while I make love to you."

Looping her arms around his neck, Lana smiled. "I like the way you think."

STAY TUNED

Stay tuned for **THE MAN IN BLACK,**
the next exciting Chimera novel!

The Man in Black picks up where *The Senator's Daughter* ends. This next chapter of Alana and Law's complicated love story solidifies their bond, establishing them as the underworld's most formidable power couple. Dark, painful secrets bubble up from Alana's past. We learn the horrors Law suffered as a child at the hands of Josef Dragovich. Their hunt for the maniac who holds the key to Law's past, gains traction. Their love for each other raises the stakes, imperiling all they hold dear...

NEWSLETTER

Subscribe to Karin's Newsletter

Join Karin's mailing list and never miss a release! While she
can't promise the news will be regular, she does promise to
update you when there is something exciting to share.

www.karintabke.com/newsletter

ABOUT THE AUTHOR

Karin Tabke is a multi-published, national bestselling, award-winning author.

Karin has sold more than a dozen stories to US publishers: Kensington, Simon & Schuster, and Penguin Random House. Her self-publishing debut, **THE CHRONICLES of KATRINA**, was met with resounding enthusiasm. Never one to disappoint her readers, Karin happily launched the spinoff series *The Bad Boys of the Bay*, featuring the heroes she knows so well–hot cops. Translation rights to Karin's books have been licensed in Japan, Thailand, Germany, France, Spain, Brazil, Italy, Portugal and the UK.

In 2008, Karin's novel **JADED** (Simon & Schuster) won the *Romantic Times* Reviewers' Choice Award for Best Erotic Romance Suspense. In 2011, her paranormal romance **BLOOD LAW** (Berkley) won the *Romantic Times* Reviewers' Choice award for Best Erotic Fiction and was the first book in her *Blood Moon Rising* series. In 2012, the second book in the trilogy, **BLOODRIGHT**, was nominated for the *Romantic Times* Reviewers' Choice Award for Best Erotic Paranormal Romance. Karin's other awards include a CAPA and the Holt Medallion, as well as a finalist nod for the Prism. Her debut single title, **GOOD GIRL GONE BAD** (Simon & Schuster), was featured in the October 2006 issue of *Cosmopolitan* magazine.

Karin's most rewarding award, however, was not bestowed

for her storytelling skills but for her mentorship of unpublished writers. She was honored to receive RWA's (Romance Writers of America) Pro Mentor of the Year award in 2008. She has served as president of her local RWA chapter in San Francisco and as Director-at-Large on the RWA National Board of Directors.

Karin has been married to her own hot cop–now licensed Private Investigator–for over thirty years and she writes what she knows. She has also started and sold several profitable businesses, but her true love is writing passionate love stories. When she isn't writing, Karin loves to travel and does so extensively, meeting readers and sharing her knowledge via workshops at writer conventions and conferences.

Head on over to Karin's website to subscribe to her newsletter for new release updates, contests and more!
www.karintabke.com/newsletter

facebook.com/karintabke

instagram.com/karin_tabke

twitter.com/Karintabke

bookbub.com/authors/karin-tabke

goodreads.com/karintabkeakaharlow

Printed in Great Britain
by Amazon

28312500R10209